The Killing Time

Also by Elly Griffiths

Elly Griffiths

The Killing Time

QUERCUS

First published in Great Britain in 2026 by Quercus
Part of John Murray Group

1

A CIP catalogue record for this book is available
from the British Library

HB ISBN 978 1 52943 338 8
TPB ISBN 978 1 52943 339 5
EBOOK ISBN 978 1 52943 340 1

Typeset in Bembo by CC Book Production

Printed and bound in Great Britain by Clays Ltd, Elcograf S.p.A.

MIX
Paper | Supporting
responsible forestry
FSC
www.fsc.org   FSC® C104740

Papers used by Quercus are from well-managed forests and other responsible sources.

Quercus
Carmelite House
50 Victoria Embankment
London EC4Y 0DZ

John Murray Group
Part of Hodder & Stoughton Limited
An Hachette UK company

The authorised representative in the EEA is Hachette Ireland,
8 Castlecourt Centre, Dublin 15, D15 XTP3, Ireland (email: info@hbgi.ie)

For Alex and Juliet

If all time is eternally present
All time is unredeemable

TS Eliot, 'Burnt Norton'

Men talk of killing time, while time quietly kills them.

Dion Boucicault

Prologue

April 1851

The carriage comes to a halt outside the London house. A coachman springs down to open the door and a woman emerges. She is dressed in the height of fashion: emerald-green silk dress with three bands of darker green fringing at the hem, a bolero jacket with a green trim and a tremendous high-poke bonnet ornamented by peacock feathers. She holds up her skirts with one gloved hand – the leather of such a pale green that it looks almost white.

'Welcome home, Lady Serafina,' says the butler who opens the door.

'Thank you, Harrison.' Her voice is low with just a trace of a foreign accent. A besotted admirer recently described her as having 'the face, voice and name of an angel'. There are rumours that she was born in Russia, in the American West, in a Glasgow tenement. Lady Serafina herself has never revealed her birthplace but she lets enough clues slip for the more informed to infer a close relationship to one of the more respectable European royal families.

Lady Serafina Jones divests herself of jacket, gloves and bonnet and glides into the drawing room to peruse the *Morning Chronicle*. A footman brings her a glass of water with a slice of lemon, a delicacy of which her ladyship is very fond.

Lady Serafina runs her eyes along the columns of tiny print until she comes across something that obviously interests her.

The Great Exhibition
Amongst the curiosities that will be available for public perusal is The Seeing Glass, a mirror that is said to be able to see into the future . . .

Idly, Lady Serafina plays with one dark curl that has escaped from her coiffure. She dips her pen in the inkwell and then writes across the page with a flourish.

The Collectors

Chapter 1

Thursday, 20 June 2024

DI Ali Dawson is late for work. She's not unduly bothered. Life at the Cold Case Unit, known to some as the Frozen People, is not exactly deadline dependent. As she crosses the Old Kent Road she considers her worries which, in order, are:

1. Her cat, Terry, who seems off his food
2. The hot weather, which has taken her by surprise and means she hasn't shaved her legs or unearthed any summer clothes
3. Her son, Finn, who has recently made ominous noises about wanting to leave London
4. Her colleague, Jones, who is currently stuck in the nineteenth century.

London, too, has been caught on the hop by the good weather. Office workers are shedding jackets and fanning themselves with copies of *Metro*. Waiters are putting tables outside restaurants, looking nervously at the rough sleepers camping nearby. Al fresco dining is fairly new to this part of the East End. Ali gives money to one of the rough sleepers, whom she recognises. She sometimes buys him breakfast but knows he really prefers cash. She has a vision, as she presses two pound coins into his hand, of a Victorian woman giving a penny to the boy sweeping the street in front of her. There's something depressingly nineteenth century about charity. It shouldn't be necessary in a properly run society. Ali plans to tell Finn this when she next sees him. He works for a Labour MP who might soon become a cabinet minister. He has more influence than Ali will ever have.

Ali takes the turn into Eel Street, where the Department of Logistics hides itself in a sixties office block, indistinguishable from those around it. The lobby seems almost designed to depress, one lift permanently out of order, the letters falling off the noticeboard displaying the names of the companies on the different floors: Quantum Mechanics, Niffenegger and Co, Wells, Pevensie Ltd.

Ali takes the stairs to the third floor. An Italian-accented voice wafts through her subconscious: *Time travel is like taking the lift rather than the stairs*. 'Not now, Jones,' says Ali, aloud. She's found that her inner monologue is increasingly making its way into spoken utterance. She needs to stop it. She doesn't want the team to think she's cracking up.

Her colleagues John and Dina are both in the open-plan area. They stop talking when she comes in, probably out of politeness, but it makes Ali feel like the boss, left out of all the fun. Technically, she *is* in charge, promoted to DI after Geoff's death, but she still feels like an imposter. John, an experienced detective, was the obvious choice, but he refused to take the job, saying that he was a better deputy. To delay going into her office, Ali offers to make drinks, a morning ritual she enjoys.

'You've got a visitor,' says Dina. 'In your office. I'll make coffee for you both.'

'A visitor?' says Ali, more shocked than she should be. Outsiders are rare in the Department of Logistics these days.

'She's called Margaret Fanshaw,' says Dina. 'That's all I know.'

Ali looks almost fearfully towards the glass cube within the larger room. Secretly, she still thinks of it as Geoff's sanctuary. She has shut his belongings – his woodland print, photographs and 'World's Best Boss' mug – in a cupboard but sometimes she thinks she hears them clamouring to get out, like in 'The Tell-Tale Heart' by Edgar Allan Poe. Ali squares her shoulders and pushes open the door.

Margaret Fanshaw is a woman of about Ali's own age, fiftyish, with ash-blonde hair in a short bob. She's wearing a smart grey dress which is too warm for the day. Ali finds this touching. Margaret has dressed up for the visit.

'Are you DI Dawson?'

'Yes,' says Ali.

'I hope you don't mind me coming in without an appointment,' says Margaret Fanshaw.

Do I look like someone with a busy diary? Ali wants to ask. Her desk is empty apart from a 'Radical Women' coffee mug. Instead, she says, 'How did you find me?' The Department is a closely guarded secret these days.

'I work as a cleaner at Imperial,' says Margaret. 'You know, the university. Well, one of the lecturers is a man called Dr Bud Sirisema. I told him about Luke – he's my son – and he suggested I contact you.'

Bud. Ali might have guessed. He's the worst in the team at keeping secrets. Except that, officially, Bud is not in the team anymore. When time travel became a forbidden activity, Bud's expertise was no longer needed and he went back to the job he had before joining the unit – teaching physics. Ali warms towards Margaret. She used to work as a cleaner and she, too, has a son.

Her visitor's next words, though, chill her to the bone.

'Luke killed himself last month,' says Margaret. Her voice is flat as if she's steeled herself by saying this many times. 'He was only nineteen. The police just wrote it off as another teen suicide but I know there's more to it than that. I'm a single mother, I raised Luke on my own, he's my youngest and we're very close. He was just a normal boy. A bit silly at times, but they all are. But then he met *him*.'

'Who?' Ali's skin crawls. She knows the statistics on young men committing suicide. It's still her darkest fear despite the fact that Finn appears to be happy and is now thirty-two.

'Barry Power,' says Margaret, almost in a whisper. 'He's a so-called psychic medium. Says he can speak to the dead and see into the future. He's very famous. Has tours all over the place. Well, Luke emailed him. At first, I thought that Luke wanted to get in contact with his grandad, who died last year, but no, it was this Victorian mesmerist called Klaus Kramer. Luke was obsessed with him. He went to see Power for a private consultation. Power went into a trance and supposedly spoke to this Kramer. Luke was rather quiet afterwards. He's always been a bit withdrawn but it suddenly got worse. One thing he said was that Power – pretending to channel Kramer's spirit – told Luke that he could fly. A week later Luke jumped from the roof of our flats.'

'Oh my God,' says Ali. 'How horrible. I'm so sorry.'

Dina comes in with the coffees, takes a look at Ali's stricken face, and backs out again.

Margaret picks up her mug and puts it down again without taking a sip. 'I want Barry Power to pay,' she says, in a stronger voice than she has used so far. 'He killed my Luke. Dr Sirisema said that you would help me. He says you specialise in cases where the police have closed their files but you know justice hasn't been done.'

This isn't quite the Department's official remit but Ali is rather touched that Bud thinks of them as champions of justice. All the same, she has to be careful not to raise Margaret's hopes.

'Power sounds like a real charlatan,' she says carefully. 'I will look into him but I have to warn you that it would be hard to make any charges stick. Luke went to see Barry Power of his own accord. It might be difficult to prove that Power committed any crime.'

'He needs to be stopped,' says Margaret. 'He's a liar and a conman, preying on vulnerable young men. You know he says he can time travel. Dr Sirisema was very interested in that part.'

I bet he was, thinks Ali.

Ali promises to do what she can and escorts Margaret out through the open-plan area. When she comes back in, Dina and John are looking at her expectantly. As succinctly as possible, Ali tells them about Luke Fanshaw.

'How awful,' says Dina. 'We must help his mum.'

'That's terrible,' says John in a quieter voice. Ali knows that John once tried to take his own life. John, an ex-murder detective, is open about his struggles with alcohol and a mental health crisis triggered by a break-up with his wife. Happily, John and Moira are now reconciled.

'We will if we can,' says Ali. 'I certainly want to investigate this Barry Power. Apparently, he says he can time travel.'

'That's impossible,' says Dina.

'Except we know it isn't,' says John.

Back in her office, Ali opens her laptop and types in the name 'Barry Power'. The results flood her screen. 'Psychic wows crowd in Wales.' 'Barry Power spoke to my grandad – and his dog!' 'How *does* Barry Power do it? Your questions answered.' There's also a website where Ali can post a question to the mystic himself.

Ali is just composing a message when her phone buzzes. It's a text from Dina.

'Alert! TCTWBN is here.' Ali stands up but escape is impossible. The only way out is back through the open-plan area. The initialism stands for The Creature That Walks By Night and it's the team's nickname for Nigel Palmer, the bureaucrat who is notionally in charge of the Department of Logistics. Ali thinks it makes him sound far too interesting. Nigel's only weapon is dullness.

Seconds later, the door opens and Nigel Palmer materialises. He's a smallish man with grey hair and horn-rimmed glasses. The team once had a competition to guess how old he was. The answers ranged from forty to sixty-five. Dina eventually found his date of birth through judicious digging online. Nigel is fifty-two.

'Good morning, Alison.'

Nigel is almost the only person to call Ali by her full name. She's been Ali since school. Even her parents use the abbreviated name.

'Hi, Nigel.'

'I was in the area and I just thought I'd check up on you . . . see how you're doing.'

The first version is probably correct. Nigel always suspects that the team are plotting behind his back. And he's usually right.

'Everything is fine,' says Ali, in the hearty voice she saves for Nigel. 'All good.'

'Have you got any further with the Payne case?'

'I was just about to put it in an email. The parents have moved to Tenerife.'

The Payne case was one of several passed to the Frozen People in order, Ali thinks, to keep them busy and stop them dwelling on past adventures. Sisters Madge and Karen Payne visited their local police station in January convinced that their father had murdered their mother. This was easily disproved, both parents were alive and well. But the Payne sisters continued to pester the police, saying that a neighbour was filling their shared flat with poisonous gas. Ali visited the house, in company with the gas board, and found no evidence of leaks. She also interviewed the neighbour, a pleasant woman whose only crime had been trying to befriend Madge and Karen. The sisters have now turned their attentions to a distant cousin whom they think is planning to kill them for their inheritance. The parents have clearly emigrated to Tenerife to get away from it all.

'I've made a referral to social services,' says Ali.

Nigel grunts. 'Good luck with that.'

'It's very sad, really,' says Ali. 'Well, they're all quite sad.'

The other cases they were given included a woman called Camille Devine who said she was the reincarnation of Marie Antoinette (it was why she had a short neck, she said), and Fred Curtis, who believed he was being followed by the ghost of Marilyn Monroe ('older of course') and ended up becoming obsessed with Ali.

'I'll see what else I can find for you,' says Nigel.

'Please don't,' says Ali. 'I've found us a case.' She tells Nigel about Luke Fanshaw.

'That's just coincidence,' he says. 'You've got nothing that links this poor boy's death to the psychic.'

'Nothing yet,' says Ali.

'Well, tread carefully,' says Nigel. 'You don't want a court case for harassment. Remember, no one is meant to know about the unit.'

'It's very difficult being a police officer under those conditions,' says Ali.

'You brought it on yourselves,' says Nigel. 'With your . . . adventures . . . last year.'

Nigel means when Ali travelled to 1850 in order to research a shadowy group called The Collectors and got stuck there. She'd had to be rescued by John who, in turn, was rescued by Jones, aka Dr Serafina Pellegrini, the brilliant Italian physicist who made time travel possible in the first place. Ali doesn't really blame Nigel for not having the words for this. At first, the government had been cautiously interested in the work of the Department but now they seem to have decided that time travel is too dangerous an experiment. Nigel has been sent to close things down, which seems to be a speciality of his. Ali sometimes thinks Nigel was put in charge of them as punishment for him as much as them. He's a high-ranking Home Office official. Surely, he should be looking forward to early retirement, not babysitting a bunch of oddballs who have managed to subvert the laws of physics.

'If you remember,' says Ali, 'it was a cabinet minister who asked me to go to 1850. We had approval at the very highest level.'

Nigel can't deny this, but his body language seems to imply that, had he been in charge at the time, Ali would never have donned a quantity of uncomfortable Victorian clothes and gone in search of a supposed mass-murderer.

He counters with, 'Well, it went badly wrong, didn't it?'

'That wasn't our fault,' says Ali. 'Well, not entirely.'

'It was somebody's fault,' says Nigel.

'Not necessarily,' says Ali. 'Sometimes things just happen.'

'That's your analysis, is it? "Sometimes things just happen"?'

'Pretty much.'

Nigel gives her an owlish look behind his glasses. 'You're a good police officer, Alison,' he says, rather unexpectedly. 'Can't you be satisfied with that?'

'One of our colleagues is lost,' says Ali. 'I can't let that go.'

'Dr Pellegrini, I am glad to say, does not come under my remit. She's a civilian and must, regrettably, be written off as a casualty of this experiment.'

'That's easy for you to say,' says Ali. 'Dr Pellegrini – Jones – is our friend.'

'Friendship has nothing to do with policing,' says Nigel, although John would definitely argue that this is untrue; he claims his friends have kept him alive.

Nigel's passing shot is, 'Remember, any more of that business and the unit will be disbanded. Good day, Alison.'

When he's gone, Ali rests her head on the desk.

'Cheer up,' says a voice. 'I've got a lead.'

Ali looks up. Dina is standing in the doorway. She looks excited, a rare emotion in the Department these days.

'Barry Power,' she says. 'He's here! At the People's Palace tomorrow night. The ad says, "You'll believe you can fly."'

Ali thinks of Margaret Fanshaw. *He told Luke that he could fly. A week later Luke jumped from the roof of our flats.*

'Dina,' says Ali, 'I think we have to meet this man.'

'I've already cancelled my date,' says Dina.

Chapter 2

Ali, too, has an appointment that evening. It's not a date; it's more important than that. Ali is having supper with her son, Finn. They meet up fairly regularly but, as Ali walks through the busy summer streets, she has a sense that this evening is, in some way, crucial. Finn works for a Labour MP called Helen Graham who, after the election in two weeks' time, might well be in government. Helen works in Westminster but her constituency is in Yorkshire and Finn has made several alarming remarks about liking the north of England and maybe even moving there one day. This evening Ali has to remind Finn not only that London is a wonderful place to live but also that he enjoys the company of his ageing mother. She must be cheerful and funny. She mustn't make jokes about the Conservative party or remind Finn of his former job as a special advisor to a Tory MP. She mustn't mock Helen Graham for her penchant for lime-green trouser suits. 'You use humour to deflect anger,' Finn told her once. Ali thinks this is probably true.

The restaurant is in Mile End so Ali can walk. She has swapped her trusty Birkenstocks for trainers and strides along the busy pavements. She has to admit that London is doing its best this evening. The sky is just darkening to azure behind the skyscrapers. Jovial drinkers are spilling out of pubs. 'Hello, Scarlett O'Hara,' says an inebriated city worker to Ali, probably in reference to her Ferrari-red hair. She ignores him but it's not an unpleasant encounter. The weather is making Londoners more cheerful than usual; some of them are even smiling. The pizza place has tables out on the pavement and Finn is sitting at one of them, frowning into his phone. Ali watches him as she approaches. Finn is tall and lean like his father, Declan, Ali's first husband. Sometimes Ali worries that Finn is getting too thin but she thinks he looks well today. He even has a slight suntan. Bloody Yorkshire.

Finn doesn't see her until she's nearly at the table but then his face brightens with a grin. Ali's heart beats faster with pure love. No one else on earth elicits this intense, tigerish devotion. Certainly, none of her husbands did.

'Hello, love. Hard at work?'

'Just checking the trains for Leeds,' says Finn, kissing her on the cheek. 'I have to be back there first thing in the morning.'

'How's the election campaign going?'

'Not bad. We're ahead in the polls. Reform might split the Tory vote.'

Ali notes that 'we' now means Labour. When he worked for Isaac Templeton, Finn was totally committed to the Conservative cause. Ali has never asked whether this was professionalism since he was working for a Tory MP, or whether Finn shared his then boss's world view. Well, Helen Graham's is very different. Far more aligned to Ali's own politics, in fact.

They talk about the election for a bit. 'Helen's constituency is in an old industrial area, lots of defunct textile factories and mills, but there's no work in those sectors now. It's all digital, fintech and medical.'

Ali has no idea what fintech is but she doesn't like the sound of it.

'Does Helen live in the centre of town?' she asks. With any luck, the area is one huge dark, satanic mill . . .

'No,' says Finn. 'She lives in the country, near Knaresborough. It's really pretty. The garden goes down to the river. Her kids have a great life there, hiking, swimming, riding. They've got a cockapoo called Dogberry and a cat called Clement Catlee.'

Ali keeps smiling although the cute names are making her feel quite nauseous. The waiter comes over and they order pizza and a bottle of house red wine.

Ali says, 'Helen must spend a lot of time in London, though.' Implication: *there's no need to move.*

'She's got a flat in Dolphin Square,' says Finn, 'but her heart is in Yorkshire. It's difficult for her, with young children.'

'It must be,' says Ali, although she knows that Helen has a devoted husband and a full-time nanny, neither of which were available to her when Finn was growing up.

'How's Georgie?' says Ali. Finn has recently started seeing a woman called Georgina, a solicitor who lives in Ealing. Ali has yet to meet her but Finn and Georgie are coming to lunch on Sunday. Ali is already counting on Georgie to keep Finn in the capital.

'She's fine. Looking forward to meeting you.'

The waiter brings their wine and Ali takes a big swig. Finn raises his eyebrows. 'Hard day?'

Ali tells him about Margaret Fanshaw and Barry Power. Finn is suitably shocked. 'How awful. That man really took advantage of Luke when he was vulnerable. That can't be right.'

'It certainly isn't right,' says Ali. 'But it might be hard to make anything stick. I'll try, though. Dina and I are going to Barry Power's show tomorrow night.'

'I bet Dina will like that.' Finn gets on well with Dina, who is near to him in age.

'We're going to invent dead family members and talk about them loudly in the queue,' says Ali. 'Just to see if Power has got spies listening. Dina will probably spoil everything by giggling.'

The pizzas arrive and the next few minutes are devoted to them. Ali is pleased to see that Finn has regained his appetite. The events of last year – his former boss Isaac Templeton dying, Ali disappearing, Finn being falsely accused of murder – have taken their toll but Ali thinks that her son is getting back to his old self. It's only when they have finished eating that Finn says, 'You haven't got any plans to do . . . the other thing . . . have you?'

'Time travel?' says Ali.

Finn looks around but the nearest diners, a group of young women and a lone man absorbed in a book, seem uninterested.

'Yes,' says Finn. He'd been astounded to discover the true nature of his mother's work. Ali knows that, when he found out that the Department had sent Ali on a trip from which she might never return, Finn tried to hit Geoff. It's hard for her to imagine.

'That's all over,' says Ali. 'Nigel came to see me today. He made it very clear. We're just ordinary cold case detectives now. No' – she lowers her voice – 'time travelling.'

'Good.'

'Hmm,' says Ali, finishing her wine.

Finn looks at her with mingled exasperation and affection. 'You miss it, don't you?'

'A little.'

'And Jones? You must miss her too.'

'Very much. It's just hard to think that she's out there some-where, probably very near here, in space if not in time, and we can't contact her.'

'She chose to go.' Ali knows that Jones talked to Finn before she went back to 1850 to rescue John. She'd give a lot to know exactly what they discussed but she thinks that, if he wanted her to know, Finn would have told her.

'I know. It's just so strange without her. She wasn't often in the office but we knew she was out there somewhere, working away. In an odd way, I think it made us feel safe.'

'What about Bud? Is he still around?'

'He's gone back to the university.'

'Is he still working on . . . Jones's projects?'

'I don't know. She was his mentor. I think he'd find it too hard without her.'

'You might see her again.'

'I might.' Ali thinks it's time to change the subject. She tells Finn about Terry's current malaise. Finn takes this seriously. He's fond of Terry and often cat-sits.

'Is it the new house, do you think?'

'It's not new anymore,' says Ali. 'It's over a year since I moved there. And I think Terry actually prefers it because of the garden.' Terry does enjoy prowling the borders of his domain but he's not a great wanderer and spends every night sleeping on Ali's bed.

'Maybe it's just the hot weather.'

'Maybe.' Though Ali isn't convinced.

The bill comes and Ali offers to pay. She wants to do it on her phone to impress Finn but, when she looks in her bag, her mobile isn't there.

'Damn. I left my phone in the office.'

'You're always leaving it around.'

'That's what Dina says. I'd better go back and get it.'

'I'll walk you to Eel House.'

'Don't worry, love. You've got an early start tomorrow.'

Ali pays with her debit card and they walk to the Tube station, where they part with a hug. Ali can't help the slight feeling of sadness that always engulfs her when she sees Finn swallowed up by London. But he's fine, she tells herself. He's enjoying work and in a new relationship. Besides, she's seeing him again on Sunday. She mustn't be a claustrophobic mother.

All the windows are dark in Eel House. Ali taps in the passcode and lets herself in. She stands in the lobby for a few minutes, under the flickering overhead light, listening. There's sometimes a faint metallic hum in this area although all the floors, apart from the third, are now empty. Ali isn't aware of it tonight but, as she climbs the stairs, she hears something else. Footsteps coming from the second floor, the area they call Pevensie, after the intrepid children in the Narnia books. Ali stops on the landing. A chair squeaks and she hears the unmistakable sound of a computer springing into life. Should she call security? But what sort of burglar breaks in and turns on a computer?

Ali pushes open the door. A long-haired man is sitting at one of the desktops, the screen filling with incomprehensible numbers.

'Bud?'

The man wheels round in his chair. 'Bloody hell, Ali! You gave me a fright.'

'What are you doing here?'

Bud pushes back his long dark hair. Usually it's constrained in a ponytail or bun. Loose, it gives him a rather wild look. Ali wonders what Bud's students make of him. As usual, Bud is wearing a slogan T-shirt. Ali peers to read it. *I never argue, I just explain why I'm right.*

'I sometimes come in at night,' says Bud. 'Just to work on things.'

Should Ali be worried about this lapse in security? Probably. But she doesn't feel that she can ask Bud to relinquish his keys. Instead, she asks, 'What sort of things?'

Bud gives her a wide-eyed look that reminds her of Finn when he can't believe just how dense his mother is being.

'Getting Jones back, of course. I'm the only one who can do it. I'm her protégé.'

This is said with some pride and Ali knows it's true. Bud was apparently one of Jones's most brilliant students at Imperial. He joined the Frozen People to work with her on the time-travel experiment. At one time all these floors were full of people bending the space/time continuum. Now there's just Bud, the sorcerer's apprentice.

'And have you made any progress?'

Bud rakes a hand through his hair. 'I don't know. Sometimes I feel very close to Jones. As if I'm in communication with her.'

Despite herself, Ali looks round, half expecting to see the elegant figure of Jones in her jeans and designer knitwear, sunglasses pushed on top of her head. But there's only the overhead light exposing the stained carpet tiles and the lone streamer hanging from the rafters, a ghost of Christmas Past.

'I had a visitor today,' she says. 'A cleaner from your offices. She said you suggested she talk to me.' She tells Bud about Margaret Fanshaw.

'Poor woman,' says Bud. 'I often work late and one evening we just got talking. I thought, if anyone can bring that man to justice, it would be you.'

Ali is rather flattered. She also notes that Bud works late at the university as well as breaking into his old workplace at night. She wonders when he last slept.

'Do you think we'll ever go through the gate again?' asks Ali. She recalls Finn saying, 'You miss it.'

'I could take you back on a short trip today,' says Bud. 'Just a couple of days or weeks. That's easy. But the 1850s? I'm not there yet. But I will be.'

It's hard to believe and yet Ali does believe it. She has proof, in the shape of a letter from Cain Templeton, whom she met in 1850. It was found in an old desk, and it implied that she'd see him again. Implied, in fact, that they became lovers. She has seen a sketch of herself, drawn by a Victorian artist called Frederick Tremain, dated 1853. Clearly, she went back through the gate at some point. Somehow, Bud must have found a way.

Chapter 3

The People's Palace is part of Queen Mary's, the university where Ali studied as a mature student. There was an older building – Victorian, which no longer seems old to Ali – but it burnt down in the 1930s and now there's an art deco auditorium that looks a bit like an old-style music hall. Ali was awarded her degree there (a first in history, no thanks to her tutor who later became her second husband). There's a rather theatrical buzz about the place this summer evening. People are chatting in the queue, some of them carrying drinks in plastic glasses and deploying purple fans emblazoned 'Power Tour 2024'.

Ali nudges Dina.

'Such a shame about Dot,' she says loudly.

'I never expected her to die like that,' says Dina. 'In a hot air balloon accident.' She makes a snuffling noise. Dina's great flaw as a co-conspirator is this tendency to giggle.

'She had no chance with her one leg,' continues Ali remorselessly. Dina snorts, spilling her Diet Coke.

'I hope she comes through tonight,' says Ali.

'The dead don't come through just for the asking,' says the woman in front of Ali. 'Conditions have to be right.'

'Have you been to one of these things before?' asks Ali.

'Have I?' says the woman and seems about to leave it at that. She has the sharp-faced look of someone who is frequently disappointed with life.

'Have you seen Barry Power before?' asks Ali again, hoping a new form of words will generate a response.

The woman relents slightly. 'I've been ten times,' she says. 'I've travelled to Manchester, Liverpool and Belfast to see him.'

'He must be very special,' says Ali, trying for a note of awe.

'He's got the gift,' says the woman with reverence. 'The things I've seen.'

Ali and Dina wait hopefully but the woman seems disinclined to say anything further. Luckily her neighbour is more forthcoming: 'He got through to my grandfather, even knew his name.'

'What was his name?'

'Alfred.'

Definitely in the top ten of grandfather names, thinks Ali. She wonders if Power tried Ernie, Bill and Harry before hitting the jackpot. She knows that people tend only to remember the correct guesses.

But she's wronging the mystic. 'He knew his cat's name too,' says her new friend. 'Beelzebub.'

That's some shot in the dark, thinks Ali, and a little disturbing that Power (and the woman's grandfather) both chose one of the names of the devil.

The doors open and Ali loses their new acquaintances in the hustle to get seats. Ali and Dina end up on the first floor, in the circle. They have a good view but are quite a long way from the stage. Ali had been hoping to see signs of trickery although she has only a vague idea of what these might be. Sleight of hand? Concealed doors? A ghostly microphone hidden amongst the stage lights?

The lights dim and a frisson runs through the audience. The anti-climax when a slight man in jeans and a golfing jumper walks onto the stage makes Dina shake with silent laughter. But, all around them, there are gasps and even a few sobs.

'Thank you, friends and seekers of light.' Power has a faint Welsh lilt which comes as a surprise to Ali and, for some reason, makes her feel more sympathetic towards him. 'Thank you for coming tonight from far and wide. Some of you from the realm beyond.'

Ali's sympathy starts to abate.

'Let us begin,' says Power, moving to the front of the stage. He then stands quite still, head tilted as if listening. The audience is completely silent. Ali finds herself leaning forwards.

'I'm listening to my spirit guide,' says Power. 'Violet. Who have you got for me, Vi? Thank you. I have a Helen. Or maybe Ellen. Yes, Ellen. She's from my part of the world. Glamorgan is my guess.' His accent becomes warmer and more pronounced. '*Shwmae*, Ellen. She was a nurse, I think. I get a strong sense of caring from her aura. She lived in a house with a view of the sea. I see the colour pink. Bright pink. Anyone recognise Ellen?'

There's a movement in the stalls. A shout of 'Yes!' A man in a purple Power Tour T-shirt hurries forwards with a microphone.

'That was my auntie,' says an excited female voice. 'She worked in a care home. Always wore pink.'

'Ah, bless you,' says Power. 'Auntie wants you to know she's very happy where she is. She's saying something about a key. Does that mean anything to you?'

'Yes,' says the woman, between laughter and tears. 'She was always losing her keys.'

'That'll be it, my love,' says Power. 'Well, no need for locks or keys where she is now. She's free as a bird now. Flying over her beloved sea.'

'She didn't . . .' begins the woman but the microphone has moved on.

'Jim,' says Power, looking upwards. 'Oh, he's a joker, Jim is. He's got me in stitches. Jim worked with his hands. Big, strong hands. Anyone recognise Sunny Jim?'

A woman two rows in front of Ali raises her hand. A purple-shirted helper is on hand with the roving mic.

'My grandad. He was called Jim. Always laughing and joking.'

'Did he work with his hands, my love?' Power is looking up to the circle, shielding his eyes with one hand against the lights.

'He was a carpenter.'

Something like a sigh runs through the audience.

'That was a bit vague,' whispers Dina. 'What are the odds in an audience this big of someone knowing a manual worker called Jim?'

'Shh,' hisses someone behind them. But Power's next words stun them both into silence.

'I've got a foreign lady here. Sara . . . no, *Serafina*. I've not had that one before. She's coming from a long way back. Or is she? It's all a little confused. She's a pilgrim soul, there's no doubt of that. Anyone know a Serafina?'

Ali and Dina look at each other.

Serafina Pellegrini. *Jones*.

'Shall we say something?' whispers Dina.

'Yes.' Ali thrusts her arm into the air. The purple-shirted man is with her in seconds. He passes her the microphone.

'Hello, my love,' says the tiny figure of Power, far below on the stage. 'I see beautiful red hair. Fiery energy. I'm guessing you're a Leo.'

Ali doesn't reply to this. She *is* a Leo.

'Serafina recognises you,' says Power. 'She's saying something about coffee.'

Jones loves good coffee but doesn't everyone these days?

'Serafina says she's happy where she is,' says Power. 'She doesn't want you to worry.'

'Where is she?' says Ali. There's a ripple of slightly disapproving laughter.

'She's in another realm,' says Power. 'But, in another way, she's still with you. In fact, she's very close to us right now. Does that make sense?'

'No,' says Ali.

The microphone is taken away from her, even as Power blesses her and promises that Serafina's spirit is flying free. But, before he moves on to the next seeker of truth, the helper presses a card into Ali's hand.

Want to continue the conversation? Contact Barry on this number . . .

That's obviously the way that Power reels in his clients. One thing's for sure. Ali's going to ring him tomorrow.

Serafina is followed by many more Elsies, Cyrils and Marys. Then, three minutes before the end, with the ushers standing ready by the doors, Power moves to the front of the stage. Ali and Dina lean forward to see better. Power raises his hands to acknowledge the applause and, with no warning at all, starts to rise into the air. It's quite eery, the steady ascent. Power still has his arms raised and, as far as Ali can make out, the same calm smile on his face. The audience gasps and applauds madly. Ali leans further forward to see if she can see the wires that must, surely, be making the trick happen, but a helpful blast of dry ice makes this impossible. Ali's eyes are still watering when she makes her way to the exit.

The crowd are all talking excitedly about the show. Several people notice Ali's hair and whisper. She senses antipathy. She clearly wasn't awestruck enough by her visitation. But the thing is, she *is* awestruck. She's actually quite shaken. Unlike Jim, Serafina is not a common name. Where did Power get it from? And he called her a pilgrim soul. Pellegrini means pilgrims in Italian. Jones has published many physics books under her own name but, perhaps unfairly, Ali can't imagine Barry Power reading them. It's possible, of course, that Power came across the name somewhere and it stuck but that seems to go against his policy of choosing English names from the mid-twentieth century (there was very little diversity in the audience tonight or in the realm supposedly frequented by 'Violet' and Power). And what about: 'She's coming from a long way back. Or is she?' That seems almost to sum up Jones's current position, a modern woman marooned in the nineteenth century. *Serafina says she's happy where she is.*

It's dark outside but still warm. Ali and Dina walk past the main entrance of the university, not talking until they can be sure they won't be overheard.

'Ali!' shouts someone.

Ali looks round and sees a tall figure running down the steps of the Queen's Building. Her heart sinks. It's not that she doesn't want to see Ed Crane. In fact, she's been seeing him quite a lot recently though is still not sure that she is *seeing* him, in the dating sense. But now's not the time. And Dina is sure to ask questions.

Ed stops a few metres away from them. He's out of breath and Ali wonders if he's run all the way from the top floor. 'Ali. What are you doing here?'

'I've just been to see Barry Power.'

'Really? I wouldn't have thought that was your sort of thing.'

'I'm full of surprises,' says Ali. She's aware that their conversation has a flirtatious edge, which is intriguing Dina.

'Ed, this is my colleague, Dina. Dina, this is Ed. He's the curator of the museum here.' This is how Ali first met Ed, who's responsible for an eclectic assortment of objects amassed by the collector Cain Templeton in the mid-1800s and now stored in the attic of the Queen's Building.

'Are you undercover?' says Ed. 'Is this a case?'

'I can't tell you or I'd have to kill you,' says Ali.

'Pleased to meet you, Ed.' Dina is obviously loving the repartee.

'You too,' says Ed, shaking hands. 'I've heard a lot about you.'

'I hope we'll meet again,' says Dina.

'I'm sure we will.'

It's all far too friendly. Ali manages to escape by promising to ring Ed tomorrow. Even so, Dina quizzes her all the way to the station.

'Is something going on between you two?'

'He's the curator of the museum. I told you about him. We met up a few times when I was researching Cain Templeton. He was very helpful.'

'He likes you.'

'Why not? I'm very likeable.'

'No, he *like* likes you.'

'Honestly, Dina,' says Ali. 'You sound like a teenager.' Although they used to be called the twins at work (because both have a small gap between their front teeth), Ali is fifteen years older than Dina and, right now, she feels it.

'Ed and Ali sitting in a tree . . .' chants Dina.

'You're being ridiculous,' says Ali, though she can't stop herself laughing. 'We're just friends.'

'It's a situationship,' says Dina.

'What the hell's that?'

'It's not quite a relationship but it's more than a fling.'

'We're *friends*,' says Ali. 'Like I said. More importantly, what did you think of Barry Power?'

'He was quite charismatic,' says Dina. 'I didn't expect that. But the rest was a bit sketchy. I mean, all that stuff about Ellen and Jim was clearly just fishing in the dark.'

'We don't even know that the woman's aunt was called Ellen,' says Ali. 'The woman just called her Auntie. And *she* didn't say her aunt lived by the sea, that was Power. I think they moved the microphone away before she could contradict him. But I know what you mean, he definitely had a presence.'

'And then there was Serafina,' says Dina. 'What do you make of that?'

'I don't know,' says Ali. 'Maybe he found out about us and knew that Jones was part of the team.'

'But no one knows about us.'

'The Department's not that secret,' says Ali. 'Bud talked about us to a cleaner at the university. But I'm definitely going to contact Power tomorrow. I'd like a chat with him.'

They have reached the station and Dina leaves Ali to start the journey to south London. Her parting shot is making a heart with both hands, clearly intended to symbolise Ali and Ed.

Ali takes the Tube back to Bow. Although it's almost eleven o'clock, she feels quite safe walking the short distance to her house. Her time spent living in Victorian London seems to have both heightened her senses and made her bolder. She remembers walking through the narrow streets, her skirts brushing against mud and worse, her head bent against the snow, assaulted on all sides by violent sounds and smells. The strange thing is, these memories bring not relief at being back in the twenty-first century, but an almost painful nostalgia. She read somewhere that the Victorians saw nostalgia as an illness and she thinks she might agree with them.

Ali's cul-de-sac is cobbled and the street lights have an old-fashioned yellowish glow. Perhaps this is why she feels at home here. She lets herself into her terraced house. Terry, her Siamese cat, isn't there to greet her, which frightens Ali for a minute. But then she sees him, asleep on her sofa, his sandy-coloured fur blending with the cushions. Ali strokes him. 'Are you OK?' Terry looks as gleaming and elegant as ever. His black nose is moist and his blue eyes – open in outrage at the nose-touching – are bright. But Ali is sure that something is wrong with her familiar. She puts fresh food into his bowl and tries not to worry. She makes herself peppermint tea and, by the time she is drinking it, Terry is examining his food, though in a desultory way. If he's not better by Monday, she'll take him to the vet.

Ali takes Barry Power's card out of her pocket and looks at it.

Want to continue the conversation?

Could the mystic really be in communication with brilliant physicist Serafina Pellegrini? Jones herself has taught Ali that nothing is impossible. Ali wishes that she could talk to Jones, who is likely only a few miles away geographically but an incredible hundred and seventy-four years ago. It makes Ali's head ache to think of it even though she has walked those same streets. Is Jones living in Hawk Street, where Ali spent several days in 1850? She can remember the exact tread of the stairs, the chiming of the clock, the smell of bread baking. She remembers the people in the house: Clara the so-called 'maid of all work' who became briefly her friend, the handsome painter Tremain, weak Arthur Moses, pianist Leonard Rokeby and his wife, Marianne. Most of all, she remembers Cain Templeton, the landlord, one of The Collectors who somehow, possibly with the help of a set of cursed chairs, had learnt the secret of time travel. Ali has met Cain only a few times and, apart from one charged moment, has never been on terms of intimacy with him. Yet she believes that they once meant something to each other. She believes that she will see him again.

Does Jones know Cain? Does she know any of those people living in Hawk Street? It's been over a year since Jones took Ali's colleague John's place in the past. Does she still have money? Maybe she's destitute, living in some hovel somewhere. No, Ali tells herself, Jones will always survive. She has to believe this.

On impulse, Ali types 'pilgrim soul' into her phone. It's apparently a quotation from a poem by William Butler Yeats, entitled, 'When You Are Old'.

How many loved your moments of glad grace,
And loved your beauty with love false or true,
But one man loved the pilgrim soul in you,
And loved the sorrows of your changing face . . .

Ali is sure of one thing. Jones will always find people to love her.

Chapter 4

Ali rings Barry Power first thing in the morning. She's not surprised to get through to an answering machine. She's sure Power has hundreds of messages on this number. Besides, it's Saturday and even mystics must take some time off. But, by the time Ali has made herself coffee and eaten half a bagel, her phone buzzes.

'Is that Ali Dawson?' Power's voice is even more melodic over the phone.

'Yes,' says Ali. 'I was at your show last night.' She's sure Power won't like this word but a show was precisely what it was. 'I was hoping to see you today.'

'I've had a cancellation as it happens,' says Power, sounding amused. 'Does two o'clock suit?'

'Perfect,' says Ali.

'I'll send you a pin to show the location,' says Power, sounding disconcertingly modern. 'It'll be good to see you again.'

I'll be the judge of that, thinks Ali. She goes to sit with Terry, who is stretched out on the sofa, showing little interest in his breakfast, even though Ali has opened a tin of salmon.

'I'm going out this afternoon,' Ali tells Terry. 'But I'll be back by four. Just rest and get better.'

Terry opens his blue eyes and blinks once, so Ali knows he understands.

Barry Power lives in Thornton Heath, a place Ali hardly counts as London. It's not even on the Tube. Halfway to Brighton really. Ali takes the Tube to Victoria and then gets an overground train. The London suburbs slide past her, the gardens with trampolines and climbing frames, the occasional glimpses into other people's lives: a patio table set for lunch, a young couple pushing a pram in the park, a girl sunbathing on a flat roof, oblivious to the trains rattling past.

Today is one of the days when Ali feels very close to her Victorian self. She kept thinking that she might spot the Hawk Street inhabitants, Clara, Tremain and Arthur, amongst the aimless crowds at the station. The man sitting two seats down from her on the train also looks familiar and vaguely nineteenth century. He catches Ali's eye and looks away. She realises that she's been staring. What would she do if Cain Templeton suddenly appeared, wearing his cape-like coat and top hat? Don't think about Cain, she tells herself.

As a distraction, Ali turns to her most twenty-first century possession: her phone. She prides herself on not being obsessed by technology. She's not on any social media and uses her phone mostly for messaging and playing word games. She often leaves it on her desk in the office, as she did on Thursday night, and would never dream of taking her phone to the loo. But Ali was shocked by how much she missed her mobile when she was trapped in 1850. She'd had to turn to reading actual hardback books, a habit she has continued. Now, she searches for the name Barry Power. She clicks into his website, and a purple banner emblazoned with tour dates appears first, accompanied by a selection of unattributed accolades. 'Mind-blowing'. '95% Prediction Accuracy'. 'Changed My Life.' There are very few actual facts, though. Even Power's Wikipedia page doesn't give his date of birth or say much about his early years, other than that he was born in Powys, Wales. There's a live psychic text service, though, which Ali vows to try later.

Ali walks to the address sent by Power. It leads her to a large Victorian villa, prosperous-looking in an old-fashioned way: monkey-puzzle tree in the front garden, porch with spiral-twist wooden pillars, stained-glass sunburst in the front door. The doorbell has a sign saying the owner won't admit door-to-door salespeople. Surely Power, with his second sight, would be able to see these coming? Ali presses hard.

Rather to her surprise, Power opens the door himself. Had she been expecting him to have a butler? Or a maid like Cain Templeton? Power is neatly dressed in chinos and a blue polo shirt. Ali feels scruffy in her summer dress and trainers.

'Ah,' says Power. 'Ali. I'd recognise you anywhere.'

'It's the hair,' says Ali, pushing her fringe back from her face. She feels uncomfortably sweaty after her walk.

'Do come in,' says Power. He has rather gracious manners. There's almost a hint of a bow.

Power leads the way into a sitting room that's as dated as the exterior of the house. Ali sits on a floral sofa that actually has antimacassars. Power offers tea or coffee and Ali asks for a glass of water. When Power is out of the room, she looks round for clues. There are framed photos on the mantelpiece and upright piano but she doesn't want to be caught examining these. There are several small oil paintings in heavy gold frames, and one massive Victorian print that looks like John Martin at his most apocalyptic. There's also an open fan in a glass case. Does Power collect Victoriana? A small bookcase contains hardbacks that look as though they were bought by the yard and a few paperbacks. The curtains are so tasselled and fringed that they might be part of a Victorian stage set. Does Power live here on his own? There's no sign of another person. The Saturday *Guardian* is open on the coffee table, folded back at the crossword. One pen, one empty coffee cup.

Power comes in with the water, tinkling with ice. Ali drinks it gratefully.

Power looks at her for a moment before saying, 'We've met before. In another life.'

'Do you believe in past lives then?'

'That's a rather simplistic way of putting it,' says Power. 'But I definitely recognise you on some other plane.'

'Really?' says Ali. 'I don't recognise you.' So far, she thinks, so standard. Claiming to recognise someone immediately puts you on intimate terms with them. She wonders if Power spoke like this to Luke Fanshaw and her heart hardens.

'But you sought me out,' says Power, making it sound more of a quest than simply following a map reference. 'Have you come to talk to me about Serafina?'

It's a shock to hear the name but Ali supposes Power must take a note of everyone who is given his card, everyone who makes a supposed spiritual contact.

'She's an interesting spirit,' he continues. 'Is she lost or found? It's hard to tell.' Then, in a slightly more businesslike tone, 'Did you bring anything of hers with you?'

'What do you mean?'

'It often helps to have something that belonged to the person who has passed. It helps me connect to their energy.'

It so happens that Ali has a pen in her bag that belongs to Jones. She found it in the Pevensie offices a few days ago, a handsome silver Parker that she remembers Jones using. She has no intention of giving this to Power, though. She says, 'You think you can contact her again?'

Power smiles. 'You don't believe, do you, Ali?'

'Why would I be here if I didn't?' counters Ali.

'I'm not sure.' Power tilts his head the other way. 'I sense that you're a natural investigator.'

'You're right,' says Ali, seeing her opening. 'I'm a police officer. And I wanted to talk to you about Luke Fanshaw.'

Power doesn't react. He is still smiling benignly.

Ali says, 'Do you remember meeting Luke?'

'I'm not sure,' says Power. 'I see so many people.'

And yet you claimed to remember me from another plane, thinks Ali. She says, 'Luke came to see you. You told him he could fly. Then he killed himself by jumping from a high building.'

She says it brutally, hoping to get a reaction. Power closes his eyes briefly.

'Do you remember now?' says Ali.

'Yes,' says Power quietly. 'His mother contacted me after he committed suicide.' Ali doesn't like the phrase 'committed suicide'. Commit sounds too much like a crime.

'He killed himself because you told him he could fly.'

Ali is failing interviewing techniques 101. PEACE. Plan, engage, account, challenge, evaluate. She has skipped straight to challenge.

'It's not that simple,' says Power.

'Why don't you tell me how it was,' says Ali, trying for a more neutral tone.

Power raises his eyes to the dusty chandelier above them. 'Luke contacted me. He wanted me to channel the spirit of a man called Klaus Kramer. Luke was very interested in Kramer. To an unhealthy extent, I thought.'

'But you still went ahead and did what he wanted.'

'I can't refuse a request made to me in good faith.'

Can't you? thinks Ali. Power is making it sound as if he signed some psychic's code of practice.

'But I was worried,' says Power. 'I know a little about this Klaus Kramer. He was a great Victorian showman. He used to hypnotise people and make them perform strange acts. I didn't think he was a suitable person to be in contact with a vulnerable young man. I know that from experience. Poor Eddie . . .' His voice trails away.

'Who's Eddie?'

Power blinks. 'No one. Sometimes random names come through.'

'Why did you contact Kramer if you knew he was dangerous?' asks Ali.

'To be honest,' says Power, leaning forward in an almost painfully sincere way, 'I didn't intend to. I intended to find a benign spirit from Luke's past and offer help that way. I asked Luke if he knew anyone who had crossed to the other side and he mentioned his grandfather, Patrick, who'd died the year before. I meant to get hold of Patrick. Paddy, he was called.'

It's an interesting insight into Power's techniques, thinks Ali. Find out about deceased relatives, use a nickname where possible, pass on a harmless message. But, in this instance, something far darker had happened.

'But instead, you got hold of Kramer,' she says.

'He came through,' says Power, opening his pale blue eyes wide. 'I couldn't stop him.'

Ali is unconvinced. 'What did Klaus say to Luke?' she asks.

Power shakes his head, apparently quite overcome. 'It's rare that I remember what happened when I'm in a trance. But I do recall one thing. Kramer said, "Now is the killing time."'

Despite the heat, Ali can feel goosebumps erupting on her arms. 'The killing time?'

'That's what he said.'

'What did it mean?'

'I've no idea but it was very much in his manner. I got the sense he likes frightening people.'

So do you, thinks Ali.

'Did Klaus tell Luke he could fly?' she asks.

'I honestly can't remember.'

'That's convenient,' says Ali. 'I noticed that flying forms a big part of your act.'

For the first time, Power looks slightly uncomfortable. 'It's a bit of theatre, that's all.'

'Clever, the dry ice covering up the wires.'

Power doesn't rise to the bait.

'It's in rather poor taste, don't you think? Using that particular bit of theatre, when a young man has died believing he could fly.'

Power gives her the intense stare again. 'Luke was in a dark place. I could sense that. Sometimes the membrane between this world and the next is very thin. Luke was in that in-between place, that liminal zone.'

And you pushed him through, thinks Ali.

'It's very sad,' says Power and he does sound sad, he's using every ounce of his stage charm. 'His poor family. It's heartbreaking. But youth is a difficult time. Particularly for young men in today's world.' He sounds about a hundred years old but the newspaper article had his age at fifty-three.

'Tell me about Klaus Kramer,' says Ali. Maybe Power's research methods are better than hers.

'He was said to have extraordinary powers,' says Power. 'He could levitate and bilocate. It was also said that he sold his soul to the devil for these gifts.'

Ali doesn't believe in the devil but it's still a shock to hear the name spoken so casually on a sunny afternoon in a respectable south London suburb. She can hear the chimes of an ice-cream van in the distance.

'Kramer sounds like a charmer,' says Ali lightly.

Power cocks his head again, as if listening. 'I know him well. As do you, Ali. You've met him and you know what he's capable of.'

'What do you mean?' says Ali, taken aback. 'I haven't met Kramer. You said he lived in Victorian times. He must have been dead for decades.'

Power just smiles his annoying Mona Lisa smile and Ali decides that the interview is over. This conversation has clearly run its course in usefulness and apart from anything else, she needs to get back for Terry. At the door, Power tries a final mind game.

'When the time comes, Ali. Remember me.'

*

The journey home seems to take for ever. The train keeps stopping for inexplicable, and unexplained, reasons. Ali rests her forehead against the window – there's no air conditioning and the carriage is stifling – and hears Power's soft Welsh voice saying, 'You've met him and you know what he's capable of.' Is it possible that she saw Kramer when she visited 1850? Was he one of The Collectors, that shadowy group of men intent on breaking down the laws of time and space? But, even if she did pass Kramer in the street or on the stairs at Hawk Street, how can Power possibly know this?

Once she gets to Victoria she learns of severe delays on the District Line. 'There's a good service on all other lines,' says the notice chirpily. Eventually Ali gets a bus and walks from Mile End. It's nearly six when she opens her front door and calls, 'Terry?' There's no answering miaow but this doesn't unduly disturb her. Terry often sulks if she's late home. It's not until she has searched both upstairs bedrooms and the bathroom (Terry sometimes naps in the shower on hot days) and every inch of the open-plan downstairs that Ali is forced to admit the truth.

Terry is missing.

Chapter 5

Ali goes into the garden. When she moved in last year she pictured this space full of fairy lights and decking but it's still a sad patch of lawn almost engulfed by overgrown shrubs. There's an apple tree at the end but Ali always forgets to pick the fruit and it ends up rotting on the ground. Ali bangs a spoon against Terry's dish and calls him. Sometimes he crouches under the bushes but, even though Ali gets down on her hands and knees, there's no telltale glimpse of pale fur. She makes a kissing noise but she doubts that Terry would be able to hear, even if he's nearby, because Tony and Christina are having a party.

Tony and Christina are Ali's next-door neighbours, a couple in their fifties with numerous children and grandchildren. They are relentlessly sociable and have been very welcoming to Ali. They even invited her to one of their barbecues last summer and she feels guilty that she hasn't yet returned the hospitality. Now she sticks her head over the fence. Christina pauses in the act of putting a tray of food on the table.

'Ali! Come and join us.'

Christina's garden actually does have decking and fairy lights as well as a pizza oven and a seating area with cushions and throws. Now it also contains a paddling pool where several small children are splashing. A young man – Ali thinks it's Christina's son Nick – is watching them, beer and cigarette in hand.

'Thanks so much,' says Ali, 'but I'm looking for my cat, Terry. The Siamese. Have you seen him?'

'Oh, I know Terry,' says Christina. She has two Maine Coone cats called Posh and Becks. 'But I don't think I've seen him today. Tony!' she calls. 'Have you seen Ali's cat today?'

Tony appears, wearing a Hawaiian shirt and carrying a sleeping baby of about a year old.

'ALI!' he yells, which is his preferred volume level. 'COME AND HAVE A DRINK.' The child sleeps on, unperturbed.

'I'm sorry, I can't,' says Ali. 'I've just got in from work and I can't find my cat.'

'You work too hard,' says Tony. He's a black-cab driver and works far longer hours than Ali. He's fascinated by the idea of her being a police officer, though. 'No rest for the wicked,' he says now, which is one of his set phrases for her.

'Have you seen Terry?' asks Ali. 'You know, my cat?'

'Terry and I are pals,' says Tony. 'He often comes and sits with me when I'm out here having a smoke.'

'Have you seen him today?' persists Ali.

'Don't think so. He keeps his distance when the family are here.'

Ali can believe this. Terry is nothing if not misanthropic.

'Well, let me know if you see him,' she says.

'I WILL,' roars Tony as, somewhere in the house, Beyoncé starts to sing about putting a ring on it.

★

Ali stays awake for hours, listening to Beyoncé, Taylor Swift and, as the older generation take over, Wham! and Queen. She keeps thinking that she can hear Terry's cat flap opening and lies waiting and hoping for the jump on the bed and the kneading paws. At two a.m. she gives up and goes downstairs to make a cup of tea. The music next door has settled to a vibrant hum that sounds vaguely foreign. Ali knows that Tony and Christina are both from Greek Cypriot families although they were born in London. Maybe this is the time of night – or morning – for thinking about the old country. Or maybe Tony's dad, Spiro, a charming octogenarian whom Ali has met once, has control of the playlist.

While the kettle boils, Ali searches every downstairs cupboard in case Terry has somehow got himself shut in. All she unearths are various items she shoved out of sight when she moved in and has never bothered with since. She takes the tea upstairs and looks out of her bedroom window. The fairy lights are still on next door and she can see the water in the paddling pool glinting. Ali's heart leaps when her security light comes on but it's only a fox returning from a night out, pausing to yawn theatrically before disappearing into the bushes.

Ali gets back into bed. She must get some sleep or she'll be no good for anything tomorrow, even searching for Terry. She tries counting the English monarchs, a trick Declan once taught to Finn, but she gets tied up in the Henrys. Her mind is running a video of Terry, as an adorable kitten, as a gangling adolescent, as a smug adult. Terry on Finn's shoulders. Terry on Ali's lap. Terry, looking furious, in a Christmas jumper.

Until Terry, Ali had thought of herself as a dog person. Her parents had always owned dogs, huge Boxers that filled the tiny house with their muscular bodies and slobbery breath. Ali had assumed that, when she grew up, she would have her own Boxer. She remembers confiding this dream to Declan, when they started going out together at sixteen. Declan thought it was hilarious. 'Get one of those awful dogs? You must be joking! They stink and they snore. I can't stand them.' Now Declan and his second wife, Nicki, have a pug which, though undeniably cute, both stinks and snores. Ali can't help thinking it's cosmic justice. When Ali and Declan divorced, she moved with Finn from their council house in Hastings to a flat in East London. There was no room, or time, for a pet, although they both wanted one. Then their neighbour, a cantankerous man called Bert, went into a home, leaving his elderly cat, Humphrey, on his own. Ali adopted Humphrey and, though he only lived two more years, it was enough to convince Ali that it was possible to have a cat in London. She acquired Terry from a rescue place when he was only a few months old. The rest is history. Oh Terry, where are you?

When she eventually sleeps, she dreams of Terry, flying over London like a bat. But, when she wakes, he's still not home.

Ali is not really in the mood for cooking lunch for Finn and his new girlfriend. But she dutifully roasts a chicken, boils some new potatoes and makes a salad. It's still hot so Ali puts a cloth on the rusty wrought-iron garden table that the previous owners left behind and hopes for the best. Then she sets off to search all the houses in the street, in case Terry is locked in someone's shed. Tony and Christina join her, accompanied by Tony's father, Spiro, who always comes for Sunday lunch. Spiro pokes at shrubs with his walking stick while Ali knocks on doors. 'WE MUST BE VERY QUIET,' bellows Tony, 'IN CASE HE'S SCARED.'

Ali feels rather ashamed that this is the first time she has met many of her neighbours. Hers is the last house in the terrace and she has really only spoken to Tony and Christina. Now she meets Irene Goldman, who has lived in the street all her life. Next to Irene are Adnan and Faaiza, who have young twins. Then there's an empty house. 'Airbnb,' said Tony darkly. The last house belongs to couple called Sean and Brian, who offer to search with them. Ali feels comforted by this neighbourly spirit, even though Terry does not materialise.

Finn and Georgie arrive promptly at one. Ali has looked at Georgie's Facebook profile so she knows what to expect – tall, blonde, sporty-looking – but, in person, she's warmer and more inclined to smile than her pictures would suggest. She's distinctly posh, though. Ali has noted this tendency in all Finn's previous girl-friends. Finn himself sounds several degrees posher than Ali, who still retains her cockney/estuary accent. Finn and Ali both went to state schools but Finn went to the LSE and works in politics. His voice now has a smooth BBC timbre to it.

'Finn told me about your cat,' says Georgie as soon as they are introduced. 'I hope he turns up. My cat went missing for a week once. Just strolled in through the door as if nothing had happened.'

'You've got a cat?' Ali adds several points to her mental score-sheet.

'Well, he lives with my parents but he's mine really. I got him for my sixteenth birthday.' Ali deducts a point. She doesn't approve of animals being given as presents.

'Georgie FaceTimes him most nights,' says Finn fondly. Ali gives half a point back.

Finn and Georgie seem easy and affectionate with each other. At one point, Ali notices them holding hands under the table. Georgie tells Ali about her work as a solicitor in a criminal law firm. Finn informs Ali that Georgie does a lot of work for clients on legal aid, knowing this will appeal to her. Ali asks Georgie how she gets on with Helen Graham, Finn's boss.

'Oh, I love Helen,' says Georgie, a touch too enthusiastically for Ali's liking. 'It's a tough job being an MP, especially if you have kids.'

Ali can think of tougher jobs (cleaner, miner, Victorian maid of all work) but she agrees and asks Georgie if she has visited Helen's constituency in Yorkshire.

'Yes,' says Georgie. 'I went to do some canvassing with Finn. It's gorgeous around there.'

'Mum's suspicious of anywhere north of Watford Gap,' says Finn.

'That's not true,' says Ali. 'I went to Oslo once and loved it.' That had been with Lincoln, husband number three, which is probably why Finn frowns slightly. Georgie says she loves Edvard Munch and the conversation moves on.

Although Ali keeps looking round, hoping to see Terry slinking into the garden, lunch is a success. Georgie and Finn eat heartily but, though they bought a bottle of white wine, don't drink much because Finn has to get the train to Leeds later. Ali limits herself to one glass because she has her book club that evening. She was tempted to cancel but she has, unusually for her, read the entire book, *Lessons in Chemistry* by Bonnie Garmus.

'Oh, I loved that one,' says Georgie, taking a sip of Ali's extra-strong coffee. 'The dog was great. What was his name? Six-Thirty?'

'Life's too short to read about a talking dog,' says Finn.

Ali and Georgie talk about books until it's time for the couple to leave. Ali watches them go with mixed feelings. She's relieved that she likes Georgie. She seems fun, intelligent and open-minded, although Ali could have done with less open-mindedness about the region she thinks of as The North. Maybe Finn was right about Watford Gap. But Finn is moving away from Ali. Technically, this happened years ago. Finn left home at eighteen to go to university and he hasn't lived permanently with Ali since. Finn is thirty-two but he won't really seem grown-up until he marries or turns fifty. There was something about Finn and Georgie that seemed settled and domestic. Ali was pleased to see this. But it also makes her feel a bit sad.

'That your son?' Tony addresses her from across the fence, his voice a few decibels lower than usual. He and Chrissie have been entertaining Spiro and assorted other relatives in their garden again.

'Yes,' says Ali. 'With his new girlfriend.'

'A new girlfriend? Maybe marriage bells soon. And grandchildren.'

'Yes,' says Ali, her spirits sinking still lower. In theory, she'd like grandchildren but not yet. She's only fifty-one, still young by today's standards. After a few more pleasantries, Ali goes back into the house to load the dishwasher. She misses Terry more than ever.

Tonight, book club is at Moira's house. Moira is the wife of Ali's colleague John and has, over the years, become a good friend. Ali is meeting another friend, Meg, on the way. Meg and Ali have been friends since university. Meg's speciality is practical but kindly advice. Ali hopes there won't be too much of this tonight.

On the way to Moira's, Ali tells Meg about Terry.

'I'm sorry,' says Meg. She's a dog person but understands about pets. 'But he might still turn up. You know what cats are like. I bet, when you get home tonight, he'll be there, miaowing for his supper.'

'I don't know,' says Ali. 'I just have the sense that he's trapped somewhere. It's as if he's sending me messages.'

'Have you tried your neighbours' sheds and so on?' says Meg, shifting her tote bag containing wine onto the opposite shoulder. 'I must say, I never knew you were psychic, Ali.'

'I'm not,' says Ali, 'though I did go to see a medium recently.'

The description of Barry Power's show lasts all the way along Clapham Common North Side and most of the way down the long street of elegant houses where John and Moira live. They moved in before this area went up in the world, John always says. He was born and bred in the East End and obviously feels slightly embarrassed about ending up south of the river.

'Did you believe any of it?' says Meg. 'Not the flying, because that must be fake, but the messages from the dead?'

'I didn't at first,' says Ali. 'It was so obvious. Lots of generic phrases like "he's a joker" or "he works with his hands". The names were pretty common. What are the odds that someone has an uncle called Jim? Everyone does. It's like having an Auntie Marge.'

'I've got an Auntie Marge,' says Meg. 'She lives in Seaford.'

'There you are then.'

'You said you didn't believe it at first,' says Meg. 'What happened to change your mind?'

Meg is an English teacher. She has a brilliant memory, especially for dialogue.

'Do you remember my colleague, Jones? The physicist?'

'The one who does the top-secret research? I think you have

mentioned her a few times.' Meg is always longing to know what really happens at the Department of Logistics.

'Well, her real name is Serafina. Power asked if anyone knew a Serafina.'

'Jesus. Now that *is* an unusual name. But this woman isn't dead, is she? Why is she talking to a medium?'

'That's what I'd like to know,' says Ali.

They've reached John and Moira's house, which has a black and white tiled path leading to a rather startling pink door. John's daughters, Hattie and Emily, painted it in a fit of teenage enthusiasm and have now gone away to university, leaving their parents to face the anger of the residents' association.

John opens the door. He's wearing a West Ham top and tracksuit bottoms.

'Welcome to the culture wars,' he says. 'So far opinions are divided on the talking dog.' John prefers non-fiction.

'Finn feels the same,' says Ali. She might have known that Six-Thirty would prove controversial with the book club. Moira's neighbour, Simone, takes anything even slightly fantastical as a personal affront.

'How was Finn?' John asks as he ushers them inside.

'Fine. He brought Georgie. She seems very nice.'

'That's good,' says John. He looks at her rather searchingly. 'Is everything else OK?'

'Oh John,' for a second Ali struggles to hold back tears, 'Terry's missing.'

Meg tactfully makes her way to the sitting room, where the meeting has started. John puts his arm round Ali.

'You poor thing. You must be frantic.'

'I just miss him,' says Ali.

'I still miss Bridie,' says John, referring to his border terrier, who died two years ago. 'It's the space. The space they occupy.'

Ali remembers, in 1850, the times when she thought she saw Terry in just those mysterious spaces occupied by domestic animals: lying against the skirting boards, on the bend in the stairs, in the patch of light on the counterpane. She has to fight a ridiculous compulsion to ring home and see if Terry answers.

After a few more kind words. John gives Ali a quick hug and escapes to his study, where he's going to watch TV. Ali goes into the sitting room and is soon absorbed into a discussion about chemistry, cooking shows and whether dogs can really learn human vocabulary. Simone talks at length about the fact that, in the TV series, the dog is a golden doodle, a breed that didn't exist in the fifties, when the book is set.

'Historical inaccuracies never bother me,' says Ali. 'I can suspend my disbelief.'

Moira gives her a look. She knows about the time travel. The Department's original charter forbade the team from discussing their work with anyone but John refused to keep a secret from his wife. 'When we got back together, we swore to always tell the truth to each other.'

'And a dog would never learn to read Proust,' says Simone.

'Are you OK?' says Moira to Ali, when they go into the kitchen to fetch the pizza that always accompanies these evenings. 'You're not your usual sparkling self.'

'I'm fine,' says Ali, 'just a bit worried about Terry.' She tells the story again.

'He'll be there when you get back,' says Moira. 'Wearing last night's clothes and looking embarrassed.'

'I hope you're right,' says Ali.

Ali almost convinces herself that Terry will be waiting at home. When she and Meg leave, at ten thirty, Ali almost runs along the road to the common.

'Slow down,' says Meg. 'I'm too full of pizza to go fast.'

Ali stops and looks back at Meg, who has dropped her now empty tote bag. Ali waits until she has rearranged herself and they start walking. Then Ali stops again.

'What is it?' says Meg.

'Did you hear that?' Ali wheels round. The long street is empty and Ali could have sworn that she heard footsteps that speeded up and slowed down to match theirs. She stands still, watching, listening. A security light comes on. A fox wanders across the road, eyes glinting.

'I thought I heard someone following us,' says Ali.

'Stop spooking me,' says Meg. 'I've never forgiven you for making me watch *Don't Look Now*.'

Ali laughs and tucks her arm through Meg's as they continue their walk. But she's still slightly unnerved. Terry will be there when you get home, she tells herself. If she says it enough times, it might come true.

But, when Ali finally lets herself into her house, it's a catless wasteland.

Chapter 6

Waking up is horrible. Ali knows immediately that something is wrong. Her first thought is Finn but then she remembers. It's her other boy. Terry is missing. Ali lies still, listening to the old house creaking. Perhaps by some miracle Terry has returned. Perhaps he's even now finishing the food that Ali optimistically left him last night. Ali pads downstairs but the kitchen is empty and the cat food is attracting flies. Ali throws it away and puts the kettle on. She looks out over the garden. The white cloth is still on the table and the wine bottle lies on its side, giving the patio a rather bacchanalian feel. Tony and Christina's trees are still gay with bunting. Ali told Meg that she sensed that Terry was trapped somewhere. Is this true? Could Terry be in one of her neighbours' sheds? Ali thinks back to the people she met for the first time yesterday. Irene, Adnan, Faaiza, Sean and Brian. They all promised to check their outhouses and keep an eye out for stray cats. What about the empty Airbnb? Should Ali try to gain access somehow? She tries to send a psychic message to her cat. Where are you, Terry?

The kettle boils and Ali makes tea. This is ridiculous, she tells

herself. She needs to move on. There's a case to investigate. Ali
needs to update Dina and John on her meeting with Barry Power
yesterday. She will never admit to anyone that, late last night, she
even considered enlisting Power's help in the search for Terry.

Ali doesn't feel like breakfast but, when she arrives at Eel House,
Dina has bought pastries. John has obviously told her about Terry.

'I'll look on all the missing cat websites,' says Dina. 'Is Terry
microchipped?'

'Yes,' says Ali. She's grateful for Dina's concern but she wishes
she didn't sound so energised at the thought of a project.

'If he's microchipped, you'll be contacted,' says Dina. 'If, you
know . . .'

If Terry's body is found, thinks Ali. Part of her hopes this will
happen. As a police officer, she knows that nothing is worse than
not finding a body. She takes an almond croissant and says, 'Let's
talk about something else. Let's talk about Barry Power. I went to
see him at the weekend and I thought he was very shifty. He said
that he recognised me from another plane of existence.'

'That's convenient,' says John. 'He didn't say which plane exactly?'

'These people never say anything exactly,' says Ali. 'It's all
vague stuff about the membrane between this world and the next.
Anyway, I told Power that I was a police officer. That seemed to
bring him to his senses.'

'I bet it did,' says Dina.

'I asked him about Luke,' says Ali. 'At first he claimed not to
remember him but then he said that Luke had come to him wanting
to contact Klaus Kramer.'

'Why did Luke want to contact this Klaus Kramer?' asks John.
'He was the Victorian, wasn't he?'

'Power said that Luke was obsessed with Kramer. "To an unhealthy extent", those were his words. He said that he thought Kramer would be a bad influence and he wanted to channel a more friendly spirit, like Luke's grandfather. But, instead, he went into a trance and there was Kramer.'

'Do you think Power really believes that?' asks John.

Ali remembers Power fixing her with his watery-blue stare. *He came through, I couldn't stop him.*

'I don't know,' she says slowly. 'All I know is, Barry Power told Luke he could fly and then he killed himself by jumping from a block of flats. I think Power should pay for that.'

There's a silence. Ali wonders if she sounds a bit too much like a vigilante. But then John says, in his calm way, 'Power has a responsibility, certainly. Luke was a vulnerable young man. As you both know, I've been in a dark place myself. There's no knowing what can push you over the edge. Sorry, that's a horrible way of putting it.'

Ali knows that John once attempted suicide. He's always been very open about his life. John became an alcoholic whilst simultaneously forging a brilliant career in the Met; 'that was the culture then'. He tried to stop when he married Moira and had children but relapsed. Moira left him and John cut his wrists whilst in the bath. It was only the overflowing water that alerted a neighbour and saved John's life. He went back to rehab and has now been sober for over fifteen years.

Dina looks up from her computer. 'Do we know why Luke was so obsessed with this Klaus Kramer?' she asks. 'I've been looking online and there's not much there. I found something in an article on Franz Mesmer, the man who supposedly invented mesmerism. It says that Kramer was one of his students.'

'According to Barry Power,' says Ali, 'Kramer could levitate and bilocate. Apparently he sold his soul to the devil for these powers.' She doesn't tell them what else Power said. *You've met him and you know what he's capable of.*

'You always hear of people selling their souls to the devil,' says John. 'I wonder what he wants with them all.'

'I read somewhere that Paganini sold his soul for the gift of music,' says Ali. 'The rumour was that he had one ordinary leg and one like a goat. I suppose he never wore shorts.'

'Don't joke about the devil,' says Dina. Ali doesn't know if she's being serious or not. Dina turns back to her screen. 'I think I've found something else. It's in a scholarly paper behind a paywall.' Ali knows that paywalls are no impediment to Dina, a seasoned hacker.

'The Shadowy Science of Energy Transfer,' reads Dina. 'Sounds like something Jones would talk about.'

'It really does,' says Ali. 'Who wrote the article?'

'Someone called Hugo Maltravers,' says Dina. 'Ever heard of him?'

'I used to be married to him,' says Ali.

Hugo was Ali's second husband. She always feels slightly embarrassed to admit that she's been married three times. It seems so *excessive*, something that belongs in the biography of a Hollywood actress or Henry VIII. Of course she didn't *plan* to be married multiple times. She met Declan at school and thought that he was the love of her life. They married when she was nineteen and pregnant. They divorced when Finn was four. Ali moved to London, to a one-bedroom flat in a Stratford tower block. She worked as a cleaner and, after school, Finn would accompany Ali on her evening shifts, at first riding on the hoover and napping on sofas in various reception areas, later doing his homework at a succession of corporate desks. Eventually Ali saved enough to enrol at Queen Mary, University of London, to study History. The plus side was that she loved university life and finally fulfilled her academic promise. The downside was that she met Hugo.

Ali remembers the first time she saw Hugo. It was at a cheese and wine party for new history students. The whole concept of cheese and wine was an alien one to Ali. It seemed an odd mix, like chalk and cheese, but the whole department was there, drinking from plastic glasses and balancing cubes of cheddar on cocktail sticks. Ali noticed Hugo at once, partly because he was drinking out of a proper glass, one containing amber liquid that clearly wasn't white wine. He was also undeniably handsome, tall and blond with hair that gleamed under the strip lighting of the common room. Ali stared, cheese in hand. Hugo, who was talking to two other men, probably lecturers, caught Ali's eye and came over.

What would have happened if she'd backed away and continued her awkward conversation about Hastings with another student from the south coast? Her life would certainly have been simpler, her time at QMUL less turbulent. But maybe Ali was ready for some turbulence at that moment. She smiled at Hugo and, when he strolled over, asked him what he was drinking.

'Whisky,' was the answer. 'You look like a woman who appreciates a proper drink.'

What did that mean? Ali wondered later. That she was older than most of the other first years? That she looked like a seasoned drinker? She was pretty sure she didn't. This was before the red hair and Ali probably looked like what she was, a thirty-year-old woman, out of her depth in the academic setting. This was what attracted Hugo, of course. He was a predator and Ali was easy prey, separated from the herd.

Hugo invited Ali for a drink that night. She didn't go because she had to get back to relieve the babysitter. This very mild resistance piqued Hugo's interest and he pursued her with theatre invitations, book recommendations and witty texts. Eventually Ali succumbed and they spent an exciting three years trying to hide their relationship. They married straight after Ali's graduation and Hugo got a job at another London university. They had made their affair public before the exams but it hadn't made Hugo very popular in the department.

Ali's marriage ended when she realised that Hugo's interest in female students was a chronic condition. She divorced him, ditched the PhD (which had never really gone anywhere) and embarked on a career as a police officer and kickass independent woman. This was only marred by her marrying Lincoln two years later. He was Ali's personal trainer during her brief period of going to the gym. Lincoln was Canadian and had an untroubled air that Ali took for good humour but later put down to an almost complete lack of thought. Finn was eighteen when Ali married Lincoln, old enough to tell her that it would be a complete disaster. He was right. They divorced after five years.

And now Hugo is a person of interest in an enquiry. Well, strictly speaking, he's not a suspect but he does have information that could be useful. Ali hasn't seen Hugo in almost eight years but they are still in occasional email contact. She messages him now and Hugo responds in ten minutes. He suggests meeting for lunch tomorrow. Ali amends this to morning coffee. After years of listening to

Hugo's dietary preferences, she vowed never to eat another meal with him. Hugo responds with an annoying thumbs-up emoji.

They meet in the courtyard of Somerset House, next to King's, Hugo's lucky new employer. This part of London isn't on Ali's usual beat and she's amazed at how much it has changed in recent years: part of the Strand is now pedestrianised and students sit at picnic tables, chatting or working on laptops; the courtyard has fountains playing and expensive-looking cafés where people are already drinking Aperol spritz and Prosecco. Two women who sound like they might be actors talk loudly at the next table. Beyond them, a man sits with a trilby hat over his nose, like a thirties spy.

Hugo, though, hasn't changed.

'Good God, Ali, what's happened to your hair?'

'At least I've still got some.'

Hugo runs a defensive hand through his fair hair. It's definitely thinning.

Ali tries to reset. 'Thank you for meeting me. How's things?'

Hugo hasn't married again but Ali knows that he's had a succession of girlfriends and now has a child with his much-younger partner.

'Pretty good.' Hugo monologues on for a while about book deals and keynote speeches at conferences. He says he's just come back from Boston.

'Boston Lincolnshire?' asks Ali.

Hugo takes the bait. 'Boston *USA*.'

'Wow,' says Ali, without enthusiasm. 'And how's . . .' She's forgotten the names of both child and partner.

'Barley's nearly five now, can you believe it?'

Ali does not find this at all hard to believe. She assumes the child is aging chronologically like everyone else. But what sort of name is Barley? She notices that his or her mother does not get a mention.

'How's Finn?' asks Hugo. 'After that . . . trouble last year.'

After Finn was accused of murder and Hugo sent an email to Ali describing him as 'basically a good kid'.

'He's fine. Working for Helen Graham, the shadow Energy Minister. So he's campaigning hard in the election.'

'I thought Finn was a Tory.'

'He's a political advisor,' says Ali. 'He advises anyone who pays him.'

'Very capitalist,' says Hugo who, having inherited a substantial private income, feels free to criticise anyone who works for a living.

'Anyway,' says Ali, feeling that she needs to call the meeting to order, 'as I said in my email, I'm interested in Klaus Kramer. I saw that you'd written a paper about him.'

'Why are you interested in Kramer?' asks Hugo. 'I mean . . . I find him fascinating but I'm an academic.'

'And I'm a police officer,' says Ali. 'Kramer's name has come up in a recent murder enquiry.'

'Kramer's name? He's been dead for more than a hundred years. I mean, I know you work with cold cases but . . .' He laughs and does the hair pat again.

Ali gives him her best stony stare. 'The details are confidential,' she says. When Ali first announced her intention of joining the police, Hugo said it was the funniest thing he'd ever heard. When she actually did it, Hugo accused her of joining a fascist organisation. They were getting divorced at the time and Hugo cited it as an example of her unreasonable behaviour. Now he seems to be back to finding it amusing.

The stare works, though, because Hugo says, in a more respectful voice, 'I just don't see how Kramer can be relevant. I mean, very few ordinary people know about him.'

Ali is sure that she counts as very ordinary. All the same, she has been wondering how Luke Fanshaw found out about Kramer in the first place. She asks Hugo if Kramer features in any books or films.

'There was a film once,' says Hugo. 'That's the rumour anyway. I've never seen it and I've searched in all the usual places. It was rumoured to be very disturbing. So disturbing that every copy was destroyed.'

Could Luke have found a copy of the film? No doubt he possessed digital powers unknown to Hugo; he was a teenager.

'Tell me about Klaus Kramer,' she says now.

'You've come to the right place.' Hugo leans back in his chair. He loves imparting information. It made him a good teacher, Ali remembers, but an irritating husband.

'Kramer was born in the late seventeen hundreds. The exact date isn't known. We do know that he studied medicine at the university of Vienna where he became obsessed with the work of Franz Mesmer, who had also studied at the university and later gave his name to the study of mesmerism, although initially he called it animal magnetism.'

'Animal magnetism?' says Ali, thinking of Terry. Despite Dina posting on various feline websites and Ali distributing leaflets locally, there have been no sightings of her beloved cat. Hope is beginning to be replaced with a dull acceptance.

Hugo frowns. He doesn't like to be interrupted.

'Mesmer used magnets to treat patients suffering from hysteria.'

'A made-up illness used to oppress women.'

Another frown. 'Hysteria coming from the Greek word hystera, meaning womb, so, yes, referring almost exclusively to women. Mesmer was also interested in the influence of the tides and the planets on the human body.'

This sounds like nonsense and yet Ali, like every police officer, knows that crime rates go up when there's a full moon.

'Mesmer tried to produce what he called artificial tides in his patients by the use of magnets,' continues Hugo. 'Later on he abandoned the magnets and just stared into people's eyes, moving his hands over their bodies but not touching them. A bit like reiki, I suppose.'

Ali has had reiki treatment and found it unexpectedly effective, although she doesn't understand how it works and therefore slightly fears it. She decides not to mention this.

'Some people thought Mesmer was a charlatan,' says Hugo, 'but he had some important admirers. He was friends with Haydn and Mozart and often used a glass harmonica in his treatments. Mozart makes a comic reference to Mesmer in *Così Fan Tutte*.'

Hugo gives the title an annoying Italianate flourish. This allows Ali to interrupt, 'What's a glass harmonica?'

'A musical instrument comprised of glass bowls,' says Hugo. 'Invented in the 1700s, I believe. It has a rather unearthly sound. There are some interesting contemporary accounts of Mesmer's treatments that say he ended the session by playing on the harmonica. The word derives, of course, from the Italian "*armonia*" or harmony.'

'Where does Klaus Kramer come in?' asks Ali, before Hugo can say any more Italian words.

'He was one of Mesmer's most ardent followers. Mesmer died in 1815 but Kramer carried on with his work. In fact, he was said to take things further.'

Hugo pauses for effect. The two women at the next table are talking about plastic surgery. 'She's literally had *everything* done,' says one.

'In what way?' Ali asks Hugo obligingly.

'Kramer thought that he could control people's minds. I suppose you might call it hypnotism. Hypnotism was supposedly invented in 1843 by a Scottish doctor called James Braid. But Kramer was a showman. He gave these great exhibitions in Paris and London. There were all sorts of rumours about him. That he made people commit murders or perform terrible crimes. That he could be in two places at once. But the big thing was that he could fly.'

'He could fly?'

'Or so he claimed. He told stories about flapping round London at night, roosting on the top of St Paul's and suchlike. He used to make people fly in his shows too. I suppose it was a form of levitation. An old magician's trick. There are accounts of as many as twenty people floating around in the rafters. Eventually Kramer fell out of favour when a young man he was treating jumped from London Bridge. It was thought that Kramer had convinced him he could fly.'

Ali remembers Barry Power, rising smoothly into the vaults of the People's Palace. She thinks of Luke climbing the stairs to the top of his apartment block. She sees the unknown boy throwing himself into the Victorian night.

'Why are you interested in Kramer?' she asks. 'I thought your field was nineteenth-century industry.'

'Well remembered,' says Hugo. 'But not enough people are interested in the Industrial Revolution so I'm thinking of branching out. I'm planning a book on shamans, conmen and time-travellers.'

'What?' Ali's voice is so loud that two pigeons take off in flight.

'Oh, didn't I tell you? That was Kramer's other thing. He claimed to be able to time travel.'

Chapter 7

Hugo suggests they have lunch at Spring, a fashionable restaurant in Somerset House, but Ali says she has to go back to work. She stops at Tesco Metro to buy a sandwich and finds herself temporarily overcome in the pet food aisle. Not that Terry deigned to eat supermarket brands – he had special food ordered over the internet – but all those cat faces peering out at her makes Ali realise how much she misses that blond fur, that black muzzle, those blue eyes. The office is deserted. Dina and John must be at lunch. Ali allows herself a brief cry in the ladies' loo. Maybe that's the thing about animals, she thinks, washing her face at the sink, they allow this release of emotion. She remembers crying over Humphrey when she hadn't over her grandparents' deaths or her divorces. Her face looks red and blotchy in the unflattering overhead light. She sticks out her tongue at her reflection to see if it makes her feel better, but it doesn't.

Back at her desk, Ali eats half her sandwich and tries to make some notes from the morning. It was a dispiriting meeting, all things considered. It's not just Hugo and his thinning hair, it's the thought that her case might not be a case after all. Luke Fanshaw must have discovered the Kramer film somehow and that sparked an unhealthy obsession that was exploited by Barry Power. It's horrible but Ali doesn't think that Power has committed any actual crime, not one that would stand up in court anyway. The trouble is, the things that fascinate Ali about Klaus Kramer are not details that can be shared outside this office. Could Kramer be a time-traveller? Could Barry Power? It sounds fantastical but Ali has walked through the streets of nineteenth-century London. She knows that nothing is impossible.

All in all, Ali is not in the best mood for her date with Ed Crane that night. It's not a date, she tells herself, they are just going to see a film. Ali is not really sure how to categorise her relationship with Ed. They haven't slept together but they've been to several films and one play, and they've enjoyed numerous meals. In the lift at the Barbican they shared a very passionate kiss. Since then, there has been no physical contact. Is this respectful or just weird? Meg says it's romantic. What did Dina call it? A situationship. The rules of modern dating are more complicated than time travel.

Ali is meeting Ed at QMUL and the sight of her alma mater, looking mellow in the golden evening light, cheers her up slightly. She crosses Library Square, heading for the café, the Novo Cemetery on her left. It's a strange corner of the university ('the dead centre of campus' the students used to joke). When the university acquired the site of the old Jewish graveyard in the 1970s, they undertook to look after the tombstones (the remains were moved elsewhere) but the place always has a melancholy feel. Now the shadows of the surrounding buildings fall across the parched grass and the flat stones are like the remnants of an abandoned city.

When she was a student Ali thought she saw a ghost here. Now she wonders if she saw a glimpse of another time.

'Ali!'

It's Elizabeth Henderson, Ali's ex-tutor, an expert in nineteenth-century history. She is carrying a tote bag, probably containing books, and a tennis racket. This last surprises Ali. She has never associated Elizabeth with any kind of sport. She doesn't exude 'just been to the gym' energy, like Ali's third husband, Lincoln, used to. Elizabeth looks as if she spends her days in libraries and examiners' meetings. It's impossible to imagine her in a tracksuit and yet, looking down, Ali sees that Elizabeth is wearing trainers, large white things with soles like tractor tyres.

'Elizabeth! Off to play tennis?'

'Yes. Meeting Tim Masters from the Law Faculty. The approach of Wimbledon fortnight always inspires us. Mind you, most academics love tennis.'

'Do they?'

'Tennis and chess. The two great tactical games.'

Hugo used to play chess. He tried to teach Ali but she'd had enough of being his student by then. It was bad enough playing Monopoly with him.

'Where are you going?' asks Elizabeth, putting her tote bag down. It *is* full of books. There's no sign of any sports clothes. Is Elizabeth going to play tennis in her sensible blue summer dress? Probably.

'I'm meeting Ed. We're going to the cinema. To see the new Vietnamese film.'

'Oh, I've seen that. It's good.' Elizabeth knows Ed because he's the curator of the museum. She doesn't ask any more questions although she looks slightly curious. Ali decides to change the subject.

'Elizabeth? Have you ever heard of Klaus Kramer?'

'Who's he?'

'A follower of Franz Mesmer. I remember you told me about mesmerism last year.'

'So I did. I haven't heard of Kramer but Mesmer had many followers. Charles Dickens was one of them.'

Elizabeth has repeatedly warned Ali not to trust Charles Dickens. Now she says, 'Going back in time again, Ali?'

'*What?*'

'You were all interested in the nineteenth century last year. You said it was to do with work.'

'Oh. Yes. No. Not really. I was just reading something about Kramer.'

'Reading can be dangerous,' says Elizabeth. 'Well, I must be off. Centre court calls.'

And with that, she walks off, making feints with the tennis racket.

Ed is waiting for Ali outside the Queen's Building. He's wearing cream chinos and a white shirt and looks slightly as though he's stepped out of a time portal, fresh from playing cricket in 1912 perhaps. Ed is extremely tall and Ali sometimes feels self-conscious looking up to him. Partly for this reason, she doesn't kiss him in greeting. Instead, she says, rather heartily, 'I've just seen Elizabeth going off to play tennis.'

'Really?' says Ed. 'I can't imagine her playing sport somehow.'

'Apparently academics like tennis.'

'Must be why I'm not an academic,' says Ed. 'I haven't played a team sport since I left school. I was always useless. No hand–eye coordination.'

'Me too,' says Ali. 'I think I had period pains for years to get out of PE.'

'Exercise is bad for you,' says Ed. 'All of my rugby-playing friends have had knee replacements.'

Ali suspects Ed of going to a minor public school. She knows that he read history at York and then did a master's in library management. That's how he ended up at QMUL, first as a librarian and then as a curator. He says that he remembers Ali from her student days, a statement she finds rather alarming, if true. Ali was thirty when she enrolled at university. Ed is only three years older but she's sure that, when she was a student, he would have seemed like one of the faculty, a *grown-up*.

They walk towards the Mile End Road. It's another warm evening and there's a carnival atmosphere, even in the least salubrious streets. People are drinking outside pubs and children play in tiny urban parks. The air smells of mown grass and petrol.

'I like London on days like this,' says Ali.

'Don't you like it all the time?' says Ed, slowing his pace slightly, rather to Ali's relief. His legs are a lot longer than hers.

'It's a bit grim in the winter,' says Ali. 'But I wouldn't move. Growing up in Hastings, all I wanted to do was escape to London.'

'I grew up in the country,' says Ed. 'Sometimes I dream about going back.'

'Really? Where?'

'Somerset,' says Ed, 'near Yeovil. It's a beautiful part of the world, though it can seem a bit far from anywhere.'

Ali thinks of Hugo, who grew up in the Cotswolds, and of Finn, currently falling in love with the Yorkshire Dales.

'I wouldn't leave London,' she says, almost in defiance.

The film is showing at the Genesis Cinema. Ali looked at the website earlier and learnt that, in 1848, the site was a pub called the Eagle, famous for its music hall entertainments. Did Leonard Rokeby, the pianist from Hawk Street, ever play here? Ali likes to think he did.

The Genesis is now ultra-modern on the outside, a stylish corner plot with neon lights and a rather space-age logo. Inside, though, there are comfortable chairs in the lobby and a bar that hints at the building's Victorian history. Ali and Ed drink gin and tonic and talk about their favourite films. Ed, *Manon des Sources*. Ali, *The Godfather, Part 2*. For a few minutes Ali feels almost happy but then she thinks about going home to a house without Terry and her heart twists. Ed doesn't notice, he's too busy talking about Emmanuelle Béart.

At any other time Ali would have liked the film, which is funny, quirky and surreal. But tonight, she feels her thoughts wandering, names scrolling across the screen of her mind. Barry Power, Klaus Kramer, Luke Fanshaw. She recalls Hugo saying, 'That was Kramer's other thing. He claimed to be able to time travel.' Once Ali would have dismissed this, now she knows that it could be true. Is there a link between Luke Fanshaw and the Victorian showman? Or is Ali just trying to make his death something other than senseless tragedy? She thinks of Barry Power conjuring Serafina, the pilgrim soul. Is she somehow nearby, in the East London of the 1850s? *Sometimes the membrane between this world and the next is very thin.*

'Did you enjoy that?' asks Ed, as they make their way out into the still-warm night.

'Very much,' says Ali, hoping he doesn't ask her to elaborate. She doesn't really remember the last half hour and thinks she might have dropped off.

'Shall we go to Pho?' asks Ed. 'A kind of homage to Vietnam?'

'OK,' says Ali. She doesn't really feel like eating but she wants to go home even less. Over their rice bowls, Ed tells Ali about his travels in Vietnam, Cambodia and Thailand. This makes Ali feel even more depressed. She has never really travelled anywhere, unless you could count 1850, which she doesn't. Growing up, her parents didn't have the money or inclination for foreign holidays. Ali and Declan, teenage parents in low-paid jobs, could hardly manage a week at Butlins in Bognor. Ali had travelled a bit when she was married to Hugo and she visited Lincoln's family in Canada but this isn't the same as the youthful backpacking adventures described by Ed.

When they leave the restaurant it's eleven o'clock. Ali announces her intention of calling an Uber. Ed says, standing in the glowing red light of a kebab shop, 'Unless you want to come back to mine?'

'Pardon?' says Ali. Hugo tried to stop her using this word ('it's so common'), but Ali refused to change her vocabulary for any of her husbands.

'Would you like to come back to my place?' Ed moves towards her and bends his head from his great height. He's going to kiss her. Two passing youths jeer and wolf whistle. A police car shoots past with siren blaring. Ali backs away.

'I'm sorry,' she says. 'I'm a bit tired. I think I need to get home.'

'No problem,' says Ed. His voice is non-committal and Ali can't see his face because it's so much above her.

Ed waits with her until her Uber arrives. Ali looks back at his tall figure, still standing by the kebab sign. *Doner and Shish, Eat In or Takeaway.* Ed raises his hand and Ali waves back. Should she have accepted the invitation and gone to the flat in Hoxton that she's never seen? In a way it would be tempting to go to bed with Ed, to lose herself in mere physical sensation. But, clearly, not tempting enough. Maybe if they hadn't been standing in the Mile End Road, with catcalling youths and squad cars screaming past. Maybe if Ed hadn't been wearing cream chinos. Maybe if he'd been in a black frock coat and cravat . . .

Entering the house is an ordeal, a physical struggle. It's as if the air has become solid and Ali has to push through it. The space feels totally different without Terry. He didn't always run to greet Ali but somehow she always knew he was there. Now she knows he isn't. On the mat is a card from Adnan and Faaiza's six-year-old twins. It shows a bright orange cat surrounded by the words, 'We hop you find Terri'. It helps, a little.

Ali is just making a cup of tea, trying not to look at Terry's empty bowls, when her phone buzzes. Finn. Why is he ringing at eleven thirty at night? She clicks 'accept'.

'Hi, Mum. Sorry to ring so late. I'm on the train back from Leeds.'

'That's OK, love. How's it going?'

'OK. I think we're going to win. The numbers are looking pretty good. The thing is, Mum . . .'

Ali waits. She knows her son.

'The thing is, if Helen wins, and I think she will, she's offered me a job as her constituency manager. Based in Yorkshire. And I think I'd like to take it.'

'What about Georgie?' says Ali, thinking, What about me?

'We'd see each other at weekends and maybe she could get a job up here too.'

Ali says all the right things. How exciting. What an adventure. But, when she sits on the sofa afterwards, she wishes fervently, despite being a lifelong Labour voter, that Helen will lose her seat. If only Terry were sitting beside her. She imagines how calming it would feel to stroke his soft fur, the tension fading with each movement, head to tail, including that all-important chin scratch. Finn didn't even mention Terry.

If only she could go back in time, just to the day that she went to see Barry Power, or the night before. She could shut the cat flap and Terry would be safe, angry at being imprisoned, but alive and with Ali.

And, as if from another lifetime, she hears Bud's voice.

I could take you back on a short trip today. Just a couple of days or weeks. That's easy.

Chapter 8

Ali joined the cold case team in 2015, and, on her first day, Geoff Bastian sent her to talk to Dr Serafina Pellegrini at Imperial College, London. Ali didn't know what to expect but Jones, stunningly beautiful with long black hair and sporting a biker's jacket, was a surprise. 'I married a man called Jones when I first came to England,' she told Ali. 'We divorced soon afterwards but his surname has been useful.' 'I'm divorced too,' Ali had told her, 'but I've gone back to my maiden name.' She had divorced Lincoln that same year but had never taken his last name, partly because it was Scrubb.

But chat about husbands soon faded into insignificance when Jones leant forward and said, 'Have you ever considered time travel, Alison?'

'Often,' laughed Ali. 'I'd like to go back to the day before I met my first husband.' Even as she said this, she'd been aware that it wasn't true. She wouldn't swap the Declan years for anything. Without them, she wouldn't have Finn.

'Time is like a sheet of paper,' said Jones, unsmiling, 'but what if you could make a pleat in that paper?'

'What if you could . . .' Ali remembers the sensation of drowning in a sea of words. If she could just grab hold of a phrase, it might save her.

'I've been working on a way of moving in time,' said Jones, briskly, 'moving the atoms of the body from one place to another. Creating a wormhole if you like.'

This was the first of many such discussions, many experiments on the secret floors of Eel House. Then, in 2020, when London was in the grip of lockdown, the streets deserted, Ali and John travelled to a side road just off Oxford Street in Jones's electric Fiat 500. It was the first electric vehicle Ali had travelled in and she remembers thinking that its futuristic hum was very appropriate for the adventure ahead. Jones, her hair now cut brutally short but still as beautiful as ever, kept turning her head while driving to address Ali in the back seat. Ali began to wonder if they'd live long enough to time travel.

John and Ali stood on the pavement. 'It's very important to come back to this exact spot,' said Jones. They didn't know then just how vital this was. 'Stand still,' said Jones. Then she got out her iPhone. Ali and John exchanged glances. Was it possible that Jones was going to change physics for ever, using a *mobile phone*? Midway through their amused eye-meet, Ali felt a jolt, as if she had tripped on a paving stone. The previously empty street was now full of people, and traffic was snarled up at the lights. Ali looked at John again and saw her amazement reflected in his face. They had travelled in time.

'I don't know,' says Bud. He spins uneasily in his chair, almost colliding with a pile of books on the floor.

'You said you could do it,' says Ali. 'You said it would be easy.' They are in Bud's office at Imperial, only a few doors away from the place where Ali first met Jones. The room is a semi-basement, lit only by a single lightbulb. The walls are bare apart from a poster of David Tennant as Doctor Who. There's no other sign that Bud has tried to personalise the space, no photographs or knick-knacks. Ali realises that she actually knows very little about Bud. He's from a Sri Lankan family, Sinhalese, she thinks. He's gay although he doesn't seem to have a partner. In his late twenties, Bud was the baby of the team and often teased for being behind on jokes. Seeing him here, in an actual office with Dr B. Sirisema on the door, makes Ali see her ex-colleague in a new light.

'I was showing off,' says Bud now, with a disarming flash of honesty. 'I don't really know if I can do it.'

'But you could try,' says Ali. 'Just a couple of hours, that's all I need. Just enough time to shut the cat flap.'

When Ali told Bud about Terry, he'd been surprisingly sympathetic. 'I like cats,' he said. 'They're smart. They know secret ways. He'll find his way home.' But now he looks completely blank, as if he's never heard of the feline species.

'I'm only talking about going back a few days,' says Ali. 'No one will even know I'm gone.'

'Just a few days,' says Bud. 'And you'll only be at home? In your house? Is that all?'

'That's all I need. Just an hour. Less than that. Just enough time to lock the cat flap.'

Bud turns to one of the two computers on the desk and presses what look to Ali like random keys. Numbers and letters spool across the screen.

'You said that you were working on a way to bring Jones back,' says Ali. 'You said you felt like you were in communication with her.'

'Did I say that?'

'Yes.'

'I know you can do it,' says Ali. 'Jones always had such faith in you.'

To be honest, Ali is not sure if Jones believed in anyone or anything but herself yet it's almost tragic to see Bud blush like a teenager.

'She always said I was her best student,' he says.

'You were,' says Ali. 'And, if we don't keep trying, what's the point of anything? What's the point of all Jones's work? All of *your* work? This is what we do. We're the Frozen People.'

The nickname was Bud's idea and Ali is pleased to see it brings a reluctant grin to his face.

'It's only an hour,' she reminds him. 'I'll be back before you know it.'

When Ali leaves Bud to the nervous-looking students waiting outside his door for a tutorial, she makes her way to the cafeteria, where she is meeting Margaret Fanshaw. She walks through the labyrinthine underground corridors, feeling slightly guilty. She thinks she has persuaded Bud. He says he will need a few days to do the necessary calculations and they have arranged to meet at Ali's house on Friday evening. But did Ali bully him, ride roughshod over his very reasonable concerns? A little, she has to admit.

Today, Margaret is in jeans and sweatshirt and blends easily into the crowd of students eating late breakfasts and working on their computers. Many of them seem to be in their thirties or forties and it reminds Ali of her own university days. She felt so excited about learning and so shocked at the casual attitudes of the eighteen-year-olds who regularly missed nine a.m. lectures or skimped on the extra reading. Ali wanted to absorb knowledge like a sponge. It's why she's still in touch with Elizabeth. There's always more to learn.

Ali buys coffee for herself and Margaret and they find a table near the entrance. Some of the students nod at Margaret as they pass and Ali asks how long she's worked at the university.

'About ten years,' says Margaret. 'I like it. I like being around young people.' She looks especially sad when she says this. Ali knows that Margaret has two other adult children but all these fresh-faced youngsters must surely make her think of Luke. Margaret tells her that Luke started at South Bank University but didn't like it and left after a term. 'He wasn't much of a one for studying but he had a job working at a gym and he loved that. He became quite vain, worked out all the time, had a special diet, always doing something called bulking or cutting, whatever they are. I just know that it cost me a fortune in chicken and spinach. And he spent a fortune on face creams and the like. His dad would have had a fit.' Ali knows that Luke's father died when he was ten. She asks Margaret how Luke got interested in Klaus Kramer.

'I don't really know,' says Margaret. 'You never know what your kids are looking at online, do you? But he started talking about Kramer, saying that he could fly and Luke wanted to learn. I didn't take much notice. Kids are always getting interested in weird subjects. Mark, my eldest, had a big thing about Ancient Rome for a while. I feel bad now. I wish I'd listened . . .' She presses her eyes with the heel of her hand.

'You can't blame yourself,' says Ali gently. 'You're a great mum. I can tell.'

Margaret sniffs and gives her a watery smile.

'There's a film about Kramer,' says Ali. 'Do you know if Luke watched it?'

'I don't,' says Margaret. 'Sorry. I'm not being very helpful.'

'As I told you on the phone,' says Ali, 'I went to see Barry Power. He claimed not to remember anything he said to Luke while in a trance.'

'Very convenient,' says Margaret, her voice hardening again.

'Exactly,' says Ali. 'If we can prove that Power told Luke he could fly, we could maybe charge him with encouraging or assisting suicide. Trouble is, Power is a slippery customer.'

'I thought that when I spoke to him,' says Margaret. 'Full of sympathy, he was, but clever enough not to take any responsibility.'

'I'll try again,' says Ali, 'but I just wanted you to know that it's quite a long shot.'

'I understand,' says Margaret. 'Thank you for trying.'

They talk about Margaret's other children for a bit. They are called Mark and Joanna so clearly there's an evangelist theme going on. Ali noticed Margaret's gold crucifix when they first met. She hopes her faith is a comfort now. As they leave, Ali asks Margaret if she knows a professor called Serafina Pellegrini.

'The Italian lady? The one with the Ferrari on her office door? Yes. I've spoken to her a few times. Very polite but not exactly friendly. She's gone away on a sabbatical, hasn't she?'

'Something like that,' says Ali.

★

It's midday by the time Ali arrives at the Department of Logistics. John and Dina both seem absorbed in work. John is writing in his notebook. He covers page after page with his beautiful italic handwriting. Ali never knows what he's recording so diligently.

'Sorry I'm late,' says Ali. 'I went to see Margaret Fanshaw, Luke's mum.'

'How was she?' asks John. 'Did you tell her you thought it might be impossible to make charges stick?'

'I did,' says Ali. 'I said I'd keep trying, though. If I can just get Power to admit that he said something inappropriate to Luke, something that could be seen as encouraging suicide, then we might have a chance. For example, Power said something weird to Luke about "the killing time". Of course he claimed it was Kramer talking through him but, hopefully, a court would dismiss that as nonsense.'

Dina looks up from her laptop. As usual, she's working on two screens at once. Ali thinks of Bud with his two computers. 'I might have found something,' she says.

'Really?' says Ali, walking over to Dina's desk. 'What is it?'

'The film about Klaus Kramer.'

'Wow,' says Ali. 'Hugo said he thought all the copies had been destroyed.'

'That's the official story,' says Dina. 'But a collector bought a box of vintage reels in an auction about five years ago. *The Mesmerist*, that's the Kramer film, was one of them. Tom, the man who bought it, wrote about it on a rare-films website. I've been in touch with him and I'm arranging to have the film digitally remastered.'

'Well done,' says Ali. 'Have you any idea what the film's about? When was it made?'

'It's a silent film, made in 1902,' says Dina.

'So it can't be the real Kramer then?'

'Not unless he was an actual vampire. When were the first films made?'

'In the late 1800s, I think,' says Ali. 'Do you know, John?'

'I don't, I'm afraid,' says John. 'Bud would know – he's the film buff.'

'Is he?' Another thing Ali doesn't know about Bud.

Dina consults her phone. 'The first public cinematic screening was in Paris in 1895. It was staged by the Lumière brothers, Auguste and Louis. The film was called *Workers Leaving the Lumière Factory*. Doesn't sound very thrilling.'

'I expect it was thrilling, though,' says Ali, 'seeing moving figures on screen for the first time. What about *The Mesmerist*? Had this Tom person watched it?'

'He said he'd watched a bit and found it quite disturbing.'

'Hugo used the same word, "disturbing",' says Ali. 'But he hadn't seen the film. Did Tom say anything more?'

'Apparently it starts with a mesmerist reading a woman's mind.'

'Bit hard to do on film, I'd imagine,' says Ali.

'Then he murders a lot of people with an axe.'

'Wow,' says Ali, 'definitely an 18 certificate. I can't wait to watch it.'

She goes back into her office reflecting that not even John or Dina had checked in again about Terry.

It's hard to wait. On Friday Ali leaves work promptly at five and is home by half past. She has asked Bud to come at ten so there are many Terry-less hours to fill. She makes herself some pasta but is too keyed up to eat it. She tidies the sitting room and the kitchen. She even washes Terry's bowls but is too superstitious to put them away so replaces them on his Top Cat plastic mat. She tries to read her Dickens book but the words swim in front of her eyes. She switches on the TV but nothing grabs her attention. Eventually she scrolls through her phone and comes across Barry Power's psychic text service.

'Ask the question that's in your heart' urges the website. 'Complicated questions may require three answers. £1.50 per message received plus standard network charges. Terms and conditions apply.'

After thinking for a few seconds, Ali texts, 'Will I find Terry?'

After a few seconds, the answer comes back. 'You will find what you seek but you may not at first recognise your heart's desire. All is not gold that glitters, not all those who wander are lost.'

A chat bot, thinks Ali. She has heard Dina talking about the way AI can mimic human conversations. This one has clearly been ransacking the book of mystic quotations. Or a Magic 8 ball.

She writes, 'Will I see Cain again?'

'If the universe wills it, you will see Cain again.'

'Thanks for nothing,' says Ali, aloud. She types her next question almost without thinking: 'Am I in danger?'

The answer comes back immediately.

'Yes.'

Bud rings the doorbell while she's still staring at the screen. He bursts into the room, looking big and chaotic, his hair loose. Ali misses Jones and her cool elegance. Bud paces around Ali's sitting room, picking up objects and putting them down again. He looks at a picture of Finn holding Terry.

'Is this the cat?'

'Yes.' Bud had met Terry before, when the team came to Ali's house-warming party, but it was a brief encounter because Terry hates visitors and spent most of the evening in hiding.

'He's a Siamese.'

'Yes.'

'There used to be Ceylon cats in Sri Lanka,' says Bud. 'My grandmother had one. He looked a bit like Terry. They're very rare now, though.'

'Do you have lots of family in Sri Lanka?' asks Ali, remembering her resolution to get to know Bud better. Bud doesn't answer. He's now browsing Ali's bookshelves and asking why they're not in alphabetical order.

At twenty past ten they go outside. Bud thinks that they will have a better chance outdoors; all the successful trips have been made this way. The street is empty although Ali can hear Tony's voice booming from inside his house. The old-fashioned street-lamps cast a soft yellow light. The air is almost as warm as it was in the day.

Ali stands with Bud on the concrete space in front of her house. Finn disapproves – the loss of urban front gardens is having a terrible effect on biodiversity, he says – but it was done before Ali bought the place.

'This is your ingress point,' says Bud.

'Great,' says Ali. 'Perfect.'

'Have you got everything? Torch? UV spray?'

'Yes.'

'I wish Jones was here,' says Bud.

So do I, thinks Ali. Jones always seemed to know what she was doing and, if she didn't, she had a variety of gnomic sayings to disguise this.

'It'll be fine,' says Ali, in the new calming voice she has adopted for Bud. 'You can do it.'

'You're going back exactly a week. To June the twenty-first.'

'That's right.'

'You've got an hour,' says Bud. 'No more.'

'I know,' says Ali. 'I got in just before eleven that night. That should give me plenty of time to shut the cat flap.'

'Be back at this exact same spot.'

'I know.'

'Remember to spray around your feet as soon as you're through the gate.'

They use an ultraviolet spray, only visible under the light of a special torch, so that they know exactly where to place their feet for the return journey.

'Let's do it,' says Ali.

'Are you sure?' asks Bud, for what feels like the hundredth time.

Ali visualises Terry looking up at her with his round blue eyes. She thinks of Finn moving to Yorkshire, of John talking about the space occupied by domestic animals, of Ed propositioning her outside the kebab shop.

'I'm sure.'

'OK then.' Bud gets out his phone.

Chapter 9

Ali stumbles forward. Was it this dark last week? She can't remember. There's no light coming from Tony's house and no sound either. Ali gropes her way to her front door, feeling in her pocket for her key. Her fingers close around her cat-shaped keyring, a present from Finn. Its eyes light up as Ali stabs the door in roughly the right place for the keyhole.

There's nothing there. Ali shines her torch. The door is plain wood, without Ali's decorative stained-glass panel. There's no bell but a brass doorknob gleams in the torchlight and, below that, an old-fashioned mortise lock. Ali backs away, confused. The house looks the same, small and symmetrical, but there are curtains at the windows instead of wooden blinds. Ali's recycling bins have gone and there's no 'Vote Labour' poster in her downstairs window.

Ali turns towards Tony's house. A hazy moon moves out from the clouds and she can see the whole street. The terraced houses are recognisable but there are no dividing walls between the front gardens. There are no street lights, no parked cars. There are no telegraph poles and no light coming from the 24-hour garage at the end of the street. This is not London in 2024.

Ali takes a step forward and trips, falling forward and banging her knee painfully. The road surface is not cobbles and it's not pavement. It feels slimy and unpleasant to touch. Ali scrambles to her feet and approaches Tony's front door. She knocks. The sound echoes loudly, which makes Ali realise how quiet everything is, but there's no answer. Ali limps towards the next house, which she now knows as Mrs Goldman's. She knocks again and, to her surprise, there's a sound of someone moving inside. The door opens and Irene Goldman stands in front of her, holding a candle like someone in a nativity play. Ali feels relief flooding through her. She hasn't travelled so far back in time after all. Her neighbour is still here. Irene is obviously dressed for bed in a long white gown. She has a grey shawl wrapped over her shoulders.

'Irene?' says Ali. 'It's Ali from two doors down. I'm locked out, I—'

Irene shuts the door in Ali's face.

Ali stumbles back as if she's been slapped. She doesn't dare knock on another door. She makes her way to the open end of her cul-de-sac. She's looking at a much wider thoroughfare. It's cobbled and there are even street lights, though very few and far between. On the other side of the road are dark edifices that look like they could be factories or warehouses. As Ali stands, not knowing what to do or even what to think, she hears the sound of approaching hooves. It's ominous somehow. The headless horseman. The four horsemen of the apocalypse. Good news never comes on horseback. But she waits. What else can she do?

A carriage pulls to a halt at the top of Ali's street. Again, it looks like something from a nightmare. Black horses, high wheels striking sparks from the stones. There's a cry and the horses come to a steaming, stamping halt. Ali can smell them, a comforting countryside smell but also one that awakens memories.

A liveried coachman springs down and opens a door. He's holding a lantern and, in its cone of light, Ali sees a woman in a long red dress. Her face is in shadow but Ali recognises her immediately.

It's Jones.

And Terry is in her arms.

'Jones!' squeaks Ali.

'Ali,' says Jones, 'for heaven's sake, get in.' Her voice is so much the same that Ali wants to hug her.

The coachman, who hasn't spoken a word, extends a hand to help Ali up the high step. She clambers in and the door is shut behind her.

'Jones,' says Ali again. 'Why are you here and why have you got Terry?' She reaches for her cat and buries her face in his fur. She's beyond relieved to see him, alive and well. He smells the same but with the addition of a floral perfume that she doesn't recognise. Terry squawks indignantly and wriggles out of Ali's grasp.

'Now you've done it,' says Jones. 'I'd only just got him calm.'

'What's going on?' says Ali, trying to tempt Terry down from the back of one of the red damask seats. There are candles in glass lanterns on the silk-covered walls. Their flickering light only adds to the strangeness of the scene. 'Bud was only meant to take me back a few days,' she went on. 'He said he could do it.'

Jones laughs. 'Bud! That explains everything. To be fair, though, there's more to this time-travel business than I ever imagined.

Emotion comes into it but it's more than that. There's some sort of link between us – the team, the Frozen People. I'm not sure quite what it all means yet but Bud was no doubt thinking of me when he did the calculations, and he brought you to me. It's that simple.'

It's not the first time that Jones has described something as simple when, in reality, it's too complicated to be comprehended by a normal human brain. Ali tries a different question. 'Why have you got Terry?'

'I knew you were coming here one day this week. I'll explain later how. I wasn't sure exactly when you'd arrive, so I've been driving around every evening. I sent James to look for you.'

'James?'

Jones points towards the place where, presumably, the coachman is now standing with the horses. The carriage isn't moving and Ali can hear snorts and the jingle of harnesses.

'It's not his real name,' says Jones, 'but all coachmen are called James. James found Terry in your garden this evening. I recognised him because he's your screen saver.'

'But how did Terry get here?'

'I don't know,' says Jones. 'It's interesting, isn't it?'

'Interesting' is another one of Jones's words. Ali finally gets Terry to sit on the seat beside her. Stroking him helps immeasurably. She tries to steady her breathing.

'*Calmati*,' says Jones. 'I must say, it's good to see you again.'

'It's good to see you too,' says Ali. And, for a moment, it is just straightforwardly good to see Jones again and to hear her softly accented voice saying things like '*calmati*'.

'So what was Bud trying to do?' asks Jones.

Ali explains about going back to shut the cat flap and Jones laughs so heartily that she almost extinguishes one of the candles.

'Now I've heard it all. You English and your pets.'

Ali strokes Terry again. He seems completely at home in this new environment. In fact, he goes well with the opulent carriage and the vision sitting opposite.

'Do you think the gate will work?' asks Ali. 'Bud says I've got an hour.'

'Let's try it,' says Jones. 'But you need to do something about your clothes. You can't be seen looking like that.'

Ali is wearing black linen trousers and a black vest with a loose white shirt over it. On her feet are white Birkenstock sandals. No wonder Irene had shut the door in her face. But why was Irene there at all? Perhaps it was her great-great grandmother. They certainly looked very alike. Irene did say that she'd lived in the street all her life. Maybe her family have always lived there. Well, Irene's ancestor was rightly horrified by the woman in black and white. To say nothing of the red hair and the nose stud. An inconsequential thought strikes Ali.

'Your hair,' she says to Jones. Her colleague's head, which was almost shaven in 2023, is a wonder of ringlets and glossy tresses, gold combs gleam in the darkness. 'How is it so long?'

'It's a wig,' says Jones. 'Very itchy too. Lots of Victorian women wore wigs. Better not ask too much about the provenance. My own hair is growing but it's not long enough for fashionable styles yet. And I'm very fashionable.'

'I can see that,' says Ali. 'But what year is it? How long have you been here?'

'It's the year of Our Lord eighteen fifty-one,' says Jones. 'It's sixteen months since I went through the gate.'

'We can get you back,' says Ali. 'Now that Bud has done this, I'm sure it means we can get you back.'

Jones laughs again. In the candlelight she's a blur of white skin and black hair, draperies of rich red silk fringed with gold.

'Ali,' says Jones, 'why on earth would I want to go back?'

Chapter 10

Dina walks slowly towards Eel House. It's another sweltering day and the sunlight on the windows is almost dazzling. Dina is only wearing a light summer dress but she's still hot. She stops to buy an iced latte. The streets are deserted because it's Saturday but, very unusually, Ali has requested a meeting. Dina has no idea what it's about but, to be honest, she's grateful for any distraction at work these days. The new IT system is full of glitches and Dina doesn't think it'll ever be rolled out across the police force. She knows that she's been given this task to keep her out of trouble. But it still leaves her too much time on her hands, even with helping out on the cold cases. Over the last year she has also stalked all her ex-boyfriends, traced her ancestry back five generations and bought a distressing number of clothes from Vinted. She doesn't know how much longer they can carry on this way. Before Ali's fatal trip to 1850, Dina had been about to travel to 1966 to track down a serial killer. She remembers how she'd felt when she was waiting for Jones to make the arrangements, a mixture of apprehension and churning excitement that was a little like falling in love. Now her days possess no such highs or lows. Her last few internet dates have been disasters. Work consists of a dreary commute, some chat and a few jokes in the office, then the Tube and bus home, a keto meal, two glasses of wine and a Netflix series.

Digging into Barry Power had felt like a breakthrough, and it had been fun to go out with Ali, but now it seems like there isn't a case at all. Barry is clearly just a conman. It has been quite satisfying tracking down the Kramer film, but Dina suspects that it will be another dead end. What could a film made in 1902 have to do with a young man taking his own life in 2024?

The streets are almost eerily silent, the windows of the offices glinting in the sunlight. Who knows what's going on behind those grim, vertical blinds, wonders Dina. She once thought Eel House contained a cold case department.

Dina is not a police officer, as she is almost tired of reminding people. She's a civilian computer forensics analyst. She studied computer science at Cambridge, narrowly avoided being recruited as a spy (or so she thinks) and didn't want to join a merchant bank, the civil service or a Californian tech giant. Her parents, first generation immigrants from Ghana, had approved of Cambridge and the computers but were baffled when Dina embarked on a master's in cyber security at Imperial. 'More degrees?' said her mother. 'When will it end?' 'There are three hundred and sixty degrees in a circle,' Dina reminded her. 'Where does a circle get you?' retorted Cynthia. Dina's mother has had very little formal education but Dina often thinks she's a lot cleverer than her daughter. At Imperial, Dina met Dr Serafina Pellegrini and the rest is history. If you can make history retrospectively.

Latte in hand, Dina types in the passcode and pushes open the doors to Eel House. She climbs the stairs because none of them trusts the lifts. Only John is in the office, drinking from his West Ham water bottle and looking out of the window towards the unsuccessful undersea mural on the building opposite.

'The octopus has ten legs,' says Dina.

'What?' says John. 'Oh yes. I see.' John has always been quiet but often, these days, he acts as if part of him were still in 1850. Dina likes John. He's the father figure in the office, despite being only five years older than Ali. But now Dina feels slightly awkward when it's just the two of them. Only Ali really understands John now.

Dina covers up her discomfort by making a meal of putting her bag on her desk, turning on her laptop and going to the kitchen to heat up her morning porridge. She throws her paper cup in the recycling and puts on the kettle. She asks John if he wants coffee but he always says no these days.

'Where's Ali? She's always up for caffeine.'

'She's not in yet,' says John.

'She's the one who called this meeting.'

'Maybe she's out looking for Terry,' says John. 'Poor Ali. She dotes on that cat.'

'He's very cute,' says Dina, 'but he bit me once because I tickled his tummy.'

'Cats' stomachs are sacrosanct,' says John. 'It's an ancient law.'

While Dina is waiting for the microwave to finish, she hears the door bang open. It's very loud, even for Ali. Dina comes out of the kitchen to see Bud standing in the centre of the room. It's been a while since she's seen her ex-colleague and she's shocked at his appearance. Bud was never the tidiest person but today he looks almost wild, his hair a mane, his clothing dishevelled.

'Bud,' says John. 'What's happened?'

'It's Ali,' says Bud. 'I've lost her.'

'And Ali never came back to the ingress point?' says John, for what feels like the tenth time. They're in Ali's office. Dina has no idea why they drifted from the open-plan area into the smaller room. Maybe it just feels safer and more secure. Maybe it reflects the seriousness of the situation. Automatically John sits in Ali's chair, Dina and Bud take the seats facing him.

'She didn't come back,' says Bud, also for the umpteenth time. 'I waited all night.' He runs his fingers through his tangled black hair. 'She was only meant to be away an hour. I took her back to the night of Power's show. Just to shut the cat flap.'

'She shouldn't . . .' begins John but stops again. This too has happened a few times. They all know that Ali shouldn't have gone back in time to save Terry. They all know Bud shouldn't have enabled her. There's no point in repeating any of this.

'That must be why she called this meeting,' says John. 'To tell us about it. After she'd done it, of course.'

'Do you know why it didn't work?' Dina asks Bud.

'No,' says Bud, doing the wild-eyed thing again. 'All the calculations should have been correct. I've watched Jones do it hundreds of times.'

That's not true, thinks Dina. Before 1850, they had only travelled in time on three occasions. First Ali and John to 2020, then again to 2021, then Dina and Ali made a trip to 1976. She thinks of her trip often: the different fashions, the strangely shaped buses, the advertisements for long-forgotten brands. For Mash get Smash. What We Want is Watney's. In those days, they hadn't been solid flesh and bone when they went through the gate. Dina and Ali weren't visible to the people around them, despite taking the precaution of wearing flares and tank-tops (Dina loves dressing up). But, when they saw a man washing his bloody hands after murdering his wife, Dina thinks that he knew he was being watched by avengers from the future. She hopes so anyway.

Ali was solid when she went to 1850. She could, in her own words, 'walk, talk, eat and piss'. No one knows why.

'We need to tell Nigel,' says John.

Dina grimaces at Bud. She's never seen Nigel express an emotional response to anything, but she doesn't think the news that Ali has, once more, disappeared in time, will make him exactly happy.

'Let's wait a bit before telling him,' she says. 'There's nothing he can do after all.'

'Ali kept saying it would work because she knows she went back again,' says Bud. 'Because of the diary and the letter.'

'Is Ali still thinking about that?' says John.

Of course she is, Dina wants to tell him. Ali knows she had some sort of relationship with a man she met in 1850. *Of course* she thinks about it. If it were Dina, she'd think of nothing else.

'I'll have to go back and get her,' says John. 'Like I did the first time.'

'Excuse me,' says Dina. 'It's my turn.'

Suddenly she wants this more than anything. It would be *something*, some tangible reward for the years of studying, for ruining her posture hunched over computers. Dina wants to be the one to save Ali. Surely, it's her turn to be the hero.

'We don't know where she is,' says Bud. 'Maybe I got that bit wrong too. She could be anywhere in time.'

It's a dizzying thought. Ali could be in 1918 or 1666 or even – Dina is vague on prehistory, she concentrated on science at school – the Stone Age. A series of outlandish pictures cross Dina's mind: Ali in a flapper dress, Ali dressed in animal skins, carrying a club. Then another idea surfaces. She's not even sure how to express it.

'If Ali only went back a week,' she says, 'won't she catch up with us? When she gets to today, I mean.'

'It doesn't work like that,' says Bud. 'Ali will always be behind us. It's a different reality now. She's in the past and that's always the past. That's what Jones says.'

Not for the first time since she joined the team, Dina struggles to comprehend. She knows, objectively, that she's got a good brain. One, moreover, that is good at probability and complicated equations. But she just can't cope with the idea that Ali will always be living a week in the past.

Frustration makes her blunt. 'You've got no idea how it works,' she says to Bud.

'You're right,' he says, humbly.

This silences Dina. No one speaks until the stand-off is broken by the phone ringing on Ali's desk. For a second, they all stare at it and then John lifts the receiver. 'John Cole.' Then he says, 'She's not available, I'm afraid. Can I help? I'm the SIO.' Senior investigating officer. It must be a police call. There's a long silence while the other person speaks. Dina feels her heart beating. Nothing good ever came of a call to a landline. The only people who call hers are scammers and her mother.

'OK,' says John. 'I'll be there in half an hour.'

Then he puts the phone down and looks at Dina and Bud.

'Ali's ex-husband has been murdered,' he says.

Chapter 11

'Hugo Maltravers,' says John. 'Did you ever meet him?'

'No,' says Dina. 'Ali was with Lincoln when I first met her.'

'Me too,' says John. 'Lincoln always seemed an odd person for Ali to marry. He only seemed to talk about going to the gym.'

'I think Ali briefly got into fitness after she divorced Hugo,' says Dina. 'She met Lincoln at the gym. He was her personal trainer. No, I couldn't see it either. Although he was rather good-looking.'

They are in an Uber on their way to Herne Hill police station. They are meeting DS Luca Venturi, who was the person who made the call earlier.

'What did Venturi tell you?' asks Dina.

'Just that Hugo had been stabbed as he walked to Herne Hill station yesterday morning.'

'If it was his usual train, then it might have been planned,' says Dina. 'Someone could have been following his routine.'

'That's true. Venturi obviously thinks there's more to it than a random attack. It didn't take him long to find the connection to Ali.'

'Is there really a connection to Ali?' says Dina. 'I know she met him a few days ago.'

'We'll find out soon,' says John, looking out of the window. 'Left here,' he says to the driver. 'I did my training around here.'

Luca Venturi is Scottish, which is a surprise. He's also young, with dark curly hair and a rather rakish moustache.

'Thanks for coming,' he says, 'though I really wanted to see DI Dawson.'

'Ali's away for a few days,' says John. 'Undercover.'

Venturi's eyes widen. 'I've heard rumours about your department.'

'They're all true,' Dina tells him with a grin.

Luca laughs but he also gives her a rather sharp look. It's news to Dina that there are stories about the unit. She thought they were entirely forgotten, shut away in Eel House, but maybe the Isaac Templeton case made some people look in their direction.

Luca takes them to his desk, which is in the centre of an open-plan area. He has tried to barricade himself in with filing cabinets and room dividers. Dina sympathises. She loves office chat as much as the next person but sometimes you want a place where you can play solitaire in peace.

'Hugo Maltravers,' says Luca, opening up a screen on his computer. 'Age fifty-five, senior lecturer in history at King's College London. Lives with Serena Richards, forty, a marketing manager. One son, Barley, aged five. Yesterday, Hugo left home to catch the seven fifty from Herne Hill to Victoria. About a hundred yards from the station he was accosted and stabbed. His body was found by another commuter at eight fifteen. Ambulance was called but he was dead at the scene. No witnesses, so far, and no weapon, although forensics think it was a domestic blade, adapted and sharpened.'

'Adapted and sharpened,' repeats John. 'Do you think this was premeditated?'

Luca shrugs. 'There's plenty of knife crime around, plenty of people carrying blades. I had a fourteen-year-old stab and fatally wound an eighteen-year-old only a few weeks ago. But there are a couple of things that strike me about this case. One, this was Hugo's usual route to work. Someone might have been watching him, planning this. The place where he was killed, it's a short cut between a warehouse and a multistorey car park. High walls on both sides, no eyewitnesses, no CCTV. It doesn't seem random to me.'

That's what I said, thinks Dina. It annoys her that Luca seems to be addressing his remarks primarily to John.

'The second thing is the link to DI Dawson. When there's a connection to a police officer, especially one involved in . . . er . . . classified work . . . that needs to be investigated. Serena, Hugo's partner, thought that he might have seen DI Dawson fairly recently?'

'They met on Tuesday,' says Dina. She remembers Ali complaining about having to go into central London and being rather grumpy afterwards. Hugo had been as irritating as ever, she said.

'Do you know why they met?' asks Luca, now giving Dina his full attention.

'It's hard to explain,' says Dina, realising that she sounds very unlike a police officer. She can't recount evidence in the wooden but efficient manner demonstrated by Luca earlier. She suddenly wishes she was wearing something more professional than a flowery dress. 'We're investigating a cold case, a death that was ruled as a suicide but might be murder, or at least manslaughter. The young man who died had contacted a psychic called Barry Power—'

'Who?' Luca speaks so loudly that the buzz of the open-plan office is suddenly stilled.

'Barry Power,' says Dina. 'Mystic to the stars.'

'I know who he is,' says Luca. 'I tried to arrest him three years ago.'

'What for?' asks Dina.

'The murder of his wife.'

Chapter 12

'She fell down the stairs,' says Luca. 'The classic murder scenario. Also impossible to prove. Husband finds wife at the bottom of the stairs. She's dead or does he just help her on her way with a twist of the neck? I've seen it hundreds of times.'

'Hundreds?' queries Dina. She thinks that Luca is trying too hard to seem a cynical, seen-it-all-before cop.

He disarms her by grinning. 'Well, once.'

'What made you think Power was guilty?' asks John.

'His demeanour,' says Luca. Another very policey word, thinks Dina. 'He seemed detached, describing the scene as if he was a witness, not a bereaved husband. And then he started talking about his past lives. I nearly arrested him there and then.'

'I saw one of his shows,' says Dina. 'He talked to a lot of dead people and then he flew in the air.' She remembers Power telling Ali that they had met before, 'on another plane'.

'That sounds like a wild evening,' says Luca. 'Was this in the course of your . . . research?'

'Yes,' says Dina. 'I'm not much of a one for mystics usually.

We're investigating the death of a young man. He killed himself after visiting Power for a consultation. Apparently Power told him he could fly and then he threw himself off a tall building.'

'And Power's wife supposedly threw herself downstairs,' says Luca. 'He's an unlucky man to be around, that's for sure.'

'I'm guessing you had no evidence, though,' says John.

'None at all,' says Luca. 'But when I looked into Power, his background seemed odd. Lots of blanks. He's apparently from Wales but I couldn't find any trace of him there. The Thornton Heath house has been in his family for generations, but Power has only lived there about ten years. Keeps himself to himself, neighbours said.'

'Classic killer behaviour,' says John with a slight smile.

'Well, exactly,' says Luca, moustache twitching in what could be an answering grin. 'Our only hope was a confession but he's a cool customer, never faltered from his story. We tried. One of our interviewing officers is a real hard case. He tried to lean on Power, but he didn't budge. Then we got a woman officer to play good cop, she even pretended to be interested in spirits. Power just kept smiling his creepy smile.'

Dina remembers the smile. It had been disconcerting even from their remote seats, high up in the balcony.

'So what was Hugo Maltravers' link to Barry Power?' asks Luca.

'Power claimed to be channelling a Victorian called Klaus Kramer,' says Dina, aware of how fantastical this sounds. 'Hugo had written a paper about him. Ali just wanted some background information.'

'Did she get anything useful?' asks Luca.

'I don't think so,' says Dina. 'Kramer's not very well-known. I've just tracked down an old film about him but it's not on public release.'

'Where did you find it?' asks Luca. 'On the dark web?'

'Yes,' says Dina, just to see his face.

Luca is obviously not sure if she's joking or not. He gives her another appraising look before saying, 'Can you send me everything you have on the case? It doesn't sound like there's any connection to Hugo's murder but just to be sure we've covered every angle . . .'

'Of course,' says John. 'Let us know if there's anything else we can do to help.'

'Thank you,' says Luca, 'but I'd really like to talk to Ali.'

Join the queue, thinks Dina.

While they are waiting for the Uber, Dina asks John, 'What now?'

'Let's go and look at Ali's place,' says John. 'There's probably nothing we can do but I can't help thinking it might be helpful to go there. When I was in . . . in 1850 . . . I kept thinking about the people who were in the same house but at different times. It was as if there was only a thin veil between us . . .'

His voice drifts away. Dina is surprised. She's been wanting to go to Ali's house all morning but hadn't known how to voice the request. Also, it's very unusual for John to mention his sojourn in the past, especially in such quasi-mystical terms. A thin veil. It almost sounds like Barry Power speaking.

'Let's go disco,' she says. It's a phrase she picked up when researching the 1970s.

The car drops them at the top of the cul-de-sac. 'The cobble-stones are hell on the tyres,' the driver tells them.

'You know,' says John, as they walk towards Ali's house, 'in Victorian times some streets were paved with wooden blocks.

I saw them when I . . . when I was there. They were incredibly slippery in the rain.'

'So these cobblestones might be relatively new,' says Dina. 'Do you know when these houses were built?'

'I think Ali said they were early nineteenth century,' says John. 'They used to house workers from the match factories.'

'They're quite smart now, though,' says Dina.

Dina has visited Ali twice before, once for a party and once on her own. She remembers being taken with the terraced house. It's small but has everything you need: two bedrooms above, one open-plan room below, a little garden. There are white walls and wooden floors but Ali has added brightly coloured sofas and chairs, as well as her famous collection of mismatched glass and china. Dina is renting a one-bedroom flat in a thirties mansion block in Streatham. It's OK but she's regularly woken up by fights outside and she's pretty sure that some drug-dealers live opposite. She really should have her own place by now.

They stop by the front door which has a stained-glass panel showing the rising sun.

'I've got her keys,' says John.

Dina is surprised all over again. They all leave a set of keys in the office, just in case something happens on a mission. But for John to have taken Ali's keys with him, that means he always planned to make this detour.

As they stand on the paved area in front of the house, a voice calls, 'Looking for Ali?'

A stocky man is smiling at them over the next-door fence. He has black hair with a rather dramatic grey streak in the middle. His voice has a carrying quality that Dina admires. At school, she was always told that her voice was too loud. It was years before Dina realised that this was, in fact, a racist microaggression but, even at the time, she resolved not to whisper and mutter like her classmates. This man assumes he has a right to be heard; Dina likes that.

'Yes,' says John, 'we're colleagues of hers.'

'Police?' says the neighbour. The word makes two passers-by stop and look round.

'Sort of,' says Dina. 'She didn't come into work today so we're a bit worried.'

'I saw her last night,' says the man. 'She was standing just where you are now with a long-haired man. It wasn't her son because I saw him on Sunday and he's short haired. I looked again a few minutes later and there was no one there. There were no lights on in the house but I thought Ali might have gone straight to bed. She's very upset about her cat, you know.'

'I know,' says Dina.

'We've all been looking for him,' says the man, 'all the neighbours. I'm Tony, by the way.'

'Dina. And this is John.'

'Pleased to meet you,' says Tony. 'Let me know if there's anything you need.'

He retreats, whistling tunelessly. John lets them into the house. It's eerily quiet. Ali's velour blanket is on the sofa, with a copy of *Nicholas Nickleby* face down beside it. A clock ticks somewhere. Dina remembers Ali once describing this sound as a heartbeat. She half expects Terry to appear, hungry and unrepentant. But the only sound is Tony talking to someone in his garden. Dina catches the word 'police'.

'Where are you, Ali?' she says.

But the little house makes no reply.

Chapter 13

John takes the long way home. Bow to Mile End, Mile End to Bank, Bank to Clapham Common, then a brisk walk along the North Side, part of the route he takes on his morning run. He knows the journey will be long and uncomfortable but he wants time to think and the constant jostle of humanity makes him remember that he's in the twenty-first century. Something he struggles with, to be honest. He's always been a diarist – journalling, they call it now – but sometimes he finds himself writing compulsively in his notebook, sometimes just page after page of the day, month and date. I'm here, now, in 2024.

When, last year, John travelled to 1850 to rescue Ali, he'd known it was the right thing to do. Ali was a colleague, a member of the team. In John's long police career, he held firm to one principle: you look out for your own people. He's heard Nigel say that policing is not about friendship but, in John's opinion, that's exactly what it is about. John would have died many times over without colleagues who shouted to be aware of the drug dealer with the gun, who shielded him with their bodies during knife fights, who listened when he was drunk and babbling on about his wife, who took him back into the fold after his suicide attempt with no questions asked and unimpaired gallows humour. So rescuing Ali was not a hard decision, but it was a painful one. He'd had to tell Moira that he was undertaking a mission from which he might not return. She'd understood it was his duty, she'd been a cop's wife long enough, but John knew that he was potentially abandoning her and his daughters, the people he loved most in the world.

Before he left, Jones had promised to save him and she had. John still remembers the moment when Clara, the maid at Hawk Street, had told him there was a visitor waiting. He'd known then it was Jones, because who else would come calling for him? He'd looked at Arthur and Tremain, still finishing their breakfast, including the mugs of ale that were a constant torment to John's teetotal soul. 'Goodbye,' he'd said, but they'd barely looked up from their beef and potatoes. They weren't to know that they'd never see their housemate again and the thought gave John an unexpected pang. He'd gone into the hallway and seen Jones, splendidly attired in red and gold.

'Jones!' He'd rushed forward. He'd wanted to hug her but didn't quite have the nerve, even if she was in the process of saving his life.

Jones had raised a gloved hand. 'I think I had better be Lady Serafina here, don't you?'

'It suits you,' said John.

'I think so too. Is there somewhere we can talk? We don't have long. The gate is only open for an hour.'

John ushered Jones into a small and stuffy chamber known as the morning room. There he had briefed her about the household although Jones told him she didn't plan to live in Hawk Street. 'I'm going to be rich, it's the only way. A rich, independent woman.'

John didn't ask how she planned to achieve this, difficult enough in 2023, surely almost impossible in 1850?

'You will come back, though, won't you?' John remembered saying.

'Of course,' says Jones. 'But I want to enjoy myself first.'

'It's a dangerous place, Victorian London,' said John. 'A man was killed near here a week ago.' Francis Burbage, a friend of Arthur's and a minor nobleman, had been stabbed outside the local inn. Arthur and Tremain had blamed the 'high mob', which seemed to be the nineteenth-century version of the mafia but, the night before he died, Burbage had visited John in his room and warned him, 'Don't trust Templeton.'

John had passed on this intelligence to Jones, soon to become Lady Serafina.

'Don't trust Cain Templeton. Don't trust The Collectors.'

'I won't trust anyone,' Jones assured him.

What is she doing now, thinks John as he finally turns into Sisters Avenue, his intrepid and brilliant colleague? Will he, as she promised, see her again? Is it possible that, even now, Ali is with Jones, both dressed in sumptuous Victorian clothes and, despite everything, enjoying their reunion?

'I'm home!' he calls as he opens the door. He still can't get used to not being greeted by Bridie. The house is too quiet these days, Hattie and Emily are both at university and, though Moira has now retired from her job as a nurse, she is always out at various charitable and leisure pursuits. Is it pickleball or Amnesty today? But no, there's a faint answering shout from the conservatory, where Moira is painting the woodwork white (to cover another of the girls' decorating experiments).

Typically, Moira is still wearing her pickleball clothes and hasn't put down newspaper to catch any drips. John is sure she was just overtaken with the need to be doing something. Or maybe she just couldn't tolerate the lime green any longer. Wordlessly, John spreads the *Guardian* on the floor. He no longer reads the news. It's just too depressing. Moira is excited about the forthcoming election; John doesn't know if he can be bothered to vote.

'How was your day?' asks Moira.

'Eventful,' says John. 'Ali is lost in time and her second husband just got murdered.'

'Bloody hell,' says Moira, sitting back on her heels, white paint dripping on Keir Starmer's face. 'You *have* got my attention.'

John tells Moira the story about Ali, Bud and the cat flap. Then he moves on to the suspicious death of Hugo Maltravers. At the end, Moira puts down her brush and goes to give John a hug.

'I'm sorry,' she says. 'That sounds tough. Does Bud think he can get Ali back?'

'I don't know,' says John. 'He obviously knows the technical stuff but I think this has really knocked his confidence. Maybe he'll think of something but he seemed really at a loss today.'

'Where's Jones when you need her?'

'Exactly. I keep thinking that if Jones is out there somewhere, maybe Ali has met up with her.'

'But I thought Bud only sent Ali back a few days. How could she end up in the 1850s? She could be anywhere.'

'It was just a thought,' says John, one which he knows has been sustaining him all the way home. He keeps thinking of Ali in Hawk Street, chatting to Tremain and Arthur, having a meal with Clara. At least she'd be with friends.

Moira goes into the kitchen to put the kettle on. John follows her, after closing the paint tin and picking up the brush.

'There are other ways to time travel,' he says, putting the brush in the sink. 'Remember I told you about the man who sat in the chair and disappeared?'

'I think you may have mentioned it,' says Moira. She must have heard this story a hundred times.

'Ali might find her own way back,' says John, aware how desperate this sounds.

'If anyone can, Ali can,' says Moira. 'Look.' She turns off the kettle. 'Let's go for a run round the common. Things always feel better after a run.'

As John goes upstairs to change his clothes, he reflects that once they would have opened a bottle of wine. He can taste it on his tongue, crisp white, warm red. And things would feel better, at first, but, after the second, third and fourth glass, they would feel much, much worse. John hasn't had an alcoholic drink now for nearly fifteen years.

Wearing running shorts and trainers, he descends the stairs into the hall. Moira is examining a letter. 'This must have been hand-delivered,' she says.

It's typewritten, addressed to 'DI John Cole'.

John opens the envelope; inside is a postcard. There's no writing on the back. John examines the image again. It's a black old-fashioned phone against a red background, the receiver hanging uselessly.

Dial M For Murder.

Chapter 14

Ali stands on the ingress point with Terry in her arms. He struggles – he's had far too much human contact in the last few hours – but Ali clamps him tightly. She can't let him escape into the Victorian night.

'Stay still,' says Jones. She's standing by Ali's front door – or the front door that will be Ali's – skirt held fastidiously above the slimy pavement. The road is too small for the carriage but Ali can see it a few hundred yards away, the spectral black horses outlined in the glow of a street lamp.

'Will it work?' she asks Jones. 'It's exactly an hour. Bud said to be back in an hour.' They have spent the last fifty minutes in the carriage, catching up on the Department and life in 2024 while the horses shifted impatiently outside.

'Who knows?' says Jones, in a bright, interested voice that makes Ali want to throw things at her.

Jones has a handsome gold fob-watch and she counts the seconds down. Ten, nine, eight . . .

The wind blows in the trees. Ali can hear the horses stamping.

Seven, six, five, four . . .

Jones's face is a pale disc. Terry struggles. Ali holds him tighter. Three, two, one.

A candle flickers in the window of the house next door. An owl hoots. Jones says, 'Interesting.'

Ali stays still although she knows it hasn't worked. She moves only when she needs to tighten her grip on Terry.

'What now?' she says.

'Let's go back to my house,' says Jones. 'At least we can get you some proper clothes.' Jones made Ali tie her shawl around her waist, so that it looks like a skirt, even though there's nobody about.

'Clothes aren't the important thing here,' says Ali.

'Clothes are always important,' says Jones. But she comes closer and puts her hand on Ali's arm. 'Don't worry, we'll get you back.'

'I've lost faith in you,' says Ali.

'The Victorian era is about loss of faith,' says Jones. 'You'll fit in nicely.'

The carriage ride through the night is like a dream but Jones's house is a fantasy. It's a blaze of light and colour: flaming lamps, red velvet curtains, myriad shiny objects. In the black-and-white tiled hallway, they are greeted by a butler called Harrison, a monumental figure in a dark suit who seems unfazed both by Ali in her shawl skirt and by Terry.

'Harrison,' says Jones, 'take this cat into the kitchen and feed him.'

'Yes, my lady.'

'Please don't let him out,' squeaks Ali, her concern for Terry trumping her fear of this imposing individual.

'No, don't let him go outside,' says Jones, 'he's very precious. He comes from the kingdom of Siam.'

Harrison bows and withdraws. Terry, awed into stillness, lies in his black liveried arms.

'Let's go to my bedchamber,' says Jones. 'My maid will find you some suitable clothes.'

Bedchamber? Maid? Ali follows Jones's red train up a sweeping staircase. She is, once more, lost in an alien world, in a time a hundred and twenty-two years before her own birth. She might never get home, she might never see Finn again. These anxious thoughts swirl around in her head but she voices the question that is suddenly uppermost in her mind.

'Jones,' she says, 'how did you get to be so rich?'

Jones turns, one hand on the banister. 'I'll tell you sometime,' she says. 'And it's Lady Serafina here. You can call me Serafina, of course.'

'Thank you,' says Ali.

And she actually means it.

Chapter 15

Jones's maid is a severe-looking woman called Frensham. Apparently, she is only ever addressed by her last name. But of course, in Ali's world, this is true of Jones too. Frensham lays a voluminous garment on the handsome four-poster bed.

'Lady Serafina asked me to give you this dressing robe,' says Frensham. 'By the morning, I will have adapted one of her ladyship's gowns for you.'

'Thank you,' says Ali. 'I'm afraid that means an awful lot of work.' Not to mention a lot of extra material, she thinks. Jones has always been slim but Victorian corsetry has given her a waist that could be spanned with two hands.

Frensham goggles at her for a second. Has Ali said something wrong? Is it the word 'awful'? Maybe it's just the fact that she said, 'thank you'. But surely Jones thanks her maid? Ali doesn't like to think otherwise.

Then, rather to Ali's surprise, Frensham gives her a shy smile and says, with quiet pride, 'Her ladyship has given me one of the new sewing machines. She saw them demonstrated at the Great Exhibition.'

The Great Exhibition. The words strike a faint chord in Ali's mind. She imagines a huge glass room full of mechanical objects. She doesn't know why this vision fills her with something like dread.

The dressing gown is purple velvet and contains so much fringing and frogging that it's quite hard to navigate. Eventually Ali finds the sash and ties it firmly round her waist. She slips on the embroidered slippers also provided by Frensham and ventures out onto the landing. Her room is on the first floor and she can see that the elegant staircase continues to swirl upwards. How big is this house? And how did Jones acquire it?

Ali descends the stairs, holding up the purple folds with one hand. Her memory of the Victorian era is of tripping up – a lot. She crosses the hallway and heads towards a door where there's a faint clink of china.

Ali follows the sound along a blue-green corridor into a room that seems full of foliage, tendrils spiralling from the wallpaper merging with pots of ferns and what looks like a small tree by the window. Jones is sitting on a green velvet sofa. Her red skirt makes her look like a Dickensian illustration of Christmas. *Don't trust Dickens.*

'Would you like some tea?' offers Jones, pointing to the teapot and bone-china cups arranged on a side table. 'I asked for some seed cakes too, in case you're hungry.'

Ali tries to remember her last meal. How long ago was it that she cooked the pasta she didn't finish? She feels too stressed to eat now. When she was in 1850, she was hungry all the time but that was partly the cold. It's summer now although the temperature in Jones's house is pleasantly cool. There's even a fire in the green-tiled grate.

Jones pours tea. 'Shall I be mother? I've never understood that phrase. But then I've never wanted to be a mother.'

Ali sips her tea which tastes mysteriously unlike the modern beverage. Maybe it's the unpasteurised milk. Jones has lemon in hers.

'What shall we do now?' she asks Jones. It still seems natural to expect answers from her.

'We must get you back,' says Jones. 'I'm beginning to realise that there are many types of time travel.'

'Really?' Ali sits up straighter, willing herself not to be lulled into accepting everything Jones says, hypnotised by the red dress, the hissing fire and the aromatic scent of tea. Suddenly she thinks of drinking iced water with Barry Power in the room that seemed more dated than this one. Of course, this decor is probably, at this moment, extremely modern.

'Yes,' says Jones. 'I've visited the Great Exhibition and seen some wonderful things.'

Again, Ali feels a slight twinge of unease. 'Time travel machines?' she asks. When did H.G. Wells write *The Time Machine*? She thinks it was later than this, towards the end of the Victorian era. Didn't he have an affair with Rebecca West, who seems very modern?

'In a way.' Jones gives one of her enigmatic smiles.

Ali looks round the room. She thinks of her four-poster bed, of all the other rooms in this house, of the servants' quarters which undoubtedly lie in the attics or in the basement.

'Jones,' she says, 'how did you get to be so rich? You can't have brought much money with you from 2023. And how come you're a lady now?'

Jones laughs. 'You have to have a title to get on in Victorian society. And you must admit that Lady Serafina sounds good. No one's ever queried how I acquired it. The money was trickier. The British Museum gave me some nineteenth-century cash. As you know, I have a contact there.'

'I remember,' says Ali. The same contact had given Ali money when she first travelled to 1850. She never knew what story Jones had spun but, in her case, the coins were enough for survival only. 'You must have had a lot more than me,' she says to Jones.

'Well, I knew I was staying longer but the most I could take would only see me through a few months. I rented this house because I thought it was necessary to present a prosperous image. I own it now, though. Then I looked around for opportunities. They weren't hard to find. This is the era of the new rich, you know. The industrial middle classes. So, with the rest of the money, I invested in steam.'

'In steam?'

'The Great Western Steamship Company,' says Jones. 'They power railways and ships. Eight years ago a man called James Nasmyth invented the steam hammer, which enables foundries to forge really large machinery. It's a growth industry. I invested in it. And in a few smaller businesses that caught my eye. Sewing machines, for example. I have money in vacuum brakes too. Another of Nasmyth's ideas. Now I own my own foundries.'

Ali thinks of Finn describing Helen's constituency: . . . *an old industrial area, lots of defunct textile factories and mills . . . now it's all digital, fintech and medical.* It seems extraordinary, and slightly disturbing, to think of Jones being part of the old industrial order.

'That's very capitalist of you,' she says, half joking. Jones always claimed to be a communist.

'This is the age of the capitalist,' says Jones. 'But if I can make sure that workers in the foundries are treated well and their children educated, well, that's all to the good.'

Ali has often wondered what Jones would be doing in the 1850s. She has never had any doubt that she would use her brilliance and retrospective knowledge to good use. But Ali had imagined her advancing the cause of women's rights or joining the Chartists, not becoming rich through the power of the steam hammer. Some of those steamships would have been involved in the slave trade. The Slavery Abolition Act was passed in 1833 but it didn't include all British territories. But Ali doesn't say any of this. She is a guest in Jones's house, after all, and wholly dependent on her.

Ali tries another question. 'How did you know I was coming back? You said you knew it was this week.'

Jones stands up with a rustle of silk. She walks over to a roll-top davenport and takes out three small, hardcover books. She places them on the table beside the tea tray.

'I've got Cain Templeton's diaries,' she says. 'Miranda Templeton gave them to me.'

Cain Templeton, the man Ali met in 1850, the man who later wrote her a letter calling her his 'time-travelling angel'. Miranda Templeton was married to his great-great-grandson Isaac Templeton and is a woman whom Ali considers almost a friend.

'How do you know Miranda?' she says, trying not to sound aggrieved.

'We became friendly after the . . . after the business with Geoff,' says Jones. 'When I knew that I'd have to go to 1850 to rescue John I asked to borrow the diaries. I didn't tell Miranda that, of course. I just said it was research.'

'And the diary says I came back in 1851?' says Ali. That sounds wrong. *I was going to come back? I would come back?* Was it Douglas Adams who said the main problem with time travel was the grammar?

'Yes,' says Jones. She opens the diary at a page marked with a ribbon.

Ali reads:

30th June 1851
Alison has returned! She is staying with Lady Serafina Pellegrini and seems mysteriously to have risen in social status. But she is still the same enigmatic personage. She told me she had arrived in London only this last week but would not say where she has been all this time. I did not say that I had travelled to Hastings in search of her. We met at the Great Exhibition by the mechanical nightingales . . .

Ali looks at Jones.

'The thirtieth of June? That's the day after tomorrow. Does this mean we have to go to the exhibition? What if we don't? Does it have to happen because it's written down here?'

Her head is spinning. She stands up, walks a few paces and almost trips up on her robe.

'*Fa'ttenzione,*' says Jones. 'Be careful, Ali.'

Ali loops the material over her arms and takes a few paces through the room, narrowly missing two tables and a glass jar containing wax flowers.

'I feel like I'm going mad,' she tells Jones.

'It's quite simple,' says Jones. That word again. 'We know what happens because it has happened before. You go to the exhibition and meet Templeton.'

'But what if I don't?'

'You do.'

Ali stops before the mantelpiece mirror. A white face stares back at her, wild-eyed, with hair like tongues of fire.

'I'll have to get a wig,' she says.

'I'll give you one of mine,' says Jones. 'Frensham can style it differently.'

Ali sits down again and picks up one of the diaries. 'Is it all in here?' she says. 'Does it say that I get back home?'

'Annoyingly, the diaries don't go much further than your meeting the day after tomorrow,' says Jones. 'But they are interesting, nonetheless. Read them later. We should be getting to bed. It's nearly midnight.'

Ali picks up the diaries. 'But you do think I get back home?'

'I'm sure you do,' says Jones, standing up. 'And I think it's The Collectors who will show us how to do it.'

'What do you mean?'

'I'll explain tomorrow,' says Jones, as the spindly clock on the mantelpiece begins to chime the witching hour.

Ali's bedroom is the epitome of cosiness. There's a fire burning in the grate and an oil lamp by the bed. Ali takes off the dressing gown and gets between the sheets wearing only her T-shirt and knickers. She thinks of her previous stay in the strange familiar/unfamiliar century: the attic room, the ice on the inside of the windows, the cold and loneliness that made her bones ache. It's different this time. That's partly because Jones is here, someone with whom Ali can discuss her predicament and who is, what's more, the only person who might conceivably save her. Jones said The Collectors will show them the way. Ali doesn't know exactly what she meant by this but she suspects that Cain Templeton and his friends have gone further down the time-travel path than they were willing to admit in 1850. Ali once saw a man called Thomas Creek, whom she believes to be one of The Collectors, sit on a chair and disappear completely. When John was stuck in 1850, he went to one of the group's secret meetings and there, too, he saw a man sit in a chair and vanish, although he reappeared almost immediately. If there's another way of getting back to 2024, Jones will find it.

But. Even so. As Ali lies between crisp sheets watching the firelight glimmer on the yellow wallpaper, she thinks of Finn lying asleep in his Pimlico flat. When he was a baby, he always slept on his side with his cheek pillowed on his hands, like an illustration in a children's book. She wonders if he still does this. Finn doesn't know that she's gone. When will he find out? Who will tell him? Will he be reassured that this has all happened before? Déjà vu is only another word for time travel, says Jones. But what if Jones fails? After all, *she* claims to have no desire to return to her own time. What if Ali never sees her beloved son again?

To stem the rising tide of panic, Ali opens one of the diaries. She has recently started to wear glasses for reading but these, of course, are in 2024. She leans close to the flickering light of the oil lamp.

25th January

Terrible day. Black day. That poor innocent Ettie has been murdered. Killed, I believe, by that . . . monster? . . . Thomas Creek. He has fled from the awful scene. I prevailed on Arthur to help me carry Ettie's body to the mortuary cart. The man was sobbing and crying. He's a weak soul but I have to say that I found it hard to suppress a tear. I remember [illegible] such a fresh, innocent flower. Hair the colour of trees in autumn. Before I left the house, in a [illegible] rage, I burnt all of Creek's paintings. They have little value anyway.

26th January

I forgot to mention, in my anger and grief, a strange manifestation yesterday. A woman calling herself Alison Dawson appeared at Hawk Street, just a few minutes after Ettie was murdered. Mrs Dawson seemed respectable enough, plainly dressed in black, but there was something about her that seemed strange, almost [illegible] uncanny? She spoke oddly and fixed me with a direct glare that I found disconcerting – and rather interesting. She fired questions at me as if she were one of those new detectives one reads about in the broadsheets. Then, suddenly, she picked up her skirts and ran. I did not think I would see her again but, a few hours later, she reappeared at the house, clearly in some distress. I offered her a room for the night and she accepted. She intrigues me.

I wrote to Ettie's parents. I doubt they can read or write but hope they have someone, maybe a local clergyman, who can help them. I sent them money for the journey to London. Doing so made me feel oddly complicit. It's almost as if [unfinished]

Dined with The Collectors. [Here a word is crossed out – very emphatically]

26th January

I saw Alison again today. There is some mystery about her. I don't know what it is. She seems to have appeared from nowhere and yet her speech and mannerisms are like no woman I've ever met. Her appearance too. She's not young and yet she glows with a strange vitality. I know she's a widow and today she mentioned that she had a son called Phin. She told me that Phin's father was called El Vis, which must be a foreign name.

Ali feels herself smiling. It's a private joke that Elvis was Finn's father but she never expected it to become a name that sounds vaguely Spanish, like El Cid. Or to see Finn become Phin, presumably short for Phineus.

27th January

I invited Alison to dine at my house. A truly respectable woman would have declined – I was alone save for Dorothy – but Alison accepted. I showed her The Collection. She was interested but not shocked, even by the murderer's brain. She described me as a magpie, drawn to glittering objects. Instead of being angry, I had the strongest compulsion to make love to her. Something that has not happened since Jane left me. She looked up at me with that challenging expression, almost as if she wanted it too. Then Dorothy interrupted to say that dinner was served.

Over the meal – she ate and drank as if starving – Alison told me that she has had three husbands. Truly, tragedy has stalked her. And she arrived, as she herself put it, at the very moment a dead woman lay at my feet. Maybe she is a harbinger of ill luck, as a magpie is said to be. But still she fascinates me.

Ali pauses. The fire has sunk to an orange glow and it's becoming harder to see the pages. After the last entry there's a gap of over a year. There's no mention of John's visit, which is disappointing. Templeton picks up his pen again in March 1851. Then on 30th June, he records meeting her, Alison, by the mechanical nightingales. Two days later, on 2nd July, he writes: *Alisoun, as I must call her now, is the love of my life.*

There's nothing else. What can happen/will happen/could have happened between the mechanical nightingales and this? Jones had said, 'We knows what happens because it has happened before.' But Ali has no idea what's going to happen between her and Cain Templeton. And then there's the spelling of her name. Ali has always been irritated that her father, when registering her birth under the influence of several celebratory pints, settled on this archaic spelling. She usually spells her name 'Alison' but it's 'Alisoun' on official documents, including her three marriage certificates. And it's Alisoun on the love letter that Ali found hidden in an old desk drawer. A love letter to her from Cain Templeton.

Ali closes the book. If the diary is right, she will meet Templeton the day after tomorrow. But what if she doesn't? Will she change the past and maybe the future? When the unit was founded, they had expected only ever to be silent witnesses, insubstantial wraiths. 'Don't interact' was one of the first laws of their charter. And now Ali and Jones are interacting like mad. Ali might even have an affair with the man who describes her as intriguing and fascinating. She can't deny a slight frisson of pleasure at the thought.

As Ali lies in bed, the diary still in her hand, something heavy lands on her legs. She stifles a scream. But it's only Terry, who has somehow evaded Harrison and tracked her down. Ali reaches out to stroke the cat, feeling her breathing calming as she does so. With Terry at her side, this strange house feels almost like home. If Finn were here, maybe Ali wouldn't want to go back either. The grandfather clock in the hall chimes once. Ali puts the book on the bedside table and blows out the lamp. She'll think about it all in the morning.

Chapter 16

Ali is woken by a uniformed maid placing a cup of tea on the marble-topped table by her bed. She hadn't drawn the curtains around her bed and the room is filled with rosy light. This is slightly different from her alarm call in Hawk Street, where a man in the street below would tap rather rudely on the downstairs window with a pole. Ali sits up, trying to hold the sheet over her disconcertingly modern vest T-shirt. At least she remembered to take her diamond nose stud out.

'Thank you,' Ali says to the maid. 'What's your name?'

'Gladys, ma'am.' The girl dips a curtsy.

'Gladys, do you know where my . . . er . . . clothes are?'

'Frensham is bringing them up now, ma'am.'

'And my cat? Have you seen him this morning?'

'Yes, ma'am. He's in the kitchen now. Mrs Beak – the cook – has given him some fish.'

Of course, Terry has made his way to the cook and, of course, he's consuming a gourmet breakfast. Time travel is obviously nothing to cats. Perhaps the answer to survival is to prioritise your own needs above everything else. Ali thanks Gladys, who casts one last scared look at Ali's head – the red hair must look even wilder this morning – and backs out of the room.

Ali drinks her tea and eats the accompanying biscuit. She then gets up and uses the chamber pot, which is concealed under the bed. In Hawk Street, she had to empty this herself but she senses that won't be the case here. She puts the lid on and pushes it back under the bed. It feels wrong, though. Someone, presumably Gladys, has filled a bowl with warm water and Ali washes her hands and face, using soap that reminds her of Jones's floral scent. This, too, is a far cry from washing in freezing water in Hawk Street, the astringent soap taking off a layer of skin. She has hardly finished when a soft knock announces the arrival of Frensham. Ali sits on the bed, trying to pull her T-shirt down to her knees.

Frensham lays several items of clothing on the chair by the dressing table, along with something that looks like a dead animal.

'I took the liberty of altering one of Lady Serafina's hairpieces,' says Frensham. 'I will assist you in dressing.'

She waits. Ali feels her whole body cringe at the thought of a stranger helping her to get dressed. She is naked under the T-shirt except for a pair of knickers.

'I can dress myself,' she says, adding, 'Thank you, though.'

Frensham gives a self-deprecating cough. 'If you will forgive me, madam, you will need help in tightening the laces of the corset.'

The corset. Ali's old enemy. It had taken her a day to work out how to remove it last time and she'd never been able to face putting it back on.

Ali gets out of bed, pulling the T-shirt as low as it can go. Expressionless, Frensham hands her a pair of white cotton drawers, beautifully sewn with lace at the edges. Ali takes off her M&S cotton pants and pulls these on, noting that the crotch is open. She knows that this is to make peeing easier but it feels very strange. Then Frensham passes over a plain, sleeveless shift. She turns away tactfully as Ali pulls off her T-shirt and replaces it with this garment. Next are white silk stockings which reach Ali's knees and are fixed in place by garters. Suspenders would be more comfortable but Ali remembers Dulcie at the Royal College of Fashion telling her that these were only invented in the 1880s. Ali stands up and allows Frensham to place the corset round her waist and pull it tight. Ali's breasts are pushed up and her waist pulled in but it's not too restrictive. She can still breathe, at any rate. Frensham indicates that Ali should sit at the dressing table. She touches Ali's hair.

'Shall I remove this hairpiece, madam?'

'What? Oh, it's not a wig. It's my own hair.'

Ali has to smile at Frensham's shocked expression, visible in the mirror before it is replaced by the customary mask.

'In that case,' says the maid, 'I will tie it back with a ribbon.' She does so. 'And place this hairpiece so.'

She puts the dead animal onto Ali's head and secures it with clips along the hairline. Then she coaxes tendrils forwards so that the join isn't visible. Ali puts up a hand to touch the hair. It feels very real. She remembers Jones saying, 'Better not ask too much about the provenance.' Did some poverty-stricken woman sell her hair because it was the only thing of value she had left? Or could it possibly be from a corpse? Ali decides to take Jones's advice. Besides, she is fascinated by her reflection in the mirror. She is transformed. She is a woman with dark brown hair which Frensham styles into a low bun, quite different from Jones's luxuriant ringlets. Ali gazes at herself. Last time she had her own hair, dyed back to its original brown before she made the journey, and keeping it clean had been one of her biggest issues. Now, this won't be a problem. Her face, she thinks, looks younger and fuller. She gives this new Ali a tentative smile.

Toilette completed, Ali stands up and Frensham hands her a succession of petticoats. They are lighter than the ones she wore last time but Ali dreads to think how warm she will be when she goes outside. It was a hot June in 2024, will it be the same here? Ali knows that global warming is making everything hotter but she seems to remember that there was a heatwave in the 1800s which was known as the Great Stink. Something to look forward to then. She slips on some blue satin shoes which are slightly too big. They must belong to Jones, who is taller than Ali. Lastly, almost reverently, Frensham drops a dress over Ali's head. The material is a faint blue pinstripe and Ali loves it immediately. She can hardly tell where Frensham has added extra panels at the sides. The dress has a high collar with a frill and several flounces on the skirt but it's fitted enough to feel quite businesslike. She touches her sides. No pockets, of course.

'You've altered it so well,' she says. 'Thank you.'

'Lady Serafina thought the style would suit you,' says Frensham. 'She is waiting for you in the small breakfast room.'

'Thank you,' says Ali again, but the maid has left the room.

As Ali steps out onto the landing, she can hear church bells ringing. It was Friday when she left 2024 but maybe it's Sunday in 1851. Ali descends the stairs, holding her skirts up with one hand. The small breakfast room. How many breakfast rooms can one house contain? She stops in the hall and hears a familiar and peremptory sound. It's Terry, miaowing in the tone that means 'hurry up'. Ali follows his self-important rear-end along a short corridor and into a room decorated in blue and white, like a Wedgwood plate. Jones, charmingly attired in primrose muslin, is sitting at a table which seems to be piled high with food and drink: covered dishes, baskets of rolls, toast rack, steaming teapot.

'Good morning, Ali. You do look nice. I knew that dress would be good on you.'

'Thank you,' says Ali. 'I love it.'

Ali sits at the table and takes a small roll, which she spreads with butter and marmalade. Jones pours her tea which is being kept warm over a flame like a small Bunsen burner. Terry jumps up onto a yellow velvet sofa and goes to sleep.

Ali sips her tea. 'Do you have coffee?' she asks. She remembers Barry Power claiming to commune with Serafina's spirit, 'she's saying something about coffee'.

'It's still quite hard to find,' says Jones. 'Strange when you think how many coffee houses there were in seventeenth-century London. I think there was some sort of virus in the coffee plantations and production has never really recovered.'

It sounds strange to hear Jones say the word 'plantation' without any twenty-first century horror. Ali remembers how hard it was to get coffee in the 1850s; last time she was reduced to buying a mug from a stall, hastily washed between customers.

The bells are still ringing in the distance. Ali says, 'What day is it?'

'Sunday,' says Jones. 'After breakfast, we'll go to church.'

'Church?' Ali stares at her colleague, sitting there in her beautiful dress, her head crowned with lustrous black curls, provenance unknown. This remark, far more than the hair and the clothes, makes Jones seem like an entirely new person. Ali assumes that Jones, being Italian, was brought up as a Catholic but, apart from the odd 'O Dio', she has never heard her mention God.

'This is 1851,' says Jones, watching Ali with some amusement. 'Everyone goes to church. All the fashionable people anyway.'

'I haven't been to church since I was married to Declan,' says Ali. 'His mum was a staunch Catholic.'

'There'll be none of that in this church,' says Jones. 'It's strictly Church of England. There's still a lot of anti-Catholic prejudice around. The Gordon Riots were only seventy years ago.'

'The what riots?'

'The Gordon Riots in 1780, protesting against the Papist Act of 1778 which was meant to end official discrimination against Catholics.'

'They were protesting because they *didn't* want discrimination to end?'

'That's right. Makes you proud to be English, doesn't it?'

This is said with a smile but Ali is stung nonetheless. She's not particularly patriotic but she's pretty sure that religious prejudice isn't unique to England.

'Dickens wrote about the riots in *Barnaby Rudge*,' says Jones. 'I was reading it the other day. Some remarkable descriptions.'

'I keep losing track of what he wrote when.'

'Me too. *David Copperfield* came out in serial form last year. I'd say Dickens is at the height of his fame. But he hasn't written *Bleak House* or *Great Expectations* yet.'

'My university tutor says not to trust Dickens.'

'Why?'

'I'm not really sure,' says Ali. 'I think because he makes stuff up.'

'That's what writers do,' says Jones. 'Are you nearly ready? We could walk to church if we leave in ten minutes.'

Ali finishes the last of her roll. Jones doesn't seem to have eaten anything, despite the mouth-watering array. Things seem to be moving rather fast. It's only nine thirty and Ali is already dressed in Victorian clothes, wearing a wig and about to participate in organised religion.

'What happens after church?' she asks. 'Are we going to talk about how I get back?'

'We can pray about it,' says Jones. Then, relenting, 'There's no sense in going back to the ingress point. I've got another idea and it involves The Collectors. Tomorrow, we'll go the Great Exhibition. We know you meet Cain Templeton there.'

'I've read the diary,' says Ali, 'but how does it work? Going to real places? Meeting real people? I know you said that we couldn't change history but that was when *we* weren't real, we were just shadows. Now we're flesh and blood. We're eating breakfast – delicious, by the way – wearing fancy clothes, using the chamber pot. Oh, I've left mine under the bed. Is that all right?'

'Fine.' Jones waves this away with a fastidious hand. 'Gladys will see to it.'

Poor Gladys, thinks Ali. She'd like to give her a tip except that she hasn't any money. She'll have to ask Jones for some, which is a rather horrible thought.

'Ali,' says Jones, in the tone she probably uses for slow students, not that she has any in her new identity, 'this has all happened before. The world is as it is because we were here. We've *already* changed history. Do you understand?'

'No,' says Ali. Her head is throbbing. Though that could be the wig.

'This happened,' says Jones. 'Whatever we do happened. We can't change it.'

'We could change it,' says Ali. 'We could just not go to the exhibition.'

'It doesn't work like that,' says Jones.

'Well, how does it work?' says Ali.

'You'll just have to trust me,' says Jones.

'I trusted you before,' says Ali, 'and got stuck in 1850.'

'I rescued you, didn't I?' says Jones.

'Yes,' says Ali. Eventually, she thinks.

The door opens, very slowly, like in a horror film, and Harrison glides in. He asks Jones if she wants the carriage sent round. Jones says, no, she and Mrs Dawson will walk to church. To Ali's surprise, Terry rouses himself and approaches the butler who – to Ali's even greater surprise – tickles him under the chin.

'He likes you,' says Ali.

'I have a great fondness for animals,' says Harrison. He departs, followed by the cat.

Before they leave the house, Frensham hands Ali a small bag that she calls a reticule. It's made of pale blue silk bordered with lace and reminds Ali of underwear. Then Ali is given a straw bonnet with a halo-like brim, and a parasol. The hat has a band of material that matches Ali's dress. Ali's parasol is blue and Jones's yellow. Does she have one to match every summer dress? But, despite this protection from the sun, Ali is boiling before they reach the end of the road. No wonder, she thinks. She left 2024 wearing only a sleeveless T-shirt, linen trousers and a loose shirt. Now she has at least four layers of clothing plus a corset. Jones, of course, is as cool as an Italian cucumber.

The air is still with almost no breeze. It's not the Great Stink but Ali can definitely smell horse manure and a sweet, rotting smell like decaying compost. Jones tells her to take the handkerchief from her reticule and hold it to her face. 'Frensham will have sprayed it with scent.' Ali does so and her nose is assailed by a lemony fragrance that reminds her of Jones.

The church, St James and St John, is an imposing structure of interlocking red and gold bricks.

'It's new,' says Jones, 'built about twenty years ago. It's all Gothic revival inside.'

'Isn't the Gothic revival Catholic?' says Ali, remembering their earlier conversation. 'Pugin and all that gang.'

'This is strictly the Protestant version,' says Jones. She nods at two women who are passing. Ali does the same. She realises that Jones is causing quite a stir as she climbs the shallow steps to the church doors. 'That's Lady Serafina,' someone whispers. Ali feels self-conscious following in her wake. Is this why Jones has acquired a taste for religion? So that people can whisper about her? It's an aspect that Ali hasn't considered before.

The church is dark inside with stone tiles, stained-glass windows and a great deal of twisted wood. It doesn't seem Gothic to Ali, so much as institutional. She feels as though she's back at school, although hers had been a plate-glass comprehensive in Hastings. They walk to a pew near the front. Is this specially saved for Jones? No one comes to join them, although the woman in front, a formidable matron in a vast, feathered hat, turns to greet Jones.

'My dear Lady Serafina. It was such an honour to have you as our guest the other night. I do hope you will grace us with your presence again.'

'I'd be delighted,' says Jones. 'This is my friend, Mrs Dawson. Mrs Dawson, this is Lady Croft.'

'How do you do?' Lady Croft extends a finger. Uncertain what to do, Ali shakes it. 'Pleased to meet you,' she replies, before remembering that this phrase is considered vulgar. The woman turns back, and Ali eases a foot out of her satin shoe and puts it on the cold stone tiles. That's the best thing about the church: it's blessedly cool.

The service seems both familiar and utterly alien. It starts with a flurry from the organ, high up in one of the soaring arches. Ali twists round and looks up. She remembers that Leonard Rokeby, who lived at Hawk Street, earned extra money playing at Sunday services. But Len had a head of bright red hair, this organist is bald.

Ali can't see much of the altar, because of the feathered hat in front. A priest leads the prayers, sounding distinctly bored and mentioning the apocalypse rather too often for Ali's taste. There are candles and incense and, whatever Jones says, it reminds Ali of going to mass with Bernadette, Declan's mother.

Jones doesn't join in with the responses or the hymns. She moves her fan continually, creating a hypnotic rhythm and a pleasant breeze. Ali feels herself almost dozing off. What is Finn doing today? He's probably out campaigning with Helen. He won't have noticed Ali's absence yet. But Dina and John will know. Are they, even now, berating Bud? Ali hopes not. It wasn't his fault.

'Come on, Ali,' says Jones in her ear. 'The show's over.'

Ali follows Jones out of the church. Once again, people greet the famous Lady Serafina and Ali is introduced, although no one seems very charmed to make her acquaintance. Lady Croft is standing in the doorway, taking up most of the space with her feathers and skirts. She, at least, seems to notice Ali.

'Are you making a long stay with Lady Serafina, Mrs Dawson?'

'I'm not sure,' says Ali. She hopes this is believable. Didn't people, in Victorian times, make visits that lasted months?

'You must come over for one of my little evenings.' Lady Croft's fan, also adorned with feathers, moves between them, almost brushing Ali's face.

'I'd love to,' says Ali.

Lady Croft leans forward, her grey-green eyes glinting behind the fan. 'Are you at all *mediumistic*, Mrs Dawson?'

'What? No. I don't think so.'

'I am,' says Lady Croft, her tone somewhere between complacency and awe. 'I frequently consort with the souls of the dead.'

'Do you?' is the best Ali can manage. Surely 'consort' is a very odd verb to choose in this context.

'I do. I am able to talk to the dead as easily as we are conversing here. Ask Lady Serafina if you don't believe me. I look forward to seeing you again.' And, using her fan to wave goodbye, Lady Croft descends the staircase in a swirl of feathers and fabric.

'Tell me about Lady Croft,' says Ali.

They are having lunch. Jones described it as a light meal but it's actually a rather sumptuous buffet: potted meat, artichokes, asparagus, fruit, cheese, pickles and seed cake. 'Most people in these times have a heavy Sunday lunch,' Jones told her, 'roast beef, potatoes, all the trimmings. But that seems barbaric to me, especially in the summer.' Ali agreed but she had a sudden memory of Sunday lunches when she was growing up. Her mum, Cheryl, hadn't been the best cook, she believed food was only edible after it had been cooked at the highest possible temperature for the longest possible time, but there had been something comforting about the ritual meal all the same. It was the only time Ali's parents drank alcohol in the house: beer for her father, a glass of white wine for her mother.

Jones surprises Ali by having a glass of champagne to accompany her lunch. Ali considers it rude not to join her.

Jones laughs. 'Oh, I saw her accosting you on the church steps. Mabel Croft is a famous medium. She runs a spiritualist society.'

'She's a spiritualist? What was she doing in church then?'

'You don't understand the Victorians yet, Ali. People believe as many as six impossible things before breakfast. Lady Croft is a highly respectable woman. She has elegant suppers in her very elegant house in Highbury. Afterwards, the guests gather in her drawing room and Mabel goes into a trance and communes with the souls of dead people. It's all very English and polite. Well, most of it. Then, on Sunday, Mabel goes to church and communes with God. There's no contradiction in her mind.'

'Lady Croft said that you'd been to one of her meetings.'

'Yes, she likes to invite guests, especially those known to be unbelievers. I suppose, as an industrialist, she thought I would deal only in facts.'

It sounds odd to hear Jones describe herself as an industrialist, rather than a physicist.

'And did you see anything at Lady Croft's to make you change your mind?'

'Not really. It was quite laughable really. Mabel shut her eyes and started groaning a bit. Then she spoke in a guttural accent and said that she was a man called Black Bob, a highwayman. I mean, talk about wish fulfilment. He's so obviously her fantasy figure. Bob claimed to talk to several people, even Mabel's dead children, but I wasn't convinced.'

Ali feels a rush of sympathy for the woman in the feathered hat. She lost a child, more than one child. Ali knows that this was fairly common in the Victorian era but it doesn't make the bereavement any more tragic. No wonder Mabel Croft wants to talk to the dead.

'Have you heard of the Fox sisters?' asks Jones.

'No,' says Ali. 'Are they top of the pops in 1851?'

'In a way,' says Jones. 'They're three American sisters, Leah, Margaretta and Catherine. They've been holding public seances in America. I've been reading about them. The dead supposedly communicate with them by rapping on tables. Some sceptics says it's the sisters themselves cracking their joints but a lot of people believe in them. Sojourner Truth went to one of their meetings in New York. Spiritualism is big business in the 1850s.'

'I went to see a medium in 2024,' says Ali. She tells Jones about Barry Power.

'And he said my name? Interesting.'

That word again.

'It was the only interesting thing about the evening really. I mean, the only thing that seemed genuinely inexplicable.'

'Everything is explicable,' says Jones. 'But I'm curious about this spiritualism craze. It occurs to me that other people might be time travelling. That might account for all the dead relatives wandering around.'

Ali shivers. 'Do you really think that?'

'I don't think Mabel Croft or the Fox sisters have the answers,' says

Jones, 'but The Collectors certainly possess some means of time travel. We'll see if we can find out more at the Great Exhibition tomorrow.'

Sunday, says Jones, is a quiet day. She suggests that Ali rests in her room after lunch. Ali has always wondered why upper-class people need to rest all the time. Surely it's Gladys, trudging up and down stairs with buckets of water, who needs to have a lie-down? But, as soon as Jones says this, a great weariness sweeps over her. Plus, she feels hot and sweaty and the thought of getting out of her corset and wig for a couple of hours is just too enticing. Frensham comes to her room and helps her to take the corset off. When she has gone, Ali takes off her wig and lies on her bed. She is woken by Gladys bringing her tea at five.

Over a light supper (does Jones eat any other kind of meal?), Ali asks if they can go to her house in Bow.

'Why?' says Jones. 'I don't think the ingress point will work if it didn't last time.'

'But we could try,' says Ali. 'We don't really know what works and what doesn't.' As the day has gone on, Ali has found herself missing home more and more, especially Finn. He might have noticed her absence by now. Maybe he is even back in London, watching Netflix with Georgie in his flat or drinking with friends in one of those dark Westminster watering holes frequented by politicians. Besides, Sunday evening is a melancholy time. It's homework and ironing clothes and back to the rat-race tomorrow. Ali feels this, even in Jones's yellow and gold dining room, eating fruit tarts and drinking another glass of champagne.

'OK,' says Jones. 'I'll ask James to bring the horses round. Lucky there's a moon tonight.'

The moon shines balefully over the terraced houses as Jones and Ali make their way along the street. Ali is carrying a wicker basket containing a furious Terry. Jones is holding an oil lamp which she shines on their feet as they negotiate the wooden pavement tiles. Ali has brought her ultraviolet torch, but she doesn't have an extra hand for it. She also has her cat key-ring, just in case.

There are no lights in any of the windows but, as Jones says, the inhabitants are probably factory workers who go to bed early. Ali thinks of Tony and Christina, with their ready hospitality, of Irene Goldman, who has lived in the street all her life, of Adnan and Faaiza and their twins, of Sean and Brian, who offered to help search for Terry. She wonders who lives in the little houses now. In the dark, they look almost the same but Ali knows that they will be lacking electric light, internal plumbing, all the things she takes for granted.

They stop outside Ali's house, the last in the terrace. Ali shines her torch and sees the shape of her footprints. Bud had told Ali to be back at this spot at eleven thirty yesterday. Could the gate open again? Ali can't help feeling a treacherous rush of hope.

'If it does work,' she says to Jones, 'thanks for everything.'

'Don't count on it,' says Jones. She checks her pocket watch. 'Eleven twenty-five.'

'I know. But if it does . . .'

'If it does, give my love to Bud. Tell him to keep the faith.'

'I will.' Ali clutches the basket, which is creaking ominously as Terry shifts his weight. An owl hoots and, looking up, Ali sees bats circling the rooftops. There are many more night creatures in Victorian London.

'Stay still,' says Jones. She counts Ali down, 'Eleven twenty-eight, twenty-nine, eleven thirty.'

Ali shuts her eyes and, when she opens them, Jones is still standing in front of her, her yellow dress glowing in the moonlight.

'I'm sorry,' she says.

But Ali hears something else. A familiar voice, loud and somewhat exasperated. It's very clear but Ali is almost certain the sound exists only in her own head.

'Where are you, Ali?'

Chapter 17

Ali dreams of churches and staircases, of bats flying in and out of her bedroom, which is a mixture of the one in Jones's house and her own familiar room in Bow. Terry and Dina are chatting, like the Mad Hatter's tea party in *Alice's Adventures in Wonderland*. 'Ali has always been unreliable,' says Dina. 'Yes,' says Terry, lighting a small clay pipe, 'but she means well.'

'Morning, ma'am,' says a slightly scared voice. It's Gladys placing the tea on her side table. Ali wondered if she'd been muttering or talking in her sleep.

'Thank you, Gladys. There's a shilling for you on the dressing table.' It has been embarrassing to ask Jones for money but at least she can now give tips. She doesn't know if tipping is expected from her but she wants to do it anyway.

'Thank you, ma'am. That's very kind of you.' Gladys must have already filled Ali's basin with water because there's scented steam in the room.

'It must be hard work carrying all that water upstairs. Do you do it for Lady Serafina too?'

'Her ladyship has a bath every day,' says Gladys, in a slightly awed voice. 'It's something they do in Italy, seemingly.'

Goodness knows how many pails Gladys has to carry to fill a bath. Ali is glad she gave her a tip.

Gladys further ventures that 'the cat' is very well. Cook has apparently boiled him some flounders for breakfast. It's going to be hard persuading Terry to leave 1851. He didn't enjoy his trip in the wicker basket yesterday.

When Gladys has departed, Ali sips her tea and contemplates her position. She is stuck in 1851, the gate didn't work and, for all her talk of there being many kinds of time travel, Jones has no idea how to get her home. Jones seems to be pinning her hopes on the Great Exhibition but Ali is not sure what she expects to find there. She remembers the faint feeling of unease she felt when the exhibition was first mentioned. Is this the déjà vu Jones was talking about? Ali knows that she's going to see Cain Templeton today. It has already happened. Maybe this accounts for the churning in Ali's stomach, a mixture of excitement and dread. Or maybe she's just hungry.

Frensham comes in and helps Ali dress. She puts on the pinstriped gown again but Frensham tells her that she's altering more clothes for her. Ali really must give Frensham some money too or is a ladies' maid too grand for a tip?

'Thank you very much,' says Ali. 'But I won't need that many clothes, will I?'

'You will need some more day dresses and an evening gown, of course.'

'Blimey,' says Ali, forgetting herself. 'When will I need an evening gown?'

'Her ladyship entertains a lot,' says Frensham repressively.

★

Jones is in the breakfast room, slowly peeling a pear. Terry is curled up on the yellow sofa. Ali strokes him.

'He had flounders for breakfast,' she tells Jones. 'I assume that's fish.'

'Yes,' says Jones. 'A flatfish, I believe. Very nice grilled with lemon.'

'You like everything with lemon.' Jones even eats lemon quarters whole.

'Has Terry recovered from yesterday?' asks Jones. Ali is beginning to understand her friend better and knows that Jones is really asking how *she* is.

'He's OK,' she says. 'I am too. It was a long shot, expecting the gate to open. You always said so.'

'I did,' says Jones. 'I really think we'll find our answers today. At the Great Exhibition.'

'I feel quite excited,' says Ali. 'Where is it? Crystal Palace?'

'It's in a crystal palace,' says Jones, 'but it's actually in Hyde Park, just round the corner from here. It's quite extraordinary really. A cathedral of glass, someone called it. The Queen opened it in May.'

It sounds odd to hear Jones say 'the Queen' and mean Victoria. Until recently, those words meant Elizabeth the Second.

'Were you there?' asks Ali.

'Of course,' says Jones. 'It was quite an occasion.'

She sounds rather complacent, thinks Ali, assuming that, if the great and good were gathered, she would be amongst them. Sometimes it's hard to remember the Jones who used to wear jeans and designer knitwear. Today, she's wearing a dress of the palest orange. Ali couldn't name the exact colour but it certainly suits Jones's dark beauty.

'Jones,' says Ali. 'What are you expecting to find at the Great

Exhibition? Will The Collectors be there? I mean, I know Cain Templeton will be. I know I meet him by the mechanical nightingales, whatever they are. But how can The Collectors help us? Do you know more than you're telling me?'

'There are rumours about them,' says Jones. 'They collect objects with special powers. Mabel Croft told me that Cain Templeton possesses a set of chairs that are somehow magical. Well, Ali. You and I saw a man sit in a chair and disappear completely.'

'We did,' says Ali. That memory is so confused with other, traumatic events, that Ali prefers not to disinter it. To gain time, she peels an apple with the same care Jones applied to her pear.

'Did I tell you that when John was in 1850 he went to one of The Collectors' meetings?' says Ali.

'You didn't,' says Jones. 'This is very interesting.'

'Cain Templeton invited him,' says Ali. 'He didn't invite me. Good old-fashioned sexism, no doubt. But John was surprised because apparently, to join the club, you have to be what people call "well born". John is the son of a cabinetmaker. He told Templeton so and he said it only made Templeton keener for him to be involved.'

'I didn't know that,' says Jones. 'About John being the son of a cabinetmaker.'

'Nor did I,' says Ali. 'I knew he was proud of being born and bred in the East End. I think I might have assumed that his family had something to do with the docks. Anyway, John went to the meeting with Templeton. He said it was in a deconsecrated church known as the Hangman's Club because executioners went there to pray before killing people.'

'Charming,' says Jones. 'Capital punishment is one of the less delightful things about the nineteenth century.'

'Yes,' says Ali. 'Anyway, Cain introduced John to the other members of the group. Some were friendly, he said, but others clearly didn't want him there. When they got to the confidential part of the proceedings, they asked John to leave.'

'And did he?' asks Jones.

'Yes,' says Ali. 'He went into a side room but there was a secret passage.'

'My God,' says Jones. 'What is this? A children's adventure story?'

'It was probably just a private way into the church,' says Ali. 'Anyway John, being the good detective he is, followed the passage, found a door and opened it, just enough to see through.'

'What did he see?' asks Jones. 'You're stringing out the story too much.'

'He saw a man sit on a chair and vanish.'

There's a brief, charged silence. The clock in the hall strikes nine. Terry yawns, stretches, jumps lightly from the sofa and strolls out, presumably in search of Cook and more flounders.

'What happened next?' asks Jones.

'John heard a noise and had to go back into the side room,' says Ali. 'But when he was shown into the church, the man was back. I can't remember his name. Something Italian, I think.'

'Of course,' says Jones.

'John says The Collectors were all talking as if nothing had happened but, on the way home, Templeton brought the subject up. He said that the chair was one of a set of four. The man who made them had murdered his own family and then killed himself. People thought they were cursed. But maybe it's more than that. I haven't told you the other bit of the story yet.'

'For heaven's sake, get on with it, Ali.'

'I've got a friend called Ed Crane.' Ali pauses briefly to wonder if Ed is still a friend, after the evening at the cinema. She ploughs on regardless. 'Ed is the curator of a museum that holds some objects from the Templeton collection. Amongst the collection is a desk and chair, once belonging to Cain Templeton. One day last year, Ed thought he saw a man appear at the table. It was very quick, one minute he was there, the next he wasn't. I think it might have been The Collector. The Italian one. The one who vanished.'

'It's possible,' says Jones, standing up and beginning to pace the room, her orange skirts swinging. 'It's simply a transfer of matter, after all.'

Simply, thinks Ali.

'If the chairs can time travel, we just need to get hold of one. We just need to understand the mechanics.'

'You said emotion comes into it,' says Ali. 'Maybe I just need to click my feet together and think of home. Like Dorothy in *The Wizard of Oz*.'

'A very good text about not trusting what's in front of your eyes,' says Jones. 'Don't dismiss emotion. It's the most dangerous thing of all.'

She takes another turn around the room and then, to Ali's surprise, she says, 'I miss John.'

'He misses you too,' says Ali. 'We all do.'

For a moment, she thinks that Jones is going to admit that, despite the wonders of the nineteenth century, she wants to come home. But, instead, Jones says, 'I think I'll ring for the carriage. It's going to be another hot day.'

★

Hyde Park is within walking distance but Ali is glad of the carriage. The open windows provide a much-needed breeze and she doesn't think she will ever tire of horse-drawn travel. She loves the jangle of harness and the sound of hooves. Jones's horses are black and beautifully matched but the streets are full of conveyances pulled by equines of all different sizes and colours. It must be hard work in this heat and, with *Black Beauty* in mind, Ali is on the alert for signs of ill-treatment. When was that book written? As with Charles Dickens, Ali is vague on publication dates. She remembers Finn crying when she read him the chapter about Ginger. He's always loved animals.

As they near Hyde Park, Ali sees crowds of people approaching the entrance. It's almost like a pop concert. Ali saw Bruce Springsteen at this self-same venue in 2023. The carriage passes between two lodges, like those by the gates of stately homes, and stops by a huge archway. Above and beyond, acres of glass reflect the bright blue sky. Ali blinks.

'Quite something, isn't it?' says Jones, taking her arm as they alight.

'It really is,' says Ali.

There are turnstiles in front of them, specially built for the exhibition, Jones tell Ali, but they bypass these and walk into a dazzling world of blue and white and crystal. There are flowers and palm trees everywhere and, at the far end of the transept, a fully grown Hyde Park elm. They enter an avenue of glass and there's a fountain in front of them. It's made of coloured glass and the air is full of rainbow prisms and shimmering water. Ali feels ashamed of her modern preconceptions. Even with her unique perspective, she has considered the Victorian age to be a sepia one, full of privation and

147

lacking in luxury. But this is Versailles, this is the Hanging Gardens of Babylon, this is how Finn must have felt when he saw Disneyland for the first time (if he'd looked up from his zombie book).

Once again, there's a frisson as Jones passes. Men bow and women nod, wide-eyed behind fans. What do they make of Lady Serafina's companion? At least Ali doesn't feel too dowdy in her pinstriped dress.

They pass giant statues of Victoria and Albert on horseback.

'You know,' says Jones, 'this exhibition led to the creation of the Natural History Museum, the Royal College of Science and, eventually, Imperial College. I should write Albert a thank you letter. This was all his idea, his vision.'

When did Prince Albert die? wonders Ali. She has a feeling that he only outlived his exhibition by about ten years. She hopes he enjoyed those years to the full. It's horrible, knowing the dates when people died, like seeing gravestones around every corner.

To the left of the fountain is a wide aisle emblazoned with flags and emblems. Above this is a balcony hung with carpets in shades of ochre, cobalt and scarlet. The general effect, combined with the glass and the crystal, is quite blindingly brilliant. Ali tips her head back – hard to do in a wide-brimmed hat – and sees people walking along the first-floor gallery.

'This is the colonial display,' says Jones. 'None of your twenty-first century sensibilities, please.'

Ali says nothing but she looks at the kaleidoscopic corridor, which seems to disappear into the distance like an optical illusion, with a less friendly eye. She thinks of the evils of Empire, of Cain Templeton and his collection, of all the wealthy Victorians wandering around the world taking whatever shiny objects catch their fancy.

They take another turn, between marble statues looking down from their plinths, their dazzling whiteness only adding to the surreal atmosphere. Ali had expected the exhibition to be full of machinery but, at first glance, it's more like an art gallery. Ali passes a group of three figures, entitled *God's Victory Over Satan*. She's not entirely sure that the battle has been won. As they move into the main aisle, Ali sees a metal cage, lit from below by a flickering gas light. Whatever is in the cage emits a glow that is both spectacular and rather sinister.

'It's the Koh-i-Noor diamond,' says Jones. 'Want to look?'

'No thanks,' says Ali. She doesn't know much about the jewel but she's pretty sure that it was looted from India.

Jones is leading Ali past the gemstones and minerals, past the display of silks – ruby red, peacock blue, imperial purple, witchy green – towards a corridor devoted, according to the brochure handed to Ali at the entrance, to 'Marvels of the Industrial Age'.

'Is the steam hammer here?' she asks.

'Of course,' says Jones, 'along with a giant model of the Liverpool docks.'

The crowd here is more masculine, full of dark puritanical suits. A bearded man hails Jones, 'Lady Serafina!' and she turns to greet him. Ali is momentarily on her own. She turns on the spot and finds herself looking into a face that is both familiar and strangely shocking.

'Good God! Mrs Dawson! Is that really you?'

'Good morning, Mr Templeton,' says Ali demurely.

Behind them, a case of mechanical birds starts to sing an unmelodic chorus.

★

'I can't believe it,' says Cain Templeton, 'I'd given up hope of ever seeing you again.'

Ali's heart races. She can almost feel it beating against the whale-bone of her corset.

'I've been away,' she says. 'My son . . . my son was in some trouble.'

'I hope the trouble has passed,' says Templeton.

'It has. Thank you.'

Templeton hasn't changed, thinks Ali. But then, only a year has passed. His face is still dark and sombre-looking, framed by greying hair and a dark moustache. For a few seconds, they simply stare at each other. Then Templeton says, in a tone of surprise, 'Lady Serafina.'

'Good day, Mr Templeton.' Jones has come to stand next to Ali.

Jones's voice is cordial but Ali senses that there is some unease between the two of them. If so, it's another thing that Jones hasn't seen fit to explain.

'Do you know Mrs Dawson?' says Jones, with a creditable pretence of surprise.

'Yes,' says Templeton, pulling himself together with what seems like an effort. 'We have met. Last year, was it not, Mrs Dawson?'

'That's right,' says Ali. 'You were kind enough to give me lodgings.'

Templeton's gaze sweeps Ali's fashionable attire. She thinks of his diary. *She . . . seems mysteriously to have risen in social status.*

'I would welcome the chance to renew our acquaintance,' says Templeton.

Me too, thinks Ali. But a modest nod seems more appropriate.

'Would you ladies care to visit the refreshment court?' asks Templeton. 'I could procure you both a glass of cool lemonade.'

Ali looks at Jones. She wants, very much, to sit and talk to Cain Templeton but is this acceptable behaviour in a companion of Lady Serafina? The lemonade sounds pretty wonderful too. She remembers John saying how relieved he'd been to discover that non-alcoholic drinks were starting to be introduced into Victorian England by the temperance movement. Up until then, John, in AA and fifteen years sober, had been offered ale with every meal. Water was potentially lethal. Wasn't it typhoid fever, caught from drinking contaminated water, that killed Prince Albert?

But Jones graciously signals her acceptance of the invitation. They walk to the far end of the transept, past the statues and the jewels and the flags, to an area where tables are placed around another fountain. Potted ferns and palm trees offer shade and a string quartet is playing. The refreshment court is crowded but Templeton finds two seats for Ali and Jones, then goes to the counter for drinks.

Jones arranges her skirts. 'Be careful,' she says to Ali.

'What do you mean?' asks Ali, trying to copy the way Jones is sitting, her rigid spine not touching the back of the chair. She feels hot and constricted and would love to take her shoes off.

'Don't give too much away to Templeton. I've seen the way you look at him.'

'I'm not looking at him in any way,' says Ali, trying for dignity.

'All right, the way you're looking at each other. Remember, The Collectors might have secrets we need to discover. We must go cautiously.'

Ali is about to respond when Templeton returns, with two glasses of yellowish liquid. There's no seat for him so he's forced to stand.

'What do you think of the Great Exhibition, Mrs Dawson?' Templeton bends down to ask the question.

'I've never seen anything like it before,' says Ali, honestly. 'It's extraordinary.' She takes a sip of her drink. It's delicious, not as sweet or as fizzy as the modern version.

Templeton's voice comes from somewhere above her. 'Lady Serafina, of course, has been here before.'

'Yes,' says Jones. 'I was lucky enough to be present at the grand opening.'

'And at an early showing of some exhibits. The Seeing Glass, for example.'

There's something going on here that Ali doesn't understand. Jones says, after a pause, 'It's a trick but a clever one, I must admit.'

Templeton laughs. 'Talking of trickery . . .' He pauses. He seems more diffident than Ali remembers him. But maybe the power balance has shifted slightly. 'I'm going to a demonstration of mesmerism tonight. Klaus Kramer. He's rumoured to be able to fly. I wonder if you two ladies would care to accompany me?'

Ali starts and spills some of her lemonade. Jones gives her a look and says, smoothly, 'We'd be delighted.' Templeton discusses arrangements which seem to include an early dinner at his house. Ali says very little and, after a few more minutes, Jones stands up, obviously ready to leave.

'We will see you tonight, Mr Templeton.'

'Farewell, ladies.' Templeton bows.

As they walk away, Ali has a compulsion to look back but Jones is steering her firmly.

'For goodness' sake, Ali. Play it cool. You'll see him later.'

'What was going on back there?' says Ali. 'What's the Seeing Glass?'

'You'll see,' says Jones. 'Pun intended.' She continues through the crowd, nodding regally to her admirers. Ali stops in front of a 'rustic summer house' made from wrought iron.

'Come on, Ali,' says Jones, with what seems like twenty-first-century impatience.

But Ali is staring through the throng, the black-suited industrialists, the butterfly skirts of upper-class women. So many faces. So many people. And, amongst them, Ali sees someone who definitely doesn't belong in 1851.

Barry Power.

Chapter 18

'You thought you saw your medium from 2024, Barry Whatsit, at the Great Exhibition?'

'Yes,' says Ali. It does sound rather ridiculous, put like that.

They are in Jones's carriage on their way back to the house. Ali is exhausted. Is this a symptom of time travel or just because she has spent the morning on her feet in stifling heat wearing a ridiculous amount of clothes? Another discomfort, one that is becoming almost too much to bear quietly, is a terrible itch around her midriff. Has she caught fleas somehow? Maybe when she patted one of the carriage horses? Ali wriggles against the seat, trying to get comfortable.

'What are you doing?' says Jones.

'Got an itch,' says Ali, squirming.

'Corset itch,' says Jones. 'Happens all the time. When we get home, Frensham will help you take it off and Gladys can bring some cold water to your room. You can sponge yourself down.'

Even the mention of cold water sounds blissful. Ali doesn't think she has ever felt so hot and *constricted*. It's as if she has been bound in fiery chains. She takes off her hat and fans herself. Jones watches her in some amusement. 'You were telling me about this man you thought you saw.'

'I did see him,' says Ali, wafting the hat more vigorously. 'I'm sure I did.'

'Ali,' says Jones, 'if I could tell you the number of times I thought I've seen you walking down the street. John too. Even Geoff. It's all part of the time-shift shock.'

'Maybe it was our ancestors you saw,' says Ali. She's quite touched that Jones has been having hallucinations about her. 'When I went through the gate this time, I knocked at the house two down from mine. A woman opened the door. I thought she was Irene, my neighbour, but then I realised it must be her great-great-grandmother or someone like that. Irene said that her family had lived in the same street for generations.'

'So maybe I've seen your great-great-grandmother,' says Jones. 'And the man at the exhibition might be a relative of this . . . Gower?'

'Power.'

'Your mind can play tricks. It's all part of the time-travel experience.'

She makes it sound like a theme park ride, thinks Ali, but maybe she's right. She recalls Jones's theory that the dead are walking the streets. 'I *thought* it was Barry,' she says, after a few seconds, 'but I could be wrong. Did I tell you that Barry Power claimed to be able to conjure the ghost of Klaus Kramer? He's the man we're going to see later.'

The sheer implication of this statement make Ali relapse into silence.

'*Dio mio*,' says Jones. 'I think I will wear my Tyrolean lace.'

The 1800s have turned Jones into quite the fashion victim.

After another 'light luncheon' Ali repairs to her room where Frensham is waiting for her. The maid helps her off with her dress and undoes her corset. Gladys had brought the bowl of water and Ali lets Frensham sponge her back. It feels blissful. Ali can see in the mirror that her skin is covered in red wheals from the whalebone.

'Lady Serafina thought you might like to rest after luncheon,' says Frensham, carefully replacing the chemise.

This time, Ali does not argue about the need for a rest. The freshly-made four-poster, with its white linen and flowery counterpane, is simply too inviting. Also, now that the itch on her body has subsided, Ali is aware of an overwhelming need to scratch her head. She takes off her wig and does so; the relief is immediate. Ali's real hair is now so flat and greasy that she can hardly bear to look at it. She lies on the bed and shuts her eyes. For a while, sleep evades her. Behind her eyelids Ali sees the gold and blue of the Great Exhibition, the marble statues, the multicoloured fountain, the great, evil diamond. She thinks of Templeton saying, 'I'd given up hope of ever seeing you again.' Then there's the – what was it called? – the Seeing Glass. There's something Jones still isn't telling her. A fly buzzes somewhere in the room. Ali sleeps.

She wakes up when a cup of tea is placed on her bedside table. This time it's Frensham, who has a mass of pinkish material draped over her other arm.

'Lady Serafina thought you might like to wear this tonight, madam.'

'Thank you. What's the time?'

'Just after five, madam.'

Ali has slept for four hours. Has Frensham spent all afternoon altering her dress? It might be pleasant being an upper-class Victorian lady but Ali thinks the guilt may well kill her. She sips her tea while Frensham brushes the wig, which Ali left untidily on the dressing table. Then she gets up and lets Frensham lace her corset and slip the silk dress over her head. Then the wig is put back on. Ali's scalp itches immediately but she has to admit that her reflection in what Frensham calls 'the looking glass' is quite pleasing. Ali doesn't think that she has ever worn pink in her life, since she started choosing her own clothes anyway, but the dusky rose is very flattering to her complexion, especially with brown hair, now arranged in a more elaborate style with tendrils framing her face. Ali has never been good at hair. She was always pleased that she had a son and never had to attempt the tight topknots that Declan's daughters sport for ballet. She thinks of Finn's curls, naturally wild but now cut short as if to demonstrate his serious character. Oh, Finn. When will she see him again?

There's a new reticule too, pink with glass beads that make a pleasant clinking sound when Ali moves. Ali transfers her fan and handkerchief. My phone won't fit, she thinks, before realising how ridiculous this thought is. But, for a second, she yearns for her mobile with its cracked screen and picture of Terry on the plastic case. If only she could text Finn to let him know she's all right.

Jones is waiting for her in the drawing room, wearing red silk. She has clearly chosen their dresses to complement each other.

'I'm nervous,' says Ali. She tries to pace around the room but, once again, her skirt keeps knocking over small tables. She sits on the green sofa.

'Don't be nervous,' says Jones, righting an ebony elephant, 'you look lovely.'

'That's not what I'm nervous about,' says Ali, although she's not sure this is entirely true.

'What is it then? Seeing Cain again?'

'Partly,' says Ali. 'Jones, what's the Seeing Glass?'

For a moment, she thinks Jones will give one of her unanswerable retorts: 'It's too complicated. You wouldn't understand.' But Jones just sighs and smooths her crimson skirts.

'I met Cain Templeton at a demonstration of a new power hammer.'

It sounds like a heavy metal concert but Ali decides not to say this.

'Afterwards,' says Jones, 'he contacted me. I thought he might be looking for me to invest in some business scheme. Since I'm known to be a . . . a venture capitalist, I get many such invitations. But Templeton said he had something – a curiosity, he called it – that might interest me. It was going to be shown at the Great Exhibition but he invited me for a preview.'

'Was it another power drill?'

'No,' says Jones. 'It was called the Seeing Glass and the idea was that it could see into the future. I'd read about it in the papers.'

'Wow,' says Ali.

'Exactly. I went along at the appointed time. It was just before the exhibition opened on the first of May. The weather had been terrible, wind and rain all week, though it cleared and was perfect for the opening ceremony. Anyway, when I arrived, a lot of the objects were still under covers. Templeton was there with another of The Collectors. I don't know his name. They greeted me, all the usual pleasantries, then they took me over to a table. There was a mirror on it. Just an ordinary looking glass, the kind that's on a stand that swivels. I sat down in front of it.'

She pauses for effect. 'What did you see?' asks Ali.

'I saw . . . myself . . .'

'Well, yes . . .'

'Myself.' Jones turns her intense gaze on Ali. 'Me. Dr Serafina Pellegrini of Imperial College, London. I was wearing jeans and my favourite Missoni cardigan. The vision was only there for a second but I saw it. I was so shocked I stood up. Templeton knew something had happened. He asked me what I'd seen. I said "nothing". He said that he'd bought the mirror from an estate in Scotland. The woman who'd owned it was said to have been a witch. She died in sixteen something.'

'Figures.'

'Yes. I'm sure I would be considered a witch by seventeenth-century standards. I made my excuses and left. But Templeton knew I'd seen something. And I knew I'd see him again. I'd read his diary.'

At that moment Harrison announces that the carriage is waiting. The butler, Ali can't help noticing, is accompanied by an adoring Terry.

Chapter 19

Ali remembers Cain Templeton's house from her first visit. Then, the door had been opened by Dorothy, the maid mentioned in Cain's diary. Cain had told Ali that he didn't have a butler in London but he certainly seems to have acquired more staff in the last year. Two liveried footmen take Ali and Jones's evening wraps (not really needed on such a warm night but Jones insisted) and usher them into the red drawing room. It seems very full of people. Last time, it had been just Templeton and Ali. He had shown her his collection, the Roman skull, the murderer's brain. She remembers the diary. *I invited Alison to dine at my house. A truly respectable woman would have declined.*

'Mrs Dawson, Lady Serafina.' Cain Templeton comes forward. The slight diffidence he had shown earlier, at the exhibition, has vanished. Now he's every inch the charming, urbane host. He is also wearing white tie and tails, as are all the other men present. They remind Ali of an orchestra but there's no doubt that the severe monochrome suits Templeton.

'Did you enjoy the Great Exhibition?' says Templeton, although he has asked her this before.

'Very much,' says Ali. 'There was so much to see. I need to make another visit. It was quite overwhelming.'

'I, too, was overwhelmed,' says Templeton, smiling down at her. What can he mean by that? Ali is sure that she's blushing. Templeton greets Jones and ushers them over to meet the other guests.

'My colleague, Giuseppe Zennaro.'

'How do you do,' says Ali, remembering that this is the only permitted response. Giuseppe. Could he be the man John saw disappear back when he was trapped in 1850? John said he had an Italian name and this is the only non-English name Ali has heard. Ali had been surprised – and pleased – to find nineteenth-century London a far more multicultural place than she had imagined but this certainly isn't reflected in tonight's company.

'And his wife, Mrs Laura Zennaro.'

'How do you do.'

'My friend, Francis Gibson . . . Lady Sonia Stevens.'

Ali bows and smiles, trying to do the right thing. It reminds her of the early days of being married to Hugo, when they'd give dinner parties and she didn't know which wine to serve or how to eat an artichoke. Jones seems perfectly in her element. Ali can hear her talking to Lady Sonia. 'It was simply too fatiguing.' What can she be talking about? Having Ali to stay?

A man who can only be the butler announces that dinner is served. Templeton apologises for hurrying them but reminds everyone that 'curtain up' is at seven thirty.

Ali follows Jones into the dining room, also wallpapered in dark red. She'd hoped to sit next to Templeton but finds herself between Giuseppe and Francis Gibson. Templeton sits at the head of the table with Jones and Lady Sonia on either side. For the first time, Ali wonders about the absence of Templeton's wife, Fedora. She remembers Templeton telling her that she preferred the countryside. Is it usual for a man to hold a dinner party without his wife?

The first course is soup, served at the sideboard and handed round by the footmen. After a quick check with Jones, Ali picks up the spoon. Soup is not the easiest thing to eat whilst wearing an evening dress and trying to ask leading questions.

Giuseppe turns to her with what seems like formal courtesy.

'Are you making a long stay in London, Mrs Dawson?' There's no trace of an Italian accent in his voice. Even Jones has slightly sing-song vowel sounds.

'Only a few days,' says Ali, crossing her fingers under the table. 'I'm a friend of Lady Serafina's.'

'Ah, Lady Serafina.' Giuseppe looks across the table. 'She's quite the enigma. No one even knows what country she hails from.'

'From your name, I'm guessing you're of Italian ancestry,' says Ali.

'I was born here,' says Giuseppe, 'but my parents were glass-makers from Venice.'

This too rings a faint bell, tinkling like Venetian glass. Ali wonders if it's unusual that the son of artisans, foreign artisans at that, is invited to dine with Cain Templeton. But then, Templeton had always seemed to prefer the company of artists to that of his own class.

'Have you been to the Great Exhibition?' asks Ali. 'I went today. It was . . .' She searches for the right word. 'Awe-inspiring.'

'Several times,' says Guiseppe. 'Some of the exhibits are magnificent. Did you see the display of stained glass of all the nations?'

'I think so,' says Ali. She remembers a gallery full of shimmering light. At that point, she had almost ceased to be amazed. 'Did you see something called the Seeing Glass?' she asks. 'I heard people talking about it today.'

She thinks she senses a movement from the end of the table which suggests that Templeton is listening. Guiseppe says, rather carefully, 'I've seen it but I'm afraid that, when I peered into the looking glass, all I saw was my plain reflection.'

He's not plain, thinks Ali. He has the dark, dramatic looks that Ali thinks of as typically Italian. His wife, by contrast, is entirely English, with a pink-and-white complexion and blondish hair.

'You didn't see into the future?' she says. 'That's disappointing.'

'From what I've seen at the exhibition,' says Guiseppe, 'the future is a dangerous place, full of furnaces and steam and terrifying noises.'

That's about right, thinks Ali. 'Maybe it's not the glass that's magic,' she says, rather daringly, 'maybe it's the chair?'

This certainly hits home. Giuseppe stares at her and Templeton lets his knife fall onto his bread plate with a clatter.

'I think you might have met a cousin of mine last year,' says Ali, ignoring Jones's attempts to attract her attention. 'John Cole. I believe he came to one of your meetings?'

Giuseppe looks across the table at Templeton, but he is now talking to Lady Sonia. Giuseppe says, 'I'm afraid I don't remember. We have many meetings.'

'You're talking about The Collectors?'

Giuseppe runs a finger around the inside of his collar but doesn't answer.

Ali says, 'Cousin John remembered this meeting because he saw an extraordinary occurrence. He saw a man sit in a chair and disappear.'

'Really?' says Giuseppe, rather hoarsely, 'How incredible. Unbelievable, one might say.'

'But Cousin John swore it was true.'

'I . . . it sounds like a trick . . . of the sort we might see tonight.'

Giuseppe gives another desperate look across the table and, this time, Templeton comes to his aid. He gestures to a footman, who comes forward to take away the soup plates. The next course is roast lamb, carved at the sideboard, with new potatoes and peas. Ali wonders if her waistband, already slightly tight, will take the strain.

'Are you looking forward to this evening's entertainment, Mrs Dawson?' asks Templeton.

'Very much,' says Ali. 'I've heard a lot about Mr Kramer.'

'What have you heard?' asks Templeton.

Ali wonders how much she might reasonably be expected to know. She replies, cagily, 'Reports of his fame have spread even to Hastings.'

'Ah yes, of course,' says Templeton, smiling. 'The famously remote Hastings.'

'Are you an admirer of Mr Kramer's?' Jones asks Templeton.

For a second Templeton's pleasant expression is replaced by something darker. 'I'm not a follower, no. But I believe in watching my enemies.'

Would Templeton be surprised to hear that he sounds like the mafia leader from one of Ali's favourite films? She realises that Francis Gibson is addressing her. The arrival of the second course seems to be a signal to talk to the person on the other side. Francis also wants to discuss Klaus Kramer.

'It's said that he can harness hidden forces within the human body. I find that a rather exhilarating thought.'

'Exhilarating?' says Ali. It seems an odd word to choose.

'There's so much that we don't understand. What does Shakespeare say? "More things in heaven and earth . . . than are dreamt of in your philosophy."'

Ali has a particular aversion to men who quote classic authors. It was one of Hugo's more annoying habits. Perhaps it's this that makes her say, 'Are you one of The Collectors?'

Francis shifts to look at her. He has a thin face with a receding chin and prominent Adam's apple. It's the sort of face that easily looks shocked, as it does now.

'What do you know about The Collectors, Mrs Dawson?'

'Mr Templeton once told me a little about them. I've seen his collection.'

That sounds like a double-entendre. Francis looks even more affronted. His chin disappears into his high collar.

'I can't see what there is in Cain's collection to interest a lady.'

'Maybe I'm not a lady.'

'Alison!' Jones calls across the table. It's breaking some etiquette rule but maybe she can get away with these things. 'I've been telling Mr Templeton about your business in Hastings. You know, as a private detective.'

There's a warning in Jones's eyes. She clearly wants Ali to change the subject but she has also landed her with an entirely fictitious career.

Ali rises to the occasion. 'Yes,' she says, 'women make good detectives. You see, we're ignored a lot of the time. Especially older women like me. But we see everything. I've often thought that an old woman, sitting quietly knitting in the corner, could solve most murders.'

Francis laughs. 'Women don't have the stomach for murder.'

'You'd be surprised,' says Ali.

She catches Cain Templeton's eye. He is looking at her with the mixture of amusement and challenge that she remembers well.

'Fascinating,' he says.

The meat course is followed by cheese and salad and then a rather tremendous milk pudding. The plates are brought and replaced quickly, presumably to allow time to reach the theatre. Ali's wine glass is topped up several times too. She's been trying to drink sparingly. It's hard enough masquerading as a Victorian lady when stone cold sober. Goodness knows what a mess she'd make of it if she got drunk. But Ali has an uneasy feeling that she has had more wine than she intended. Part of the problem is that she is thirsty and there's no water on the table. When the party stands up to leave, Ali sways slightly. She sees Jones watching her.

'Be careful,' says Jones in her ear, for what feels like the umpteenth time, when they collect their wraps in the hallway.

'I'm fine,' says Ali.

Templeton holds the door open for them. He smiles at Ali in a rather sardonic way. Jones is right. She has to be careful.

Klaus Kramer is performing at the Theatre Royal, Drury Lane. Ali has been to this venue once before, to see *Jack and the Beanstalk* with Finn. That must have been around 2000 or 2001, a date which she is sure would sound unimaginable to Templeton and company. She has a memory of ushers in scarlet livery, of gilt and velvet that continued all the way up to their seats, which were the highest (and cheapest) in the house. The pantomime had been the traditional sort full of innuendo and good old-fashioned sexism. Ali had enjoyed it more than she should.

She's surprised how familiar the outside of the theatre looks: steps, classical portico, colonnade. All that's missing are the black cabs and red buses that generally clog the wide street. In their place are carriages and two-wheeled hansom cabs, which dart between the larger vehicles. Ali can't help noticing that some of the horses look thin and unhealthy, wild-eyed as they negotiate the traffic. Templeton helps Ali down from the carriage and gives her his arm as they cross the street. The rest of the party follow, Giuseppe giving one arm to Jones and one to his wife.

'Have you been to the Theatre Royal before?' asks Templeton.

'No,' says Ali. She thinks this is safest.

'It's one of our oldest theatres,' says Templeton. 'It burnt down in the sixteen hundreds and again at the turn of the century.' Ali remembers that 1800 is the supposed year of her birth. She nods solemnly. 'The theatre was rebuilt about thirty years ago,' Templeton continues. 'It's fully gaslit now.' He obviously thinks this is a good thing but it doesn't make Ali feel exactly confident about fire safety.

'It seems a huge venue for one man to fill,' says Ali.

'Yes,' Templeton bows her through one of the sets of double doors, 'but Kramer is popular.'

'Not with you, I gather.'

'No,' replies Templeton and Ali gets the impression that he is choosing his words carefully. 'He stole something of mine and I mean to get it back.'

'Something valuable?' asks Ali.

'Potentially.' They are walking up the red-carpeted stairs and, with an air of changing the subject, Templeton says, 'I think the management here will do anything for an audience. They've had a run of failures recently. Too many worthy plays, not enough melodramas.'

'I do like a melodrama,' says Ali.

'I'm in agreement,' smiles Templeton. He points at a framed poster on the wall. *The Cataract of the Ganges; or, the Rajah's Daughter*. 'I saw that here as a young man. There was a real waterfall on stage and, in the last act, the heroine escaped on horseback. I dreamt about it for weeks.'

In *Jack and the Beanstalk*, when the titular plant emerged from the floorboards and rose jerkily until it reached the rafters, Ali remembers gasping in pure pleasure. Finn's eyes had been like stars. Once again, she feels a kinship with Cain Templeton.

They have reached the first landing which forms a circle looking down on the horseshoe-shaped bar below. Ali peers over the balustrade and sees waiters pouring wine and champagne. Tailcoats and tiaras abound. Around the walls there are niches containing marble statues, their shadows made monstrous by the giant candelabras. Ali feels a faint stirring of unease. Or maybe it's just indigestion.

'This way,' says Templeton, pushing open a door marked, 'Royal Box'. They are certainly not in the cheap seats this time. The box is luxurious, with velvet seats and swagged curtains above. It is rather crowded with seven of them in it, though, and uncomfortably hot. The famous gas lighting emits a faintly sulphuric smell. This, combined with the red curtains, puts Ali strongly in mind of hell fire. She whispers this to Jones, who says, 'Say a Hail Mary then.' But Ali has no idea how this prayer goes. If only she could ask her one-time mother-in-law, Bernadette.

The lights dim, flickering demonically, and the curtains go up, revealing a man on the stage, sitting at what looks like a giant sewing machine. He moves his hands over it and music starts. The sound is like a piano but much eerier, the notes echoing and re-echoing around the vast theatre. Is this a glass harmonica? It's rather beautiful but Ali finds herself longing for the noise to stop. It's as if it is plucking at something just out of reach, something familiar but also deeply disturbing. Uncanny, she thinks. *Unheimlich.*

The music stops and the man stands. He's a far more impressive figure than Barry Power, tall and thin with grey hair worn just slightly too long. He's wearing evening dress and a crimson-lined black cloak.

'Friends and seekers of light,' Klaus Kramer begins. Ali starts. Aren't these the exact same words that Power used? Kramer continues, looking up at the gallery, 'Are you ready to leave the earthly realm and enter the divine?'

There are shouts of 'Yes!' – and 'No!' Ali is surprised at the level of audience participation. She also marvels at the way Kramer is able to project his voice. There's no microphone, and he's not shouting, but she can hear every word. Kramer asks for volunteers and three people, two men and a woman, make their way on stage. Kramer talks to them in his pleasant German accent. He asks them if they have any unfulfilled ambitions. One man says to marry his sweetheart. There's laughter at this, the audience is warming to him. The second man says that he wishes he could fly. Jones and Ali exchange glances. The woman says that she's always wanted to sing.

Kramer asks the three volunteers to lie down on the stage. The woman does so with reluctance, arranging her skirts around her. Then Kramer passes his hands over them, in much the same way that he played the glass harmonica. The woman rises to her feet, in one sinister, slow movement. She opens her mouth and a sound comes out that, like the music earlier, is almost, but not quite, perfect. It gets louder and louder until many people have hands over their ears. Then it stops and the woman lies back on the stage.

Kramer raises the second man. 'Is your sweetheart here?' he asks. 'Yes,' says the man, in a very different voice from the cheerful falsetto earlier. 'Ask her,' says Kramer. 'Milly!' booms the man, 'will you marry me?' There's more laughter and a shout of 'Yes!' from the gallery but Ali has no way of knowing if it's 'Milly' or not. The man, too, lies back down. Then Kramer approaches the third man. He lifts both hands as if he's a puppeteer and, slowly and steadily, the volunteer rises from the stage, completely horizontal. Ali peers forward, looking for hidden wires, and sees Templeton doing the same. But the man rises higher and higher, until he's almost level with the box. Ali can see his face, looking exactly as if he's asleep, eyes closed, lips relaxed. Kramer goes back to the harmonica and starts to play. The floating figure drifts downwards.

The audience applauds madly.

Chapter 20

After the spectacle of the floating man, the rest of the first act is an anticlimax. Kramer invites more people up onto the stage and demonstrates that he can guess what they are thinking. Ali watches the volunteers closely. They don't look like plants but, then again, they wouldn't, would they? Then he plays the harmonica again and disappears – literally – in a puff of smoke.

Templeton asks Ali and Jones if he can fetch them some lemonade. Ali accepts gratefully. She's still feeling thirsty and the soup, meat and milk pudding are churning unpleasantly in her stomach.

'I'd really like some fresh air,' she says. The theatre is now stiflingly hot, the seats below are fluttering with fans and enthusiastically plied programmes. The auditorium is one vast brandy snifter intensifying an overpowering smell of gas and sweat.

'Come with me,' says Templeton. 'There's a covered walkway where you can wait while I get the drinks.'

Giuseppe escorts Ali, Jones and his wife, Laura, down the stairs and out through a side door while Templeton goes to get the drinks. Francis Gibson and Lady Sonia remain in the box.

It's wonderful to be outside in the cool night air. Many other people have had the same idea and there's quite a crowd of colourful skirts swishing up and down between the Greek columns. Ali and Jones walk behind Giuseppe and Laura.

'What do you think of him?' asks Jones.

'He's quite a showman,' says Ali. 'But it could all be faked, I suppose.'

'I meant Giuseppe,' says Jones, lowering her voice, nodding towards the man in front of them. 'Is he the man in the chair?'

'I think so,' says Ali. 'He seemed shocked when I mentioned the meeting John went to.'

'You can't just blurt things out like that.'

'What about you, saying I was a private detective?'

Jones laughs. 'I had to do something to change the subject. Quick work, though, thinking of Miss Marple. It's a good cover story. You always ask too many questions. This can be your excuse.'

Ali is thinking up a reply to this when a voice calls, 'Mrs Dawson!' Templeton is approaching with several glasses on a tray. He is accompanied by a shorter man with dark hair and a neat beard.

'Lady Serafina, Mrs Dawson,' says Templeton, proffering the tray, 'may I present Mr Charles Dickens.'

Ali almost drops her glass. Charles Dickens. *The* Charles Dickens. This is the moment, she thinks, when time travel has jumped the shark and descended into truly Dickensian melodrama. She is meeting the man who invented Oliver and Nancy and Fagin, Mr Micawber, Little Dorrit and Miss Haversham, the man who practically invented Christmas. He doesn't know that his name is now an adjective or the words to 'As Long As He Needs Me'. He has never heard of *The Muppet Christmas Carol* and Ali doesn't think there are enough words in the lexicon to explain it to him. He doesn't know that every actor in England longs to be in a Sunday night adaptation of his books. If only Ali could tell him.

She stares so long that Jones gives her a slight nudge. 'How do you do, Mr Dickens,' says Jones, inclining her head regally. 'I'm a great admirer of your stories in *Household Words*.'

'I'm planning to write an article about this evening's entertainment,' says Dickens. 'What do you ladies make of it?' His eyes move from Jones to Ali. They are extraordinarily dark and bright, like those of a bird.

'Quite a spectacle,' says Ali, amazed that her voice works. She is speaking *to Charles Dickens*.

'Ah, you're a sceptic, Mrs Dawson,' says Dickens, sounding amused. 'Let me tell you, mesmerism works. I have seen the great Franz Mesmer at work. He was a protégé of my friend, Dr John Elliotson. Indeed, I have performed a mesmeric experiment myself. Shall I tell you about it?'

'Please do,' says Ali. Try stopping you, she thinks.

'I have a dear friend called Emile de la Rue. His wife, Augusta, suffered from terrible headaches and choler. Both husband and wife begged me to help her. So I visited Madame de la Rue at home. I made a pass at her . . .'

'I beg your pardon?'

Dickens smiles. 'That is the mesmeric term for the laying on of hands. I laid my hands on Madame de la Rue and she became agitated. Then she fell into a deep sleep. She told me later that, whilst asleep, she dreamt that she was being pursued by a terrible phantom. The figure was clearly connected with the distresses in her soul. But, when the lady awoke, the ghost had vanished, never to return.'

He rocks back on his heels, clearly delighted with himself. Ali has many questions. Just where did Dickens lay his hands? What exactly is his relationship with Madame de la Rue? How does he know the phantom will not return? Instead, she says, 'That sounds rather different from making a man fly. How do you think Klaus Kramer managed that?'

'Ah,' Dickens smiles again. 'Do you suspect hidden ropes and pulleys?'

'Yes, I do,' says Ali.

'As do I,' interjects Templeton.

'My dear Cain,' says Dickens. 'You are a cynic. Now I – I believe in magic.'

Ali feels that she should be applauding, as the crowd does to keep Tinkerbell alive in *Peter Pan* but, before any of them can react, the bell rings for the start of the second act. Templeton gives Ali his arm as they climb the stairs. 'What did you make of the great writer?' he asks.

'I love his books,' says Ali, 'but I wouldn't want to be married to him.'

Templeton laughs so much that she knows she's said something inappropriate again.

Klaus Kramer seems different when he comes back on stage. His movements are more staccato, his accent thicker. Can he have been partaking of recreational drugs in the interval? wonders Ali. Opium maybe? She knows that the drug is prevalent amongst upper-class Victorians. Templeton's mistress died of an opium overdose. The audience temperature – both actual and emotional – has risen too.

There's now an orchestra in the pit and every move of Kramer's is met with clashing cymbals and glissando-ing violins. He makes people sing and dance on stage. He capers too, his cape floating behind him. Finally, he stands centre stage, sweating under the gas-powered footlights.

'My dear friends. Thank you for coming this evening. Perhaps you have seen things that make you wonder. And wonder is a great thing, ladies and gentleman. Wonderful, in fact. Perhaps I have made you think about heaven and hell and how little separates them. Perhaps I have made you feel that the other realm is very near. The membrane is very thin. Reach out, you can touch it.' Once again, Ali is taken aback to hear an almost exact echo of Barry Power. *Sometimes the membrane between this world and the next is very thin.*

Kramer stretches out a hand. The auditorium is silent apart from the fluttering of fans.

'I hope I have made you experience the impossible. And now, now I take my leave.'

He reaches out the other hand and, without any further warning, rises into the air. His cloak flaps out on either side. It is almost identical to Barry Power's closing spectacle. Like the audience in the People's Palace, the crowd gasps and cheers. Kramer ascends, as if he is on an invisible escalator. He passes the box. Templeton says, 'By God! He *is* flying.' Ali cranes her head as the small figure with scarlet wings swoops past the chandelier and is lost in darkness. The applause is ragged and shocked.

As they leave the box Ali can hear exclamations of amazement all around her.

'How did he . . .'

'Did you see . . .'

'Devilment . . .'

'Conjuring . . .'

The crowd surges down the stairs. Ali would have been swept along with them if Templeton hadn't grasped her arm tightly. 'Stay close to me, Mrs Dawson. You don't want to be trampled.' Ali can smell his cologne – sandalwood and lime – and feel the heat from his body. She holds up her skirt with one hand but, even so, almost stumbles twice. When they reach the portico, the street outside is full of carriages and hansom cabs; horses stamping, coachmen shouting. A nineteenth-century taxi rank.

'I told James to wait around the corner,' says Templeton, still keeping hold of Ali's arm.

Jones was right. All coachmen *are* called James.

They cross the street. Jones follows with Francis Gibson and Lady Sonia. Giuseppe and his wife are a little way behind. Beggars call out for money and Ali thinks how terrible it is that this same, sad ritual still occurs when you leave a theatre in 2024. Surely, they should have solved homelessness and poverty by the twenty-first century? Charles Dickens would definitely think so. She remembers a scene in *A Christmas Carol* that didn't feature in the Muppet version. The two children cowering beneath the robes of the Ghost of Christmas Present. *This boy is Ignorance. This girl is Want. Beware them both* . . . Ali can't see the famous writer in the crush, but she hopes that she will get to read his article about the night's entertainment. As they walk along Catherine Street, Ali sees a carriage go past. It's drawn by two black horses and seems to be moving too fast for the crowded thoroughfare.

Street urchins are forced to jump out of the way and somebody swears. Ali gets a brief, chaotic glimpse of the occupants. One is Klaus Kramer, still wearing his scarlet-lined cloak. The other is, unmistakably, Barry Power.

Chapter 21

Dina wakes from a confusing dream about cats and teapots to hear two people arguing at the bus stop below her window.

'. . . and he never said that . . . he never . . .'

'. . . are you calling me a liar because, I swear . . .'

Dina rolls over to look at her phone. Six a.m. She half expects to see a message from Ali saying she is safely back in her little house but, instead, there are two messages from her mother and a notification that the day's *NYT* puzzles are ready to play. Dina does Wordle in four and gets stuck on connections. She goes to the bathroom and then pads into her tiny kitchen to make tea. The arguers are still hard at it.

'. . . it's disrespect, that's what it is . . .'

'. . . don't talk to me about disrespect . . .'

Dina peers out of the window but can only see the top of their heads. Two young women, probably in their late teens or early twenties. Dina is torn between telling them to be quiet or joining in the argument. Maybe she should just call them an Uber. She has a feeling that there won't be a bus for at least another half an hour. Have the girls been out all night?

It seems a long time since Dina has been to an all-night party. Now she's thirty-six, living on her own and making tea like a spinster. Dina's friend, Shawna, is trying to reclaim the word spinster but using it, even to herself, makes Dina feel slightly sorry for herself. It's Sunday. Dina's mother and father will be at church and they would definitely think Dina should be doing the same. She should be doing something wholesome and fun: going to a pottery class, meeting friends for brunch, volunteering at a charity. She should, at the very least, be off for a park run.

Dina makes her tea and goes back to bed. The quarrelling girls seem to have moved away but now Dina has thoroughly woken up. Should she message John, work out what to do about Ali? But John will be at home with his wife Moira. They have a very close relationship, which would be sickening if Dina didn't know how much they'd both gone through. Should she see if anyone is playing *Dungeons and Dragons*? Or she could do some work on her farm in *Stardew Valley*. She decides that all these things can wait until she has finished the day's puzzles. She is just reaching for her phone, planning another attack on connections, when a message comes up. Unknown number.

Hi Dina. Its Luca. Want to meet to discuss case? There's a place near me that does great breakfast burritos 😊

He has included a location pin. Dina waits for ten minutes before replying. It's quite hard, though.

★

The café is in Tooting, not far from Dina's Streatham flat. She knows she should walk there but spends too long deciding what to wear so ends up running late and having to catch the bus. The weather is still hot so she decides on a T-shirt and floaty skirt. She'd like to wear flip-flops but she hasn't painted her toenails so settles on white trainers.

Luca is sitting at a table outside the café. He's on his phone and Dina catches the telltale *NYT* site.

'Wordle in one?' she greets him.

'Four,' he says. 'I've never got it in one but I always have the same starter word, just in case.'

'What's your starter?' The geek version of foreplay, she thinks, as she settles herself in the chair across from him.

'Adieu.'

'Mine's "stare". Statistically, it's more helpful to get the consonants in place.'

'And has that ever come up?'

'No.' They both laugh, which makes the whole sitting down and ordering thing easier than usual.

They talk about puzzles for a bit and Dina says that she and all her software developer friends are mad about board games.

'Like Scrabble?' says Luca.

'More things like Ticket to Ride where you create train routes or Carcassonne where you build castles.'

'I play video games,' says Luca. 'Strategy stuff like Civilization V.'

'Me too,' says Dina. She also enjoys social deduction games like Mafia but decides not to mention this.

'Hope it wasn't too hard to get here,' says Luca. 'Bit selfish to choose somewhere on my doorstep.'

'It's OK,' says Dina. 'I live in Streatham.'

'Did you grow up in London?'

'Yes. Well, Croydon. Which sort of counts. What about you? I'm not sensing much of a London accent.'

'I'm from Portobello,' says Luca. 'It's on the coast near Edinburgh. A lot of Italian immigrants settled there. My grandad was a prisoner-of-war in Scotland.'

'My grandparents emigrated from Ghana,' says Dina. 'Do you speak Italian?'

'Not very well,' says Luca. 'My mum's Scottish so we didn't really talk Italian at home. I support Italy in football, though.'

'Smart move,' says Dina. 'How did you end up in south London?'

'Came to London for university and just stayed. Joined the police as a graduate trainee. What about you?'

'I'm not in the force,' says Dina. Their burritos arrive which delays her explanation but, eventually, she says, 'I'm a civilian data analyst, seconded to a cold case team.'

Luca's eyes widen. They are dark brown with surprisingly long eyelashes. 'Are you going to tell me about the top-secret team?'

Dina takes a bite of burrito. It really is delicious. 'It's just cold cases,' she says. 'We call ourselves the Frozen People because our cases are so cold they're frozen.'

'There must be more to it than that. DI Cole is a famous murder detective. DI Dawson . . . well, there's some mystery about her. Lots of her personnel files have been redacted.'

'Have you been digging then?'

'Of course.' Luca grins. He has very white teeth, emphasised by the olive skin and black moustache.

'Look,' says Dina. 'Some of our cases are classified, so obviously I can't talk about them, but mostly we sit around in an

East End tower block, going through old files and driving each other mad.'

Luca tries the grin again but obviously decides to move on. 'Thank you for sending me the files on Barry Power,' he says. 'I wish there was some way of pinning something on him.'

'He's too slippery,' says Dina. 'Even if he was responsible for Luke's death – the young man who killed himself – there's almost no way of proving it. The CPS would never bring a charge against him.'

'You said you'd been to see his stage show,' says Luca. 'What was that like?'

'On the face of it, very easy to dismiss. Lots of lucky guesses with the audience. Playing on their desire to believe. Lots of business with the spirit guide and all that. But he did say something about one of our colleagues that made Ali and me sit up a bit.'

'What was that?'

Dina wonders how much to tell Luca but decides it can't hurt to say, 'He mentioned the name Serafina and said she was a pilgrim soul. Well, we have an advisor called Serafina Pellegrini, which means—'

Obviously, Luca knows this much Italian. 'Pilgrims,' he finishes. 'Is that Dr Serafina Jones from Imperial? I heard she'd disappeared.'

Dina's heart beats slightly faster. 'You *have* been doing your research.'

'I may not be an expert but I can use a computer.'

This seems slightly pointed.

'Jones . . . Serafina . . . is away working on a case,' says Dina. 'That's all I can say. Is that why you invited me here, to ask questions about the team?'

'Partly,' says Luca, 'and partly because I wanted to see you again. Also, I wanted to update you on the Hugo Maltravers case.'

Dina is still getting over 'I wanted to see you again'. She says, as if she has never heard the name before, 'Hugo Maltravers?'

'Ali Dawson's ex-husband?' says Luca. 'Found murdered in an alleyway? Ring any bells?'

'I remember,' says Dina, trying for a bit of dignity, not helped by the fact that she's spilt some tomato sauce on her top.

'Hugo's partner, Serena, collected his stuff from his office at King's,' says Luca. 'Amongst his papers she found a postcard of the actor Christopher Lee, dressed as Dracula. On the back was a handwritten message. "I'm going to kill you."'

'Gosh,' says Dina, trying surreptitiously to erase the stain, 'did she know what that was about?'

'No. Apparently Hugo had never mentioned any death threats to her. It could have been a joke, of course. Or maybe Maltravers got messages like that from disgruntled students all the time. But I just thought you should be aware of it.'

'Do you think it's significant?'

'A man dies and we find a message threatening to kill him, we have to take it seriously. The postcard's with forensics now but I doubt if they'll find anything. It's been handled by so many people and, even if we did get prints, that wouldn't help unless they matched some on file. The same with DNA. We'll have a handwriting expert look at it too but I never think those people tell you much. "May have been a man, may have been a woman."'

'Sounds a bit like Barry Power's mind-reading techniques,' says Dina. 'I suppose you can check it against his fingerprints. You must have them on file.'

'I'll certainly do that,' says Luca. 'Anyway, I thought maybe we could do some research.'

'What sort of research?' says Dina. Maybe Luca is only interested in her IT skills after all.

'I thought we could see a Dracula film tonight,' says Luca. 'They're showing *Nosferatu* at the BFI.'

After making arrangements to meet that evening on the South Bank, Dina pays half the bill and leaves to walk down Tooting High Street. She tells Luca that she has shopping to do but really she just wants to be on her own for a while. She feels acutely aware of her body; her legs underneath the thin skirt, the touch of the cotton T-shirt on her skin, even her feet in the clumpy trainers. Is it because of Luca? Is it the thought of a date, if that's even what this is? She stops to look in the window of an artisan bakery and her phone buzzes. Is it Luca saying he's missing her? No, Dina's heart sinks, it's Finn.

'Hi, Finn.'

'Dina. Hi. Sorry to bother you. It's just . . . I've been trying to get hold of Mum since yesterday and I thought . . . well, I'm sure it's fine . . . just . . .'

Dina waits just a second too long before answering.

'Oh no,' says Finn. 'Really?'

Finn had been horrified when, last year, he learnt the true nature of his mother's work. Dina remembers him storming out of Eel House after, allegedly, attempting to punch Geoff. She doesn't know if Ali promised him that her time-travelling days were over. She suspects not. She doesn't think Ali would lie to Finn.

'It's OK,' says Dina. Though it isn't, not by a long way. She stares, unseeingly, at a plate of cinnamon buns.

'She went through the gate again?'

'She only went back a few days.'

'Then why isn't she back?'

Dina can't think what to say and settles on the truth. 'I don't know.'

'Jesus,' says Finn. 'I can't believe it. After last time, why on earth would she go back again? Was it to try and save Jones?'

'No, I think it was to save Terry.' Dina explains about shutting the cat flap.

Finn gives a bark of humourless laughter. 'Oh my God. I know she was upset about Terry. I just never thought . . . What shall I do? I'm in Yorkshire with Helen Graham. Should I come back to London?'

'No,' says Dina. 'There's nothing you can do. You're better off keeping busy.'

'It is quite manic here,' says Finn. 'I can't believe the election is next week.'

'Nor can I,' says Dina. The atmosphere in London is curiously flat. There are very few party posters up. Dina, to her secret disappointment, hasn't been canvassed once.

'Ali will be back by then,' she says, trying to insert some confidence into her voice.

'Nothing will stop her casting her vote,' says Finn.

Dina laughs and they part on a more cheerful note but, for Dina, the day has lost its glow. She's almost tempted to ring Luca and cancel the film.

Chapter 22

But she doesn't. At six o'clock, Dina is on the bus. One of the drawbacks of living in Streatham is that it's not on the Tube. She will have to change at Clapham Common and get the Northern Line to Waterloo. To pass the time, Dina googles *Nosferatu*. She learns that it was made in 1922 and is 'a silent German impressionist film'. Her heart sinks slightly at the thought of an hour, or an hour and a half (timings depend on the version and transfer speed apparently), of watching men suck women's blood in silence. At least it's in black and white, which she hopes will be less gory than colour. Dina is not really a fan of horror. Although she considers herself agnostic, she was brought up in a Christian family that took the devil and the occult very seriously. She thinks of *The Mesmerist*, the film about Klaus Kramer, made twenty years before *Nosferatu*. Tom had described it as 'disturbing'. Will that too be full of violence against women, disguised as art?

On impulse, Dina texts her friend Shawna. 'On date. Meeting at NFT. Will text when home.'

Shawna replies immediately, as Dina knew she would. 'A date! OMG! What's he like? Did u meet online?'

Dina texts back. 'No. IRL. He's a cop. Half Italian. Cute.'

'Did u meet at work?' Dina imagines Shawna typing, her long nails tapping the screen.

'Yes. Murder enquiry!'

She knows this will get Shawna, who is fascinated by crime. Shawna's the one who should have been a police officer but she left school at sixteen after getting pregnant. She's now a single mother, supporting her son by working as a beautician. Dina is very proud of her.

Shawna sends four texts in quick succession.

Murder??? U need to tell me all!!

Then:

Name?

So I can stalk him and check ur safe.

Have fun.

Dina smiles and types in Luca's name, adding 'thx' and a heart emoji. She has to admit that she's pleased someone knows where she is. She can't tell her parents because they'd overreact, her mother would want Luca's entire biography and her father would warn her against all men but especially half-Italian police officers from Portobello. Her brothers would offer to beat Luca up, although neither of them has been in a fight since school. Her sister, who has been with her partner since teacher training college, would offer sensible advice guaranteed to suck the fun out of any situation. Or situationship.

At seven o'clock Dina is walking along the South Bank. She's wearing a red dress and flat sandals and is satisfied when she catches sight of her reflection in windows. She has even painted her toenails although she was in a rush and they are rather streaky. The banks of the Thames are busy, people are eating at tables outside restaurants and cafés, others are just strolling, listening to buskers and staring at the so-called 'living statues'. Dina finds these rather scary, the performers painted gold or silver, Charlie Chaplin with his cane, Britannia with her crown, waiting for the moment when a child puts money into the box and the effigy moves, with alarming suddenness. Dina walks past quickly, holding her phone tightly in case of pickpockets.

Luca is waiting by a real statue, Laurence Olivier. The famous actor is in dramatic pose, holding a sword up to the sky. Luca, wearing shorts and a pale blue shirt, provides a very pleasing contrast. He was the one who suggested the meeting place and Dina had been slightly worried that he'd turn out to be a fan of actors who played Othello in blackface. But, after complimenting Dina on her dress, Luca says, 'Can't stand all that Shakespearean stuff. Henry the fifth, the English winning all the battles. Give me Dracula any day.'

'What about Macbeth?' says Dina. 'He's Scottish.'

'I'm pretty sure it's unlucky to mention him so near a theatre,' says Luca. 'Let's get something to eat. The film doesn't start until nine.'

They eat at one of the crowded tables. They both choose noodles, which aren't ideal for a first date, but Luca is remarkably good at winding the strands round his fork. Dina supposes he's had a lot of practice with spaghetti. She manages all right and, at least, doesn't spill food on herself. They drink Aperol spritz, which adds to the celebratory feel. Dina is glad that Luca didn't insist on some dourly-named ale instead.

It's only when they take their seats in the cinema that Dina starts to have doubts. What is she doing, sitting next to an almost stranger and, what's worse, a serving police officer? She has always tried to avoid the forces when internet dating. And why on earth did they choose a horror film for their first date? If it even is a date.

The music starts. Luca looks at Dina and grins, with a flash of those white teeth.

'Scared?'

'Of course not.'

To her surprise, Dina enjoys *Nosferatu*. Although there is no spoken dialogue, there's plenty of music. The film is subtitled, 'A Symphony of Horror'. The plot seems very similar to what Dina remembers of *Dracula*. She read the book at Cambridge whilst going through a slightly Gothic phase.

Max Schreck, as Count Orlok, is too much of a pantomime villain, with his bald head and claw-like hands, to be really terrifying. There are some memorable scenes, though: the carriage on a snowy mountain road, the sea voyage, black waves against white cliffs, rats running through medieval streets. Dina is very conscious of Luca beside her. Is he going to put his arm round her, as boys used to do when she was at school? But both Luca's hands are resting on his knees. Dina even gasps once, to see if he tries to comfort her, but Luca seems intent on the screen.

The last shot of the film shows Orlok's castle in ruins. Luca and Dina emerge into the summer night.

'Another drink?' says Luca.

'Why not?'

They go to an old-fashioned pub by the side of the river. This time Luca drinks beer and Dina has a gin and tonic.

They discuss the film. Luca says that he read that the producer, Albin Grau, had been influenced by his experiences of serving in the German army in the First World War. 'He saw the war as a vampire that was drinking the blood of young men.'

Dina is pleased that Luca, too, has been googling. 'People always believe more in the occult during wartime,' she says. 'There was a rise in belief in spiritualism after the First World War. Everyone wanted to see their dead relatives again.'

'And spiritualists took advantage of that,' says Luca. 'Charlatans.'

Dina remembers Barry Power conjuring the ghosts of Jim and Auntie Ellen. She thinks of Ali, lost somewhere in time, and the moments when she has had to believe the impossible. She decides to lighten the conversation.

'I haven't seen a horror film since I was at school. *The Amityville Horror*. I had to lie about my age to get in. I must have been about sixteen.'

'Tell me about the young Dina,' says Luca. 'I bet all the boys fancied you.'

'They really didn't,' answers Dina. 'I was a nerd, going to computer club every lunchtime. My family didn't have much money and I never wore the right sort of clothes. I was terrible at sport too and that counted in my school. My sister was in all the teams. She's a PE teacher now. What about you?'

'All the girls fancied me,' says Luca, grinning. 'I think it was because I didn't have any spots. British boys are often spotty.'

'You don't think of yourself as British then?' Dina ignores the boast.

'I'm Scottish and Italian. The word British doesn't mean much to me.'

'I think of myself as British,' says Dina. 'Partly because so many people try to tell me I'm not.'

'Does that still happen?' asks Luca.

'All the time,' says Dina. She thinks it's a naive question but at least Luca didn't dismiss her experience, as so many people do. She remembers tutors at Cambridge who asked about her 'culture' or her family 'back home'. 'Do you mean Croydon?' she used to say.

The pub is closing so they walk back over Waterloo Bridge. Late-night revellers are wending their way home. A busker is singing 'Waterloo Sunset'.

'Shall we share a taxi?' asks Luca. 'Tooting first and then Streatham.'

'OK.' Dina feels slightly deflated. She has no intention of sleeping with Luca on their first date but she would like him to show a little interest. She walks on for a few paces before realising that Luca has stopped.

'What is it?' She walks back to him.

Luca looks at her and Dina feels her insides churning. She moves closer and, unsmiling, Luca leans in to kiss her. The midnight traffic roars past, unnoticed by either of them.

Chapter 23

Dina gets to work early on Monday, which is just as well because there's a malign presence lurking by the sink.

'I was beginning to think this was a ghost ship,' says Nigel Palmer, 'and the hot tap doesn't work.'

'It's never worked,' says Dina. 'Not as long as we've been here anyway.'

'Where is everyone?' says Nigel. He looks rather peevishly at the kettle but doesn't seem to have switched it on. Dina flicks the switch. She has a feeling they will need caffeine soon.

'It's only eight thirty,' she says.

'What time do you normally start?' asks Nigel, selecting a cup from the cupboard. If he's looking for one without stains, he'll be doomed to disappointment.

'Nine o'clock,' says Dina, although, in truth, this is a movable feast these days. Ali and Dina often wait until after rush hour to make the journey. John is usually punctual, though.

Nigel selects Bud's *Doctor Who* mug. 'Where's DI Dawson?' he says.

Dina thinks fast. 'She's taken a few days' leave. To see her son in Yorkshire.'

'I thought Finn lived in London?'

It's a surprise that Nigel knows Finn's name, much less where he lives.

'He works for a Yorkshire MP,' says Dina, 'so he's living in the constituency at the moment.'

'Does DI Dawson know her ex-husband's been murdered?'

Dina is saved from answering by the outer door banging open. She looks out of the kitchen and sees John making his way to his desk, looking rather hot and bothered. He must be sweltering in jeans and a polo shirt but John, like Paganini, never wears shorts.

'John!' Dina gives him a warning look. 'We're in here. Me and Nigel.'

John raises his eyebrows at her and approaches the kitchen.

'I've just been telling Nigel about Ali visiting Finn in Yorkshire.'

'Oh, yes,' says John, going to the sink to fill his water bottle. 'Yorkshire.' For a detective, he's a bad liar.

'And I was asking if DI Dawson knew that her ex-husband had been murdered,' says Nigel, pouring hot water on a tea bag. Dina notes he hasn't offered anyone else a drink.

'We haven't told her yet,' says John. 'Didn't want to spoil her holiday. In Yorkshire. With Finn.'

They move into the open-plan area. Ali's shut door looks like a reproach. Nigel sits, without asking, at Dina's desk. Dina and John remain standing.

'DI Dawson must be informed,' says Nigel. 'There could be a connection. She could even be in danger.'

'I spoke to the DS in charge,' says Dina, avoiding John's eyes, 'and he said that Hugo Maltravers had received a possible death threat. A postcard of Dracula with the handwritten message, "I'm going to kill you".' She has a sudden flashback to the *Nosferatu* film: mountain passes, white on black, rickety bridges over chasms, a galleon on a storm-tossed sea.

John makes an inarticulate sound. Dina thinks he's annoyed that she's spoken to Luca. She knows she should have told him about the postcard but, somehow, didn't find the time yesterday.

But John says, 'A postcard of Dracula?'

'Well, the actor Christopher Lee as Dracula.'

'I had a postcard too,' says John. 'Hand-delivered, envelope addressed to me.'

'A postcard?' says Nigel. 'What are you talking about?'

'A picture of the poster for the film *Dial M for Murder*,' says John. 'I looked it up. It came out in 1954 and starred Grace Kelly and Ray Milland.'

'And you didn't think it was worth reporting?' says Nigel. 'A detective of your experience?'

'It only happened on Saturday,' says John, although Dina thinks he sounds slightly embarrassed.

There's a silence broken, once again, by a door slamming. They hear footsteps running up the stairs, then the second door crashes open and, before Dina or John can say anything, Bud bursts into the room. 'Is there any news? About Ali? Is she still missing . . .' He stops.

Slowly, wordlessly, Nigel stands up.

★

'So she's been missing since Friday night?' says Nigel.

'Yes,' says John. They are still grouped around Dina's desk. Nigel looks from one to the other like a disappointed headmaster.

'And when were you going to tell me?'

'We thought she'd be back,' says Dina, aware how unconvincing this sounds. Bud, after his first outburst, has sunk into silence.

'Regardless of that,' says Nigel, 'you should have informed me immediately. As you're no doubt aware, any *extra-curricular activities* are expressly forbidden.'

Extra-curricular activities. It sounds like a sixth form trip to the Globe. Dina thinks it might be physically impossible for Nigel to utter the words 'time travel'.

'We've got this capability,' says John, unexpectedly, 'you can't expect us not to use it.'

'Funnily enough, DI Cole,' says Nigel, 'that's exactly what I expect.'

'But we have to do our best to get Jones . . . Dr Pellegrini . . . back . . .'

'Dr Pellegrini is not a government employee and so not my business,' says Nigel. 'Besides, it's my understanding that DI Dawson only planned to go back three days and so this *jaunt* had nothing to do with retrieving Dr Pellegrini.'

None of them have dared to mention closing the cat flap.

'So,' Nigel fixes his eyes on Bud. 'You facilitated this . . . Mr . . .'

'Dr,' says Bud. 'Dr Sirisema.'

Nigel rolls his eyes as if another doctorate is more than he can bear. 'You facilitated this. You must get her back.'

'It's not that easy,' says Bud. Today's T-shirt reads, 'I found this humerus' over a picture of a bone. 'The technique developed by

Dr Pellegrini involves an exchange of particles. A gate is created through which one person can pass. At first we thought that only a person with identical molecules could use the gate in either direction but events have . . . er . . . shown that not to be true. Last year someone else used Ali's gate. Then DI Cole returned using Dr Pellegrini's gate.'

'You'll just have to create another gate.'

'Whichever way I do it,' says Bud, 'someone will be left behind.'

This explanation seems to enrage Nigel. He says, sounding more impassioned than Dina could have believed possible, 'This should never have been allowed. It's madness. Stark raving insanity. I don't know what the PM was thinking. Dr Pellegrini seems to have bewitched everyone.'

'She does do that,' says Dina.

'Tell me the truth,' says Nigel, staring at Bud behind his thick glasses. 'Is there any way of rescuing DI Dawson?'

Bud pushes his hair back. 'I honestly think the only way is for Ali to rescue herself.'

When Nigel has left, frustration oozing from every pore, the team escapes to a nearby café for proper coffee.

'I wouldn't have thought Nigel could get that angry,' says John. In honour of the occasion, he actually orders a non-decaf latte.

'What do you think he'll do?' says Bud, dithering over the chai options.

'I don't think there's much he can do,' says John. 'They can't disband the unit because we know too much.'

'They could kill us, though,' says Dina. 'Joking,' she adds, for Bud's benefit.

'Maybe Nigel's been sending the postcards,' says John.

'What do you mean?' says Bud, sounding aggrieved as he always does when he feels he's been left out of things.

Dina explains about the *Dracula* and *Dial M for Murder* postcards.

'Grace Kelly,' says Bud. 'The most beautiful woman in the world.'

'Did DS Venturi have anything else to say?' asks John.

'Not much,' says Dina. Instead of a taxi, she and Luca caught the night bus and kissed all the way back to Dina's flat. By the time Dina remembered her vow about not having sex on the first date, they had made love twice. They plan to meet again this evening.

'Luca . . . DS Venturi . . . thinks he might have murdered his wife,' says Dina. 'Maybe he killed Hugo too.'

'DS Venturi didn't have any proof,' says John. 'And, besides, spousal murder is very different from assaulting someone in the street.'

Spousal murder is another police officer phrase. For some reason, it makes Dina feel angry.

'I think we should carry on investigating the death of Luke Fanshaw,' she says. 'We know Luke saw Power before he died. I think I should go and talk to him.'

'Seeing Barry Power won't bring Ali back,' says John.

'According to Bud, nothing can bring her back.' Dina is annoyed to find her voice wobbling.

'I didn't say that.' Bud takes a thoughtful sip of masala chai. 'I said Ali would have to rescue herself. In the days before she . . . she went back . . . Jones was talking about other ways to time travel. She said she'd seen someone sit on a chair and disappear.'

'I saw that too,' says John. 'In 1850.'

'Great,' says Dina. 'All Ali has to do is find a time-travelling chair. Why don't we ring Enid Blyton and ask if she's got a spare one.'

'Who?' asks Bud.

Dina makes the trip to Thornton Heath the next day. What else is there to do? She now has the remastered film about Klaus Kramer owned by the rare-films collector, Tom, but she doesn't want to watch it in the office. And she doesn't want to sit in Eel House, staring at John and pretending to work.

On the train, Dina does a bit of light stalking of Luca. He was born in 1989 which makes him a year younger than her. He attended a state school in Scotland and studied sociology at Imperial. His time there overlapped with Dina's by a year. It's tempting to think that they might have passed each other in a corridor one day or queued for half-price beer in the student bar. Luca doesn't post on Facebook but he's friends with his mother, Tina, who only shares pictures of cats, and his brother, Matteo, who seems obsessed with the football club Hibernian. There are no relationships listed but he is tagged in a post shared by a woman called Marie Blue, which is a pseudonym if Dina ever heard one. The photo shows Luca and (presumably) Marie drinking cocktails on a beach. Luca is wearing a Ferrari cap which obscures most of his face. Marie looks irritatingly glamorous, which is obviously why she posted the picture. It's captioned #blessed, which makes Dina feel quite nauseous. She turns off her phone.

Power is expecting her. It's not psychic precognition; Dina rang to say she was on her way (the number was in Ali's notes).

'Another visitor,' he says, ushering her through a dark hallway into a sitting room that reminds Dina of her grandmother's. 'I must have made an impression that evening.'

'It was very interesting,' says Dina. 'I'd never been to anything like that before.'

'Ah,' says Power, 'you're a new soul. I thought that immediately. Everything is new and exciting to you.'

'What does that mean?' says Dina. 'That I haven't been reincarnated?'

'That's a crude term,' says Power. 'But some people have definitely been here before. DI Dawson for one. Tea? Coffee?'

Dina asks for mint tea, which arrives in a cup and saucer. Dina asks how long Power has lived in Thornton Heath. She remembers Luca talking about the strange gaps in Power's biography.

'I'm thinking about moving,' she says, 'and I like south London.'

'I've been here about ten years,' says Power. 'I moved to London from Wales after I got married.'

'Is your wife a medium too?' asks Dina innocently.

Power doesn't blink but he makes an odd movement, as if warding something off, a fly or maybe an errant spirit.

'She passed over three years ago,' says Power.

'Passed over' seems an odd phrase. Dina is used to 'passed away' and an evangelical friend of her mother's uses the baleful 'gathered'. Passing over definitely implies a journey of some kind.

'How did she die?' says Dina, trying to sound sympathetic rather than merely nosy.

'An accident,' says Power shortly. 'She tripped and fell down the stairs.'

'I'm sorry,' says Dina. 'How horrible.' She had glanced at the stairs when they went past. They were steep and somehow sinister with a dark banister and narrow red carpet. For the first time Dina thinks that she might well be in the room with a murderer. She wishes she had told Luca, or even Shawna, where she was going.

'It *was* horrible,' says Power. 'I was in bed. Vi got up, maybe to go to the loo. I don't know. Then I heard her say "No", really loudly. I ran out onto the landing. Violet was lying at the bottom of the stairs. Dead.'

'Who do you think she was talking to?' asks Dina. She is shivering, despite the hot day.

'I don't know,' says Power. 'I have my suspicions but . . .' He turns away and blows his nose on a real, linen handkerchief.

The significance of the name has just dawned on Dina. 'Violet,' she says. 'Isn't she your spirit guide?'

'Yes,' says Power, wiping his eyes. 'I am lucky that I can be in contact with my love. We have travelled through many lives together.'

Lucky is one word for it. Power seems to pull himself together and says, 'Well, I'm sure you didn't come here to discuss my wife, Miss . . .' He looks at Dina's card. 'Miss Appiah.'

'No,' says Dina. 'I wanted to talk about Luke Fanshaw.'

Power gives her a look that seems marginally less spiritual than his previously calm gaze.

'As I told Alison . . . DI Dawson, I only saw Luke once. I'm desperately sorry about what happened to him but it's nothing to do with me.'

Dina takes a sip of tea. It tastes slightly odd or maybe that's just because it's real mint. She can see the leaves at the bottom of the cup.

She says, 'When you saw Luke, you allegedly went into a trance and conjured the spirit of Klaus Kramer. You talked about the killing time. What did that mean?'

'I didn't mean to contact Kramer,' says Power. 'He just came through. He does sometimes.' He looks round, as if he expects the mesmerist to be hovering in the doorway. Dina shivers again. It's broad daylight, she tells herself, you can get up and leave any time.

'Why was Luke so obsessed with Kramer?' asks Dina.

'I don't know,' says Power. 'He wasn't a good person for a young man to associate with. Trust me on that.'

And Dina almost does believe him. For a second Power sounds like he knew Kramer well. Which is impossible, of course. Isn't it?

'There's a film about Kramer,' she says, 'it's called *The Mesmerist*. Have you seen it?'

'No,' says Power. 'That doesn't sound like a film I'd like to watch.'

'Do you think Luke watched it?'

'I have no idea.'

'Have you heard of a man called Hugo Maltravers?'

'I don't think so. It's not a well-starred name, though. Mal means evil. I suppose it could translate as evil crossing.'

'Hugo was Ali's ex-husband. He was killed last week, not far from here.'

'An evil crossing indeed,' says Power.

'Hugo was also an expert on Klaus Kramer.'

'Really?' says Power. 'An unusual speciality.'

'He was a historian,' says Dina, 'and he wrote a paper on Kramer. "The Victorian Art of Conjuring". Have you ever read it?'

'No,' says Power. 'Interesting title, though. Conjuring is often associated with the devil.'

Dina feels that the conversation has gone off the rails. The trouble is, she has no new information apart from the discovery of the film and Hugo's murder, neither of which are directly linked to Luke Fanshaw or Barry Power.

Power is watching her almost with amusement.

'Let me ask you a question, Miss Appiah,' he says. 'Where is Alison Dawson?'

Dina falls back on the lie she told Nigel. 'She's in Yorkshire for a few days, visiting her son.'

'Because to me you look like a woman who is searching for someone or something.'

'Really?'

'Really.' Power gives her his best mediumistic stare. 'Do you believe in time travel, Ms Appiah?'

'What?'

'What would you say if I told you that I'd met Alison before, in a very different time and place? In nineteenth-century London, to be precise.'

'I'd assume you were joking.'

'Would you?'

'Yes,' says Dina, although her heart is beating so fast that she wouldn't be surprised to see her T-shirt vibrating. 'How is that possible?'

'In another life, I worked for Klaus Kramer,' says Power. 'I met Alison in 1851. She was in the company of a woman called Lady Serafina Pellegrini. The pilgrim soul herself. Oh, and a certain Cain Templeton.'

Dina's head is spinning. How could Power know these names? Could his story possibly be true? But he's a conman, she tells herself, a conjuror.

'I don't know what you're talking about,' she says.

'I think you do,' says Power. 'And you'll come back. Because I can help you. I can help get Alison back.' He hands Dina a piece of card. 'Here's my mobile number. Call me.'

Before she leaves, Dina asks if she can use the loo. It's a trick she has learnt from John. 'You can learn a lot from the bathroom in a suspect's house.' But all Dina learns is that Power uses Molton Brown liquid soap and his hand towel appears freshly laundered. But, as she emerges into the dark hallway, she stops in front of a framed poster. It shows a white-faced man with abnormally long fingers and nails. A ship in full sail cuts its way through the title. *Nosferatu, a symphony of horror.*

'Are you interested in old films?' Dina asks Power.

'Not really,' he replies, 'but I'm fascinated by the legend of Dracula. It's the ultimate story of eternal life.'

'Is it?' says Dina, thinking of the film. 'I seem to remember that Orlok, or Dracula, dies at the end of the film.'

'Vampires never die,' says Power. 'That's why the story keeps being told.'

'It's a bit of a pain, though, isn't it?' says Dina. 'All that sleeping in coffins and drinking blood.'

She speaks lightly but in truth there's something unsettling about Power in that moment. He is standing in shadow but the afternoon sunlight shining through the stained glass in the front door casts a strange red glow on his face. Dina remembers Ellen dying at the end of *Nosferatu*, sacrificing herself to the monster. She thinks of Luca saying that he was certain Power had killed his wife. *He seemed detached, describing the scene as if he was a witness, not a bereaved husband.*

On the doorstep, Dina asks Power if he's heard of a police officer called Luca Venturi. For the first time, the medium's mild expression vanishes, to be replaced with something altogether colder.

'I've encountered him,' he says. 'For a man whose name means bringer of light, he's a force of darkness. My advice is to steer clear of him at all costs.'

Dina walks quickly down the suburban street, eager to get as much distance between her and Barry Power as possible. How on earth can he have known about Cain Templeton and the link to Serafina Pellegrini? Dina tries to remember what Ali said about her visit to Power. Hadn't Power said something about knowing her from another plane of existence? Could Ali possibly have mentioned Cain Templeton then? It seems unlikely but it's the only explanation. Isn't it?

Then there was the story of Violet's death. Power hadn't sounded detached when he told it; he'd sounded scared. Dina thinks of the woman calling out 'No!' and then falling to her death. Did Power want Dina to believe that Violet had seen Klaus Kramer that night? Was he the demonic figure who had pushed her to her death? *He just came through. He does sometimes.*

There's undoubtedly something creepy about Power, with his milky gaze and his calm talk of travelling through many lives. *I'm fascinated by the legend of Dracula. It's the ultimate story of eternal life.* Dina thinks of watching the film with Luca, of the kiss on the bridge and all the subsequent kisses. Power had called Luca a force of darkness. Luca had clearly suspected Power of killing his wife and admitted that he had questioned him aggressively. Dina doesn't imagine that he is top of Power's Christmas card list. But there is something rather chilling about hearing your boyfriend described in that way. If he even is her boyfriend.

Dina arrives at the station to find that she has just missed a train. The next one is not for twenty minutes. She buys a Diet Coke from a kiosk because she can still taste Kramer's mint tea. The can is wonderfully cold and Dina presses it to her forehead. The day is hotter than ever, the sky an oppressive yellow colour that promises thunder later. Dina puts in her EarPods, planning to listen to some soothing podcast, when her phone buzzes. Luca.

Want to meet tonite?

Dina hesitates, watching a group of children congregate on the opposite platform. It must be the end of the school day. Funny how the day seems so long when you're at school but in reality three p.m. is only just after lunch. Not that Dina's had any today. Maybe that's why she's feeling slightly odd.

She calls Luca. He answers in his police officer voice which she can't help finding rather sexy.

'Want to watch a scary film tonight?'

'I do. Aye.' She can't believe he said 'aye'.

'Come to mine after work. Bring snacks.'

Luca brings pizza, which is a meal rather than a snack, but Dina is not complaining. She contributes two gins in a tin and some crisps. The pizza has to wait, though, because they start kissing in the hallway and inevitably make their way into Dina's bedroom. So they eat the pizza and drink the gin in bed with Dina's laptop between them.

Dina has just loaded the film when a sudden gust of wind blows the curtains inwards. Far across London she hears the first, faint rumble of thunder. She gets up to shut the window. Large drops of rain are starting to hit the pavement. Three people are huddled in the bus shelter where the girls were arguing on Sunday morning.

'That's our summer gone,' says Luca, pressing pause on the film.

'Spoken like a true Italian,' says Dina, getting back into bed.

'I'm Scots Italian,' says Luca. 'I'm used to not seeing the sun for months on end.'

'Well, it was good while it lasted,' says Dina, pressing play. 'The nights are drawing in now.'

Dina had been slightly scared to see the film but, watching it with Luca, the jerky images, the silhouetted figures and clutching hands outlined against the night sky, seem more amusing than terrifying. There's no sound, which doesn't help with the atmosphere. Dina remembers the stirring music of *Nosferatu*. Now all she has is Luca's laconic Scots narration: 'Och, now he's looking for someone else to murder . . . be careful with that axe, sonny . . . now he's off for a bit of flying . . . watch out for the bats . . . too late . . .'

The short film is so lacking in plot as to appear almost postmodern. The first five minutes focus on the Mesmerist's face as he stares into the mid-distance. Gradually it becomes clear that he is in a room with a woman who seems to be in a trance. The Mesmerist's hands hover over the woman's body and she rises into the air (you can see the strings). A minute later the woman is conscious again and locked into an embrace with the necromancer. Then, without much explanation, the woman is running away, a rather nightmarish sequence up and down staircases which, Escher-like, never seem to reach a destination. There's one rather effective shot where the woman and the Mesmerist are standing by an open window. The woman's hair and gown fly backwards as though blown by a fierce wind. Her face is not shown but it appears that she is still in a trance. The writing on the screen, white against black, says, 'You can fly.' The man pushes and the woman falls forwards. The screen goes black and the next sequence shows the Mesmerist, now wearing a cloak and top hat, prowling through the streets of London, armed with an axe. There's a potentially horrible part where he pursues a woman, his shadow merging monstrously with hers, but the camera moves away at the critical moment. After killing a policeman ('That's a whole life term,' says Luca), the murderer eventually escapes by flying over St Paul's.

'When was it made?' asks Luca, when the screen fades to black. No credits.

'The turn of the century, apparently,' says Dina. 'There were lots of experimental films made then. I watched one about trying to photograph a ghost.'

'My Neapolitan *nonna* regularly saw my *nonno*'s ghost,' says Luca. 'He used to pull her feet out of bed, apparently.'

'Why would he do that?'

'Who knows?' says Luca, looking at Dina in a way that makes her forget ghosts, vampires and even Ali for quite some time.

Dina finds it hard to sleep. When she eventually dozes off, she dreams about the cats again but now they can fly, sprouting leathery little wings behind their shoulder blades. She's woken up by Luca's phone buzzing. She thinks it's morning but it's only half past midnight. She nudges Luca, none too gently.

'Your phone.'

Luca sits up and answers the call. 'Yes? What? When? OK . . . I'm on my way . . . fifteen minutes.'

He turns to Dina looking, despite the fact that he is naked, medallion buried in his black chest hair, every inch a cop.

'Barry Power's been murdered.'

Chapter 24

Ali sleeps late. When she wakes up, her cup of tea, presumably delivered by Gladys, is stone cold. She drinks it anyway. The elegant little clock on her dressing table says ten past nine. Ali gets up, uses the chamber pot, washes her hands and dons her purple dressing gown. The house is silent but, on the black-and-white tiled landing, she finds Terry, asleep in a patch of sunlight.

Ali strokes him. 'Where is everyone?'

A gentle cough makes her jump. 'Lady Serafina is in the breakfast room, madam.'

'Thank you, Harrison.'

How can he just materialise like that? He's the one who should have a show at the Theatre Royal, Drury Lane.

Jones is, as usual, cutting a piece of fruit that she shows no intention of eating. She looks up and smiles at Ali.

'Good sleep?'

'Almost too good,' says Ali, reaching for a bread roll. 'I slept like I'd been knocked out.'

'It means you're getting used to the time jump,' says Jones, 'like jet lag.'

'I don't want to get used to it,' says Ali. 'I want to go home.'

Will they be missing her yet? In 2024 it will be Monday today. Finn often rings for a catch-up at the weekends. Will he be worried when she doesn't answer her phone? What about the team? Bud will be panicking but will John remember The Collectors and wonder if there's another way? Dina will want to go through the gate herself. Ali hopes that John dissuades her. There are just too many variables now.

'What did you think of last night's entertainment?' asks Jones.

They hadn't had much time to talk afterwards. Ali didn't want to say anything in Templeton's carriage and, back at the Kensington house, Harrison and Frensham were always nearby. One of the minor inconveniences of being rich is never being on your own.

'It was quite a show,' says Ali. 'Especially that last trick. There must have been cables holding him up but I couldn't see them. Anyway, that's not all. I saw him again. Barry Power. He was in the carriage with Klaus Kramer.'

'Are you sure it was him?' says Jones. Her sceptical expression annoys Ali but, before she can answer, there's a soft tap on the door and Harrison emerges.

'Sorry to bother you, my lady, but there's a Mr Cain Templeton in the drawing room. He is asking for Mrs Dawson.' He hands Jones a small, printed card. Jones looks amused. 'You'd better get dressed, Ali.'

Ali puts her hand to her head. She realises that she has forgotten to put on her wig and her red hair, unwashed now for three days, is on show.

'I'll send Frensham to you,' says Jones.

Frensham has altered another dress for Ali. This one is dark blue and Ali doesn't like it as much. She thinks it makes her look like a matron in a hospital. But she can't really complain when Jones is donating so many of her clothes. Frensham does arrange Ali's wig in another flattering style, though. The hair is lighter than Jones's and Ali asks about this. 'I dye them black, madam,' says Frensham, 'that being her ladyship's natural colour.' Ali can hardly remember what her own natural shade is but she likes the soft brown of the hairpiece. If only it wasn't so itchy.

Cain Templeton stands up when she enters the drawing room. 'Please forgive such an early call,' he says. 'But I was anxious to see you.'

Ali's heart beats faster behind her corset. There's something in Templeton's tone that makes it almost believable that one day he could call her his time-travelling angel.

'I wondered if you would walk in the park with me,' says Templeton. 'Since I can't invite you to my home without a chaperone.'

That hadn't bothered Templeton before, thinks Ali, when she was an indigent widow living in a rented room in an artists' house. Now, as Lady Serafina's protégée, it seems that her reputation must be preserved.

'I'm rather old to need a chaperone,' she says. 'I'm fifty-one.' Jones would be shocked. Her own age is a well-kept secret but Ali thinks she must be in her mid-forties.

'As am I,' says Templeton with a smile. 'We will be perfect walking companions.'

It's another hot day and Ali doubts that Jones's parasol will afford much protection. But Hyde Park, with its avenues of shady trees, is pleasant indeed. Ali tries to think how the Victorian park differs from the modern version, still a green oasis in the centre of London. Well, there's the glittering glass dome of the crystal palace, for one thing. Ali wonders why the exhibition centre didn't stay here, in Central London, rather than departing for Sydenham Hill (was that a replica or the actual building rebuilt?). Not for the first time she misses Wikipedia. The Albert Memorial is an edifice yet to come. But most of the park is recognisable, trees and grass don't change and, once you are used to the clothes, as Ali almost is, there's something very familiar about families out walking with children or older people sitting on benches watching the world go by.

'My children like to come here,' says Templeton. 'And Kensington Gardens, of course. It's where all the nannies congregate.'

This is a useful reminder that Templeton is married and has, Ali thinks, at least five children. She personally knew his great-great-grandson, Isaac. She knows, too, that Templeton has had at least one mistress, a woman called Jane who died of an opium overdose. She's the Jane mentioned in his diary.

'I can't imagine having a nanny,' says Ali. 'I brought up my son on my own.' More on her own than she thinks Templeton could imagine.

'Your son, Phineas, isn't it?'

'Finn. Yes.' She's slightly mollified that Templeton has (almost) remembered the name.

'What does Finn do?'

'He works for a politician.'

'That must be an interesting world,' says Templeton, 'though more cut-throat even than art. Is he a Whig or a Tory?'

'Whig,' says Ali. 'Well, his boss . . . employer . . . is.' It sounds better than saying Tory and she knows that the Whigs were the predecessors of the Liberal Party. The British Labour Party, of course, has yet to be formed. When was Keir Hardie elected as the first Labour MP? Ali thinks it was around 1906.

'He sounds like a clever young man,' says Templeton.

'He is,' says Ali proudly.

After walking on a little further, the Serpentine glinting through the trees, Templeton says, 'Mrs Dawson, you must be wondering why I wanted to speak to you.'

Ali doesn't answer. Templeton stops, forcing Ali to halt too. She raises her eyes to his face and something in his gaze makes her look away in some confusion. 'Mrs Dawson,' says Templeton, 'Alison, if I may. I feel there is some mystery about you. After you disappeared last year, I went to Hastings but I could find nobody there who knew you. The other Hawk Street residents – Arthur, Tremain, Clara – they didn't know what had become of you. You didn't correspond with them. Or with me. And now you're back in London and you appear to be on intimate terms with Lady Serafina. She says you're a private investigator. Won't you let me into the secret?'

Ali thinks fast. For a second, she is tempted to tell Templeton the whole story: the Frozen People, Jones, the cat flap, everything. But surely, he would just think she was mad.

'I am from Hastings,' says Ali. It's not a lie, she tells herself. 'And I am an investigator. My investigation concerns The Collectors. I'm afraid I can't say more.'

'What about your cousin, John Cole?' says Templeton. 'He disappeared too. Was he really your cousin?'

'No,' says Ali. 'John is also an investigator.'

There's another silence. The sounds of Victorian London seem to fade and Ali has the strangest feeling that she can hear the roar of traffic in the background.

Templeton says, 'Can I ask how you know Lady Serafina?'

'She was a friend of my second husband's,' says Ali. 'The teacher.'

'Of course, you have lost three husbands,' says Templeton. 'You have known much tragedy.'

'Haven't I just.' Ali feels slightly bad about killing off Declan. Less so about Hugo and Lincoln.

Templeton says, lifting his hat to a passing female, 'You know, there are rumours about Lady Serafina.'

'What sort of rumours?' says Ali, though she thinks she can guess.

'Well, her origins are rather a mystery. She is obviously of foreign nobility.'

Ali doesn't answer. As far as she knows, Jones was born in Naples and her family aren't particularly aristocratic.

'And then there's her wealth. She's one of the new industrial rich, of course, but I've heard disturbing things about her business interests. One of her foundries is known as the devil's furnace, because of the terrible conditions.'

Could this be true? Ali remembers Jones saying, 'If I can make sure that workers in the foundries are treated well and their children educated, well, that's all to the good.' Is Jones really the caring employer she pretends?

Ali says, 'Successful women always face criticism. Successful men, less so.'

'That's true,' says Templeton. 'But I'm very interested in factory reform. I met Robert Owen last year. You know, he won't permit any child under ten to work in his factories? He builds houses and schools for his workers. He has set up a society to look after their interests. A trades union, it's called.'

'He sounds like a good man,' says Ali. It's a bit of a shock to hear that most places routinely employ children under ten. Does Jones do this?

'I believe he is,' says Templeton. There's another silence. A child with a hoop bowls past. What happened to hoops? thinks Ali. They seem to have become exercise accessories rather than playthings.

She says, 'Lady Serafina tells me that she met you at a demonstration of a power hammer. Such things are a mystery to me.' That, at least, is true.

Templeton laughs in a slightly condescending way but at least he adds, 'I'm not sure I understand them either.'

'And then you and Lady Serafina met again, at a demonstration of the Seeing Glass?'

Templeton says, 'I heard you talking about the Seeing Glass with my colleague Giuseppe Zennaro last night.'

'It sounds very intriguing,' says Ali. 'A mirror that can see into the future.'

She thinks she senses Templeton making his mind up about something. They walk on for a few paces in silence, past more hoops and perambulators, then Templeton says, 'Would you like to see the glass, Mrs Dawson? The exhibition is but a few hundred yards away.'

'Why not?' says Ali.

Once again, a steady stream of humanity is passing through the famous turnstiles.

'It sometimes seems as if all the world has seen the Great Exhibition,' says Templeton. 'Thirty thousand people visited on the first day. One hears of whole villages in remote parts of the country setting up collections in order to attend.'

Ali doesn't think that any of the crowd look as if they come from small rural communities. Most look almost as well-dressed as Lady Serafina herself. She asks if Templeton was at the opening ceremony.

'I was,' he says. 'The Prince gave a very long and boring speech. Have you ever heard the rhyme about how he had the idea for the exhibition?'

'No,' says Ali.

'I can't remember all of it,' says Templeton, 'but it begins:

> *His Highness Prince Albert woke up one day*
> *'Twas four in the morning*
> *The grey light was dawning*
> *And he said to himself as he sleepless lay*
> *It's a desperate bore*
> *I can't doze any more . . .*

And so on. Lots of fustian about "every class of British art having its part".'

Ali can't think of a suitable response. This, she thinks, is how people entertained themselves before Netflix.

They walk along the glass corridor lined with palm trees but this time they turn towards another avenue dominated by an enormous block of coal, so dark it seems to absorb the light around it.

'From the Coed Talon mine in Wales,' says Templeton. 'It required chains and gears to lift it into place.'

The coal is followed by mining equipment and mineral products. A sculpture court demonstrates rather more artistic use of stone. The statues – humans, animals and heraldic beasts – remind Ali of the scene in *The Lion, the Witch and the Wardrobe* when the Pevensie children free the creatures turned to stone by the White Witch. But, of course, this seminal time-travel book has yet to be written.

Next is an agricultural room containing a wonderful selection of beehives, one shaped like a tall town house. Templeton reads aloud from the label, '"John Milton's beehives demonstrate how individuals labour together for the good of society." What do you think of that, Mrs Dawson?'

'It's a nice idea,' says Ali. 'But there's always a Queen Bee, isn't there? And a lot of drones.'

Templeton laughs. 'You're an extraordinary woman, Mrs Dawson.' It's like the Dickens conversation all over again. She didn't mean to be *that* interesting.

Eventually, they reach a room full of furniture: tables, chairs, low sofas, ornate cabinets. Near the centre is a mirror on a stand. Two women are reading the description, and, with much laughter, one takes her place in the accompanying chair.

'What can you see, Ethel?'

'Nothing, Maud. Just my ordinary, workaday face.'

'How disappointing, my dear.'

More laughter. When Maud and Ethel have departed, Ali and Templeton approach the mirror.

'What will I see?' asks Ali, suddenly slightly scared.

'Probably, like those two ladies, just your reflection. Not that yours is ordinary or workaday.'

'Thank you,' says Ali. 'I think.'

'The looking glass comes from Scotland. The woman who owned it was thought to be a witch. She would tell fortunes by looking into the glass. She claimed that she could see into the future.'

'That sounds harmless enough.'

'The other rumour was that she could summon devils. Hellish faces would appear and demonic voices would be heard.'

Ali takes her seat. She realises that she is trembling. What if this is a magic chair, like the one that briefly transported Guiseppe into another time? But nothing happens. Ali raises her eyes to the glass. What will she see? Her nineteenth-century reflection with its elaborately coiled hair or the twenty-first century incarnation? Or maybe she'll see something even more terrifying. Herself as an old crone, perhaps? A witch in the making.

'Look in the glass, Mrs Dawson,' says Templeton.

Ali does so. Her anxious face looks back at her. For a second, she thinks she sees a flash of bright red hair and the glint of a diamond around her nostril. But she raises her hand to her head and she's Victorian Alison again.

'Just me,' she says, trying to sound amused.

'What a relief,' says Templeton. He offers her his arm and they walk back through the glass corridors, past the statues, the farming implements and the great elm tree.

In the park they walk in a silence that seems more companiable than before. Then, at the gates, Templeton stops. 'Can I see you again?'

'If you like,' says Ali, trying to keep her voice light.

'Do *you* like?'

'I'd like to see Hawk Street again,' says Ali.

Templeton laughs. 'That can easily be arranged. Why not dine there with me tonight? Arthur and Tremain are still in residence. Still painting, still not paying any rent.'

'That sounds like fun,' says Ali.

'Fun,' repeats Templeton. Ali wonders if she's used the wrong word again.

Templeton included Jones in the invitation but she said that she thought Ali would probably find out more on her own. 'You know these people, I don't. See if you can find out about the chairs.' Ali had almost forgotten about the chairs in the excitement of her second visit to the Great Exhibition. She has to admit that she is rather relieved that Jones is staying at home. She's looking forward to seeing her old housemates again and Jones's elegant presence would be a constraint. Besides, she feels uncomfortable about the devil's furnace revelations. She remembers feeling disappointed that Jones did not seem to be using her time in the nineteenth century to further the cause of women's suffrage and workers' rights. But is it worse than that? Is Jones actually exploiting the poorest people in society? Ali's instinct is to confront Jones but what would happen if Jones threw her out? Ali has nowhere else to go and her only money is in the purse given to her by Jones. It will be easier to be apart for a few hours.

It's strange to drive to Hawk Street in Jones's carriage. When Ali was here before, she trudged along the snowy pavement, past the street-sellers peddling hot sheep's feet and baked potatoes. Now the horses pull up outside the door with the griffin knocker and Ali is helped to descend by the efficient 'James'. She looks up and down the street. She suddenly has the strangest feeling that she's being watched. It reminds her of the evening when she went to book club at John's house, the footsteps that had faded away into the night. There's no one suspicious in Hawk Street, unless you count a woman with a shawl, carrying a bundle of firewood. Even the stray dogs seem to have found pastures new.

Ali knocks on the door, pleasantly aware that she's wearing a truly splendid dress, apple-green with emerald fringes. Clara actually backs away when she sees her.

'Goodness me, Mrs Dawson. You're a sight for sore eyes.'

For her part, Ali is so overcome with emotion at the sight of the housekeeper that she enfolds her in a distinctly twenty-first-century hug.

'Get along with you,' says Clara, but she doesn't seem displeased.

The grandfather clock in the hallway is wheezing its way towards six o'clock. Ali remembers this timepiece well. Each number is represented by a scene, most of them macabre in the extreme. Six is an owl. Twelve is hell itself. Ali looks up, remembering the first time she climbed the stairs, making her way to a room where a woman lay dead at her feet.

'This way, Mrs Dawson,' says Clara. 'I'm sure you haven't forgotten.'

Ali follows Clara into the drawing room where Templeton, Arthur and Tremain are all gathered. Arthur bows low. He looks the same, fair-haired and somehow insubstantial. Tremain is rather better dressed than before and still has plenty of his old dash.

'Good Gad, Mrs Dawson, you look a vision.'

'A vision in green,' agrees Templeton, bowing over her hand.

'It's wonderful to see you all again,' says Ali.

'Where did you go?' says Tremain, as Ali takes her seat on the sofa. She had once thought this room the grandest in the house but it looks distinctly shabby compared to Jones's abode. 'You just disappeared.'

'I went back to Hastings,' says Ali.

'And you're staying with Lady Serafina,' says Tremain. 'I'd love to paint that woman.'

Tremain once did a drawing of Ali. She has seen it, a tender pencil sketch dated 1853. Ali still finds this hard to comprehend.

'Tremain's work is attracting quite a following,' says Templeton. 'I live in hope that one day he will pay his rent.'

Tremain ignores this. Ali knows that, in 2024, Frederick Tremain is considered a very collectable artist. She's pleased that he found fame in his own lifetime.

'Where are Marianne and Leonard?' she asks. 'Do they still live here?'

'They have lodgings in a different part of town,' says Templeton. 'I believe they have several rooms, which is a blessing because they now have two children. Leonard still finds plenty of work in the music halls.'

'I went to church with Lady Serafina on Sunday,' says Ali. 'I thought Leonard might be playing the organ.'

'I wouldn't have had Lady Serafina down as a churchgoer,' says Templeton. 'I'm a freethinker myself.'

'Me too,' says Ali, though she doesn't quite know what this term means. 'But Lady Serafina assures me that all fashionable people go to church.'

Templeton laughs. 'God preserve me from fashionable people.'

Ali doesn't know if this is meant to be ironical. She says, 'It must seem strange here without the piano playing.' The sound of

Leonard's scales, up and down, up and down, often accompanies her dreams.

'It's much quieter,' says Arthur. 'But I do miss Marianne.'

Marianne had been Tremain's muse, Ali remembers, but he does not add his own reminiscence. Instead, he asks Ali a stream of questions about Hastings and Lady Serafina. Ali struggles to answer coherently. She sees Templeton watching her rather sardonically.

They eat in the dining room. It's the first time Ali has seen Templeton sit down with his tenants. Clara serves them but does not join them at the table. Ali suddenly wishes that she was eating with Clara in the kitchen, sharing swigs from her mysterious black bottle. Supper is less elaborate than last night's pre-theatre meal but Ali enjoys it more. There's steak-and-kidney pie served with vegetables and something called mushroom ketchup. Templeton pours red wine and the table is lit with many candles, although it's still daylight outside. Ali wonders if this largesse is in her honour.

The conversation turns to Klaus Kramer.

'He's a charlatan,' says Tremain. 'I saw his show and I could distinctly see the wires lifting him into the air.'

'So you don't believe the rumours that he can actually fly?' says Templeton. 'All those gullible people who see him flapping over the town at night.'

But, at the theatre, Templeton had said, 'He really is flying.' So he'd been fooled, even if only for a minute.

'It's ridiculous,' says Tremain, who seems more confident than he did last year. Or maybe it's just because he's drunk the best part of a bottle of burgundy. 'Men will never fly.'

'I thought you and Kramer were deadly enemies, Mr Templeton,' says Arthur. He was always making sly comments like this, Ali remembers.

'I objected when he tried to abduct a young lady of my acquaintance,' says Templeton.

Ali remembers Templeton saying that Kramer has stolen something of his. She hopes he didn't see this unnamed woman as a possession. *He stole something of mine and I mean to get it back.*

Ali says, 'Is this something Kramer does often? Abduct young women?'

'I'd forgotten how blunt you are, Mrs Dawson,' says Tremain. 'Yes, in my opinion, Kramer uses his so-called mesmeric powers to seduce innocent girls. In this case, Mr Templeton alerted the young female's guardian and she was rescued.'

'I heard something about a young man who fell from a roof because Kramer told him he could fly,' says Ali.

Her dinner companions look at her blankly. Ali realises that this tragedy hasn't happened yet. Hugo hadn't mentioned Kramer preying on young women. But, remembering the capering figure on stage, Ali can believe it.

'Have you heard of a man called Barry Power?' she asks. 'I think he's an associate of Kramer's.'

Templeton gives her a quizzical look. Tremain says, 'Barry? What sort of a name is that?'

It is a very un-Victorian name, thinks Ali. She guesses most Barrys were born in the 1950s or 60s.

'Short for Bartholomew?' she hazards.

'My father was a surgeon at St Barts,' says Tremain, inconsequentially. He's not boasting. Ali knows that being a doctor was not considered a very genteel profession.

'Mrs Dawson and I saw Kramer perform yesterday,' says Templeton. 'We were both of your opinion, Tremain. Dickens, on the other hand, thought it was magic.'

'Oh, Dickens,' says Arthur. 'Who cares what he thinks?'

'He's a fine writer,' says Templeton, 'but I'm not sure he is to be trusted.'

How strange, thinks Ali, to hear Templeton agreeing with Elizabeth. She thinks it's time to ask the question that has been bothering her since her return to the 1850s. Last year, Ali couldn't return to her own time because her gate had been taken by someone else. She believes this was a man called Thomas Creek. She also believes that Creek followed her to the twenty-first century, tried to kill her and escaped on one of Templeton's chairs.

'When I was here last,' she says carefully, 'there was talk of a man called Thomas Creek. You suspected him of killing Ettie, as I remember, and then he disappeared.'

The men exchange glances. Ettie was an artist's model, Arthur's muse. When Ali first arrived at Hawk Street, it was to find Ettie's dead body in the attic bedroom.

Templeton drains his glass. 'He disappeared for a while,' he says, in an almost off-hand voice. 'But he reappeared a few weeks later. He went to trial for Ettie's murder.'

'And what happened?' says Ali.

'He was found guilty and he went to the gallows,' says Templeton. 'More wine, Mrs Dawson?'

After supper, Tremain and Arthur are obviously keen to go to a tavern and continue drinking. 'I remember going to the inn with

John,' says Tremain. 'He was pleasant company, even though he had taken the pledge. Will you give him my good wishes, Mrs Dawson?'

'I certainly will,' says Ali. She has got to believe that she will see John again.

'John was with us when poor Burbage was murdered,' says Arthur. 'I'll never forget the sight of his body, there in the lane behind the tavern.' He shivers.

'Did you ever find out who killed him?' asks Ali. John, the detective, will want to know this.

'It was the high mobsmen,' says Arthur. 'I believe Burbage owed them money.'

John was never satisfied with this explanation, thinks Ali, but Tremain is clearly in need of more alcohol and practically hustles Arthur out of the door. 'Farewell, Mrs Dawson,' calls Tremain from the hall, 'no doubt we'll meet again.'

When the two artists have gone, Templeton and Ali are left in the dimly lit parlour. Templeton is drinking brandy. Ali, although she longs for a stiff drink, is sticking to tea. The clock strikes nine. Should Ali be thinking of going home? She clears her throat but, just at that moment, Templeton says, 'Did John, your fellow investigator, tell you what happened when he attended a meeting of The Collectors?'

'Yes,' says Ali. 'He did. He told me that he'd seen a man, Giuseppe, sit on a chair and vanish into thin air.'

'John was not in the room at the time,' says Templeton, 'but it's true that this happened.'

'Do you know why?' asks Ali.

'I think it was to do with the chair. It was one of a set of four believed to have certain powers.'

There's a silence. Ali thinks that they are, at last, getting to the core of the mystery. She can hear the clock ticking in the hall. Someone once described this sound to her as the heartbeat of a house. The telltale heart. Ali thinks of Hawk Street in its modern iteration, the top floor converted into a flat occupied by medical students from St Barts. She wonders if they ever hear music playing on the stairs. The same grandfather clock is still in the hallway.

'What happened to the chairs?' asks Ali.

'Two of them are in my house in the country,' says Templeton. 'One was stolen from me. But the other is upstairs in your old room. Would you like to see it?'

Should Ali refuse to accompany Templeton upstairs? Maybe she should but she doesn't. They climb the three flights to Ali's attic bedroom, the place where Ettie was murdered. Templeton holds his oil lamp high and Ali sees the bed, now covered by a single sheet, the wardrobe and the easel. The small, round window emits a soft evening light. It's still not fully dark outside.

'There it is,' says Templeton. A single chair is marooned between bed and wardrobe. It's leather-backed and its arms form a comfortable half-circle. Not speaking, Ali crosses the room and sits in it. There's no place like home, she says to herself, there's no place like home.

She hadn't realised that she had shut her eyes but, when she opens them again, Templeton is looking down at her.

'What were you thinking?' he asks softly.

'I was trying to get home,' says Ali.

Templeton reaches out a hand. Ali takes it and stands, facing him. After a second, his lips touch hers.

If Templeton had made any move towards the bed, Ali knows she would have followed. Instead, after the kiss, which seemed to go on a very long time, he says, 'Mrs Dawson, I think I'm in love with you.'

'You can't be,' says Ali. 'It's impossible.'

'Impossible things do happen,' says Templeton.

'Tell me about it,' says Ali.

She is still standing very close to him. Now she backs away and says, 'I have something to tell you.'

Templeton says, 'Are you going to let me into the secret?'

Carriage wheels in the road outside, the cry of a night-watchman.

Ali says, 'What if I told you I was a time-traveller?'

'A time-traveller?' repeats Templeton.

Something reckless surges through Ali. She kissed Cain Templeton, he said he was in love with her. All this has happened before.

She says, 'I'm not from Hastings. Well, I am but that's not the important part. I'm from the future. From 2024, to be exact.'

'Twenty twenty-four? What does that mean?'

'The year two thousand and twenty-four. We've found a way to time travel. Well, Jones has. Lady Serafina has. Oh God, I'm telling it all wrong.'

'Sit down.' Templeton sits on the bed and gestures for her to join him. There's nothing passionate in his manner now. He seems almost businesslike. Ali takes her place next to him on the white sheet. 'Jones is a professor. A brilliant physicist. She found a way to time travel. Last year I travelled from 2023 to 1850. I came to this house, met you and the others. Then I got stuck here. John came to save me but Jones had to save him. She stayed and became Lady Serafina. Now I'm here again and I can't get back to my own time.'

She has left out a lot but the relief of telling so much brings tears to her eyes.

'I don't expect you to believe me,' she says.

'I do believe you,' says Templeton.

'You do?' Ali edges closer but Templeton stands up and begins to pace the small room.

'This explains so much. You always seemed strange . . .'

'Thanks,' says Ali.

'You talk differently. John did too. You didn't seem to understand money or how to eat certain food. And I knew, through The Collectors, that it was possible to travel from one world to another. Guiseppe remembers suddenly being in a room with strange white light.'

'I think that was a museum at Queen Mary's, in my time,' says Ali. 'Our lighting is like that.'

'That chair,' Templeton points to it. 'Did you think it would take you back?'

'I hoped it would.'

'Do you want to leave?'

'Yes,' says Ali. Templeton comes to her side again. He lifts her chin with one hand. 'No,' says Ali. 'Yes. No. I don't know.'

Chapter 25

Jones is in bed when Templeton's carriage brings Ali home. Frensham is waiting up, though, which adds guilt to Ali's maelstrom of emotions. Ali sleeps heavily but wakes when Gladys brings the tea the next morning. With Frensham's help she dresses in her favourite pinstripe and goes downstairs to join Jones.

'What happened last night?' asks Jones, cool in pale lavender in the blue-and-white breakfast room.

'I slept with Cain Templeton,' says Ali, helping herself to tea.

'*Dio mio*,' says Jones, 'you are certainly corporeally present in this world.'

Ali's interest is piqued. 'Have you slept with anyone while you've been here?'

'One man,' says Jones. 'It wasn't very satisfactory.'

'This was,' says Ali. '*More* than satisfactory. What's more, I told him about being a time-traveller and he believed me.'

She thinks about Cain's diary entry. Written today, she realises. *Alisoun, as I must call her now, is the love of my life*. Last night, she had told him the secret of her name. 'If you write with that spelling,

I'll know it's from you.' He does write, she knows it. *We know what happens because it has happened before.*

'You're a risk-taker, Ali,' says Jones. She puts her fruit knife down. Ali is glad. It made her look rather murderous.

'We both are,' says Ali, 'that's why we're here. But I thought there was a good chance Templeton . . . Cain . . . might believe me. He knows there's some secret about the chairs. He saw his friend Giuseppe disappear, that time when John was watching. That's what The Collectors are all about, I think. Finding a way to time travel using so-called magical objects.'

'Did you see the famous chair?'

'Yes, I sat in it and nothing happened.'

'Disappointing,' says Jones. 'There must be another element that we're missing. Maybe the chair needs to be in a certain place, maybe a certain number of people need to be present . . .'

'We'll just have to work it out,' says Ali.

Jones raises one eyebrow. She's very good at this. Ali suspects her of practising in front of a mirror. 'Are you so keen to go back?'

Ali remembers Templeton asking her the same question. She remembers what came afterwards and how she hadn't thought about her old life at all.

'Of course,' she says now, rather too loudly. 'I want to get back and see Finn, the team, everyone. It's my life, where I belong. I can't understand why you *don't* want to go back.'

Jones is silent for a moment, examining a sliver of apple. Then she says, 'My parents are dead. I'm an only child. I don't have children of my own. I'm not in a relationship. Jones, my ex-husband, might as well be dead. I never see him. I have less at stake than you.'

'But your work,' says Ali, 'surely you want to continue your work at Imperial? You're so brilliant. You could win the Nobel Prize one day.' She wonders if she's overcompensating because she found Jones's previous comments rather sad.

'There's work I can do here,' says Jones. 'That reminds me. I thought we might visit one of the foundries today. I sense that you're slightly uneasy about the welfare of my workers.'

Does Jones know what Templeton said about her? Maybe he's not the first. Ali is pleased that Jones seems willing to show her around the foundry, even if 'my workers' sounds rather feudal.

'Shall we go this morning?' Ali asks.

'This afternoon,' says Jones. 'I've got a treat for you this morning. We're going to visit Klaus Kramer.'

'Klaus Kramer! How did you manage that?'

'What Lady Serafina wants, Lady Serafina gets.'

'Watch out,' says Ali. 'It's a very bad sign when you start referring to yourself in the third person.'

Klaus Kramer lives in Dulwich which, Jones says, is suspicious in itself.

'Why?' asks Ali. 'It's a very nice area. My friend Meg lives there.'

'That's in 2024,' says Jones. 'It's basically just a village now. Almost in Surrey.'

Ali remembers having the same thought about Thornton Heath. Depressing that metropolitan snobbery is still alive and well.

'Maybe Kramer likes the quiet life,' she says.

Dulwich certainly looks bucolic in the July sunshine. They travel in Jones's open-top brougham. Ali remembers when Hugo had a convertible Mini Cooper. She'd teased him about it at the time but she had to admit that there was something exciting, almost daring, about bowling along with the wind in your hair. This is the same. It's not as stiflingly hot today, or maybe it's just that they are out of central London. A gentle breeze riffles through the trees, making it look as if they were painting the sky a brighter blue. The carriage passes Dulwich College (which probably hasn't changed much between 1851 and 2024, thinks Ali, still a public school, still single sex) and draws up outside a large house, set back in what is almost a park of its own.

'There's obviously money in mesmerism,' says Ali. The house is white and square with a small turret at each corner. Ali has her own views about people who want to turn their houses into castles. Even Declan now lives in a bungalow called 'Balmoral'.

'There's always money in fraud,' says Jones, rearranging her skirts and unfurling her parasol. 'Shall we?'

The front door is opened before they reach it and, to Ali's shock, the opener is none other than Barry Power.

She stops, tripping slightly on her skirt. Jones turns to look at her, raising that eyebrow.

'Welcome,' says Power. 'I'm Balthazar Power, Mr Kramer's associate.'

Balthazar! That solves the Barry question anyway. And what does 'associate' mean? One thing is certain: from the look on Balthazar's face, he has never seen Ali before in his life.

Power ushers them into the house and a maid appears to take their parasols. They keep their hats on, a Victorian habit that always feels odd to Ali.

'Thank you, Violet,' says Power to the maid. The name sparks a memory in Ali and, with it, comes a feeling of unease. Where has she heard that name before?

Klaus Kramer is waiting for them in the airy drawing room, which has French windows and views across lawns to an ornamental lake.

'Lady Serafina, what an honour. And Mrs Dawson too.'

Talk about afterthought, thinks Ali. Kramer's German accent is more pronounced here, in his own home. On the other hand, Power's Welsh lilt seems fainter. Kramer is dressed in a tweed suit but, even without his crimson-lined cloak, he still has a certain dark glamour. His shoulder-length hair is grey, almost white, but his eyebrows and eyes are black. He gives them both a stare. Ali thinks of Barry Power, that afternoon in his Thornton Heath house: *You know him and you know what he's capable of.* Had Power known then that they had met before? Can Barry Power, the medium, really be the same person as Balthazar Power, showman's associate? Because, if so, it can only mean one thing. Power knows the secret of time travel.

These thoughts mean that Ali doesn't play much of a part in the small talk that accompanies them taking their seats. Kramer offers refreshment and Jones accepts tea for both of them. Once again, Ali longs for strong coffee.

Jones says that they enjoyed the show at the Theatre Royal.

'Is "enjoy" the word?' twinkles Kramer.

'It was certainly a spectacle,' says Ali, feeling as if it was time that she spoke.

'People need spectacle,' says Kramer, 'it's an escape from their humdrum lives.'

'Bread and circuses,' says Jones.

'Exactly,' says Kramer. 'But instead of gladiators I give you a man who can fly.'

'I don't suppose,' says Ali, 'that you can tell us how it's done.'

Power laughs. 'He can fly, that's how it's done.' His status in the room is uncertain, thinks Ali. He sits next to Kramer but with his chair pushed slightly back. He thanked Violet for bringing the tea but poured it himself. Is he some sort of servant? But Ali thinks that, once or twice, she sees Kramer looking at Power before he speaks, almost as if asking for permission.

Now Kramer leans forward and takes one of Ali's hands. She's wearing gloves (another strange convention) but, even so, she experiences a slight electric shock.

'Mrs Dawson,' says Kramer, 'do you believe in magic?'

'No,' says Ali, trying to withdraw her hand.

'But I believe you do,' says Kramer. 'And, what's more, I believe that you have experienced it yourself.'

Ali thinks of going through the gate, that jolt of excitement, the modern city giving way to its older form. She recalls the times when she was just a wraith, invisible to people for whom the past was the present. She tries to stare calmly back. 'I'm not sure what you mean.'

Kramer lets go of her hand and, in quite a different voice, he says, 'I believe you attended the theatre in the company of Mr Cain Templeton.'

That name gives Ali another jolt. She's relieved when Jones says, with just a hint of hauteur, 'We were in Mr Templeton's party, yes.'

'Was Mr Templeton interested in the show?'

'He's a sceptic, like me,' says Ali. A freethinker, she remembers.

'I had a letter from Mr Dickens this morning,' says Kramer. 'He said I had made him believe in magic. He said that he had started to doubt the meaning of life after losing his daughter in April.'

Dickens lost a daughter only three months ago? Ali thinks of the cocksure figure, bouncing on the balls of his feet as he told of his adventures in mesmerism, but this time with compassion. Losing a child would make you yearn for something, anything, that proves this life is not the end. It might even, like Lady Croft, make you believe in the ghost of a highwayman called Black Bob.

Jones is still interrogating Kramer. 'If you can fly, and do all those other things, how did you learn?'

'You must allow me some secrets, Lady Serafina,' says Kramer, sounding amused again. 'But I studied at the feet of the great Mesmer himself. I have refined his theories, of course, with the help of Mr Power here.'

This gives Ali a chance to look at Power, who has pushed his chair further back so he's almost in shadow. He looks the same, she thinks. In fact, the neat Victorian suit becomes him better than modern-day clothes. She remembers the house in Thornton Heath, full of Victorian furniture. And the John Martin print which, she realises, was of Belshazzar's Feast. Was this a link to his previous name?

'What is your role in the magic, Mr Power?' asks Ali.

'Certain logistical things,' says Power. 'Mr Kramer has very real gifts but they need to be displayed in the right way. The audience needs to know where to look, what to see.'

Misdirection, thinks Ali. She's willing to bet that Power organised the ropes and pulleys which lifted Kramer into the air.

'Are you a mesmerist too?' Jones asks Power.

'He has the gift of second sight,' says Kramer. 'He's Welsh, you know. They are a mystical people.'

'My father had a caravan at fairs,' says Power. 'He used to tell fortunes. There are tricks, of course, but some of it was real.'

Ali remembers the audience at the People's Palace, only too ready to think that Power could commune with Grandad Jim and Auntie Ellen. *People must be amused.* She's willing to bet that Power learnt a few tricks from his father. Or is this Power the great-great-grandfather of the one she met? Her head starts to spin and, for a second, the room becomes hazy, full of wavy lines like an old-fashioned television losing its signal.

'Are you quite well, Mrs Dawson?' asks Kramer.

'Oh yes,' says Ali, shutting her eyes tightly and then opening them again. The lines are still there. 'It's just the heat.'

'And you have travelled a very long way,' says Power sympathetically.

'Only from Kensington,' says Jones.

Kramer suggests a walk down to the lake, 'maybe some fresh air will revive you, Mrs Dawson.' Ali and Jones unfurl their parasols. Kramer walks with Jones and Ali follows with Balthazar – or Barry – Power. She's surprised that Violet the maid also accompanies them, carrying a tray with glasses and a bottle of champagne. What is it with Victorians and daytime drinking? Ali's head aches and she longs for a fizzy drink like the lemonade Templeton bought at the Great Exhibition and the Theatre Royal.

'Do you live with Mr Kramer?' Ali asks Power. She thinks that this question will not carry the same implications as it would in 2024.

'Yes,' says Power. 'He's been very generous to me. He's known for taking in waifs and strays.' He says this rather coldly, with a distinctly sardonic tone.

'Are you a waif?' asks Ali.

Power smiles, again without much warmth, and says, 'I was thinking of Violet and her brother, Edward. They were urchins, living on the meanest streets of London. Kramer took them in and trained them. Edward works in the gardens here.'

There's something about the word 'trained' that Ali doesn't like, although she supposes that life as a maid and a gardener must be better than living on the streets.

'Of course,' says Power, 'they are useful subjects for him, being young and innocent.'

This is even worse.

'What about you?' says Ali. 'How did you meet Mr Kramer?' She hopes that she isn't asking too many questions, but this might be her only chance to talk to Power on his own. They are almost at the lake.

'Mr Kramer contacted me,' says Power. 'He had heard about my father and knew that I'd worked with him.'

'It sounds like you help Mr Kramer with his act too,' says Ali.

Power looks at her. It's the same mild, blue gaze that she remembers from Thornton Heath. Surely, he must be the same person?

'It's not an act,' he says. 'Mr Kramer possesses magical powers.'

'Oh, come on,' says Ali, with perhaps rather too modern emphasis, 'you can't expect me to believe that he can fly.'

To her surprise, Power laughs. 'Oh, flying is an easy illusion. Every pantomime director knows that.'

'Is it the mind-reading then?' says Ali.

'Kramer has a charismatic personality,' says Power. 'It's easy to convince people that you know what they're thinking, particularly when they already want to believe.'

Ali thinks of Power on stage at the People's Palace. That audience had wanted to believe. *Auntie wants you to know she's very happy where she is. She's saying something about a key.* There's something about that memory that's bothering her. Something hovering on the edge of consciousness . . .

'Have you heard of a group called The Collectors?' she asks.

Power laughs but Ali gets the impression that he's not amused. 'Of course, Cain Templeton is a leading member of The Collectors. I applied to join. I'm interested in their work. But apparently, I'm not well-born enough.'

There's definite bitterness now. In this instance, Ali finds herself siding with Power against Templeton. She's had enough experience of being overlooked because of her London accent and working-class background. For the first time, she's ashamed of last night. What does she really know about Cain Templeton? she thinks, in sudden panic. He belongs to a secret society that is, at the very best, misogynistic and snobbish. He's married and she knows he's had at least one mistress. Has time travel destroyed Ali's moral compass?

They have reached the water's edge. It shimmers in the sunlight, willow trees providing dappled, impressionistic shade. A pair of mallard ducks glides over the surface. A table and chairs are situated under a pagoda hung with what look like hops. As Violet puts the tray down, she trips on an exposed tree root and almost falls. Power is at her side in seconds, a hand under her elbow.

'Careful, Violet,' says Kramer. 'That's expensive champagne, you know.'

He laughs but Ali thinks that Violet gives him a rather scared look. She's an attractive girl with red hair piled on top of her head. It must be natural, thinks Ali, but it's almost as vibrant as her own dyed hair. Looking across the lake, she thinks she sees the glint of a similar colour, russet amongst the dark evergreens. Is that Edward, the gardener brother?

Kramer opens the champagne with an explosive sound that sends the ducks squawking into the air. Violet hands round the glasses which aren't flutes but the shallow kind that Ali associates with Babycham. She takes a sip and feels as if the liquid has travelled straight to her headache, intensifying it and making the surroundings glow in lurid technicolour: the green trees, the blue water, the mauve of Jones's dress. Jones arranges herself elegantly in her chair. She hasn't touched her champagne.

'Are you performing tonight, Mr Kramer?' she asks.

Kramer laughs again. 'Performing? Is that what you'd call it?'

'What would you call it?'

'I'd call it communing with the unknown,' says Kramer. 'Mr Templeton knows about that, doesn't he, Mrs Dawson?'

'I don't know what you're talking about,' says Ali, rather too shortly for a polite Victorian lady.

'You can tell Mr Templeton that I'm hoping to add another magical object to my collection.'

The word 'collection' can't be accidental, surely? Ali is still standing but, suddenly, feels as if her legs are giving way. She moves towards the chair and, without warning, the grass and the sky change places. Ali hears Violet scream as she falls to the ground in a confusion of skirts and spilt champagne.

Chapter 26

'Are you all right now?' says Jones.

Ali thinks it's a good thing that her friend chose academia rather than one of the caring professions. There's a distinct note of impatience in her voice.

Ali's faint had only lasted a few seconds. She came round to find Power fanning her and Kramer saying, from what felt like a long way off, 'It's a long time since I've made a lady swoon.'

Power helped Ali into a chair and offered to get her some brandy. 'No thank you,' said Ali. 'Could I possibly have some water?' At that moment, she didn't care if was polluted or not. She just wanted to drink something non-alcoholic. Violet was dispatched for some water and, after a few sips, Ali felt well enough to get to her feet. Jones announced that they would be leaving immediately. 'Mrs Dawson needs to rest.'

Now they are in the carriage and the cool air is refreshing, although there's still a tight band of pain around Ali's forehead.

'I do feel better,' she says to Jones. 'I don't know what it was. Time travel vertigo perhaps.' She remembers Jones warning her of this when she first went through the gate. It's been absent this time until now.

'Kramer is an unpleasant individual,' says Jones. 'I'm not surprised he made you feel queasy.'

'Yes, he's horrible. Sinister too. But it was more the other man. Barry Power. Balthazar, or whatever he's called now. I'm sure he's the man I saw in 2024. Or else I met his great-great-grandson who's an exact replica.'

'That could be the case,' says Jones. 'I'm said to resemble my *bisnonna*. She was a great beauty,' she adds complacently.

'I'm sure she was,' says Ali. 'But this feels like the same person. And, if it is Barry Power, he must have travelled in time.'

'He didn't seem to recognise you,' says Jones.

'Not this time,' says Ali, 'but, in 2024, he acted like we'd met before. In fact, he told me to remember him. Of course, in 1851, we've only just met. Oh God, this is making me feel dizzier.'

'Breathe,' says Jones. 'Where's your fan?'

Ali fumbles in her reticule. 'I think I lost it.'

Jones unfurls her own fan and wafts it vigorously.

'Better?'

'Yes,' says Ali. Though it isn't, really. 'There's another thing,' she says. 'The maid, Violet.'

'What about her? She had very pretty hair, I thought. Pre-Raphaelite.'

'When I saw Barry Power at the People's Palace, he kept talking to his spirit guide. Her name was Vi. Short for Violet.'

The memory came back to Ali just before she lost consciousness. She thought she heard Power say, in that lilting Welsh voice, 'Who have you got for me, Vi?'

'I thought Kramer was the one with his eye on Violet,' says Jones. 'He never stopped watching her.'

'Kramer has a bad track record with women,' says Ali. 'Last night, at Hawk Street, someone said that Templeton stopped Kramer abducting a young woman.'

'What a hero,' says Jones, at her most sardonic.

Is Cain a hero? wonders Ali. Last night she'd been prepared to think so but Templeton is still the man who didn't let Power join the Collectors because he wasn't posh enough.

She doesn't mention this to Jones. Instead, she says, 'Kramer doesn't like Templeton. You heard him just now, talking about adding another magical object to his collection. That's clearly a dig at Templeton and The Collectors. At the theatre, Cain told me that Kramer had stolen something of his.'

'Do you know what it was?'

'I think it was one of the chairs. Cain said one was stolen. I didn't see anything similar in Kramer's sitting room. The furniture looked older. Lighter. More Regency.'

'Yes,' says Jones, 'it was an elegant house.'

Jones is silent for a while, furling and unfurling her fan. Ali wonders if she's thinking about interior decorating but, after a minute or two, Jones turns to Ali and says, 'You know why I think it didn't work last time?'

'What? Oh, the gate. Why?'

'It was because you had that wretched cat in your arms. That gate was for you. Only you. Terry was another entity. Another set of atoms.'

Ali remembers standing in the street, holding Terry tightly. Jones is right, she thinks. Terry was the complication. Typical.

'I have to take him with me this time,' she says.

'Ali,' says Jones, 'be sensible. If you get the chance to go back, take it. You can't wait until you have Terry with you. It will be OK,' she says in a gentler voice, 'Terry is happy here. Harrison loves him. He'll look after him.'

Ali sees the outskirts of London through a haze of tears.

Back at the house, there's a huge bunch of yellow roses from Cain Templeton.

'There you are, Ali,' says Jones. 'He still respects you in the morning.'

Ali ignores this. The flowers are beautiful, still gleaming with dew. Where did Templeton get them? Ali wonders. Are there florists in Victorian London or does he have his own greenhouse somewhere? The accompanying note says, 'I meant what I said last night.' Ali puts it in her reticule.

Ali goes up to her room where Frensham helps her off with the pin-stripe, now stained with champagne and grass, and on with the dark blue number. Ali wishes she could ask for an aspirin. For the first time, she contemplates the thought of being ill in 1851. With no pain relief and no antibiotics, even flu could be serious and an infection fatal. Will she be protected by the flu jab she had last year? Ali doubts it. She's not often ill but suffered from tonsilitis as a child. She still has her tonsils and, although they haven't troubled her for years, what if they make a comeback now? No wonder Victorian heroines are always swooning and having the vapours. Ali has joined their ranks now.

It's not just her health that's worrying Ali. She keeps thinking about Terry. Can she really leave him here, in this strange world?

There's no doubt that he seems to have acclimatised to life as an indoor cat in a mansion, but won't he miss Ali? Sadly, she thinks she knows the answer to this.

Another light lunch is laid out in the small dining room. Jones eats nothing and Ali very little. When Harrison clears away the plates, Ali asks about Terry.

'He's very well, madam. He caught a mouse this morning so Cook was very pleased with him. She gave him some salmon as a treat.'

No, Terry won't miss her at all. Ali asks if she can go to the kitchen and see him. Harrison looks surprised but says she is welcome, of course.

'Don't be too long,' says Jones. 'I'll have the horses brought round at two. They're expecting us at the foundry. If you're up to it, that is.' Ali assures her that she is.

It's the first time Ali has been 'below stairs' and she half expects the kitchen to be like the one in Hawk Street, a cosy but chaotic room with an open range and objects suspended from the ceiling on a system of ropes. This kitchen seems far more organised, with dressers along one wall and a scrubbed oak table in the centre. It doesn't have the same smoky smell either. This, Cook tells her, is due to the new kitchener, or closed range.

'The smoke goes straight up the chimney. There's a water boiler too. It's wonderful, isn't it? Her ladyship saw it at the Great Exhibition.'

Jones is certainly making the most of the new inventions, thinks Ali. The kitchener is rather monstrous, a solid black presence taking up half of one wall with several iron doors and a fire glowing in the centre. Terry is curled up in a wicker basket nestled against the side of the stove. He blinks at Ali but doesn't get up.

'We've given him Whiskers' old basket,' says Cook, almost apologetically. 'He seems to like it. I think it's because it's warm.'

The room is certainly warm. In fact, it verges on extremely hot. Ali can feel sweat trickling down her back and her corset is itching again. Mrs Beak, the cook, a small woman wearing a spotless white apron, seems not to notice the temperature.

'I placed a freshly laundered blanket in the basket,' says Harrison.

'Mr Harrison loves animals,' says Mrs Beak.

Jones was right, thinks Ali as she trudges back upstairs, after thanking the cook and Harrison profusely; Terry will be fine here, sleeping by the range and being rewarded for catching mice. It's just that Ali will miss him dreadfully.

'Cheer up,' says Jones, as Ali climbs into the brougham, which has its hood up this time, 'it might never happen.'

'But it probably will,' says Ali.

Jones seems in a very good mood. Perhaps it's the thought of a visit to the beating heart of her empire. She hums as she looks out of the window. 'Cruel Summer' by Taylor Swift.

'You should be careful,' says Ali. 'I don't suppose there are many Swifties in 1851.'

'Oh, I don't know,' says Jones dreamily. 'I'm beginning to think that everything's cyclical. Maybe Taylor Swift has happened before.'

'That sounds mystical,' says Ali. 'You always used to warn us against getting mystical about time travel.'

'That was before I did it myself,' says Jones. 'There is something very metaphysical about being almost a ghost in the world, present in space but belonging to a different time. Everything has happened before, everyone around you will be dead long before you were born.'

'And you still want to stay?' says Ali. 'You don't miss Taylor Swift, Netflix and your iPhone?'

She says it lightly but there's a serious question there and Jones responds in kind.

'I do miss them,' says Jones. 'Everything's still in my Islington flat, you know. I didn't have time to sell it before I left.'

Who has the key? wonders Ali. She thinks of Jones's silver Parker pen which is still in Ali's sitting room. Will she ever see her house again?

But Jones is still talking, 'Sometimes I still catch myself swiping at a book cover as though it's an iPad. But life is richer here. I've read more in the last year than I have since I was a student. A few months ago I heard a Liszt étude played for the *very first time*. I love living at a time when new things are happening. New ideas, new inventions. It's refreshing to be living in a world where technology is exciting. Before we all got cynical and worried about the planet.'

To be honest, Ali doesn't remember Jones worrying much about the planet in the 2020s. Her electric Fiat was almost her only concession to the green agenda. But, when they arrive at the foundry, Ali can see exactly why Jones finds it exciting. It's also horrific.

At first sight, when the carriage clatters under the high brick archway, it doesn't look so bad. The factory, which manufactures iron railings, is just off the Whitechapel Road, on Ali's route to work, in fact. She amuses herself by thinking how stylish these tall industrial edifices are considered now, all spiral staircases and kitchen islands, with just the occasional stretch of exposed brick coyly hinting at the building's past life. The foundry even has a winch outside, like all the trendiest Clerkenwell apartment blocks.

Inside, though, it's a different matter. The noise is indescribable, a crashing and grinding that sounds almost demonic. The air smells ferrous, like blood, and Ali's thin shoes crunch over what feels like sand. She holds her skirts as high as she can. Fine soot falls from the rafters and Ali copies Jones in putting up her parasol. Jones strides on ahead, talking to the foreman, introduced as Mr Wilton. Ali has no idea how they can find their way. It's a huge space but it also seems monstrously crowded. Eventually they climb a flight of open stairs, almost a ladder, onto a narrow platform. There, Ali has a grandstand view of the whole process.

She thinks of ruin and destruction, of the devil building Pandemonium, the last days of Pompeii. Hurrying figures are outlined against fiery furnaces, a towering chimney spews out what looks like molten lava, a nightmare railway track circles the walls, vibrating constantly to shake the grit from metal castings. And always there's the noise, ear-splitting and constant, like tectonic plates smashing together. Ali wipes her forehead, which she knows is dripping with sweat. Her glove comes away black with soot.

'Isn't it wonderful?' says Jones.

'Awe-inspiring,' says Ali. She thinks of the original meaning of the word: terror or dread. There *is* something thrilling about the sheer scale of the place but it also feels inhuman, lacking in light, air or peace, any of the essentials of civilised life. Ali thinks of Cain Templeton. *One of her foundries is known as the devil's furnace.*

When Jones has asked Mr Wilton a series of technical questions, they descend from the platform and leave through the double doors at the far end of the foundry. There they cross a courtyard – Ali's ears throbbing in relief – and Jones shows Ali a schoolroom where about twenty children are copying letters onto slates. Ali is willing to accept that Jones is trying to educate the children of her work-force, and she has to admit that she didn't see any minors labouring in the foundry itself but, even so, Jones is beginning to seem an entirely alien figure. There's almost nothing left of the university lecturer who drives an electric Fiat 500. Instead, there's a queenly figure in a long mauve dress, poring over discarded castings and asking accusatory questions about wastage.

They don't speak much on the journey home. Jones is humming again and Ali's head is aching. Back at the house, she goes upstairs to her bedroom and takes off her wig. It feels good to be able to scratch her scalp but there's still a band of pain across her eyes. Frensham appears, heralded by a soft knock.

'Would you like me to help you off with your dress, madam? I could take it away and brush it.'

Ali looks at the hem of her dress, which has a black rim about an inch deep. She thinks it will take more than brushing.

'It's very dirty,' she says. 'I'm sorry.' That's the second dress she's ruined in one day.

'I'm used to it, madam,' says Frensham. 'Her ladyship is always going to visit manufactories.'

Ali is not sure if her tone is proud or disapproving or somewhere in between. She allows Frensham to help her take the blue dress off and, when the maid has gone, she lies down. Her head is still pounding but, a few minutes later, Frensham comes back with a strip of material soaked in water and vinegar.

'Put it across your eyes, madam. It will help.'

Presumably mind-reading is an essential quality in a lady's maid.

Ali puts the cloth over her face and the headache eases instantly. She closes her eyes. She wakes to Gladys bringing her a note.

'This has just been delivered, ma'am.'

Dearest Alison, meet me at my house tonight.
I'll send a carriage at midnight. CT.

Chapter 27

Ali changes into her pink evening dress.

'You're getting all dressed up,' says Jones. 'It's rather daring, meeting him at midnight. There's not much moon either. I hope the carriage has good lanterns.'

'It's probably a very bad idea,' says Ali. She has no intention of not going, though.

'I say it again,' says Jones. 'You're a risk taker.' But she doesn't sound as if she seriously disapproves. After supper, Jones announces her intention of going to the library to work. 'Today's visit has given me some ideas about speeding up the casting process.'

'Is that all?' says Ali.

'What do you mean, "is that all"? It's very important.'

'I thought you might be . . .' Suddenly Ali is reluctant to say it.

'What?' says Jones, with that edge of impatience again, her hand on the door.

'Time travel. You said, that evening when I came through the gate, that there was more to time travel than you realised. I thought you might be working on a new way of doing it.' Jones gives her a look that is hard to read. Ali thinks she sees irritation, amusement and, more surprisingly, embarrassment.

'I am working on it,' says Jones at last. 'It's difficult without any of the right equipment. No computers, for one thing. But The Collectors have obviously managed it. I wish I understood more about the chairs. Ali, if you get the chance at Templeton's house, sit in the chair again. It's worth a go.'

'I will,' says Ali. Then, as Jones turns to go, she adds, 'If I do, you know, manage it. Thanks for everything. It's been great spending time with you. I've always wanted to, you know.'

'I've enjoyed it too,' says Jones. 'But I think you'll be back tonight. Or early this morning.'

'But if I'm not,' says Ali. 'Thank you. And thank Frensham too. She's been very good to me and I never even gave her a tip.'

'I'll pass on your message,' says Jones. 'Goodnight, Ali.'

Left alone in the sitting room, surrounded by yards of silk and lace, Ali has the usual problem of occupying her time. The little clock on the mantelpiece says ten thirty. Ali thinks of the timepiece at Hawk Street. Sometimes, when she can't sleep, she imagines its face, the sinister pictures floating beside each number. Ten is the dark tower.

Ali has brought a book from Jones's library. *Barnaby Rudge* by Charles Dickens, the one with the Gordon Riots in it. Ali tries to concentrate on the meeting of four friends in a country pub but her mind keeps wandering. She thinks of the author, bright eyed and bombastic. *Indeed, I have performed a mesmeric experiment myself. Shall I tell you about it?* It reminds her of Klaus Kramer. *Mrs Dawson, do you believe in magic?*

Ali tries to pace the room, once again having trouble negotiating her full skirt through the maze of furniture. Is there really a chair somewhere that could convey her back to 2024? She imagines seeing Finn again, hugging him, ruffling his hair, and she starts to tremble. Sit in the chair again, Jones said. Has Templeton arranged this midnight meeting because he has a plan for getting her home? But that would mean never seeing him again. Ali sits down. It's not a difficult choice between Finn and Cain – Finn wins every time – but Ali does find herself wanting just a few more days. Just a few more days of wearing pink dresses and having her hair in elaborate coils. Just a few more days of having servants and riding in carriages. Just a few more days of being loved by Cain Templeton. *Is* he in love with her? Is *she* in love with *him*? He called her the love of his life in his diary but Cain is married. He has never shown any sign of leaving his wife. All Ali knows is that he once wrote her a love letter and carved their initials on a tree. Has she been infected by some Victorian disease where you fall in love after only having seen someone once or twice?

Ali opens the book and shuts it again. Not for the first time, she misses her phone. She has tried to limit her usage since going cold turkey in 1850 but, right now, it would be good to play a game of solitaire or Two Dots. Something mindless and satisfying. Make a square of the coloured dots, stack King, Queen, Jack, ten. Click, click, click, click. Ali fiddles with her ringlets. Is it ridiculous to have a style like this at fifty-one? She remembers being worried that the wig would come off in bed. It would be very disconcerting to stroke someone's hair and have it come off in your hand. She has a feeling that Cain would just have laughed.

Ten to twelve at last. Terry enters the room and sashays up to Ali. She strokes him from ears to tail, the way he likes it.

'Will you forgive me, Terry, if I have to leave you here?'

Terry purrs, which she takes as assent or, most likely, indifference. Ali wipes away a tear with her lace glove. Don't be pathetic, she tells herself. You must get back for Finn's sake. But Finn wants to leave you to go to Yorkshire, says a weaselly voice in her head. Terry has never let you down.

The clock strikes midnight and Ali hears the coach and horses outside. It's all rather Cinderella, she thinks.

The first thing Ali notices is the darkness. Ali thinks of Jones's remark about the moon and the lanterns. Certainly, the lamps by the driver's seat don't seem to cast much light. Ali can't even see the horses.

The coachman offers a gloved hand to help her into her seat.

'Thanks, James,' she says. It's really awful to give them all the same name. The men are even starting to look alike.

Ali remembers the first time Templeton sent a carriage for her. Then, it had seemed like a prop from a horror film, the black horses, the crimson-lined body like the inside of a coffin. Now, she feels the same frisson of fear. The horses seem to be travelling very fast, the vehicle swaying from side to side. Ali holds on to the window strap and hopes for the best. At least it's not far to Templeton's house, which is also in Kensington. She could have walked. She should have walked.

Surely the journey is taking too long? It reminds Ali of getting a taxi in Central London and feeling sure the driver is taking the long way round. The cabbie usually has some answer to hand. Tony, Ali's neighbour, has a whole store of them. *East to west, Embankment's best.* But Ali can't call out to James. She can only hope that the horses slow down soon.

When they do, Ali feels quite dizzy. She descends from the carriage holding on to her pink, beribboned hat. It's only when she looks up that she realises that, instead of a London town house, she is facing a grand portico with steps and columns. It looks familiar. The moon makes a fleeting appearance and illuminates a man wearing a long, black cloak.

'So glad you could join me,' says Klaus Kramer.

'What's going on?' says Ali. 'What are you doing here?' She looks round for the carriage but it has already driven away. A surge of fear, almost of panic, sweeps through her.

'I knew you couldn't resist an invitation from Cain Templeton,' says Kramer. 'And midnight too. So romantic.'

Ali turns to run but trips again on her stupid skirts. Kramer helps her to her feet and guides her, with a strong hand gripping her arm, through the open doors of the theatre.

Ali decides that her best bet is to go with Kramer. If she runs, he is sure to catch her. In jeans and trainers, she might be able to get away, but not in long skirts and satin shoes. If Kramer relaxes, maybe she'll be able to distract him, use a bit of Power's misdirection. Where is Power anyway?

It's a frightening thought, not being able to contact anyone. If only she had a phone and could ring Jones or Templeton. Even as Kramer marshals her up a set of dusty stairs, she spares a thought for her Victorian sisters. It's hard enough being a woman in 2024, what must it be like when you've almost no agency and are imprisoned by your clothes?

They are obviously in a part of the theatre that is not on public view. Floorboards creak underfoot and the paint is peeling from the walls. There's no light apart from a candle held in Kramer's hand, the one not clutching Ali. *Here comes a candle to light you to bed, here comes a chopper to chop off your head.* Up and up. It reminds Ali of the staircase leading to the secret Templeton Collection at Queen Mary's. She can't help thinking of Luke, who fell to his death, supposedly whilst possessed by the spirit of the man beside her. *You've met him and you know what he's capable of.*

Eventually Kramer pushes open a door and they are in a room that is obviously at the very top of the building. The only furniture is a bed and a chair. A round window reflects the night sky. Kramer puts the candle on the floor and opens a door that Ali hadn't previously noticed. He pulls Ali towards the open aperture. It leads onto a narrow ledge. The moon moves behind clouds and Ali sees rooftops and domes. Something flies past, very close. A bird or a bat?

Kramer says, 'And now we're going to see if you can fly.'

'No!' Ali manages to push him away and rushes to the other door. It's locked. Ali hadn't seen Kramer with a key but then he's an illusionist so she wouldn't, would she?

Kramer is watching her with something like amusement. 'Cain Templeton thinks he can interfere with my private life, I'll interfere with his.'

Ali looks round for something to throw at him but there's nothing except the chair. She edges towards it. 'What do you mean?' she says, trying to sound calm. 'I hardly know Mr Templeton.'

Kramer laughs. 'I saw you go into Hawk Street yesterday and come out several hours later. Hardly the behaviour of a respectable woman.'

'You saw me?'

'Yes. Don't you know I can be in two places at once?'

More likely, Kramer was disguised as the woman in the shawl

with the firewood. Who needs firewood – or a shawl – in the middle of summer? And, now that she thinks of it, the note had said 'Alison', not 'Alisoun'. Ali should have guessed. Some detective she is.

'You're mad,' says Ali.

Kramer keeps smiling and then, without warning, lunges towards her and grabs both her arms. He's pulling, almost dragging, her towards the door to the sky.

'Help!' shouts Ali, although she knows there's no one to hear. She tries to grab hold of something to stop her inexorable progress but there's nothing to hand. Kramer grasps her round the waist and bundles her out, through the open doorway, and onto the ledge.

It's only just wide enough to stand on. A chunk of plaster crumbles from beneath Ali's foot and plummets downwards. How high are they? Across the rooftops, the spire of St Mary-Le-Bow seems almost at her eye level. The wind whips her hair back against her face, although she hadn't noticed a breeze earlier.

'You can fly,' whispers Kramer. 'Think how wonderful it will feel.'

'No!' Ali pushes back and manages to get one foot inside the door frame. But Kramer is hideously strong. She supposes all those magic tricks are like a workout. He must have performed them on stage tonight, only hours earlier. He's standing close behind her and she can smell the sweat, horribly mixed with strong cologne.

'You're not getting away from me,' says Kramer. 'Send my love to Mr Templeton.'

He pushes her forwards onto the ledge again. One hard shove is all it would take to make her lose her balance and fall. Is she going to die, here in 1851? Ali closes her eyes and hears a voice shout, 'Kramer!'

Kramer loosens his hold and Ali manages to step quickly back into the room, where Balthazar Power is standing by the now open door.

'Kramer! For God's sake! This is madness.'

'You can't stop me this time.' Kramer really does seem mad at that moment, his teeth bared in what looks like a snarl.

'Mrs Dawson,' says Power. 'Sit in the chair.'

'What?' Ali is heading for the door, but this makes her pause.

'Sit in the chair. Trust me. Remember me.'

Dazed, Ali does as he tells her. Kramer hurls himself forward, bellowing.

And the world goes dark.

Chapter 28

Dina goes in the squad car with Luca.

'After all, I'm part of the investigation.'

'You're not even a police officer,' says Luca but he doesn't put up too much resistance. Dina thinks he's already absorbed in the case. Her mind, too, is racing. She saw Barry Power only yesterday. Was she the last person to see him alive? Can his death be linked to Hugo Maltravers' murder? She remembers Power's words, the soft Welsh accent that almost lulled her into belief: *What would you say if I told you that I'd met Alison before, in a very different time and place?* Power told her that she'd be back, that he knew how to save Ali. Well, it's too late now.

As they drive through the dark streets, Luca is getting updates from the scene.

'Looks like Power was killed on his own doorstep,' he tells Dina. 'Stabbed.'

'Same MO as Hugo Maltravers,' says Dina.

'Aye.'

The rain has stopped but there's still a strong wind blowing rubbish across the streets and setting off car alarms. Apart from a group of young people weaving their way along Streatham High Road and a large fox, full of urban attitude, near Norbury station, they don't see a living soul. They reach Thornton Heath in under fifteen minutes. A uniformed officer is standing by the gate of Power's house. Dina averts her eyes from the huddled shape by the front door.

'Are SOCO on their way?' asks Luca.

'Yes, guv,' says the uniform, who looks about twelve.

'Were you the first on the scene?'

'Yes. My partner and I were in the area. A neighbour heard an altercation and dialled 999. My partner and I found the deceased on the doorstep. Ambulance arrived and paramedics ascertained life extinct. Then they left and I called CID.'

There's a lot here for Dina's list of police words: altercation, deceased, ascertained, life extinct. She's fascinated to see Luca at work. He seems calm but he's drumming the fingers of one hand against his leg. It seems almost impossible that, only a few hours ago, they were in bed together.

'Where's your partner now?'

'She's checking round the back.'

On cue, a woman emerges from the side of the house. She, too, looks hardly old enough to drive but she has an urgency and sense of purpose that appear to be lacking in the male officer. She introduces herself as PC Rachel Dent.

'Nobody in the back garden,' she says.

'Have you checked with the neighbour? The one who called it in.' There's a light on in the house next door. Dina can imagine the inhabitants inside, sitting together, terrified and intrigued, not wanting to look out of the window, for fear of seeming insensitive.

'Yes, I took an initial statement. Gentleman called Jaswinder Singh. Mr Singh heard a scream, looked out of the window and saw a dark figure running away. He thought there was someone lying on the ground – couldn't be sure who it was – so he called police and ambulance. David and I asked Mr Singh if he'd come and look at the body from a distance. Mr Singh was able to identify Mr Power, the owner of the property.'

'Have you been inside?' For the first time, Dina notices that the front door is ajar. Had the assailant rung the bell and, when Barry Power came to open it, stabbed him? It seems a horribly simple way to kill someone.

Rachel says they haven't been into the house and Luca nods, as if this was the right answer. They wait for the scene-of-crime team, Luca frowning into his phone, his face illuminated by its light. Dina feels cold in her hoodie (Trinity Fencing 2008) and wishes she hadn't come.

Eventually a van appears – more lights going on in neigh-bouring houses – and two alien figures in paper suits get out. They hand a suit to Luca, who puts it on, pulling overshoes onto his feet and tucking his hair into what looks like a bath hat. Rather to Dina's surprise, she too is given a suit and she climbs into it, copying Luca. She hasn't showed her ID to anyone and assumed she'd be left outside with the officers, both of whom look frozen but resigned.

Dina follows Luca up the path and edges past the body on the doorstep. She gets a glimpse of a livid white face, no blood that she can see. One of the SOCO team bends over the body. The deceased.

Luca advances slowly but purposefully into the house. Of course, thinks Dina, he's been here before, investigating the death of Power's wife, Violet. She glances up at the dark staircase. There's no sound anywhere, not even a ticking clock. Luca moves into the sitting room.

'Don't touch anything,' he says to Dina.

Luca's phone torch illuminates the dark furniture, the sofa with antimacassars that reminded Dina of her grandmother's. The beam searches every corner of the room. Is Luca expecting the killer to be hiding here? For the first time, she feels scared.

'I'm going upstairs,' says Luca. 'Wait here.'

Dina wants to go with him but she has to keep seeming like the professional police officer she isn't. She stays in the dark sitting room listening to Luca's footsteps above. That same slow, steady pace. Dina locates her phone and switches on the light

Just in time to see a woman in a pink dress materialise in front of her.

'Ali?' whispers Dina.

She now sees that the figure is sitting in a chair. She rises and Dina realises that it really is Ali. She is so pleased to see her that relief almost overpowers surprise.

'Ali. Oh my God. Is it really you?'

Ali looks around her. She seems almost in a trance. Dina remembers this from her own trip to the 1970s. If travelling to the past is a shock, that's almost nothing compared to returning. But Ali doesn't have time to be dazed. She has made her comeback right in the middle of a murder scene.

'Where am I?' asks Ali.

At that moment, Luca shouts from upstairs. 'Dina! Who are you talking to?'

Dina doesn't answer. How can she? The footsteps come downstairs again, much faster this time. Luca hurtles into the room and then stops.

'Who the hell are you?'

'Ali Dawson,' says Ali, sounding more like her old self. 'Who are you?'

'Ali Dawson,' repeats Luca. '*The* Ali Dawson?

'I suppose so,' says Ali. 'What's going on here?'

Luca pulls himself together with what is clearly an effort. 'I'm DS Luca Venturi. I'm investigating the suspicious death of Barry Power.'

Ali sways and almost falls. Dina goes to her side. 'It's OK, Ali.' She has no idea if it is or not, but the main thing is that Ali is here, in July 2024, and not lost in time.

'Is Balthazar dead?' asks Ali.

Both Dina and Luca stare at her. 'Who?' says Dina, after a confused pause.

'Balthazar Power. Barry Power.'

'A man we believe to be Barry Power was stabbed to death at this location,' says Luca, falling back on police speak. Then, more naturally, 'Where did you come from? There was no one in this room a few minutes ago. And why are you dressed like that?'

Ali puts her hand to her eyes. Dina doesn't know if she's really feeling faint or just playing for time. Luca, though, has been filling in some of the gaps for himself. 'Did Power keep you here?' he says. 'Were you his prisoner? Did he force you to dress like that?'

Ali does the only thing she can do. She says, in a feeble voice, holding on to Dina's arm for support, 'I don't remember.'

'We need to get her home,' says Dina. 'I can take her.'

'We need a statement,' says Luca.

'She's in no fit state,' says Dina.

'Then she should go to hospital.'

'I don't believe you can force me,' says Ali, lapsing back into her real voice. 'Unless I'm under arrest.'

Luca glances at Dina, clearly wondering if Ali *should* be under arrest, but in the end he says, 'Give your name and address to the officer at the door. Dina will see you home.'

'Come on, Ali,' says Dina. 'Let's get you out of here.'

Dina calls an Uber. She doesn't want to wait for a squad car and hear Luca talk about ambulances and hospitals. Luckily, back-up arrives from Luca's team and he's almost too busy bossing them around to notice Dina and Ali go. It's 2.15 a.m. The street is in darkness again apart from lights set up around Power's house, which has rapidly become a crime scene; police tape, screens and all.

The Uber driver takes one look at Ali and says, 'Fancy dress party?'

'Yes,' says Dina.

'Well, you haven't made much effort, have you?'

'I'm a fencer,' says Dina. 'It's better with a sword.'

Dina's flat is closest but she doesn't want to leave Ali on her own, so she asks the driver to take them to Bow.

Ali says, 'The last time I was in a vehicle it was pulled by horses.'

Dina glances at the driver but he has turned the radio on and seems to have lost interest in them.

'Did you go back to the 1850s then?' she says. 'Did you see Jones?'

'I certainly did. She's called Lady Serafina now.'

'Gosh,' says Dina, inadequately.

She looks at Ali, who is staring out of the window, obviously still partly in a dream. Dina didn't see Ali in her Victorian clothes last time and she's surprised what a difference they make. Ali looks younger, probably due to the wig, and curvier, almost definitely due to the corset. But she seems unapproachable too, isolated by her oceans of skirt, like a bride on her wedding day.

'How did you get back?' asks Dina.

'On a chair. Must have been one of Templeton's set. Power helped me. He saved my life.' Ali puts a gloved hand up to her eyes. 'I can't believe he's dead.'

'He was killed last night,' says Dina, 'or this morning. There might be links to Hugo Maltravers' murder.'

'What?' Ali turns as quickly as her undergarments allow. Her face, illuminated by passing headlights, is deathly pale.

'Oh my God,' says Dina. 'I forgot you didn't know. I'm so sorry, Ali. Hugo was killed last week. Stabbed. Luca, the police officer you met just now, is investigating it. He contacted us because he knew you'd been married to Hugo. He was looking for you. That's one reason why he was so shocked just now.'

'Hugo,' says Ali. 'I can't believe it.'

'I'm sorry,' says Dina again.

'I only saw him a few days ago,' says Ali. 'It seems like another lifetime. Poor Hugo. Did you say he was stabbed?'

'Yes. He was ambushed on his way to work. No witnesses.'

'He had a partner and a child. I don't know whether it's a boy or a girl.'

Ali's rambling now, thinks Dina.

'The main thing is, you're back,' she says. 'Finn will be so happy.'

'Does he know?' says Ali.

'Yes,' says Dina. 'He's really worried. He's in Yorkshire but we've talked on the phone.'

'He's still in Yorkshire?'

'He asked if he should come back but I said there was nothing he could do here.'

'I suppose not. Does Nigel know?'

'Yes. He came into the office. John and I tried to bluff it out but Bud let the cat out of the bag.'

'Typical,' says Ali.

They both laugh and, for a moment, everything is almost back to normal. After a few minutes, Ali says, 'I just can't believe that Barry's dead. "Remember me." That's the last thing he said to me.'

'He told me that he'd met you in 1851.'

'Yes. I met Klaus Kramer too. He was just as charming as we'd imagined.'

Ali is silent until the car bumps over the cobbles of her street.

'Here you are, ladies,' says the driver. 'Two Cinderellas home from the ball.'

Dina forces herself to laugh. She doesn't want to lose her five-star Uber rating.

Ali says she's lost her cat key ring but she remembers there's a spare one under the loose paving stone by the front door.

'It was probably still there in 1851. This street was almost the same then. I even met one of my neighbours.'

'Gosh,' says Dina. Ali's not making a lot of sense but the important thing is to get inside the house. The key works and Ali stands for a moment in the doorway, her skirts filling the frame. Then there's a sound, a skittering noise somewhere in the darkness. Ali falls to her knees. She's laughing and crying. Dina doesn't know what to do or say. At first, she can just see the top of Ali's elaborately curled head but then she edges past and spots the creature in Ali's arms. A purring Siamese cat.

Terry.

Chapter 29

Ali wakes to rain outside and Terry lying across her feet. She lies back on her pillows, so flat after the Victorian feather versions, and looks at the time on her clock radio. 7.08. For a moment, she almost reaches out to see if Gladys has brought her morning tea. But there's nothing on her bedside table apart from a lamp, the radio and her phone, which is glowing with messages. Last night, after sitting on the floor crying over Terry, Ali had got up and texted Finn. 'I'm home. Mum xx.' Then she'd gone upstairs to bed. Her pink dress is a pool of silk on the floor. Next to it lies her wig, looking like roadkill.

Finn's texts chart his progress from relief to anger.

Thank God! Where r u?
R U in your house?
What happened?
??
Why aren't you answering
I've been so worried
What the hell were you thinking???

Ali texts Finn quickly. 'I'm fine. At home. I'm so sorry for worrying you, love.' She almost tells him about Terry's miraculous appearance but decides that he might have had enough of hearing about the cat. Dina said she'd told Finn about the reason for Ali's latest trip through the gate. He laughed, said Dina, he understood. Even so, Ali doesn't want to push Finn too far. He'll be up to his eyes in the election which, Ali checks her phone, is tomorrow. All the same, Ali is slightly hurt that Finn didn't come rushing back to London when he found out she was missing.

First things first. She must have a shower. She was too exhausted last night but hasn't had a full-body wash for five days. Jones showed her the bathtub, which was positioned on a plinth in a room otherwise decorated no differently from the other bedrooms, curtains, wallpaper, chandelier and all. Ali longed to use it but still couldn't bring herself to ask Gladys to fill the tub for her as well as Jones, especially after she'd already toiled up three flights of stairs with water for Ali's basin. So Ali had contented herself with soap and flannel, adding some of Jones's lavender scent for good luck. Ali's hair, crammed under the wig, has fared worse. It's lank and greasy and seems to have acquired a layer of soot from the foundry.

Ali takes off her pyjamas and steps onto the landing. Then she remembers that Dina is sleeping in the spare room and goes back for her dressing gown. It hadn't seemed worth Dina going home last night. They've got a lot to talk about. But hot water, shower gel and shampoo first.

The shower is blissful. Ali can practically feel the dirt streaming out. She washes and washes until the whole room is steamy. Then she goes back into her bedroom and dresses in jeans, T-shirt and a cotton jumper. The hot weather has gone and the day looks almost as cold as winter. The trees in the garden are heavy with rain and Tony's bunting, put up for the barbecue, flaps forlornly. Terry yowls from the landing, reminding Ali that he hasn't eaten since . . . since when? Since Cook gave him salmon for catching a mouse? Just how did Terry appear here, in 2024, when Ali left him in 1851? Ali remembers Bud saying that he liked cats because they were smart, 'he might find his way home.' Bud, it seems, is the smart one.

Jones said there was more to time travel than she had imagined. *Emotion* comes into it, she had said, sounding surprised. Does this explain how Ali got back? Was it just because she wanted it so much? But, the first time, she had longed to go home and nothing had happened. Interesting, as Jones would say.

Ali feeds Terry and he rushes out through the cat flap to do his ablutions. Ali doesn't want to let him go but she has to trust him. After all, Terry has shown himself to be an expert in the art of getting back home. Ali makes herself some toast and Marmite. The bread is a bit stale but fine when toasted. After all, she's only been gone a week. Ali remembers last time, when she returned from the 1850s, modern food had seemed far too strongly flavoured. The Marmite, with its yeasty saltiness, is a shock to her system. Delicious, though. Ali is about to take another bite when there's a knock on the door. Ali is surprised to find her heart thumping. Who does she think will be there? Klaus Kramer? The ghost of Balthazar Power? Charles Dickens?

'ALI! YOU'RE BACK! WANTED TO TELL YOU I THOUGHT I SAW TERRY IN THE GARDEN JUST NOW.'

It's Tony, in towelling dressing gown and sliders, hair wet from the shower.

'Yes,' says Ali. 'When I got home last night, he was waiting for me. Isn't it wonderful?'

'It's a miracle,' says Tony. 'Chrissie prayed to Saint Francis.'

'That must be it,' says Ali. Stranger things have happened, after all.

When Tony has flip-flopped away, whistling cheerfully, Ali goes back to her toast. She's just contemplating a second slice when Dina appears.

'God,' she says, 'what a night.'

'Toast?' says Ali. 'Marmite?'

'Yes, please. I love Marmite.' Ali is pleased. She slightly distrusts anyone who doesn't.

Dina is wearing yesterday's leggings and the T-shirt Ali lent her to sleep in. She looks younger than usual and remarkably bright eyed. Considering.

Ali puts bread in the toaster and coffee in the cafetière. She jumps when Terry clatters back in through the cat flap, looking outraged because his fur is wet.

Dina bends to stroke him. 'Isn't it wonderful that Terry came back? Where do you think he's been all this time? He doesn't look thin or bedraggled.'

'I know where he's been,' says Ali. 'When I arrived in 1851, the first person I saw was Jones holding Terry in her arms.'

Dina stares at her. 'What?'

'I don't know how he got there,' says Ali. 'Even Jones couldn't explain it. But he settled in remarkably well. Jones's butler and cook both loved him. That was the only thing that persuaded me to leave him behind.'

'But Ali,' says Dina. 'How can it have been Terry? It must just have been a cat that looked very like him.'

'Siamese cats weren't imported to the UK until the end of the nineteenth century,' says Ali. 'But, anyway, I knew it was him. Same coat, same markings, everything.'

Dina still looks dubious and Ali knows she doesn't understand. Dina doesn't have any pets. She doesn't realise that Ali would know Terry anywhere. It's not just his colour and markings; it's his essence, his very Terryishness. She would know him even if he was disguised as a ginger tom, just as she'd know Finn if he dyed his hair or had plastic surgery.

They drink their coffee in silence for a few minutes – Ali savouring the caffeine – and then Dina says, 'Well, go on. Tell me everything. About Lady Serafina and her butler and cook. Everything.'

So Ali does. She tells Dina about the house in Kensington, the lady's maid, the pinstriped dress, the Great Exhibition, Cain Templeton, Klaus Kramer, Charles Dickens and Balthazar Power. She tells her about watching Kramer read people's minds, about the reunion at Hawk Street and the moment when she stood on the ledge at the top of the Theatre Royal and wondered if she could fly. The only thing she doesn't tell her is that she slept with Cain Templeton.

'Bloody hell, Ali,' says Dina, when she's finished. 'That's a lot.'

'It felt like a lot,' says Ali. 'It was terrifying but it was also . . .'

'Fun?' suggests Dina.

'Not exactly. More exhilarating. As if the world was suddenly in technicolour.' She thinks of Jones saying, 'Life is richer here.' She looks out of the French windows and sees a drab, rain-streaked morning. OK, this world has Finn it in, Dina and the team too, but there's no denying that it doesn't look its best today.

'We should go into the office,' says Ali, glancing at the railway clock over the breakfast bar. 'John will want to hear all this.' She had texted John last night too and he had contented himself with a heart emoji and a simple, 'I'm so glad.'

'Yes,' says Dina. 'I've texted Bud to meet us there too. He'll be so pleased to see you. He felt really guilty about the whole thing.'

'He shouldn't have,' says Ali. 'It was all my fault. I strong-armed him into it.'

Dina goes on, 'I need to bring John up to date on Barry Power too. I'll see if Luca has any more info.'

'You seem to be quite friendly with Luca,' says Ali.

'We're sleeping together,' says Dina. She tries to sound casual but can't stop herself grinning.

'Is that a situationship?' asks Ali.

'I don't know what it is,' says Dina. 'But I'm enjoying it.'

The short journey on the Tube seems terrifying to Ali. The noise, the darkness, the constant messaging: departure boards, advertisements, disembodied voices telling her to mind the gap and to report suspicious packages. See it, say it, sorted. Can she really have forgotten all this in just a week? Even Dina seems nervous, constantly checking her phone although she can't have any signal underground. Ali emerges into drizzly Whitechapel with a sigh of relief. It's nearly ten o'clock so most of the commuters have gone. There's a grey, depressed feeling to the empty streets. Apart from a headline on a discarded copy of the *Telegraph* ('It's not too late to stop Labour'), there's no sign that a general election is happening tomorrow. As far as Ali knows, Labour still has a massive lead in the polls but there's none of the excitement she remembers from 1997, the last time Labour won with a landslide.

There's plenty of excitement in 14 Eel Street, though. John and Bud cheer when Ali comes through the door. John embraces her warmly and even Bud manages an awkward one-armed hug. 'I'm sorry,' he says.

'Nothing to be sorry about,' says Ali. 'It seems there are more variables than we thought. Jones said that feelings and emotions play a part in it. It's not just about physics. You must have been thinking about Jones so you brought me to her.'

'Tell us about Jones,' says John. 'Is she well? Is she happy?' Dina thought to stop for pastries and they are all eating them in Ali's office. The world seems slightly less grey.

Ali takes a bite of almond croissant and almost gags at the sweetness. She puts it to one side, thinking about Jones in her beautiful dresses, sailing through the Great Exhibition or watching her furnaces burn. Is she happy? Ali really doesn't know. She says, 'She's well. She's become very rich. She lives in a beautiful house. She says she doesn't want to come back.'

Bud chokes on his cinnamon swirl. Ali wishes she had put this more tactfully. She'd forgotten Bud's feelings for Jones. She's his mentor but also his idol. He adores her.

'She sent her love to you,' she tells Bud. 'You were the only one.'

'Really?' Bud brightens so quickly it's almost painful to see. 'Did she really?'

'Give my love to Bud, she said. Tell him to keep the faith.'

Bud closes his eyes as if picturing the scene. 'I will,' he says, almost to himself, 'I will.'

'Why doesn't Jones want to come back?' asks John, still looking rather troubled.

Ali doesn't repeat what Jones told her about not having a partner or children. She says, 'It's an exciting world. Jones invested in the new industries. I went to see one of her foundries and it was incredible. Terrifying but incredible. You can imagine what that's like for someone like Jones, being in the forefront of scientific discoveries. It's thrilling for her.'

'I bet she's fighting the good fight for women's rights too,' says Dina.

'I'm sure she is,' says Ali, although she isn't sure at all, 'whilst wearing some very gorgeous clothes.'

'The dress you were in last night was pretty fancy,' says Dina. 'I hardly recognised you. It makes me want to have a Victorian-themed party. Have you still got the clothes you wore, John?'

'I burnt them,' says John. He exchanges a look with Ali. Neither of them loves Dina's costume parties.

'How *did* you get back, Ali?' says John. 'Dina says that you turned up at Barry Power's house in the middle of a crime scene. I can't believe he's been killed.'

'Nor can I,' says Ali. 'I'm only here because of him.' She tells them about Klaus Kramer and the ledge in the sky.

'You saw Barry Power in 1851?' says John.

'Yes,' says Ali. 'I'm sure it was him. When I met him the first time, he said something about knowing me on another plane. That must have been what he meant.'

'He said something similar to me,' says Dina. 'Did I tell you I went to see Barry Power, Ali?'

'No. You didn't.'

'I might have been the last person to see him alive,' says Dina. 'It was all very weird. Power said he'd seen you, Ali, in another time and place.'

'Power wanted to join The Collectors,' says Ali. 'I think he wanted to learn how to time travel. And he did.'

'It must be the chair,' says John. 'Probably the same chair I saw. Or one of the same set. I suppose that Power had one of the chairs in his house, that's why you ended up there.'

'Maybe,' says Ali, thinking of Power's sitting room, crammed with outdated furniture. 'Perhaps Power took the chair that Kramer kept at the theatre and moved it to his own house. Cain told me that two of the chairs were in his country house, one of them must be the chair that Thomas Creek used that time. The other one, or the one in Hawk Street, could have ended up in in the Templeton collection at QMUL. I remember Ed telling me that he saw someone appear there and then vanish the next minute. I think that must have been Giuseppe at the meeting you attended, John.'

'I'll never forget it,' says John. 'It was so simple, like a switch flicking. One minute there, one minute gone.'

'I met Giuseppe,' says Ali. 'He seemed nice, but he didn't want to talk about The Collectors.'

'Was Klaus Kramer one of The Collectors?' asks John. 'Is that why he had the chair?'

'No,' says Ali. 'Kramer hates Cain Templeton. I think he stole the chair from him. That's why he tried to kill me. To get back at Cain.'

There's a second's silence. Then John says, 'Why did Kramer think killing you would be getting back at Templeton? Did he know that you knew him?'

'Yes,' says Ali. 'Jones and I went to the theatre with Templeton, to see Kramer's show. Kramer knew that. Maybe he thought there was something more to our relationship.' She hopes she isn't blushing.

'It wasn't just the chair,' says Bud suddenly. He hasn't spoken since the revelation about Jones. 'There must have been another factor. I've been thinking about what Jones said about emotion. Strong emotion can produce a burst of energy. Maybe that was it.'

'Maybe,' says Ali. 'Templeton had one of the chairs in Hawk Street. I sat on it and nothing happened. But maybe the emotion wasn't strong enough. When I sat on the chair in that room at the top of the theatre, I thought I was going to be killed. That must have increased the adrenaline.'

John is distracted. 'Did you go to Hawk Street? How was everyone?'

'Fine,' says Ali. 'They all asked after you. Tremain is becoming famous. Len and Marianne have moved out, they've had another child.'

'It's so odd, you and John talking about them like this,' says Dina. 'It's like you're watching a Netflix series that Bud and I don't know about.'

'And I hate feeling left out,' says Bud, unnecessarily.

'Sorry,' says John. 'We should talk about the Barry Power murder too.' He leans forward and touches Ali's arm. 'I'm so sorry about Hugo, Ali.'

'Thanks,' says Ali. 'I still can't believe it. I wasn't on the best terms with Hugo but . . .'

'It's still a shock,' says John.

'It is,' says Ali. 'And he had a partner and a child. It's terrible for them.'

After another pause, John says, 'I'm raising it now because the local police – I think you met Luca Venturi last night? – believe there might have been a link to you, Ali. And there's something else. Hugo was sent a postcard of an old Dracula film. I got one too. *Dial M for Murder*. I didn't think much of it at the time but . . .' John glances at Dina, 'I got sent another one yesterday.'

'Oh my God,' says Dina. 'What did it say?'

'Same as last time. No message, just the postcard. *Some Like it Hot*. I've got it in my bag.'

'Marilyn Monroe, Tony Curtis and Jack Lemmon,' says Bud. 'Great film.'

'Was there a stamp on it?' asks Dina.

'No. It must have been hand-delivered. I sent the first one to SOCO to test for fingerprints but they haven't come back with anything.'

'And, even if there are prints,' says Ali, 'that won't help unless we have them on file,'

'Exactly.'

'You'll have to tell Luca,' says Dina. She looks at her phone. 'Oh, he's on his way over now. He wants to talk to you, Ali.'

'I thought he might,' says Ali.

'Do you know how Power was killed?' John asks Dina.

'I'm not sure,' says Dina. 'But it seems like someone knocked on Power's door and then stabbed him when he answered it. I saw his body.' She shivers.

John looks at Ali. Dina isn't a police officer and she's rather squeamish. Usually, they both try hard to keep her away from the more gruesome aspects of policing.

'I'm sorry, Dina,' says John. 'That must have been horrible to see.'

'I tried not to look,' says Dina. 'I followed Luca into the house and then Ali just appeared. I couldn't believe it. Then Luca came in and, well, you can imagine. At least I had some idea that Ali *might* appear from nowhere. Luca looked like he'd seen a ghost.'

'What did he say?' asks John.

'He asked if Power kept her locked up in the house, dressed like that.' Dina starts to giggle. 'Sorry, it's not really funny. I haven't slept much.'

'It has its amusing side,' says Ali.

'What are you going to say to Luca?' John asks Ali.

'I'll have to get Nigel to scare him off,' says Ali.

'Do you think he will?' asks John. 'We're not his favourite people at the moment. When I told him you were back all he said was "About time too."'

'I think he'll have to,' says Ali. 'He's not going to want me called as a witness.'

'I'm not surprised Luca thought Power was behind it somehow,' says John. 'He already thinks he killed his wife.'

'What?' says Ali.

'Barry told me all about it,' says Dina. 'It was very creepy. He said that his wife Violet . . .'

'What was her name?' says Ali.

'Violet. Vi. Do you remember that was the name of his spirit guide?'

But Ali is thinking of a lake and a red-haired woman almost falling as she placed champagne on a table. Barry Power had been at her side in an instant.

Dina is saying, 'Barry heard Violet say "No!" but, when Barry came out onto the landing, there was no one there and Violet was dead at the bottom of the stairs.'

'Did you believe him?' asks John.

Dina hesitates for a minute. 'I think I do,' she says. 'He sounded quite haunted by it.'

'I have to say,' says John, 'if Barry came up with that story when I was questioning him, I'd want to send him down for twenty years.'

'You're such a cop, John,' says Dina. She looks at her phone. 'Luca's on his way up.'

Chapter 30

Ali goes into her office and calls Nigel. There's no answer but she leaves a voice message. 'Hi, Nigel, it's Ali. I'm back! I just need your help with one tiny thing. Call me?' She imagines Nigel's face when he hears the cheery interrogative tone. He'll be furious but Ali thinks he'll support her. What choice does he have?

She has hardly put her phone down when Luca rings the doorbell downstairs. Dina goes to meet him, presumably for some private conversation on the stairs. Ali sits behind her desk and tries to look like a cool, calm professional.

Ali is interested to properly meet Luca Venturi, the man who is investigating her ex-husband's murder and also seems to have stolen her friend's heart. As Dina shows him into her office, Ali has to admit he's quite good-looking, tall, with dark, curly hair and a rather Victorian moustache. But there's something about Luca that makes Ali feel a little wary. He's perfectly polite but she thinks that she detects an edge, almost an anger, beneath the charming Scottish accent.

'DI Dawson,' says Luca, 'I've been wanting to talk to you for some time.'

'I've been away,' says Ali.

'So I heard,' says Luca, leaning back in his chair in a way that seems slightly too comfortable. It's Ali's office after all. 'It was quite the surprise when you turned up last night.'

Ali says nothing. She tries her own power play, unsmiling, straight-backed. She doesn't want to do the leaning thing because her chair is slightly unstable and she thinks falling flat on her back would lose her some Jane Tennison points.

'Are you going to tell me what happened?' says Luca. 'I checked that room myself and it was empty. I went upstairs and, the next thing I hear, you're chatting to Dina.'

'Why was Dina at the crime scene?' says Ali. 'She's not authorised personnel.'

She wants to wrong-foot Luca, not get Dina into trouble, and is gratified when he flushes slightly.

'She's involved in another case,' he says, losing some of his poise.

'The death of my ex-husband.'

'Yes. My condolences.'

Ali acknowledges this with a nod. Luca says, 'DI Dawson. Ali. Help me out here. I know you're involved but I just don't know how. Your ex-husband is killed. Now a man you're investigating is killed in the very same way.'

'Same MO?' says Ali.

'Looks like it. Single stab with a sharp-bladed weapon. I'm hoping to get some DNA from the scene. And I'm hoping it's not yours.'

'I'm sorry, DS Venturi,' says Ali. 'I can't tell you why I was at Barry Power's house last night. That's classified information.'

'And the fancy dress?'

'That's classified too.'

Luca gives a bark of laughter, tipping back his chair in the way that Finn used to do when he was younger. It's all Ali can do not to tell him to sit properly.

'Later today,' says Ali, hoping this is true, 'you'll get a call from Nigel Palmer at the Home Office. He'll explain. Or rather he'll explain why he can't explain.'

The chair bangs back onto four legs. 'Is this the secret work your department does?' Luca suddenly sounds younger and much less guarded. 'Is that what all this is about?'

'Yes,' says Ali. 'But I can't tell you any more.'

'Dina wouldn't tell me either,' says Luca, sounding aggrieved now.

'Quite right too,' says Ali.

Luca laughs again, making Ali like him slightly more. 'What the hell can it be? What sort of secret assignment involves dressing up like . . . like that?'

Ali says nothing and Luca says, more thoughtfully, 'Dina really didn't know where you were. I'm sure of it. DI Cole too. There's something seriously weird going on.'

'Don't try to work it out,' says Ali. 'It'll send you mad.'

She means it too.

Luca leaves the office with just a cursory word to Dina. Ali hopes her appearance hasn't ruined their burgeoning romance. But Dina seems quite cheerful.

'Did Luca try to arrest you?'

'I think he'd like to but hopefully Nigel can scare him off.'

'Does Luca have any theories about Barry Power's death?' asks John.

'He thinks it's the same MO as Hugo,' says Ali. 'Single stab with a sharp blade. How was Hugo killed?' It still sounds strange to say it aloud like that. Hugo, handsome, pedantic, annoying, sometimes well-meaning Hugo, is dead.

'Assaulted on his way to work,' says John. 'It seems likely that the assailant knew his route. He was attacked in an alleyway with no CCTV. Looks professional and premeditated. The same with Power. It takes some nerve to kill someone on their own doorstep with a single stab. No witnesses there either.'

'Barry Power's neighbour mentioned a dark figure running away,' says Dina.

'Those dark figures,' says Bud. 'They've got a lot to answer for.'

'And the postcards,' says Ali. 'If they were sent by the killer, that also means premeditation. It's stalker behaviour. Do we know if Power got a postcard?'

'I didn't ask him . . .' says Dina. She stops and her eyes widen. Dina has the worst poker face of anyone Ali has ever met. 'Wait.' She fumbles in the backpack, a strange object with rubber spikes that she takes everywhere. 'Look!' She proffers a small piece of card. 'Power wrote his mobile number for me on this. Look at the back of it.'

Ali, John and Bud peer forward. It's part of a postcard that shows a man's eye and a finger raised as if pressing down on a lever.

'*Rear Window*,' says Bud. 'James Stewart and Grace Kelly.'

'What are the films again?' says Ali. She takes a piece of paper from the printer and starts to write. 'Dracula . . .'

'Which Dracula film?' says Bud. 'There are loads.'

'Luca didn't say,' says Dina. 'I'll ask him.' She taps out a quick text, using her thumbs. At moments like this, Ali definitely notices the age difference between them.

'*Dial M for Murder*,' says Ali, writing. '*Some Like it Hot. Rear Window*. Bud, you're the film expert. Is there anything that links these films?'

'Luca says the Dracula film was *Scars of Dracula*,' says Dina. 'He sent a photo.'

She shows a tiny image on her phone, a man in black looming over a woman on a bed. They are pictured against a background of red velvet curtains that reminds Ali of the Theatre Royal, Drury Lane.

'When was Dracula written?' she says, almost to herself.

Dina does a lightning google and reads: '"*Dracula* is an 1897 Gothic horror novel by the Irish author Bram Stoker".'

So Klaus Kramer can't have been modelling himself on the prince of darkness. Maybe it was the other way round? Ali wonders if Bram Stoker ever attended one of Kramer's performances.

'Barry Power said he was fascinated by the Dracula legend,' says Dina. 'He had a poster of *Nosferatu* in his hallway.'

'The silent film or the later version?' asks Bud.

'The silent film,' says Dina. 'A symphony of horror. I went to see it with Luca.' Her poker face is letting her down again.

'*Nosferatu*'s not Dracula,' says Bud, 'but it might as well be. The Bram Stoker estate sued the film-makers for copyright violation. All copies of the film were meant to be destroyed.'

'Like the Klaus Kramer film,' says Dina. '*The Mesmerist*.'

'Did you watch that one too?' asks Ali.

'Yes,' says Dina. 'It wasn't that scary really although there's one horrible scene where he kills a woman with an axe. Luca said . . .' She stops.

'Luca Venturi?' says Bud. 'The policeman who was here just now? Are you dating him then?'

'We've been out a few times,' says Dina, trying to sound casual.

Ali takes pity on her. 'OK, Bud,' she says. 'Tell us about these films.' She's trying to involve Bud in the investigation, to make him feel valued, and she thinks it's working. Bud sits up straighter, pushes his hair back from his face and examines Ali's handwritten list.

'I don't know much about *Scars of Dracula* but from the picture I think it's one of the later ones, 1970s perhaps. Christopher Lee first played Dracula in the 1950s. *Dial M for Murder* is a Hitchcock film. It's about an ex-tennis player – Ray Milland – who pays an old university friend to kill his rich wife. That's Grace Kelly. It goes wrong and the wife stabs the friend with a pair of scissors. She's convicted of murder but, in the end, the husband, Tony, gets his comeuppance. Something to do with a key and a handbag.'

'She stabs him with scissors,' says Ali. 'That's a bit like our killer's MO.'

'Nothing else fits, though,' says Bud, going back to the list. '*Rear Window* is Hitchcock too. A masterpiece. The hero – James Stewart – is confined to a wheelchair. He thinks he sees a murder in the apartment block opposite. There's a really good scene where he fights off the killer using camera flash bulbs. Grace Kelly's in this one too. She's the girlfriend, Lisa.'

'Sounds a bit stalkerish,' says Ali. 'I think our man's a stalker.'

'What about *Some Like It Hot*?' asks Dina. 'I thought that was a comedy.'

'It is,' says Bud. 'Jack Lemmon and Tony Curtis are on the run because they witnessed a mafia shooting. They dress up as women to join an all-girl jazz band. Tony Curtis falls in love with the singer, Marilyn Monroe, and an elderly playboy falls in love with Jack Lemmon. It's very funny.'

'Thanks, Bud,' says Ali. 'You ought to be on *Mastermind*. Can you see any link between the films?'

Bud is silent for a minute. 'Grace Kelly's in two of them. Two are directed by Hitchcock. But there's nothing else really. They're all quite mainstream. The sort of films any film nerd would know. The only thing I can think is . . .' He pauses, which is an annoying habit of his.

'What?' prompts Ali.

'Heat,' says Bud. '*Some Like it Hot*. And there's a heatwave in *Rear Window*. That's all I've got.'

For a second, Ali thinks of Jones's foundry, the devil's furnace. She says, 'We've been having a heatwave here, haven't we? Though it's freezing today.'

'Was it hot in 1851?' asks Dina.

'Boiling,' says Ali. 'I got corset itch.'

'Sounds nasty.'

'It was.'

'Could our man be triggered by hot weather?' asks Dina. 'I'm assuming it is a man though I suppose it could be a woman.'

'You wouldn't need much force to stab someone like that,' says John. 'It's all about being taken unawares and knowing where to put the blade.'

'Medical knowhow?' suggests Ali.

'I'm thinking more of iron nerve and indifference to consequences,' says John. 'Classic psychopath behaviour.'

'So we're facing a psychopath,' says Ali. 'Always good to know.'

'But he didn't choose the film *Psycho*,' says Dina. 'Maybe that would be too obvious.'

'Another Hitchcock film,' says Bud. 'Anthony Perkins and Janet Leigh.'

It's worse than book club, thinks Ali.

By lunchtime Ali is exhausted. She only had a few hours' sleep last night and is suffering from time-travel jet lag. Nigel rings just as she's wondering if it's worth having a cat nap at her desk.

'So, you're back then,' says Nigel.

'I'm fine,' says Ali. 'Thanks for asking.'

'I did warn you when we last spoke that this sort of . . . adventure . . . goes totally against the new departmental guidelines. It's a disciplinary offence. I could sack you.'

Go on then, thinks Ali. She doesn't think Nigel would want her out of a job. She thinks Nigel wants her where he can see her.

'How did you get back?' says Nigel, in a slightly more conciliatory voice. 'When I came into the office your supposed expert, Bud Whatsit, seemed totally at a loss.'

'I found a new way,' says Ali. 'I'll write you a report. There's just a slight problem.'

Nigel groans. 'I knew there would be.'

Ali tells him about turning up in the middle of a crime scene. Nigel groans again.

'So can you tell DS Venturi to back off?' asks Ali.

'I suppose I'll have to,' says Nigel, 'assuming you didn't kill this man.'

Ali hopes this is a joke. Nigel rings off without saying goodbye. Ali is contemplating sleep again when Dina appears at her door.

'What about some lunch? Let's go to the Bag O'Nails to celebrate.'

'Celebrate what?'

'Your safe return, of course.'

Ali doesn't feel like celebrating but she picks up her bag. Maybe a glass of wine will cheer her up.

The four of them descend the stairs. Bud also seems more cheerful now. Maybe he's pleased to have contributed his film knowledge. Or maybe he's just relieved that Ali is back. Only John seems pre-occupied. But, as they leave the building, Ali sees something that makes her spirits soar higher than a flying mesmerist. A tall, slim man is loping towards her. He's wearing a large Labour rosette.

'I wanted to check that you're really here.'

Finn.

Finn joins the team for lunch and, afterwards, John and Dina insist that Ali goes home.

'You must be exhausted,' says Dina. 'And you'll want some time alone with Finn.'

Finn has to go back to Yorkshire early in the morning but he agrees to spend the night at Ali's house. Ali can't remember the last time he stayed there, not counting the period when she was lost in 1850. She tries to make an event of it, stopping on the way home from the Tube station to buy the ingredients for spaghetti and meatballs (Finn's favourite childhood meal) and a bottle of red wine.

Terry greets them both with indignant yowls. While Finn strokes the cat, Ali tells him about Terry's double life as a Victorian mouser. Unlike Dina, Finn doesn't tell Ali that it must have been another cat. He knows that Terry is Ali's familiar. But he does say, 'What's it like, being there? I can't imagine. Well, I *can* imagine – carriages, crinolines, top hats, all that – but I can't get my head round actually *being* there. You, my mother, existing in 1851.'

Ali doesn't tell Finn that crinolines weren't fashionable until later in the 1850s. She's thinking about the question. It seems that Finn is asking something deeper than whether it was hard to walk in a long skirt and if the streets smelled bad.

She says, 'It's odd because it does feel dreamlike. Jones says it's like déjà vu; after all, everything really *has* happened before. I think, if I hadn't felt like that, slightly out of it, I would have been freaking out all the time. I mean . . . the thought of not seeing you again . . .'

'Even though you had Terry?' says Finn, grinning.

'Even then. You mean more to me than Terry.'

'Don't listen, boy.' Finn puts his hands over Terry's ears. Terry, who had been sitting on Finn's lap, gets up and walks away, stiff-legged with outrage.

'You should have seen him in 1851,' says Ali. 'Ignoring me and sucking up to the butler.'

'Just when I think I'm getting to grips with it, you say stuff like that. You were in 1851. You had a butler.'

'He was Jones's butler,' says Ali. She wonders if Finn is going to ask more about Jones, if he feels about her the way Bud does, but he seems more concerned with the mechanics. 'You just sat in a chair. I don't get it.'

'Nor do I,' says Ali. 'I'd sat in a similar chair, one of the same set, the day before and nothing happened but, this time, as soon as I sat down, everything went black. I found myself in a completely different room. In a completely different time.'

'In the middle of Dina's murder investigation.' Dina had told Finn the story over lunch.

'Yes, it was really weird. DS Venturi, the investigating officer, thought that I was the prime suspect. I had to set Nigel on him.' Nigel texted Ali half an hour ago: 'Told him. You won't have any more trouble.'

'What about Isaac Templeton's great-great-grandfather?' says Finn. 'Cain Templeton. Did he think it was odd, seeing you again?'

'He did,' says Ali. 'I had to fall back on the old "I was in Hastings" excuse.'

She doesn't tell Finn that she told Cain about the time travel. She certainly doesn't tell her son that the only time she felt really alive, and not in a dream world, was when Cain Templeton was making love to her.

They eat early and watch an episode of *Succession*, a new obsession of Ali's and an old favourite of Finn's. At nine thirty, Ali is yawning so much she says she'd better go to bed.

'You stay and watch TV.'

'No, I'll go up too,' says Finn. 'I've got an early start in the morning.'

'I can't believe it's the election tomorrow,' says Ali. 'I'll get up early too and get my vote in.'

'I've already done mine by post,' says Finn. Ali doesn't ask how he voted. She'd like to think Labour because he works for Helen but, when Finn had worked for a Tory MP, she hadn't assumed he voted the same way.

Finn heads for the spare room. Ali hasn't changed the sheets after Dina but hopes he won't notice they've been slept in. She locks the doors and puts on the dishwasher. She locks the cat flap too, just to be on the safe side. Terry is asleep on the sofa.

In her bedroom, Ali picks up the pink dress and puts it on a hanger. It fills half of the wardrobe but, for some reason, Ali wants to shut the door on it. Should she burn it, as John supposedly did with his Victorian clothes? That seems too drastic and yet Ali can't imagine donning the costume again, even for one of Dina's fancy dress parties. Her undergarments and corset are still on the floor. Ali picks them up and sees a small pink object underneath. Her reticule. Somehow she escaped being murdered, travelled in time and still managed to hold on to her handbag. Who says women don't have super powers? Ali puts the underwear into a drawer and opens the reticule, which is a small drawstring pouch, decorated with beads. It was attached to her wrist by a ribbon, which is obviously why it wasn't dropped on the way. Ali opens the bag. Inside is a comb, given to her by Jones, and a purse containing sovereigns, guineas, florins and shillings. There's also a small piece of card. On it is written, in Cain's now familiar writing, 'I meant what I said last night.' Something like a moan escapes Ali. Clutching the card, she runs back downstairs into the sitting room and searches the book-case for her copy of *The Pickwick Papers*, a book she brought with her from Hawk Street in 1850. There, wedged between the exploits of Nathaniel Winkle and Augustus Snodgrass, is a letter that was found in a desk once belonging to Cain Templeton.

Alisoun, my time-travelling angel. I don't know when I will ever see you again but I must trust that fate will bring us together. I carved our names on a tree today, Cain and Alisoun. Maybe one day you'll see it. There will never be anyone like you, in my past, present or future. No one like you in heaven or earth. If you're an angel, I'm a devil and my hell is being away from you. I hope that one day I will see your face again . . .

Two days ago, Ali told Cain the true spelling of her name. She also said that she'd see him tomorrow. Almost for the first time Ali realises that Cain is dead, that he has been dead for over a hundred years.

She sits on the floor and cries and cries.

Chapter 31

Dina also leaves work early. Her late night is starting to catch up with her. In fact, it seems days ago that she was in bed with Luca watching *The Mesmerist*. The subsequent events: the midnight drive to the murder scene, the body on the doorstep, Ali's reappearance, the few hours' sleep at Ali's house, the meeting with the team at Eel House, seem to unroll like experimental film, all close-ups and unexplained gaps. Did Ali really appear in front of her, wearing a flouncy pink dress? Did Luca really come to Eel Street and interrogate Ali? And, most of all, is Barry Power really dead? Dina can't forget that she might have been the last person to see him. She remembers standing in the hallway, the *Nosferatu* poster behind them, and Barry saying, 'I'm fascinated by the legend of Dracula. It's the ultimate story of eternal life.' She can't forget, either, that Barry warned her against Luca.

Before he left the office, Luca had whispered to Dina that he'd see her later. Dina is not sure whether she feels up to this. She'd really like to sleep for twelve uninterrupted hours. But she also wants to know what's going on with the case. 'Detective fever', she once heard Ali call it.

By four o'clock, she can hardly keep her eyes open.

'Go home,' says John. 'You look exhausted.'

'I think I will,' says Dina. 'Text me if anything exciting happens.'

'More exciting than Ali coming back from 1851 on a magic chair?' says John. 'I promise I will.'

Dina laughs. 'See you tomorrow.'

'See you tomorrow,' says John. 'Sleep well, love.'

It's the first time John has ever called her 'love' and he immediately looks embarrassed. It must be something he says to his daughters.

'Bye,' says Dina, shouldering her spiked backpack.

She falls asleep on the Northern Line and ends up in Morden. There's a reason why it sounds so much like Mordor, thinks Dina, trudging across to the northbound platform. Her love for *The Lord of the Rings* was another thing that made her uncool at school. Did J.R.R. Tolkien ever venture to south London? Tooting sounds a bit like a place where hobbits would live. Dina takes the Tube back to Clapham Common but can't face waiting for a bus to Streatham. She calls an Uber and is home before six. Not even bothering to take off her trainers, Dina crashes out on the still rumpled bed and falls into a deep sleep.

She wakes to a text from her friend Shawna. 'R U OK? How is it going with 🔔' For a moment Dina feels quite disorientated and imagines that she's back in her childhood bedroom in Croydon. She almost expects to see her sister on the other twin bed and their Steps posters on the walls.

Dina checks the time on her phone. It's seven thirty-four but feels much later. The curtains are drawn but she can see light filtering through the gap. She's been asleep for just an hour and a half. Dina texts back a laughing face and a heart. She can't face a longer message. She knows that Shawna would love to hear that Dina had been present at an actual crime scene but the details seem too serious for a text somehow. 'A man was stabbed. I saw his body.' Emojis are safer. Dina scrolls down her phone. Two missed calls from Luca. Should she respond? Instead, she goes into her kitchen and makes tea.

Dina drinks her tea looking out of the sitting room window towards the common. It's a beautiful evening, pink and blue with the occasional feathery cloud tinged gold by the setting sun. Parents and children walk back from the park, trailing scooters and abandoned anoraks. Several groups of secondary-school-age children slouch past. Exams must be over. Dina remembers the feeling of the summer stretching ahead, results still too far in the future to cast a shadow. Dina always worried about exams despite invariably gaining top marks. As she watches two boys play-fighting at the level crossing, she sees something fly across the sky. It's so quick, left to right, just a blurred impression of wings and darkness, too big for a bird and too close to be a plane. Was it a bat? Another *Lord of the Rings* reference comes into Dina's head. The Nazgûl, Ringwraiths who start off on horseback but, by the second book, have become horrifying winged creatures. Dina cranes her head but none of the passers-by seem to have noticed anything out of the ordinary. The boys have abandoned their fight and are now throwing grass cuttings at a group of girls. This time Dina thinks of the lines from *Alice Through the Looking Glass. Just then flew down a monstrous crow, As black as a tar-barrel; Which frightened both the heroes so, They quite forgot their quarrel.*

There's a buzz from the answerphone by the front door. Dina lets out a small scream. She must get a grip. It's a summer evening, what she saw was just a trick of the light.

'Hello?' Her voice sounds shaky.

'It's Luca. I've brought a takeaway.'

Dina presses the button to open the door.

Luca comes in bearing a quantity of silver foil containers.

'Are we having a party?' says Dina. Her dad says this to her mum before almost every meal.

'It's awful not having enough,' says Luca. He puts the containers on Dina's coffee table, which is the only place in the house to eat. She goes to get cutlery and a bottle of red wine that Bud gave her for Christmas. It's been in the rack all this time – Dina prefers cocktails or beer – and she hopes it hasn't gone off. At least it's Italian.

But Luca has bought two bottles of Peroni.

'This will go better with curry,' he says. Dina slightly resents his high-handed attitude but she agrees so she puts the wine on the floor and accepts the beer. Luca doesn't mind sharing dishes (one of Dina's tests) and they chat about food whilst piling their plates. Dina feels herself starting to relax.

Then Luca says, 'I had a call from a Nigel Palmer at the Home Office. He informed me that Ali Dawson was nowhere near Barry Power's house on the night of second of July.'

'Then she wasn't,' says Dina, tearing off a piece of naan.

'I don't suppose you're going to tell me what all this is about,' says Luca. 'It's just so . . . so bloody weird. Why was Ali there? Why the hell was she dressed like that? She seemed strange too. Almost like she'd been drugged. She was totally different when I saw her in the office today.'

Time travel can do that to you, thinks Dina. She says, 'I really can't talk about it. I don't even know everything. I'm just the IT girl.' She hates it when Bud calls her this but it seems to defuse the situation. Dina says, 'Do you have any idea who killed Barry Power?'

'SOCO got some DNA from the body,' says Luca. 'Don't quote me on this but looks like the killer spat on the corpse. We saw the same thing with Hugo Maltravers. We haven't had the DNA analysis back yet but we're working on the assumption that it's the same perpetrator.'

Another police word, thinks Dina. She says, 'They spat on the corpse? That sounds very . . . very personal. It's obviously not just a random killer.'

'No. These victims were obviously carefully selected. There's a degree of forethought and planning. Looks like the victims have been stalked beforehand. And then there are the postcards. Your information was very useful there. We found the rest of the *Rear Window* postcard in Power's house.'

'We were trying to think of a link between them,' says Dina. 'Bud knows all about old films.'

'Yes,' says Luca. 'He looks the type.'

Dina bristles in defence of her colleague. 'What do you mean by that?'

'Nothing,' says Luca. 'He just seemed . . . intellectual.'

'I'm intellectual,' says Dina.

'Of course you are,' says Luca placatingly. 'And did you find a link?'

'Not really,' admits Dina. 'Two of the films were Hitchcock, two have Grace Kelly in them. But one thing I should tell you, John – DI Cole – he's had another postcard.'

Luca snaps back into police mode. 'Another postcard? Another film?'

'*Some Like it Hot*.'

'What's that about?'

'Jack Lemmon and Tony Curtis dress up as women to join a jazz band. Marilyn Monroe is the singer.'

'Bit less murderous than the others.'

'Yes,' says Dina. 'It's worrying, though, isn't it?'

She hopes Luca will tell her not to worry but, instead, he says, 'Maybe we need to get DI Cole some police protection. He's a pro, though. He won't take any risks.'

'He doesn't seem very concerned,' admits Dina.

'Well, he's seen it all before,' says Luca. 'He's a legend in the Met, you know.'

'He's a lovely man,' says Dina.

'I heard he'd had a few problems,' says Luca. 'Drink and so on. Happens to a lot of coppers.'

'That's in the past,' says Dina. 'John's a health freak now. He goes running on Clapham Common every morning.'

'It's a tough job,' says Luca, 'but there are compensations.' He bats his eyelashes at her. Once again, Dina is very conscious of her body: her skin touching the T-shirt she borrowed from Ali, the breeze from the half-open window playing on her scalp between her braids. Luca puts down his plate and stretches out a hand. Dina moves closer to him and they kiss. But, when Luca's hand moves under the fencing hoodie, Dina says, 'I think you should go home.'

'Why?' says Luca, still searching for her bra strap.

Dina moves away to sit on another chair. 'I'm exhausted and I'm sure you are too. And I think things are going a bit fast.'

'I thought you liked me,' says Luca, trying the eyelash thing again.

'I do,' says Dina. 'That's why I want to take it slowly.'

For a second, Luca looks mutinous, eyebrows lowered. Then he smiles at her. 'I like you too,' he says. 'I'll call an Uber.'

They finish the food and take the dishes out to the kitchen. When Luca gets a message to say that his cab has arrived, he kisses Dina on the cheek and says, 'See you soon.'

Dina watches from the window as Luca gets into the car. She waves but doesn't think he sees. It's nine thirty and the street lights are coming on. Dina stays looking up at the darkening sky for some time but the winged creature doesn't return.

Chapter 32

John hasn't quite got to the stage where he's happy to get up at five a.m. for his early morning run, but he's definitely getting there. 'What's the time?' mutters Moira. When he tells her, she grunts crossly and rolls over. John raises the blind an inch. It's getting light, the sky a soft grey that promises more rain later. John dresses quickly in shorts, running top and trainers. The girls brought him an armband to hold his mobile phone but he feels silly wearing it and leaves his phone charging by the bed. His daughters can't believe that he can run without listening to music or podcasts but John prefers silence. Besides, all the news today will be about the election. John isn't conscious of thinking much on his runs but, often, when he gets home, he finds that he has solved some problem he didn't know he was worrying about, so something must be going on up there.

John kisses Moira on the cheek. She raises a hand, either to swat him away or to wave. John smiles to himself. Moira has never been one for overt gestures of affection but, in her steadfast devotion, she has saved his life many times.

He runs lightly downstairs. The house is very quiet. Moira says they should move, somewhere more manageable for the two of them. They don't need four bedrooms, a study and a conservatory. It's obscene really. But, then again, according to the features Moira listens to on *Woman's Hour*, a whole generation of twenty-somethings are back living at home with their parents after university. John is ashamed of how much he longs for this to happen to them.

John leaves the house, jogging along the black-and-white tiled path and breaking into a run when he hits Sisters Avenue. He always takes the same route, across the common, skirting past Mount Pond and turning for home before he reaches the Windmill pub. There's a nice café on the way, where Moira and John sometimes go for breakfast, piling on all the calories he's burnt. But he's not doing this to lose weight, John reminds himself, as he takes the path by the outdoor gym, the machinery looking forlorn and almost sinister in the dawn-washed light. He's running for his mental health, to help him come to terms with the fact that he once travelled in time.

I'm here, now, in 2024, John thinks as he runs. It's all very well to go through the gate, as Ali always says, you have to come back. Well, Ali has come back and, what's more, she has brought news of Jones. John has felt guilty about Jones ever since she took his place in 1850. Should he feel better now that he knows she's a rich industrialist? Maybe, but he doesn't. He noticed that Ali didn't answer his question about whether Jones was happy.

John always sees the same few people on his run. The man with the greyhound, neither of them hurrying, the man resting his hand on the snake-like head as they wait by the traffic lights, despite the fact that the road is always completely clear. The two women runners, one with all the gear, the other moving much more easily despite the fact that she's often wearing a skirt or summer dress. Sometimes there's a rough sleeper on a bench by the pond. John always feels guilty because he's never carrying any money.

There's no one on the bench today. The pond is glassy and green, even the ducks are still asleep. At the bandstand he pauses, catching his breath. When he first started running, he did this several times, now there's just the one stop. John can hear his heart pounding. Just for a second, he thinks he hears another sound, maybe footsteps, but, when he turns, the path is deserted. John heads for home, running between a short avenue of trees, their summer foliage thick and green. It's cool here and he tries to up the pace. He's often noticed that, even when there's no wind, the leaves move and murmur to each other. But, today, everything is still.

I'm here, now, in 2024.

The light looks bright at the end of the tunnel of trees. The figure appears with absolutely no warning. John's last thought is a confusion of light and shade and a sudden vision of Moira, Hattie and Emily, laughing by the sea, as clear as a screensaver. Then the dagger and the blade to the heart.

Chapter 33

Finn leaves at six a.m., planning to catch the 7.03 from King's Cross to Leeds. Ali sees him off in her dressing gown but doesn't feel like going back to bed. Last night's tears over Cain have left her feeling strangely detached and weightless. Or is this more time-travel jet lag? Ali decides to shower, dress and go to vote. Then she can come home for breakfast. She bought yoghurt and muesli for Finn but he said it was too early to eat.

Vote early, vote often, Ali thinks to herself as she walks to the polling station, which is in a local primary school. Ali likes the school, which is full of colourful children's drawings and signs saying welcome in several languages. In retrospect, she looks back on Finn's primary school years with fondness. Yes, she'd been worried about money all the time, doing several cleaning jobs to keep afloat, but Finn had enjoyed school and it had seemed a safe place, unlike the slightly scary comprehensive that had followed. Finn had liked it, though, preferring it to the much smarter state school in Chalk Farm, the one he'd attended during the Hugo years. Ali still feels guilty about disrupting Finn's education but he'd done well, getting top grades in his A levels and going on to the LSE. Now he works for what will almost definitely be the next government. Ali can relax and be proud of him.

She's one of the first to arrive and is given a warm welcome by the election officials. There are three tables set up, with street names on boards behind them. Ali confirms her address, shows her ID (a new development and one she disapproves of) and is given her ballot paper. She goes into the booth, takes the pencil provided and puts an X by the Labour candidate.

It's all over in minutes. As Ali walks home, she thinks that it really is a very civilised process. One pencil cross and, tomorrow, there'll be a new prime minister in Downing Street. The people she passes – shopkeepers opening up, refuse collectors emptying bins, parents starting the school run – do not seem excited or worried about the seismic change that is taking place. And that, Ali thinks, is how it should be.

At the corner of her road, she checks her phone to see if Finn has messaged to say he's on the train. She's surprised to see that Dina is calling her.

'Hi, Dina. What's up?'

Dina is making a noise like nothing Ali has heard before, a hysterical keening that sounds almost like a wounded animal.

'For God's sake,' says Ali. 'What's wrong?'

'It's John,' sobs Dina. 'He's been stabbed.'

Ali goes straight to the office. On the Tube, she wraps her arms across her stomach and tries to keep calm. Is John dead? Dina was almost incoherent but Ali just about made out that John was stabbed on his morning run across the common. The alarm was raised by a rough sleeper who knew John well from his daily runs. Even in her agitation, Ali thinks how typical it is that John obviously took time to talk to this man. Ali thinks of going to church with Bernadette, of sitting beside Jones at St James and St John, her fan parting the incense-filled air. Please God, let John be alive.

Dina and Bud are both in the office but Ali is surprised to see Luca Venturi there too, patting Dina's shoulder rather ineffectually. Bud looks shell-shocked. 'I can't believe it,' he keeps saying. 'I know,' says Ali, doing some patting of her own. 'It's like a nightmare.'

'What happened?' Ali says to Luca.

'DI Cole's body was found by a rough sleeper at five forty-five this morning. The man didn't have a phone but he ran to a nearby café, which was opening up for the day, and they called police and ambulance. DI Cole was taken to King's College Hospital with serious wounds to his chest and lungs. His condition is apparently critical.'

Bud makes a strangled noise and Dina starts crying again.

'For God's sake, call him John,' says Ali. 'What do you know about the assailant? Is he in custody?'

Luca gives her a very straight look, rather at odds with his earlier compassionate manner.

'We don't have the assailant in custody and there are no witnesses to the attack. DI— John was stabbed with a bladed weapon. Same MO as the attacks on Hugo Maltravers and Barry Power. We know that he also received postcards . . .'

'You said you'd get him police protection,' bursts out Dina. 'You said.'

'I'm sorry,' says Luca. Then, after a pause, 'It looks like DI Cole always took the same route for his morning run. It would have been easy for our perp to track him.'

'Oh, John,' says Ali. 'How could you be so stupid?'

'Police officers always think they're immune,' says Luca. 'We're all devastated at the station. DI Cole was a hero to all of us.'

'Don't use the past tense,' snaps Dina. 'He's still alive.'

'Of course he is,' says Luca. 'I'll keep you updated. His wife is with him now. His children are on their way.'

Ali thinks of tough, no-nonsense Moira, sobbing by John's bedside. Of Hattie and Emily on their way from Edinburgh and Bristol, checking their phones for news as they start their convoluted journeys. She realises that she has always thought of John as having the perfect family. And now this could be shattered. One person with a knife is all it takes.

'I've got to get back to the station now,' says Luca. 'I just wanted to give you the news myself. I promise I'll keep you informed.'

'Thank you,' says Ali. 'We appreciate it.'

Luca kisses Dina on the cheek, whispers something to her, straightens up and says, 'I'll be in touch.'

'Thank you,' says Ali again. As the door shuts behind Luca, she turns to her colleagues. They are both sitting at their desks, looking utterly derelict.

'Well,' she says. 'We know what we've got to do.'

'What?' Dina raises a tear-stained face.

'Go back in time to save John, of course.'

'We can't do that,' says Bud.

'Bud,' says Ali. 'I went back in time to save my cat. You helped me. I'm going back to save John.'

'We can't,' says Dina. 'Can we?'

'Why not?' says Ali.

'We can't change history,' says Dina, 'however much we want to. Remember our charter? Rule three. "Don't interact".'

'We've gone way beyond "don't interact",' says Ali. 'I was fully present in 1850 and 1851. I met Charles Dickens. I slept with Cain Templeton.'

Despite everything, this gets a response from Dina. 'You did?'

'Yes,' says Ali. 'I don't know how that's changed history, if it has, but I'm willing to run the risk for John.' She looks at her colleagues. 'Come on, this is John. He remembers our birthdays. He sends us jokes about *Strictly*. Remember when he made us all go to that terrible play Emily was in? Remember when Hattie knitted him that hideous jumper that was way too small but he wore it all the same?'

Dina starts crying again. Bud is standing against the wall, as if he has been backed there. His red T-shirt says, 'I might be colour blind, but I know I look good in green'. He says, 'It's too big. It's too big a thing to change.'

'Bud,' says Ali, 'remember what Jones said? Keep the faith. We have to keep the faith with John.'

It's unfair but Ali is prepared to play dirty. Bud shuts his eyes, as he did when Ali first conveyed Jones's message.

'Bud,' says Dina. 'Can you do it?'

Bud opens his eyes. 'I don't know,' he says. 'It went wrong last time.'

'I only couldn't get back because I was holding Terry,' says Ali. 'That's what Jones said.'

'That makes sense,' says Bud. 'Terry is another set of particles, another essence.'

'But Ali,' says Dina, 'that wasn't all that went wrong. You ended up in 1851 rather than 2024.'

'It's to do with emotion,' says Ali, 'that's what Jones said. Well, today we're all feeling the same emotion. Remember, Bud, you said you felt like you were in communication with Jones? That's why you brought me to her. And I think that means we *can* change time when it's to do with one of us. The Frozen People.'

There's a moment's charged silence. Rain spatters the windows.

'We need to be quick,' says Ali. 'The more time, the more damage.'

'So much has happened already,' says Bud.

'We can change it,' says Ali. 'Keep the faith.'

'Yes, OK. I'll go to Pevensie and work on the coordinates,' says Bud. He leaves the room. Ali and Dina look at each other. 'Are we really going to do this?' Dina sounds scared.

'If we can,' says Ali. 'What's the point of having this power if we don't use it?'

'In that case,' says Dina, 'I want to do it. I want to go back and save John.'

'No,' says Ali.

Dina looks shocked. It's probably the first time that Ali has ever used that tone with her.

'I'm in charge,' says Ali. 'I should do it.'

'It's my turn,' says Dina, sounding more like an eight-year-old than a thirty-something computer genius.

'Tough,' said Ali. 'I'm going.'

Dina glares at Ali for a few more seconds then sits back down at her desk. It's a capitulation of sorts. Ali wants to say something nice but there just isn't time. Instead she says, 'Can you give me Luca's number?'

Wordlessly Dina shares the contact. Ali dials the number, looking out at the undersea mural, a lanternfish regarding her with its globular eye. 'Luca. It's Ali Dawson. Look, I know you're busy but could you tell me the exact route John took this morning?'

It takes Bud two hours to do whatever he has to do. By ten o'clock, Ali is standing under the cover of the bandstand, Bud two steps below. They left Dina back at Eel House, torn between terror, excitement and lingering resentment of Ali's high-handed approach. 'Ring me the minute you see John,' Ali told her. 'Then we'll know it will have worked.'

There aren't many people on the common this rainy midmorning. Jones always claims that the 'moment of transfer' is so quick that it can't be comprehended by the human eye. Even so, Ali is glad that she doesn't have to perform her conjuring trick in front of yoga-ing women or a pack of dog walkers.

'Ready?' says Bud.

'Yes,' says Ali. 'You can take me back to five a.m.?' That was when Luca said John set out, Moira remembered him leaving.

'I think so,' is the less-than-reassuring response.

Bud looks at his phone. Ali closes her eyes and concentrates very hard on John, her friend. She thinks of his serious voice and sudden laughter, his West Ham water bottle, the moment when he turned up in Clara's kitchen to save her, his face when he talks about his daughters.

Ali opens her eyes. There's no sign of Bud and the light tells her that it's early. There's no rain but it's definitely colder. The common is deserted but, as she watches, two women run along the path to her left, one of them wearing a long floral skirt. Ali looks at her phone but it's not working, a regular occurrence with time travel.

She sprays around her feet and waits. A plane cuts its way across the sky. A heron flies low across the pond, a weirdly Jurassic sight. Then a figure appears, jogging easily along the path, grey hair lifting in the breeze. Ali waits until he's almost at the bandstand.

'John!'

He gasps and she's scared he's going to have a heart attack. 'Ali! What are you doing here?'

'Turn back now,' says Ali.

'What? Why?' John stares at her and then his eyes widen. 'Oh my God. Have you come back in time? Are you trying to warn me?'

'You need to go home now,' says Ali. 'I'll walk with you.'

There are signs that Clapham is waking up. More joggers on the paths, a few commuters holding takeaway coffees.

'What happened?' says John. 'What do you know? God, this is weird.'

'I'm not sure I should tell you,' says Ali. 'I think it would mess with your head too much.'

'Come on, Ali. You think my head isn't a mess already?'

'OK. You were stabbed on your run today. Police think it was the same person who killed Hugo and Barry. At this moment, in the time I just left, you're lying critically injured in King's College Hospital.'

There's a silence and then John says, 'I thought that nothing could be stranger than going back to 1850, but this is. I mean, you changed time.'

'I think so,' says Ali. 'I hope so. I've still got to go back, of course.'

'Did Bud do this? For me?'

'Yes,' says Ali. 'We all love you. You know that.'

At the zebra crossing a man is waiting, holding a greyhound on a string lead. John says hello to him. It's strange to hear his voice sounding normal. Ali crosses the road with John but, when she can see his house, she stops.

'Go home,' says Ali. 'I'll wait until you're inside.' She sounds like an anxious parent.

'Ali,' says John, 'Thank you . . .'

'Just go,' says Ali.

She waits until John reaches the pink door. He turns, waves, and disappears inside. Then Ali walks back across the common. She's got at least half an hour before she needs to be back for the gate. Should she try to apprehend the perpetrator? That's what her detective instincts say but what if she's killed? That would be time having its revenge in a big way. She decides that she should at least see if she can get a look at John's assailant.

She approaches the copse from a different angle. By her reckoning, the assailant should already be there. Ali waits by the first trees, listening. Although there's a cold wind blowing, everything seems very still. No birdsong, no traffic noise. Then Ali hears footsteps behind her, they are coming steadily closer, moving in a slightly erratic way. Ali turns and sees a man wearing stained and dirty clothes, carrying a sleeping bag. For a moment she thinks this is the knifeman but then she realises he's probably the rough sleeper, the man who found John's body.

'Morning,' he says, incongruously cheerful.

'Don't go that way.' Ali points to the tunnel of trees.

'Why not?' The man still seems polite, looking at Ali with interest rather than alarm.

'It's not safe,' says Ali. She searches in her jeans pocket and – thank God – finds a tenner. 'Look, take this and get yourself some breakfast.' She can see lights through the branches. The café must be opening soon.

'Cheers, thanks,' says the man and heads off in the opposite direction. Ali walks towards the trees. Should she go closer? She could apprehend the attacker but, of course, he hasn't attacked anyone yet. She could still arrest him, though. He'd be carrying a knife, which is an offence in itself, and maybe he'd crack under the shock of the arrest and confess everything. But that would take time and time is what Ali doesn't have. She turns and heads back towards the bandstand. When she's a good hundred metres away, she looks back at the small patch of woodland. Is that a movement she sees, a flutter of white amongst the evergreen? She can't be sure. Ali takes the circular route back to the ingress point. As she passes the pond there's a flurry of indignant quacking. The heron must be back.

Ali climbs the steps to the bandstand and stands carefully on her footprints. It has to work, she tells herself. And, if it doesn't, she's only a few hours behind. But will she ever catch up? The past is always the past, that's what Jones says.

Her stomach lurches and she almost falls forward. She sees a flash of red and realises that it's Bud's T-shirt.

'Are you all right?' says Bud. 'Did you see John?'

'Yes,' pants Ali, suddenly breathless. She raises her head and feels the rain on her face. Or is she crying? She doesn't know. Ali pulls out her phone, watching as the Apple logo glows back into life. A call from Dina.

'Dina,' says Ali.

'John's here,' says Dina. 'He's just walked into the office.'

Chapter 34

Ali and Bud get the Tube from Clapham Common and change at Bank. The commuters have gone and the only travellers are secretive-looking people deep in newspapers or in the music of their headphones. The headlines are all about the election but, because it's actually happening today, there's nothing new to say. There won't be a hint of the results until the exit poll at ten p.m. Ali thinks of Finn, campaigning with Helen in Yorkshire. They'll be getting the last of the vote out. Ali remembers the routine from her campaigning days: offering lifts to elderly party members, knocking on doors reminding potential supporters to make their way down to the polling station. It seems years since Ali stood in the colourful primary school and put her cross on the ballot paper.

Just over an hour ago Ali was in a world where DI John Cole, a detective with a long and distinguished career in the Met, was stabbed while on his morning run across Clapham Common. It hadn't hit the papers yet, by the time that Ali went through the gate, but it would have been on the evening news, although low down on the agenda because of the election. This morning Moira would have been woken by a knock on the door and two uniformed officers with fear in their eyes. Now, Moira is at home drinking coffee and listening to *Woman's Hour* or off doing one of her many voluntary projects. Hattie and Emily are working in libraries or lounging in common rooms or sleeping off hangovers. Did it ever happen? Will there be a memory of the tragic events that unspooled but have now rewound? Is there a world out there where John is still critically injured? But this is the multiverse theory and Ali has always hated having too many options. She can't stand long menus or Choose Your Own Adventure stories. There's just one world and she's living in it.

Bud can't sit still. He jiggles first one leg and then the other. He gets up and paces the carriage, swinging on the poles as if he's about to start belting out 'Singin' in the Rain'.

'We did it,' he says, coming back to stand opposite Ali. 'I did it. We kept the faith.'

'We did,' says Ali. 'Sit down, for heaven's sake.'

'Jones would be proud.'

'She would.'

'I didn't think it would work but you just vanished. And then you came back at exactly the right time. It's a triumph.'

'It is.'

'We have to go through the gate again. We can't just lose this power.'

This is very much what Ali said to persuade Bud to open the gate the first time. But now such talk scares her. Bud is starting to sound like Geoff. Ali gives him a warning glance. Most of their fellow travellers are still absorbed in their own worlds but one young man has taken off his headphones and is unashamedly eavesdropping. At least nothing will make sense to him. Ali isn't sure it makes sense to her.

Back at the office, they find Dina looking excited and rather scared.

'I wrote it all down,' she says. 'I knew that . . . if it worked . . . I wouldn't remember anything because it wouldn't have happened. We changed time so those hours, those hours when John was injured, they didn't happen. Look.'

Dina thrusts a piece of paper at Ali. It's covered with her round, surprisingly childish, handwriting.

John has been stabbed. Ali has gone through the gate. If John arrives in the office, RING ALI IMMEDIATELY.

Underneath is a list of timings.

Approx 5.15 a.m. John stabbed.
5.45 a.m. Body found.
7.10 a.m. Luca arrives at Dina's house and drives her to Eel House.
7.15 a.m. Dina rings Ali.
7.16 a.m. Dina rings Bud.
7.45 a.m. Dina and Luca arrive at Eel House.
7.50 a.m. Bud arrives.
8 a.m. Ali arrives.
10 a.m. Ali goes through the gate.

Ali looks at Dina. 'Where's John now?'
'Gone out for a walk. He said he needed air.'
'Did you tell him? Did you show him this?' Ali waves the paper.

'Yes,' says Dina. 'Do you think that was wrong?'

'I don't know,' says Ali. She looks at Bud, who shrugs. Not for the first time, Ali wishes Jones were there. She, at least, would pretend to know what to do.

'And you really can't remember any of it?' says Ali. 'Any of the things you wrote down?'

'No,' says Dina. 'It's weird but I have completely different memories of this morning. I remember waking up, having a shower, doing Wordle. I went to vote at Dunraven School and then walked to the bus stop.'

'Do you think that actually happened?' says Ali. 'Do you think you really did vote?'

'I'm sure I did. I remember it all. That school smell. One of the election officials said he liked my backpack.'

They all jump as the door opens. John appears, looking rather pale but so obviously alive that Ali can't resist hugging him.

'I'm so glad you're OK.'

'So am I,' says John. 'Obviously. But it takes a bit of getting used to. Was I really stabbed when I was on my run?'

'It happened,' says Ali. 'I remember it.' Although, in truth, the morning's events seem to be becoming fainter in her mind: Finn leaving for the train, Ali going to vote, the phone call from Dina, praying on the Tube, standing on the bandstand steps, walking across the common at dawn. *Don't go that way, it's not safe.*

'I'm not sure you should have done it,' says John, taking a gulp from his West Ham bottle. 'But I'm very glad you did.'

'We had to,' says Ali. 'We agreed, didn't we?' She looks at Dina and Bud but, although they both nod in agreement, they look rather dazed. Dina obviously can't remember any of it and Bud looks like he's forgetting by the second.

'Let's all do what Dina did,' says Ali, 'and write it down. I think, because we've changed time, we're losing our memories. We're getting new ones.'

'We only remember memories,' says Bud. 'Not what actually happened. That's what Jones says.'

'The collective unconscious,' says Dina. 'Humans share memories that might not even have happened to them personally. That's why it's meant to be easier to do Wordle at the end of the day, because so many people will have done it before you. The answer is out there in the collective unconscious.'

Ali has never got into Wordle and she doesn't intend to start now.

'Write it down,' she says. 'Write everything you remember from this morning.'

For the next few minutes, they are all scribbling at their desks like students in an exam. Ali goes back into her office and writes in the feminist notebook that was a present from Meg. It's the first time she's used it and her sprawling handwriting fills several pages. When she gets to the point of walking John home and then returning to the ingress point, she wonders if she should she have waited in the trees until she saw the attacker's face. But then she might have missed her gate. Then she thinks: she has one big advantage in this case. She knows what the killer's next move would have been. He killed Hugo and Barry Power and would have killed John. He *did* try to kill John. What's the link here? The postcards, obviously, but there must be more than that.

Ali thinks of walking across the common with John this morning, of seeing the man with the dog, of watching John disappear behind his pink front door. She remembers walking along that same road with Meg, hearing the footsteps that speeded up and slowed down with theirs.

'John,' she says. 'Do you remember the night of the book club?'

'What?' says John, sounding more bemused than ever. 'Oh, yes. The book with the talking dog.'

'When Meg and I were walking to the station afterwards,' says Ali, 'I was sure we were being followed. When I went to see Barry Power that first time, there was a man on the train. I thought he was watching me. I think I saw the same man at Somerset House, when I was having a coffee with Hugo. He was at the next table with a hat pulled down over his face. Oh my God, I know the link between the murders, and the attack on John.'

'I still can't quite get used to hearing that,' says John.

'What's the link?' says Dina.

'Me,' says Ali. She goes back into her office and clicks onto her desktop computer. There's a folder of the cases Nigel asked them to investigate. One file is labelled 'Curtis'.

Fred Curtis, 43, was cautioned by police after following a woman to her home. When questioned Curtis said he believed the woman to be the rein-carnation of Marilyn Monroe. Referred to social services and, later, to the Department of Logistics. Interviewed by DI Dawson. Curtis later returned twice, on the last occasion displaying fixated behaviour towards DI Dawson. Interviewed by DI Cole and referred to mental health services. Date of last contact: 16 May 2024.

There's a contact number and address.

'I'm going out,' says Ali.

Chapter 35

The address is in Poplar, not far from Ali's house. She thinks it'll be quicker to get the bus rather than wait for an Uber but it seems to take ages, the lumbering double-decker stopping at lights and roadworks every few minutes. Ali texts Luca from the top deck. He has a longer journey from south London but he might still get there first.

Leaning forward, willing the bus to go faster, Ali tries to remember Fred Curtis. The problem is, he wasn't very memorable. She has trouble recalling his face. At the time, he had seemed sad, rather than frightening. True, he'd followed a woman home but he'd seemed genuinely confused when questioned about it. Curtis had been in the army and Ali had wondered whether he was suffering from PTSD. Moira, who volunteers at a homeless refuge, says that a lot of rough sleepers are veterans and many of them are suffering from undiagnosed mental health conditions. Ali can't remember what job Curtis is doing now and, when she tries to google, she doesn't have any mobile phone connection.

Eventually, Ali can't stand it any more. She gets off the bus and walks. Her phone's satnav gets disorientated by the tall buildings and she takes a few wrong turns before she arrives at the block of flats. It's the sort that has a balcony running along each floor. As Ali watches, a man emerges from Curtis's apartment. He's wearing a panama hat. Ali remembers the trilby in the courtyard at Somerset House. That must be him. Ali scans the surrounding streets and the area of rough grass in front of the flats. No sign of Luca. This time she won't let Curtis get away.

Curtis moves quickly. He's only forty-three and seems fit. Ali won't be able to keep up if he starts running. She watches Curtis descend the outer staircase and walk swiftly across the grass. She ducks into the darkness of the stairwell, wishing she wasn't so conspicuous with her red hair. When Curtis has passed by, Ali sets off in pursuit. The white panama takes a right turn and stops at a bus stop. Curtis could be going anywhere. Ali isn't going to let him get away again. She starts to run. Curtis hears footsteps and turns. His face splits into a smile.

'It's you! I knew you'd come to me eventually.'

For a second, Ali is taken aback, then she pants, 'Fred Curtis, I'm arresting you for the murders of Hugo Maltravers and Barry Power. You do not have to say anything . . .'

At first, Curtis just stares at her. Then he turns and runs. Straight into Luca Venturi.

'I'll take it from here, Ali,' he says.

Slightly reluctantly, Luca allows Ali to watch the interview remotely. Curtis sits at the table, seeming quite calm and relaxed. He really does have a bland face: regular features, dark eyes, greying-brown hair that looks almost colourless. Luca and his colleague, DS Laura

Volks, sit opposite. Curtis has declined a solicitor in the same polite tone that he refused a cup of tea.

After preliminary questions, Luca shows Curtis CCTV footage from Clapham Common that morning. He'd seemed amazed when Ali had suggested he look for this. 'How on earth can you know that Curtis planned to attack DI Cole?' he'd asked. 'John saw someone lurking in the bushes,' extemporised Ali, 'I suddenly thought it might be Curtis.'

Luca addresses Curtis, his lilting Scottish accent now sounding quite clipped and formal. 'Is this you in the picture, Fred?'

'Yes,' says Curtis, without hesitation.

'If I zoom in,' Luca touches the screen, 'you can see a blade in your hand. Why are you carrying a blade?'

'I was going to ambush DI Cole,' says Curtis simply.

The prompt reply seems to surprise Luca. He says, after a second's delay, 'Why were you going to do that?'

'He was too friendly with Ali.'

'Ali?'

'Alison Dawson. DI Dawson. You know her. She was here just now. I'm in love with her. She's like Rita Hayworth.'

Ali snorts loudly, glad she's on her own. It must be the hair again.

'And did you kill Hugo Maltravers for the same reason?'

'Yes. I saw Ali having lunch with him. I'd been following her for a while. I've got her on Find My Friends. I did it when I was in her office. She went out of the room and left her phone on the table. Her password's her birthday. I looked it up.'

Ali can hear Dina and Finn upbraiding her in a reproachful chorus. *You're always leaving your phone lying around. Use a password manager.*

'And Barry Power?'

'I saw Ali leaving his house. She's mine, you see.' Curtis smiles pleasantly at the two officers. 'I can't let these other men get too close. I saw her having a pizza with Finn but that was all right. They are obviously mother and son. These others? Sorry, they had to go.'

'What do we know about Fred Curtis?' asks Dina. 'Other than that he was obsessed with Ali, as any normal person would be.'

They are back at Eel House. Fred Curtis has been charged with the murders of Hugo Maltravers and Barry Power, also with possession of a bladed weapon with intent to kill. Luca has made a statement on the steps of Herne Hill station, looking very handsome as he described Curtis's arrest. 'This person was known to police and social services and is believed to have killed Hugo Maltravers and Barry Power because of his obsession with a female police officer. Our thoughts are with their families today.' Ali had thought of Serena and Barley, Hugo's partner and son. She feels bad now for mocking Barley's name. Because of her, he is growing up without a father. Objectively she knows it's not her fault but the fact remains that Curtis killed Hugo and Barry, and would have killed John, because he believed they were rivals for Ali's affections.

'Curtis is an unassuming chap,' says Luca, 'as so many of them are.'

'In your wide experience of serial killers,' murmurs Dina.

'In my limited experience,' says Luca, lifting an eyebrow, which reminds Ali of Jones. 'He's forty-three. He served in the army. Saw action in Iraq and Afghanistan. Until recently he worked as a postman.'

'A postman?' says Dina.

'Ideal job for him as it left him most of the day free for stalking. He was dismissed by the Royal Mail because of inappropriate behaviour towards a female colleague. He said she reminded him of Jane Russell. When officers entered his flat they found it full of movie stuff. Posters, memorabilia, toys. Mostly Marilyn Monroe – there was an almost life-size statue of her in the hall, you know the one with her skirt lifting – but there were lots of other actors and actresses, from old films, in the main. He had a stack of postcards, like the ones he sent to Maltravers, Power and DI Cole.'

Did Ali once tell Luca to call DI Cole John? She can't remember.

'Curtis put a tracker on my phone,' she tells Dina. 'I think I saw him on the train when I was on the way to Power's house. He could have been at Somerset House too, when I met Hugo. The thing is, he hasn't got a very memorable face.'

'Curtis was fixated on you,' says Luca to Ali. 'You heard him in the interview. He was convinced that somehow you were in a relationship with him and that Maltravers and Power were trying to seduce you.'

'When I went to John's house for my book club,' she says, 'I thought someone was following me along the road. That could have been Curtis.'

'Probably was,' says Luca cheerfully. 'He'll probably plead diminished responsibility, but I think the CPS will fight that. There were several knives at the property, all sharpened to a murderous point, plus maps and pictures of his victims. It was all very carefully planned, plenty of malice aforethought.'

Ali thinks of the words 'malice aforethought'. Like many legal terms it has a nineteenth-century ring. Ali knows the definition by heart. 'The intention to commit a crime without just cause or provocation.' Ali thinks of Klaus Kramer, who wanted to kill her to be revenged on Cain Templeton. Barry Power had saved her, only to be murdered himself because of his connection to Ali. There's a kind of awful circularity to it. 'Things seem predestined,' Jones said once, 'because they *have* happened before. Time travel is advanced déjà vu.' Barry could supposedly see the future but could he see into the past too?

Luca and Dina are talking about where to go for dinner. They invite Ali (it feels like an afterthought, though) but she says that she wants to go home. 'I'm feeling a bit tired, what with one thing and another.' Dina says something sympathetic but she's too busy twinkling at Luca to pay much attention to Ali.

Back home, Ali eats the muesli she intended for her healthy breakfast. Already she has a slippery false memory of going home after voting, eating breakfast and strolling into work at nine thirty. That didn't happen, she tells herself. She still has her feminist notebook and, whilst spooning up her cereal, she reads her account of the morning's events. *Dina rang to say John had been stabbed, I took the Tube to E House. Dina and Bud were both there . . .*

Ali feels exhausted but she's too strung-up to sleep. No rest for the wicked, she tells herself. She sits on the sofa, half reading *Nicholas Nickleby* and half watching TV. The exit poll appears on the ten o'clock news, preceded by a sonorous countdown, like New Year's Eve. A Labour landslide is predicted. 'Hooray,' says Ali to Terry, but her heart isn't in it. Terry sleeps on. He's one of nature's Tories.

Ali dozes on the sofa all night, Terry beside her. At two a.m. Helen's result comes in. She has won. Ali watches as Helen makes her victory speech. The camera pans to her team, cheering and waving Labour flags. Finn is grinning from ear to ear. He looks like a man who is planning to move to Yorkshire and get a dog.

Ali turns off the TV and goes to bed.

Chapter 36

Ali expects to sleep late the next morning. Instead, she wakes up at seven and looks up to see Terry balancing on her headboard. He opens his mouth in a silent but commanding miaow. Ali closes her eyes and wills sleep but it doesn't come. She gets up and checks her phone. She sent Finn a congratulatory text last night and he responded with a heart and a smiley face. Ali goes downstairs to feed Terry and make herself tea, sending a message of fellow feeling to Gladys as she does so. She is sure that Gladys's day started far earlier than seven.

Ali switches on her old-fashioned transistor radio. The first five minutes are devoted to the election: record win for Labour, record loss for the Conservatives, Reform jubilant, the Liberal Democrats quietly pleased. Then, 'The Metropolitan Police have announced that they have charged a man with the murders of university lecturer Hugo Maltravers, and popular TV mesmerist Barry Power. Fred Curtis, forty-three, was arrested yesterday at his home in Poplar, East London. He was also charged with the attempted murder of a third man. Arresting officer DS Luca

Venturi says that Curtis is believed to have murdered the two men, and attempted to kill the third, because of an obsession with a female police officer.' Once again, Ali is not named. She turns off the radio.

Ali wonders whether to go back to bed with her tea but she knows that she won't sleep. She eats more muesli and decides to go into work. She thinks that she'll be the only one there but, when she pushes open the door to the Department of Logistics, she finds Dina and Bud drinking takeaway coffee and eating pastries.

'Hello,' says Dina. 'I thought you'd sleep in. I bet you stayed up all night watching the election. I saw that Helen won. Finn must be pleased.'

'I'm sure he is,' says Ali. She has bought coffee too and pulls up a chair to join them.

'I should be at the university,' says Bud, 'but I wanted to come here first. I keep wondering whether it really happened. We did do it, didn't we? We did go back in time and save John.'

'We did,' says Ali, although, already, this seems a strange thing to say, as if she's recounting something that happened in a dream.

'I rang John just to check he was still alive,' says Dina. 'He wasn't pleased. It was six a.m. Moira must think I'm nuts.'

Ali laughs although she had had the same impulse.

'I kept wondering if it would affect the results of the election,' says Dina. 'That I'd wake up and find that Reform had won.'

'Bloody hell,' says Ali. 'I never thought of that.'

'I don't think it changes something like that,' says Bud. 'I really think that we can only change things between the four of us. Five counting Jones.'

Ali wonders if he's joking but Bud looks perfectly serious, like a professor explaining a problem in quantum physics. He even looks quite professorial today, in a blue linen shirt rather than his usual slogan T-shirt. His hair is pulled back into a ponytail.

'I think it's about biorhythms,' Bud continues.

'What?' says Ali. She has a vague idea that biorhythms have to do with getting enough sleep. But Bud carries on as if she hadn't interrupted.

'All living organisms have time-measuring devices that affect their development and lifespan. You can roughly categorise these as hourglasses or oscillators. Lifespan is measured by an hourglass, for example, menstruation by an oscillator. Each cell in your body effectively has its own clock.'

'Why do I always get up late then?' says Dina.

Bud ignores this. 'I think our biorhythms, the four of us, are uniquely in sync. That's why we can do the things we do. That's why I took Ali to Jones without meaning to. That's why we were able to go back in time to save John.'

'It doesn't explain why Terry was able to time travel, though,' says Ali. She doesn't look at Dina. She knows that Dina still thinks the cat Ali encountered in 1851 was an entirely different animal.

Bud, though, takes this seriously.

'Like I said before, I think cats find their own way. I don't think your cells can be in sync with Terry's. After all, you couldn't go through the gate when you were carrying him.'

'There's still such a lot we don't know,' says Ali. 'Jones would say it was interesting.'

Bud laughs. He seems in an unusually upbeat mood today. He finishes his coffee, lobs the cup into the recycling and heads for the door, announcing that he has a ten o'clock tutorial. But, on the threshold, he stops and looks back. 'Ali? Do you think we'll ever see Jones again?'

Ali wants to say yes, to promise him this much but, in all honesty, she has to fall back, once again, on, 'I don't know.'

'It's just,' says Bud, 'I've got a lot to tell her. I've been working really hard on her programs. I think I've made some progress.'

He sounds like Finn when he was nine, wanting to show Ali the book he was writing about about alien hamsters. Ali's heart breaks a little.

'She'd be proud of you, Bud,' is all she can manage.

Ali goes into her office intending to catch up with her emails. Instead, she rests her head on her desk and falls asleep, an uncomfortable stiff-necked doze full of confused images of yellow roses, herons and Finn's smiling face. She jumps when Dina opens the door.

'Ali! I think I've made a breakthrough.'

'What?' Ali wipes her mouth with the back of her hand.

'It's about Luke Fanshaw. Come and see.'

Dina has Luke's enlarged photo on her desk.

'Look at his face,' says Dina. 'What do you see?'

Ali has looked at the picture many times over the last few days. Luke was blond, with hair that was probably curly but cut so short that it's hard to tell. He has soft, indeterminate features and a shy smile. He's wearing a bow tie so it's probably his prom photo, which makes the picture all the more poignant.

'A young man,' says Ali. It shouldn't be like this, she thinks. Luke shouldn't be immortalised in this photo, for ever nineteen.

He should have got older, found a partner, got a job, moved to Yorkshire.

'He's got spots,' says Dina.

'What's that got to do with anything?' Ali feels offended on Luke's behalf. He would have grown out of his spots, if he'd had a chance.

'I thought of it just now,' says Dina. 'On our first date, Luca said that all the girls fancied him at school because he didn't have any spots, unlike the British boys. I remember one of my brothers saying something similar about white boys. I emailed Luke's mother and asked if he was taking any acne medication. She said he was and she told me the name. It's a pill called Glabellus. I looked it up and one of the side effects is "suicidal ideation".'

Ali thinks of Margaret talking about Luke's job at the gym and his new-found vanity. *He spent a fortune on face creams and the like . . .*

'He went to the gym,' she says. 'Maybe he was taking steroids or something that, combined with the pills, affected the balance of his mind.'

'It's possible,' says Dina.

'And you really think this is what killed him?'

'Well, maybe a combination of the pills and Barry Power,' says Dina. 'I'm not ready to let him off completely.'

Ali remembers Kramer saying, 'You can fly, think how wonderful it will feel.' She can feel the night air on her face as she looked down on Victorian London. However tragic it is that medication caused Luke's death, it's better than imagining him with this voice in his ears.

'Let's do some more research,' says Ali. 'And write to the manufacturers. They should take the medicine off the market or at least make sure people are aware of the side effects.'

'We could start a campaign,' says Dina. She loves a good cause.

'It won't bring Luke back, though,' says Ali.

John comes in at midday, looking slightly hollow-eyed but otherwise very much his old self.

'It's funny,' he says to Ali in the kitchen, making himself a cup of decaffeinated coffee. 'Since 1850, I've felt odd, as if I was stuck somehow, but yesterday changed that. I don't have to write the date down any more.'

'You're not making much sense,' says Ali. 'Should I be worried?'

John laughs. 'None of it makes much sense, does it? But you saved my life yesterday. It's the third time I've come back from the dead, really. Moira saved me, then Jones, then you. I've got so much to be thankful for.'

Ali feels moved by this but doesn't know how to respond. She decides to change the subject.

'Bud says it's all to do with biorhythms.'

'What is?' John looks confused in his turn. Dina comes in just as Ali is trying to explain. Her rather more technical explanation, involving photoperiodism and the endocrine glands, loses both John and Ali, who exchange baffled looks.

'Basically it works because we're all so close,' says Ali. 'The four of us, including Jones.'

'I think that's true,' says John.

Dina abandons biology and starts to tell John about Luke Fanshaw and the acne medicine.

'I'm glad you've found a possible explanation,' says John, 'but that's so sad, knowing it was preventable. Have you spoken to his mother?'

'I'll do it now,' says Ali, her heart sinking. Sure enough, Margaret's first reaction is to feel guilty. 'I should have checked the small print,' she says. 'I knew he was taking stuff for his acne.'

'It wasn't your fault,' says Ali, for what feels like the hundredth time. 'You weren't to know.'

Ali clicks off her phone feeling sad. John might be alive but Luke is still dead and Margaret is still grieving. Then her phone buzzes. Finn. He sounds tired but still elated.

'Hi, love. How are you feeling this morning?'

'Great,' says Finn. 'I haven't been to bed. We had Champagne for breakfast.'

'Well done,' says Ali. 'You deserve it. You worked so hard. All of you.' She braces herself.

'Mum, you know Helen offered me the job of constituency manager? Here in Yorkshire?'

'Yes.'

'Well, I've decided not to take it. I want to keep on working as a special advisor in the House of Commons. I don't want to move away from Georgie. Or you.'

Ali is ashamed of herself for bursting into tears.

Chapter 37

A week later, Ali attends the funeral of Hugo Maltravers. Finn comes with her and Ali is glad of his company. It's a short, humanist service in a crematorium. Serena, a good-looking blonde in a black suit, sits at the front next to a young boy with long, blond curls. Barley.

'Hugo was always nagging me to cut my hair,' Finn whispers to Ali. 'Remember?'

'He must have softened in his old age,' says Ali. 'His hair was thinning. Maybe that's why.'

She remembers Hugo sitting opposite her in the stylish café, the arches and pediments of Somerset House behind him. He'd been irritating that day but he *had* agreed to meet her and he *had*, briefly, asked after Finn. Although Ali might have wished death on Hugo a few times, he didn't deserve to die, stabbed in an alleyway like a Dickensian villain, like Francis Burbage, in fact.

'Poor Hugo,' she says now.

'Yes,' says Finn, non-committally, adjusting his long legs in the narrow pew. 'Poor Hugo.'

Afterwards, Serena thanks Ali for coming. 'He talked about you often,' she says. 'He was still very fond of you and Finn.'

'He talked about you and Barley when we last met,' says Ali, which isn't strictly true. Serena didn't get a mention. 'He seemed very happy.'

Serena puts a protective hand on Barley's curls. 'That's good to hear. I hope he was happy right up to the end. The police said that it was very quick. Hugo wouldn't have known a thing.'

The police always say that, Ali knows. But she assures Serena that this is true and they part with an awkward hug.

Ali wants to go to Barry Power's funeral too, but she is told that the body was cremated with no service. Did Power have any family? Ali doesn't know. Dina had told her that Luca suspected Power of killing his wife and also that Power's early history was suspiciously blank. Is this proof that Power somehow travelled to the twenty-first century from the nineteenth? The Thornton Heath house had, apparently, been in his family for years. Had it once belonged to his father, bought with the money earned from telling fortunes at fairs in the early 1800s? But Barry Power had been in the modern world long enough to amass a reputation and a fortune himself. According to Luca, all the money has been left to Battersea Dogs and Cats Home. For Ali, this is a further sign of his innocence.

Ali has many unanswered questions about Barry Power, but she thinks she can solve one mystery. She asks Luca if he could find out the colour of Violet Power's hair. If Luca is surprised, he doesn't show it. He comes back two days later to tell Ali that a sample of Violet's hair was taken for DNA testing. 'She was a redhead, apparently,' says Luca, 'rather an unusual shade. "Auburn", the forensics officer called it. Never knew SOCO were so poetic.' For Ali this proves it. Violet must be the woman she met at Klaus Kramer's Dulwich mansion. The urchin saved from the streets. The woman who seemed scared of Kramer. The woman Power had rushed to help when she fell. Did Barry and Violet escape from Kramer together? Power obviously knew how to make the chairs work. Did they sit on them one day and find themselves transported to the Thornton Heath house, surrounded by familiar-looking furniture but with twenty-first century London outside? Ali thinks back to that sitting room. She remembers the framed landscapes and the open fan in the glass case. Could that have been her fan, the one she left in 1851? Ali really must stop leaving her belongings lying around.

Ali has her theories about Violet's brother Edward too. She remembers, when she first talked to Power about Luke Fanshaw, he'd said, 'Kramer wasn't a good person to be in contact with a vulnerable young man. I know that from experience. Poor Eddie . . .' Ali hadn't followed this up at the time but now she thinks that Edward, whose red head she had glimpsed through the trees, might have been the man who had jumped to his death when Kramer told him he could fly. Kramer probably thought of the brother and sister as his personal property, objects for experimentation. Power described them as his subjects. Could this have been the final straw for Violet and Barry? Was this why they made their getaway?

And what about the voice on the landing? Violet had cried out 'No!' and the next minute she had fallen to her death. Could this have been Klaus Kramer, travelling through time to have his revenge? Had Kramer's ghostly hand pushed his former protégée downstairs? Ali thinks she knows what Barry Power believed.

Ali has also researched Bram Stoker, the author of *Dracula*. She learnt that he was the personal assistant of the actor Henry Irving and once managed the Lyceum Theatre, just around the corner from the Theatre Royal, Drury Lane. It wasn't impossible that Stoker could have known Klaus Kramer. Was Kramer the model for the Count who drank the blood of innocent women in order to gain eternal life? In some versions Dracula can fly, as well as scaling walls like a spider. Dina told Ali about the mysterious winged creature she thought she saw from her window. Was this Kramer, flapping his way across south London? Ali has believed stranger things.

Kramer was guilty of many crimes, abducting Ali being one of them. What about Barry Power? He was a showman and almost certainly a conman. He contributed, albeit unknowingly, to the tragic death of Luke Fanshaw. He devised the illusions with which Klaus Kramer mesmerised Victorian London. But he was also a time traveller and he saved Ali's life. Ali wishes that they could have had just one proper conversation about it all, but she hopes that somewhere, on some spiritual plane, Barry and Violet are together.

At the end of July, John and Moira go on holiday to Sicily. Finn disappears to Sweden with some of his political advisor friends. Dina and Luca are talking about Greece. Even Bud takes a long weekend to go to a *Doctor Who* convention. Ali feels restless and dissatisfied. So, she's in the right frame of mind to receive an invitation from Ed Crane, inviting her to a talk at QMUL given by her ex-tutor, Elizabeth Henderson. It's part of a series of summer lectures and is entitled, 'Knobsticks and Spinning Jennies: the role of women in the Industrial Revolution'.

Ali hasn't heard from Ed since the Vietnamese film. It was only four weeks ago but Ali feels that she has lived several lifetimes since then. She has even slept with another man, although that man is long dead.

But Ali is in a cheerful mood as she walks along the Mile End Road to her old university. The rainy summer weather has given way to sunshine once more. Ali strides along in her linen trousers, loose top and her new Birkenstocks, remembering the torture of wearing a corset in hot weather. She misses some things about 1851 but not the clothes.

Ed is waiting for her in the lobby of the Queen's Building. Ali had wondered if it would be awkward seeing him again. After all, she had, in a way, rejected his advances. Ali has no real idea why she did so or why she followed Cain Templeton upstairs to the attic bedroom. On balance, she would rather have fallen in love with the man who is still alive but you can't have everything.

There is a slightly difficult moment when they are not sure whether to kiss hello or not. In the end they settle for a brief hug.

'It's good to see you, Ali,' says Ed.

'You too,' says Ali and she means it. These days she values friends like Ed and Meg who have no idea that time can be reversed.

'Do you want to go for a drink?' asks Ed. 'We might need one to get through the lecture.'

'Sounds like a good idea,' says Ali, 'but could I ask a favour first?'

'Of course,' says Ed, though he looks wary. 'What is it?'

'Could we have a look at the Templeton collection?'

There's a slight pause before Ed says, 'Why not? I'll get the key.'

As they climb the stairs, Ali recalls previous upward ascents: the climb to her top-storey bedroom at Hawk Street, accompanied by scales (the Italian word for stairs) played on Len's piano; the grand staircase at Jones's Kensington house; Klaus Kramer opening the door that led to the sky. Jones might say that time travel is taking the lift rather than the stairs, but Ali has always been afraid of elevators.

On the top landing, Ed produces an antique-looking key and opens the door. Flickering overhead lights reveal dusty display cabinets. Ali walks between them: the Roman skull, the mummified cat, the jet necklace, the murderer's brain preserved in formaldehyde. What does this motley assortment tell her about Cain Templeton? That he was someone who liked to keep his possessions together and gloat over them in private? Did he want to add Ali to his collection? He was married, after all. Was she just another conquest? She sees Cain's face looking down on her as they lay together in the single bed. She can imagine his hands on her body.

'Are you OK?' says Ed. 'You look a bit pale.'

'I'm fine,' says Ali. 'It's just the heat.'

The low-ceilinged room is certainly airless. Ali walks over to a desk and chair in the far corner. It's identical to the chair in Hawk Street and the one in the Drury Lane theatre. Cain Templeton once told John that there were four in the set, all believed to have magical powers. One is here, one is in the Sussex mansion once belonging to Isaac Templeton, one is in Barry Power's house in Thornton Heath. Where is the last one?

'Do you remember when you thought you saw a man sitting in this chair?' she asks Ed.

'I'm not likely to forget it,' says Ed. 'Since then, I've been reading about stone tape theory, the idea that the very fabric of a building can hold a memory. Have you heard about it?'

Ali recalls standing in front of her house in 1851 and hearing, clear as day, a voice saying, 'Where are you, Ali?' Dina confirmed that she'd used almost exactly the same words, standing in almost exactly the same spot, in 2024.

'No,' says Ali. 'But I believe in almost anything these days. Shall we go down?'

Elizabeth's talk is fascinating. She discusses the Industrial Revolution of the eighteenth and nineteenth centuries. The new factories meant work for women and payment for their labour but they were usually employed in unskilled capacities. Women had always weaved and spun in the home but, in the new factories, they were reduced to working small power looms or cotton processing machines. Despite its feminine name, the Spinning Jenny was actually too heavy for most women to operate. Ali thinks of standing with Jones, looking down at the foundry. The whole thing had seemed too hellish and chaotic for Ali to identify any of the individual jobs. Were there women amongst that workforce? She didn't know.

It is only at the end of the lecture that Elizabeth explains the 'knobstick' of the title. It comes from *North and South* by Elizabeth Gaskell. In the novel, Margaret, an upper-class girl, is forced to relocate to the fictional industrial town of Milton. There she meets a factory owner called Thornton and shocks her mother by her knowledge of factory jargon. 'Why, Mamma, I could astonish you with a great many words you never heard in your life. I don't believe you know what a knobstick is.' This gets a laugh from the audience, but Elizabeth makes the point that the factories were phallocentric and Victorian society strongly patriarchal. 'There were, in fact, some women factory owners,' says Elizabeth, 'but they are shadowy figures in history. One of them was an Italian woman called Lady Serafina but we know little about her apart from her name.'

Afterwards, Ed and Ali congratulate Elizabeth, but they don't go to the cheese and wine party that follows. The very name reminds Ali of the gathering where she first met Hugo. Elizabeth wrote to her when Hugo died, offering her condolences, although Ali knew she wasn't his biggest fan. She doesn't want to talk about Hugo tonight. Ed suggests that they walk across campus and have supper in a Lebanese restaurant he knows. It's nine o'clock but not yet dark. The statue of Clement Attlee looms in front of the Student Union. 'Hello, Clem,' says Ali, as she always does. It's the holidays so the campus is almost deserted. Ali and Ed walk together in companionable silence. As they pass the Novo Cemetery, Ali thinks she sees a tiny light moving between the flat tombstones, almost like a laser, the sort that Elizabeth used to point at illustrations in her talk.

'Did you see that?' she asks Ed.

'What?'

'That light. Look! There it is.'

Ali steps over the low wall and walks across the dry, summer grass in the direction of the light. Halfway across the cemetery, it vanishes. Ali looks down at her feet and sees that she's standing on one of the gravestones. She moves hastily and then she reads the name.

Dedicated to the memory of Lady Serafina Pellegrini. Died 1875.

Acknowledgements

Thanks, as always, to my wonderful editor, Jane Wood, and agent, Rebecca Carter. Thanks to all at Quercus especially Stef Bierwerth, Katy Blott, Jon Butler, Charlotte Gill, Florence Hare, Ella Horne, David Murphy, Ella Patel, Emily Patience, Vanessa Phan, Megan Schaffer and Beth Wright. Thanks to Liz Hatherell for her matchless copyediting and to Chris Shamwana for the beautiful cover.

Thanks to Jeramie Orton and the team at Pamela Dorman Books in the US: Anna Brill, Ivy Cheng, Tricia Conley, Natalie Grant, Brianna Lopez, Jason Ramirez, Elizabeth Yaffe and Claire Vaccaro. Thanks to all the publishers around the world who have taken a chance on the new series.

Over the last couple of years I've read a lot about the nineteenth century. For this book I'm particularly indebted to *The Great Exhibition* by John R. Davis (Sutton Publishing). Thanks to Emma Bragg for her insights into the life of a computer expert.

Love and thanks always to my husband, Andy, and our now grown-up children, Alex and Juliet. This book is for you, A and J. I couldn't be more proud of you.

Thanks to Pip who, if he knows the secrets of the universe, is keeping them to himself.

Thank you to all the bookshops and libraries who have supported me from the very beginning. And thanks to you, the readers who have come with me on this new journey. I appreciate you more than I can say.

EG 2026

RAISING READERS

Books Build Bright Futures

Dear Reader,

We'd love your attention for one more page to tell you about the crisis in children's reading, and what we can all do.

Studies have shown that reading for fun is the **single biggest predictor of a child's future life chances** – more than family circumstance, parents' educational background or income. It improves academic results, mental health, wealth, communication skills, ambition and happiness.[1]

The number of children reading for fun is in rapid decline. Young people have a lot of competition for their time. In 2024, 1 in 10 children and young people in the UK aged 5 to 18 did not own a single book at home.[2]

Hachette works extensively with schools, libraries and literacy charities, but here are some ways we can all raise more readers:

- Reading to children for just 10 minutes a day makes a difference
- Don't give up if children aren't regular readers – there will be books for them!
- Visit bookshops and libraries to get recommendations
- Encourage them to listen to audiobooks
- Support school libraries
- Give books as gifts

There's a lot more information about how to encourage children to read on our website: **www.RaisingReaders.co.uk**

Thank you for reading.

hachette UK

---

[1] OECD, '21st-Century Readers: Developing Literacy Skills in a Digital World', 2021, https://www.oecd.org/en/publications/21st-century-readers_a83d84cb-en.html

[2] National Literacy Trust, 'Book Ownership in 2024', November 2024, https://literacytrust.org.uk/research-services/research-reports/book-ownership-in-2024